A Wilderness of Mirrors

Book 1 of the Australian Spy series.

A Wilderness of Mirrors

GILLIAN LONG © 2025

All rights reserved.

First Published, 2025

ISBN: 9781763804111

Millaa House Publishing
PO Box 89
Millaa Millaa,
Queensland 4886

Table of Contents

A Wilderness of Mirrors

Just as Chris Davis resigns himself to the doghouse,
fate stirs up more trouble than he could have imagined.

. . . .

Gillian Long

Also, by Gillian Long

The 9ᵗʰ District

(Book 1 in the Mark Anders series)

Greenwash

Becoming Helen

The Trouble with Maggie

Watershed

Dying Days

Forthcoming in 2025

An Uncivil War

(Sequel to *The 9ᵗʰ District*)

1. Misdirection

Morning wept its soft yoke over the horizon, sending muted light across the sill through windows now unshuttered since the storm had passed. The rest of the room was shrouded in gloom, except for one corner where a table lamp remained burning next to a cold fireplace. Imprisoned in its glow, Harvey Kashton, the well-known billionaire, who had dined last night with the New South Wales Premier, sat or rather lolled in a wing-back chair. On the floor beside his feet, next to an overturned glass, lay a newspaper. The headline proclaimed a shadowy mercenary group was creating havoc in the Central African Republic. The paper was dated 23 February 2017. Yesterday's edition.

Mr Kashton's blue eyes bulged as if in shock. Thinning blond hair lay in disarray, while his mouth fell slack with a dried substance in its corner. His wire rimmed reading spectacles had slipped down to rest on his chin. The top buttons of his shirt were open, with bowtie lank on a damp and glistening chest. He reeked of whisky.

The housekeeper, Mrs. Susan Ainsworth, had an urge to straighten his glasses. It was an indignity he shouldn't have to suffer, but she knew better than to touch the body. Instead, she stood back; her gaze travelling in a distracted way, through and beyond the windowpane, to the racing gunmetal sky.

The three-storied building, or four if one included the garret, had once been her family home. It was now a discrete private hotel, modelled in the manner of an exclusive London club, where she and Martin had once stayed.

Mr Kashton had a suite with a private sitting room and balcony overlooking the sea. The same one he always demanded when he stayed at the hotel, which until now had been often.

Susan's daughter had once called him a privileged prick. It was the vulgarity of the language that had offended Susan, for surely, with that amount of money, privilege is taken for granted. Besides, who else would stay here? Bancroft House was a favoured haunt of the establishment. A place designed for the fortunate few, where they could drop their guard for a moment and know that what happened inside Bancroft House stayed in Bancroft House.

Bancroft House Rules was a phrase gaining currency among the leaders of industry and government. Susan prided herself on that. The house rules encouraged the guest to network, collaborate, and strategize. They unashamedly upheld British tradition and shunned publicity. Susan had never allowed a known journalist inside its doors. Of course, it was different for those who owned the presses. They had become the establishment, although privacy trumped all in her opinion. Fourth Estate or not, journalists and the press were mere journeymen and women, not the cream of society as some of them now thought themselves to be.

Yet, she acknowledged the world had changed, and she felt left behind, bewildered by modern societal values. Duty, honour, and respect for authority had all but vanished, replaced by the personal and the private. Self-care on public display. Truth and reality subsumed beneath the supposedly greater integrity of the lived experience. Now, there was the dreadful arguments over same sex marriage, which would go to a plebiscite later in the year. Susan didn't want to have to think about such things. They were private matters, and she was heartily sick of what she saw as media created conflict.

Rather than aspirations towards the professions, doctor, lawyer and such like, the everyday person now desired to become a star of film, television, or a social media influencer. In place of intelligence, breeding, and grace, Susan was faced with fame, notoriety, and self-absorption. The world was no longer a safe space for the ruling class, but Susan had determined it was her job to provide a refuge from a destabilised world. Bancroft House gave sanctuary with unparalleled guests' services, even for those with rather eccentric tastes or requests.

The current Premier of New South Wales was a frequent visitor. In fact, one could claim with certainty that Bancroft House's policy on its guests' fraternisation and collusion was instrumental in the Premier's rapid rise to his current position. Besides, he lived nearby, so the hotel was convenient for entertaining guests at minimum disruption to his wife's busy schedule.

A swarm of water droplets rifled across the windowpane distorting Susan's view and bringing her back to the moment. Without making a conscious decision, she scurried out of the room and concealed herself in a niche along the well-appointed hallway where she huddled over her mobile phone.

When the person she had contacted answered, she said in a voice barely above a whisper. 'Thank goodness I caught you before you went to court, Cassie darling.'

'I'm not in court today. What's the matter Mum?'

'Can you come over right now, dear?'

'Why? What's wrong?'

Susan glanced down the hallway in the direction of the gentlemen's withdrawing room. She should have locked it to prevent someone from entering. The guests rarely used the room until after dinner, but someone might take it into their head to barge in.

'Mum. Are you still there?'

'Yes, dear.'

'What's the matter? Are you okay?'

'I just need you here.'

'Mum, I have to go to work.'

'I know, but you are not in court today. You just said.'

'Tell me what's wrong.'

'I can't. Not on the phone. You must come here but use the private entrance. The Chief Justice is in residence, and I know you won't want to bump into him.'

Susan heard the lift door ping and said, 'I have to go. Come as soon as you can.' She dropped her mobile into her apron pocket and scuttled back along the hallway. With a furtive glance over her shoulder, she slipped back into the withdrawing room, locking the door behind her.

When she had found Mr. Kashton this morning she had immediately known he was dead, although she had never seen a dead body before, but this man was most emphatically deceased. Her first thought was, what a pity—such a handsome man. But what does one do when one finds a dead man in one's house? She had run from the room before reason had kicked into action but that had been a mistake.

The situation required careful contemplation. She plonked down onto a chesterfield sofa opposite him and stared at a large painting hanging above the fireplace. It was one of Martin's favourites, Joseph Highmore's *A Club of Gentlemen*. Of course, this was a reproduction. Martin had tried, unsuccessfully, to buy the original. The only reason Susan had kept it was its relevance to the purpose of the room. Now a man in the painting appeared to be staring in accusation, as if demanding she explain this indignity. *How could she treat such a valued guest in this way?*

As if it was anything to do with her. Yet it was the second time in her life she didn't know what to do. The first time was after her forty-eighth birthday, when Martin had left her. Yes, for that age-old cliché of the younger woman, although she had not suspected a thing. Susan hadn't the right sort of mental equipment to deal with the shock then, and now, well, she had to think of the scandal.

Rain continued to batter the windows, and she could see the terrace and the little used smoking area were running with water. So much wind and rain. The obvious course of action was to call the police, an ambulance, or an undertaker, but she couldn't do any of those things. Each of the guests held a position in society and they would not thank her for embroiling them in something so vulgar as a guest's death. Besides, any gossip would spell the ruination of her plans for her home to become Australia's most elite and exclusive private hotel. In this, there were no second chances.

She glanced at her watch. Soon, the guests would sit down to breakfast. Most might leave by ten or eleven o'clock. Of course, guests arrived at any time. Often on weekends they would arrive for lunch, but usually the time between 11:00 am and 12 noon was quiet. Plenty of time for the undertakers and ambulances to do their job and let the hotel return to normal. Or was it?

The most important thing was to keep the dead man quiet. She shook her head at the contranym. What she really meant was no ambulance or police sirens. This was merely an unfortunate death, probably by heart attack, of a guest who had stayed only one night and did not die in any of the beds. That was an important point to note.

An idea struck her. He had arrived in his yacht, now moored to the jetty below the cliffs. He should, in all good grace, have died on it. Not in the hotel. Clearly that was the solution. She hurried out of the room to find the majordomo.

The majordomo, Mason Bronson, was her second cousin and his loyalty to her was absolute. They had grown up together, almost brother and sister, and he had never revealed to a soul that she was not merely a humble housekeeper but owned Bancroft House. An ex-policeman himself, he would know what to do and how to keep this quiet. She messaged her daughter to tell her not to worry; she had resolved her problem and went off in search of Mason.

2. The Spy Master

Less than a week after Susan had disposed of her problem, the chief, or Devin Royce as his mother had named him, entered the Canberra Commonwealth Club on Forster Crescent at 7.30 pm. This wasn't his natural stomping ground, and he was a member more for his job than for personal leisure. To him, this place was a bastion of the past just like the person he was here to meet—his predecessor Myles Delahanty, although he kept such thoughts to himself.

He spotted Myles at a table next to a plate-glass window, which during daylight hours showed a view of Lake Burley Griffin. Devin saw the lake as Canberra's soggy heart, centred on a desiccated landscape of blazing heat or freezing air, and ringing with the eerie silence of what he saw as the quintessential Australia.

Tilly his ever-practical wife, had explained that his description was inconsistent. Silence could not ring, and the landscape, fed as it was by the Molonglo River, was lush not desiccated. Yet this was a perspective he felt compelled to correct, pointing out that Canberra had a foot in two camps. Watered, treed, and grassed in the pastels of Europe, interspersed with moments of dry straw, rust and the slate green of the bush. He could see both worlds, but the latter occupied his soul.

She had retaliated by calling him an unromantic pessimist and blamed his job for doing the damage. She was wrong, but it was pointless for him to try to explain. It was a feeling; a sense of belonging, but in his line of work you didn't give voice to such nebulous and sentimental emotions. He refocused on the issues at hand.

Sitting opposite Myles was Dr. Huma Sharapova, a woman once touted as the next chief. Lucky for Devin, she had been moved sideways into a job lecturing at the National Security College although she hankered to return to the office. Not that she had a choice with the Chinese threats to her relatives.

Two years ago, 2015 if he recalled correctly, Myles had moved her to the university position, in which she had excelled. Mid last year, when Myles had taken up the role of Chair of the Foreign Investment Review Board, she had become his deputy. She was expected to take over the position of chair when Myles cashed in his superannuation next year, although she would still retain her lecturing job.

As Devin approached, Myles stood up, clutching a linen napkin in one hand, and smoothed his hair across his pate with the other. 'Devin, good chap. Punctual as ever.' He held out his hand to include Dr Sharapova. You know Huma don't you? If I recall correctly, you and she were at the Kabul mission in 2013 together, neck and neck for the top job.'

Miles Delahanty smiled at Huma as if she were a young relative, rather than a woman in her late thirties, highly intelligent, and as sentimental as granite. Huma might be tough, but she was a striking woman with shoulder-length hair that was neither blonde nor brunette, but a bewildering mix of the two.

Tilly had explained the effect was called highlighting—an understatement of epic proportions in his view. Still, not much about her looks or demeanour betrayed her claims to her mother's Meskhetian heritage, although her sloe eyes had a slightly eastern cast, more reminiscent of the near, rather than the far, east.

Devin recalled an acute case of unrequited lust for her back in the day, but Huma hadn't seemed to notice him. Not surprising. He was a middle-aged man, and she was still in her prime. Still, going unnoticed had always been his superpower. Or at least that was Tilly's opinion.

He nodded a greeting and sat down at the table.

After the pleasantries and ordering of drinks were over, Devin waited for Myles to get to the point. What was the urgency and why this venue? He didn't have to wait long.

Myles took a deep slug of his whisky and soda, glanced across at Huma, inhaled and said, 'Huma and I were at Bancroft House in Sydney last week, for a dinner with potential investors in the new bauxite mine.

'The one making front-page headlines?' Devin frowned. Protesters were making a fuss over mining in an area of ecological significance, but what had that to do with him? This couldn't be why Myles wanted to meet.

'One and the same, although its ecological value is not my concern. Foreign investment is, and this one is shaping into a quagmire.'

'I thought XNT had the front running.'

'They did, until the Brits opened an investigation into serious fraud, and the Americans claimed violation of U.S. anti-bribery laws, while the company was operating in western Africa. Treasury doesn't like the smell. Which is why Huma, and I stayed at Bancroft House last week to help the Premier persuade Harvey Kashton he wanted to invest.

'And?'

'He was thinking about it, but mining was never his thing, despite his father making a fortune in the Pilbara.'

Devin went along for the detour. Myles wasn't known for getting to the point quickly. 'Harvey Kashton, a keen yachtsman if I recall. Took line honours in the Sydney to Hobart last year. Makes his money in shipbuilding and import/export. Do I have that right?'

Myles nodded. 'And munitions. He has become involved with David Wilson's Democritus-Australia. They are designing Uncrewed Air Systems, which was why he was thinking about the mining venture. The bauxite company comes with processing facilities, ship loaders, an export wharf, its own power station, and a rail network. Of course, aluminium to armaments is like a pelt to a fox.

'Okay. Pegged the man. So, what's the problem?'

'Kashton's vanished. He attended the Premier's little dinner party last Wednesday night, and Huma and I arranged to meet him again the next morning. I must confess I favoured his position as an Australian investor. I'm not keen on foreign investors getting their hooks into more of our resources. Not in the current global environment.' He paused and drank the last of his whisky before ordering another round of drinks.

Devin waited, unobtrusively observing the other members in the room. He felt Huma's eyes on him and glanced towards her, but Myles had resumed his story.

'Kashton didn't show for our meeting. The Bancroft House majordomo said he'd gone out earlier for a sail, but he didn't return.'

Devin said, 'Maybe he had someplace else to be.'

'The most obvious explanation.' Myles had that superior tilt to his sagging jaw as if to say Devin was still an idiot. He continued. 'We rang his office, but again, he was a no show.'

'You think he changed his mind. Not sure what I can do about it.'

'It's more than that. The morning was a tad blustery for a leisure sail. A low-pressure system in the Tasman Sea. It brought confounded weather to Sydney for a few days. But he didn't go home either. Neither that day, nor the weekend following. His younger son got married on Saturday and he missed the wedding. His ex-wife said that was really out of character. He apparently wouldn't have missed that for quids. She called the police to report him missing.'

'Well, probably the best course, in the circumstances.' Devin thrummed his fingers on the table. The entire conversation was odd, but why Myles thought he should involve Devin was what intrigued him most. This seemed like a police matter. 'What else is going on, Myles?'

Huma interjected. 'Myles and I fear for his safety. There may be other investors who want him out of the way.' She drew a breath, glanced at Myles, and then said, 'there was another person at Bancroft House that same night. One whom I think I've met previously in my former capacity.'

Devin gazed at her, amused by her formality, waiting for the rest. He took in the tiny crows' feet around her eyes, and the faint lines ringing her neck, but none of that mattered. She could still set a man's blood racing. She touched her hair as if aware of his thoughts, and he pulled himself together. 'Intelligence?'

'I think so.'

'At the dinner?'

'No. Possibly unrelated.'

'Well, are you going to tell me, or shall I guess?' He smiled, but she didn't return the compliment. Instead, she glanced again at Myles as if seeking his approval.

Devin and Huma had been colleagues once, although she was always the flyer. Myles might be gracious enough to say they were neck and neck, but she was definitely the favourite, despite Devin being her ranking senior.

Devin considered himself an average plodder who got results from perseverance. She seemed to magic them from her fingertips. Then, the Chinese government threatened her family if she refused to provide them with the intel they wanted. He wondered what had happened to the family once Myles had moved her out of harm's way.

Huma's family, or at least those still in China, were victims of Uzbek nationalist violence in the Fergana valley in the late 80s. The story on her file outlined a sorry saga of relatives fleeing to Xinjiang, the Uygur Autonomous Region in North-western China, while the Soviet government transported Huma and her parents, along with 70,000 others, across seven countries of the former USSR. Huma's mother had died somewhere along that route, but Huma and her father, a Lithuanian by birth, ended up back in Lithuania.

After the fall of the Soviet Union, they made their way to America. In America, Huma's father married a woman fifteen years his junior. The daughter of a wealthy Australian industrialist. They had waited for Huma to finish school and then moved to Sydney, where Huma attended the ANU. She excelled in foreign languages and subsequently joined the service.

A long journey for anyone. Perhaps that was why she seemed so focused. The only time he'd ever seen humour soften her eyes was in dealing with Myles. He had been the chief back in their Kabul days. There were rumours and inuendo about Myles and Huma's relationship, but Devin had never subscribed to them. She was years younger than him, and as professional and talented an officer as he'd ever come across. Anything she had achieved in those days, and now, arose through her own effort and ability. If they'd had a dalliance at any point, well lucky Myles was all Devin could say.

Myles leaned forward, arm on the table. 'Huma thought she recognised the bloke from her stint with the British Mission in London about fifteen years ago.'

Devin sat forward. 'SIS?' There had been no communication about an operation on Australian soil. Yet, it was possible, especially if they had concerns about compromised operations. Those compromised operations were now resolved although they had kept Devin awake at night, but Myles didn't need to know about that. The question was, what were they after and why were they interested in the sale of a bauxite mine?

Huma shrugged. 'I can't be sure, and perhaps it was a coincidence.'

'Who are the other investors?'

Myles reeled them off. 'Michael Baliston the Rio chair; Robert Sullivan, chair of the XNT Group; an Argentinian Investment banker by the name of Elias Aguirre. The Chinese aluminium company Căihóng brought two attendees, the chair, David Cho, and General Aiguo Liu. I suspect Liu is Cho's babysitter. You know who Liu works for don't you?'

Devin nodded.

Myles continued. 'There was also a British Investment Banker by the name of James Sinclair.' He pushed a folded piece of notepaper across the table. 'They're all on there.'

'Were all of them staying at the same hotel?'

'Yes. The dinner was an informal briefing and get-to-know-you affair. Most of those attending hoped to lobby the Premier's and my support. You know how it goes. Unfortunately, the media had got wind of the dinner, put two and two together as they do, and splashed it all over the Sydney news.'

'What about other guests?'

Myles nodded. 'A few. Thomas Hawkins, the NSW Chief Justice, was in residence with his wife, Elizabeth. Not at the dinner. I understand they were celebrating their 40th wedding anniversary.' They attended the opera that evening. There was also an American pharmaceutical bloke, his wife and a few others. Then there was the second British chap, Walker Fitzsimmons, who Huma thinks is five eyes, but the rest... Well, you would have to get the register if you wanted to investigate all the guests from that night.'

Devin rubbed his forehead. Investigate? He remembered Walker Fitzsimmons, but he'd retired from the service years ago. Besides, who the hell did Myles think he was dealing with—the local coppers? He shook his head. Then an idea popped up. He might play the MI6 angle for the Secretary's *Perseus Project*, and... Well, that would become another ball of knitting altogether as his dear old mum used to say.

3. An Australian Spy

The ride from the Canberra suburb of Reid across Lake Burley Griffin to the office near the Australian parliament took twenty minutes, but not if he went the scenic route, which was his preference. Autumn was well on its way, and a long overdue storm had washed summer's dust from the sky. This was his favourite time of year although he missed Beijing. A surge of bitterness galvanised him and he stood on the pedals. Sunshine, clear sky, and russet leaves were no compensation for the excitement and frenetic activity behind that particular veil of smog.

A white Nissan Dualis passed him. The driver was Huaren or maybe Zhongguoren, but definitely a Chinese man staring straight ahead through the vehicle's windscreen. Same as yesterday and the day before. In fact, the same for the past few weeks. Was he interested or was it coincidence? Chris Davis barely bothered with counter surveillance measures. Australia was making him lazy.

Who would be interested? He did this ride to work every day. No one was trying to recruit him. Not that this sort of recruitment was the Chinese style in any case. They preferred using the diaspora, particularly those whom they could control through blackmail. Besides, no one wanted him dead except perhaps the former ministerial staffer, whose quiet sacking had not come a minute too soon. How she had got away with it beggared belief, but there were no laws in Australia to cover that kind of treacherous indiscretion, as his boss called it. Although he had also indicated that would soon change.

Not quickly enough in Chris's opinion. Yet despite her departure, the Chinese still seemed to be one step ahead of them. Chris was certain there was someone else involved, but the investigation hadn't found any trace of a mole in the service. Still, he was convinced she had been a patsy, duped into her role, but she was their patsy and maybe they wanted revenge.

She was lucky to be in Australia. If the same thing had happened in China she would have simply disappeared. Sacking was a relatively light sentence for betraying her country, never mind wrecking his career by possibly exposing his role at the Australian Embassy in Beijing.

His ambition had been a posting to Moscow, but now that was unlikely. Still, he blamed himself. He'd known there was something wrong when she had accompanied the minister to Beijing in 2015 for the signing of the Free Trade Agreement.

He should have done something about it immediately, but he was the new boy, an outsider, hadn't been in his job long, wanted to be sure before he made any such allegations. The minister went ballistic; made no secret of the fact she wanted him fired and he wasn't sure she wouldn't get her way. Perhaps he should resign, but then what? He liked this job or at least had done before they brought him back to a Canberra desk.

It was true he supposed. It was his fault. He'd waited too long, fearful of acting without evidence and now no one knew if the policy officer had compromised his position or not. It was not something they were prepared to gamble on, and his immediate director had said as much. Told him he was a lame duck.

He would never make that mistake again. Not if he ever got another chance, but second chances were few in this life. He dismounted at the back of the building and made his way to the side door before removing his helmet and folding his bike to carry inside. The Dualis passed again, going in the other direction. No point hiding. If they were following him, they already knew who he was, but he'd make the report, same as yesterday.

Inside, the office had an air of overnight abandonment. It was still early. The best time of day to catch up before anyone arrived. He sorted through some papers while his computer booted, glanced through his email, then went in search of the office coffee making equipment in the small kitchenette. The morning ritual was one he no longer noticed after two months back in the country. Humans seemed able to adapt to most things, even endless boredom although that was likely to push him into the void.

When he arrived back at his desk, the phone was ringing. He picked up the receiver.

'Davis speaking.'

'Come up to my office please, Mr Davis.'

'Yes sir.' He hung up, took a slurp of coffee, put the mug on the desk, and took the lift to the upper floor.

13

The chief was a mild-mannered and conservative looking man, although Chris could see his agitation showing by the way he sat one arm folded across his chest, elbow of the other arm resting on it, hand covering his mouth. It was his thinking stance but thinking when he didn't have the answers.

Two other men sat across from him. Chris guessed, one was Australian Federal Police, although the man wore a dark civilian suit, white cotton/linen mix shirt, pale grey tie, Tag Heuer watch. Expensive. Must be brass. No matter the rank, there was something about the gaze of a policeman that gave them away every time. Chris had never liked the police much, spent too much time dodging them as a teenager, and now as an adult, well... Old prejudices remained hard-wired.

The other man was in another league altogether. Grey suit, white shirt, silver tie, sandy hair. Unremarkable in height, build or colouring. It was the eyes that showed who he was. Hard, shrewd, and calculating, missing nothing. Chris knew him by sight only. In Britain this would be MI5, and Scotland Yard meeting with SIS or MI6. In American terms, the CIA, and the FBI.

Open on the desk between the two men lay an official file marked secret and headed *The Perseus Project*. Next to it was his personnel file. What the hell was this about? He waited; feet apart, hands behind his back, features parked in neutral.

The two men stood up. Neither acknowledge Chris, but the presumed AFP officer said to the chief, 'We'll leave it with you Devin.'

The chief watched them leave the office before he said, 'Thank you for coming up so promptly, Mr Davis.'

'Of course, sir.' What the hell, when the chief called you responded pronto, but then this guy was unfailingly a gentleman.

He pulled the personnel file towards him and opened it. 'It says here your politics are progressive, but you ascribe to many aspects of conservatism.' He shook his head. 'How do you reconcile such competing values?'

Chris shrugged. 'I don't really. I'm pretty much an ideological agnostic. I prefer to ascribe to those things I think are good for humanity and the planet. You will find my self-assessment outlines my argument that conservatism literally means to conserve.'

'Explain please Mr Davis.'

Chris ran his hand across the back of his neck before he said, 'Well, my view is that the word conservative has become corrupted to mean populism or worse, religious fundamentalism. I subscribe to the type of conservation that is good for humanity, traditions which are mutually beneficial to a healthy planet and population. I don't think change for change's sake is always a good option, but when it is required, it needs careful evidence-based consideration to get the right results.'

The chief said, 'That strikes me as ideological.'

Chris opened his mouth to explain, but the chief held up his hand. 'Enough. Too much actually... what I suppose I really want to know is where you peg loyalty to the Crown?'

Chris reflected before saying, 'I take my oath seriously sir.'

'Of course, but do you think we should be a republic or a monarchy?'

'Sir, that's not my decision, nor one I need to contemplate.'

The chief sighed.

Chris frowned. He wasn't trying to be obscure, but he didn't have any clue where this interrogation was going.

'Okay. What's your opinion on the Royal family.'

Chris wondered what he could say. He wanted to be honest even if he didn't know why the chief was asking. He admired the man, but he also knew his answers would create a profile that would influence his perspective, his decision making, and thus Chris's prospects. He tried to balance a fine line, leaning towards the establishment, but not as a sycophant.'

'I see my job as protecting the Crown and what it stands for, at least the Australian version of it.' 'What about your personal views of royalty.'

Devin waved his hand. 'What about your personal views of royalty.'

'Sir, I think Queen Elizabeth provides a standard of grace and elegance worth conserving. The monarchy along with the preservation of history, historic sites, and monuments remind us of who we are and what has shaped us. This includes the good and the ugly including, I must add, the avarice and cruelty of British imperialism and its dispossession of some Australians for the gain of others. The latter is a cautionary warning of the dangers of seeing only one side of society, and one side of history, among a plurality of perspectives. This does not mean we should destroy our past for a better future but acknowledge it. If we extinguish history because it offends us, we leave society in danger of repeating it. Chaos loves a vacuum, sir. The aftermath of the fall of Soviet Russia is an illustrative case.' Chris's face remained in neutral, but his brain whizzed. What was with the pop quiz? Was he going to be posted. Please, please, make it so.

Devin smiled. 'I'm sorry I asked. Why on earth did I imagine you were the strong, silent type? He paused. 'I'll get to the point. Do you think you could merge into the furnishings of an ultra-conservative venue, and make friends with a British guest, apparently a distant member of the royal family, without confusing the fuck out of him by demanding the British ban fox hunting or something?'

'They banned fox hunting in 2004, sir.'

The chief laughed. 'Anyone ever told you how annoying being corrected is? You know very well what I mean.'

Chris grinned, ran his fingers through his hair, plastering it back from his brow, and with a luminosity lighting up his face, he seemed to morph into another person entirely. Dark, supremely confident with the stance of wealth, and privileged. In a languid Oxbridge drawl, which extinguished his Australian accent, he asked, 'Received pronunciation or Standard Southern British, sir?'

The chief raised his eyebrows, and said, 'Smug bastard. Remind me.'

'Prince Charles, or Prince William. Although I must advise, the upper classes have become anathema in Britain.'

'Yet they flourish. William will be fine.' He paused and scrutinised Chris. 'I must say, although I had heard of your ability, I didn't realise it was quite so good. Ever thought of taking up acting as a career?'

Chis grimaced. Perhaps, rather than another posting, this interview was the prelude to firing him. He forced himself to relax and said wryly, 'It's helped me survive.'

'In Beijing?'

'School mostly.'

Devin glanced at the file. 'You grew up in Darwin. Why did you return—to Britain, I mean?'

'I thought I might fit in better in the place I was born, sir.'

'The lot of many immigrants I hear.' Devin looked down and read the file. 'You joined the Royal Navy and flew choppers with Commando Helicopter

Force in the Fleet Air Arm. You requested a transferred to Intelligence after your fiancée died in the 2005 London terrorist attack.'

Chris blinked the memory away and swallowed the instant lump in his throat, but his eyes glistened. 'I wanted to stop attacks before they killed innocent people.'

'But instead, you resigned your commission.'

'My commanding officer was reluctant to approve my application to transfer. We didn't see eye to eye. sir.'

Devin cleared his throat, put his chin on his fist, and gazed at Chris. 'I'm curious. Why return to Australia?'

'It's all in my file, sir.'

'Yes, your mother got sick, but afterwards you stayed. Why?'

'There was nothing left for me in the UK. Here was as good as anywhere, so I enrolled in a master's at ANU. Needed a career change.'

'Why not fly private helicopters or some such thing? Big money in it.'

'I tried. Too boring. The jobs are mostly glorified bus-driving for billionaires. I don't have a lot of use for big money at any cost, and besides, I got a more interesting job offer, and I still get to fly with the Reserves.'

'Are you enjoying the role, Mr Davis? Being desk bound was never your chosen position.'

'Nothing's for ever sir, not even the doghouse.'

The chief's eyebrows rose briefly. 'You are right, but I'm afraid the job I have for you is more Canberra-desk than the icy streets of Moscow. I know you had hoped for a transfer, but it's unlikely now, given the circumstances... Sydney will have to suffice for the moment.'

'What's with the 20 questions, sir?'

'You have not been in Canberra long enough for me to know who you are, or how you operate. All I have on you are self-reports or reports written by other people. I prefer to make judgements about my staff myself. So mostly, I am trying to understand what motivates you.'

'I'd be keen to know that myself, sir.'

Devin gazed at Chris for an uncomfortable minute. 'I think you know enough about yourself to work it out.'

Chris let the observation go. 'What's the space you want me to infiltrate, sir?'

'You were born in London.'

'Yes, sir.'

The chief glanced down at Chris's personnel file again. 'British mother—Patsy Davis—a radical and former punk rock singer, who later immigrated to Australia where she took up the study of Australian Indigenous art.' His eyebrows rose. 'She was adopted into a family of the Larrakia Nation.' He stared at the file, a tick in his jaw twitching. 'Your father was either French Algerian or Spanish Argentine...' He glanced up at Chris's face, questions lingering in his eyes.

'Only speculation, sir. My mother refused to answer that one. I found two candidates after she died, but there were others I haven't yet got around to tracking down. It's not terribly important to me. What's the place in Sydney?'

The chief shook his head before glancing at the file marked Project Perseus. 'Bancroft House, a small but very exclusive private hotel with some interesting characters in residence, one of whom has gone missing, a police matter, but one or two of the others are not who they seem to be. Look, read the file and when you've digested it, come and talk to me—no one else. My colleagues and I are not convinced the leaks have stopped, so keep it under wraps, including your director. I'll let him know you are working on something rather delicate. In fact, I'll have a space made for you on this floor, so you can keep me informed. You will report solely to me on this one, eyes only. Collect your things, then pick up the file from my desk. I don't want it to leave this floor.' He opened another file and became absorbed in its contents. It was as though Chris had already left the room.

'Sir...'

Without looking up, the chief asked, 'Something else, Mr Davis?'

'Yes sir. Why us? If it's a Sydney investigation, wouldn't the AFP or ASIO deal with it?'

'You saw my colleagues here earlier. They are not sure that the leak is plugged. There are ongoing investigations within their own agencies, but that's classified. They have asked us to handle it. A one-man cross agency project, so to speak. But, as I said, Mr Davis. Read the file.'

Chris returned to his desk, coffee cold, the open space now a bustling multidisciplinary hive beginning their day's work. He was a spare part. Until this morning, he had been a senior project officer with no project and no team, hanging around like an unwelcome smell, trying desperately to engage in meaningful work.

No one quite knew what to do with him since he had exposed the ministerial policy officer. He was now both hero and embarrassment in one brittle husk. Yet despite the investigations, the chief had intimated the Chinese had more than one oozing source, but where and from whom?

Zoe Wilson had come across from Defence. Chris had helped her settle in, but all he really knew about her was that she spoke Bahasa, Malay and Mandarin, her grandmother had been Malay-Chinese, and she had a PhD in the history and political implications of the Chinese Cultural Revolution on the CCP, or Chinese Communist Party, today.

She sat in the desk adjacent to his, which was useful as he could speak to her in Mandarin, a means of keeping himself practiced in the language. It was too easy to become rusty. Chris had spent five years learning Arabic, Chinese, and Russian and brushing up his French and Spanish, all the while trying to persuade his commander in the Royal Navy to support his transfer to intelligence. When his mother got sick, he figured he'd wasted enough time and told the man where he could shove his last ten years of service.

Zoe lit up when he arrived at his desk and said in Mandarin, 'Dr Elgar wants to see you.'

Chris grimaced. Robin Elgar's mother-in-law was the minister, Marianna Laidley. Elgar seemed to share her attitude, blaming Chris for her policy officer's treason. Elgar was the one who had let drop the minister's desire to get rid of him. Chris didn't like his chances of seeing another overseas posting, although he had posited that if the minister wanted him gone, another posting would do the trick. Elgar hadn't been amused.

This new project's internal secrecy and cross departmental nature was likely to bend Elgar's nose further out of shape. He picked up the phone and dialled Elgar's executive assistant. 'Hello. Davis here. The director asked to see me.'

He listened, nodded and replaced the phone in its cradle before smiling at Zoe, speaking again in Mandarin. 'If I'm not back in half an hour, send out a search and rescue mission, will you?'

Her forehead creased, and she glanced around the room as if looking for deliverance.

'I'm kidding,' he said in English, wondering if that was actually true.

When he entered Elgar's office, he noticed the man still had shaving cream in the crease of his neck. Perhaps crease was the wrong word. Crevasse might me more descriptive. Elgar had once been a major in the army, played rugby in his day, and was built accordingly. Although the muscles may have become softer with age, he was still a large and imposing specimen, some claimed handsome or that may have been the power he exuded.

The Public Service medal he had received a month ago, was framed and hung on his wall. Oddly, for an intelligence operative, status and prestige were important to him, but then he'd never been in the field. In Chris's experience it was only after a near-death experience people came to recognise the meaninglessness of status.

The man's army career had only ever consisted of roles as aide de camp to Australian dignitaries, or military attaché during foreign excursions to friendly countries—building capital for his curriculum vitae. From gossip Chris had heard, his subordinates had uniformly loathed him. Nothing had changed, and status symbols were no endorsement of character in Chris's book.

Elgar held up the report Chris had written. It was a desktop assessment of the security situation for the various Australian diplomatic missions in the region. Boko Haram were running rampant across Nigeria and countries adjacent. Earlier in the year, they had pledged allegiance to Islamic State and rebranded themselves as the Islamic State in the West African Province.

Chris's report gave a detailed account of the terrorist group's capability and reach as well as its factional in-house conflict. He concluded that increasing international involvement seemed to have resulted in spreading the terrorist militancy to countries across the Sahel region. The Sahel is an east-west corridor comprising a horizontal and continent-wide wedge between the Sahara Desert and tropical Africa. The threats to regional stability had exacerbated a growing humanitarian crisis, which in turn worsened violent extremism, and human displacement. He had ended the report with an outline of what he considered was a new threat rising from the vacuum left by the demise of Muammar Gaddafi's old order.

Russian interests were now capitalising on the regional upheaval. Since the United Nations embargo on arm sales to the Central African Republic, a gold and diamond-rich country, Russia had defied UN sanctions to fill the vacuum by smuggling armaments, along with military trainers to prop up the government. It was something, he knew, both the CIA and MI6 were concerned about.

In the conclusion to his report Chris had warned that Russia was using the militant violence and unrest to infiltrate and control the Sahel. The Russians, he argued, were intent upon developing political influence and control in Africa, not only as a form of President Putin's megalomania to place himself in charge of a new empire, but also in a quest to garner support for Russian interests in the United Nations. Furthermore, Russia wanted to control the resources needed to increase their own armament manufacturing and in the process make a few more oligarchs wealthier than they had already become.

Chris stood in front of his director's desk, watching Elgar contemplating the words on the paper in front of him, a ploy to keep his subordinate on edge. Light from the window bounced off his smooth dome, and Chris figured the man had an excess of testosterone if you believed the adverts claiming it was responsible for baldness. It would certainly account for his erratic temper. He wasn't reading, that was for sure—didn't have his glasses on. Still, Chris could wait. It was a game with which he had become familiar.

Eventually, Elgar threw the file onto the desk. 'Is this what you have been wasting your time on?'

Chris remained mute.

'I suppose you think bringing in the Russian angle will get you a transfer to Moscow.'

Or Europe, even North Africa, Chris thought, but didn't say. Anywhere out of this rancid office...

'Your sympathies are showing.'

Chris frowned. What was that supposed to mean?

'Your father was an Arab, wasn't he?'

Chris opened his mouth, but before he could respond, Elgar was off again.

'You're fluent in Arabic, aren't you? For all I know, you are a closet Muslim.'

Chris said nothing. What was wrong with being Muslim? Other than the same thing that was wrong with all religions, but Elgar was off again.

'What else am I supposed to think when your report dismisses the Muslim extremism causing the problems in Africa. First, you blame it on the UN then you target Russia, for Pete's sake? Never mind the jihad being run in that region by the so-called Islamic State of the Great Sahara.' Spit frothed in one corner of his mouth, and he took a breath. 'It would be interesting to know what the French would make of this, this... I certainly don't know what to call it, especially given the enormous efforts by the UN to stabilise the region since 2013. Not forgetting the G5 Sahel's counterterrorism task force.'

'It's not working sir...'

Elgar ignored him. 'The Russians! For Pete's sake. Why? What conceivable motive could they have?'

'Protecting the right allies, undermining the West, expanding territory and access to resources to create a new Russian empire, are all possibilities, sir.'

Elgar scowled. 'This is becoming a pattern.'

'Excuse me?'

Elgar's eyes narrowed. 'Last week at the team meeting, I understand you argued right-wing extremism is becoming more of a threat in Australia than Islamic extremism.'

Chris inhaled as if to speak.

Elgar held up a hand. 'Tell that to Khan's victims in Minto last year. Or the Martin Place café siege victims in 2014.'

'Monis was mentally ill, sir.'

'Officially declared an act of terrorism, Davis. Don't forget that.' He waved his hand as if brushing the issue away. 'Who asked you to prepare this report anyway?'

'You did, sir.'

'What?' His voice rose a decibel. 'I asked you to carry out a desk top assessment of the Islamic threat to Australian consulates in West Africa.'

'Yes sir, you said since President Buhari's election promise that he would get rid of Boko Haram, you wanted to understand if the threat remained. My report shows it does and there is another threat growing through it, one that has greater implications for Australian interests in the region, particularly mining, but it's the human right abuses...

'You seem hell-bent on ignoring the Muslim threat, to focus on anything but.'

Chris shook his head. He didn't think he was ignoring anything, just raising intel on a significant new threat that was exploiting the chaos left in the wake of the Arab Spring.

But Elgar was off again. 'Who next, the Chinese? Oh, no...' He laughed. 'They're on to you, aren't they? I do read your little morning reports, you know. Are you sure it's the Chinese, and not some poor Asian/ Australian you keep running into on your way to work? Or perhaps you, in fact, are the problem. Are you a Chinese mole Mr Davis? It wouldn't surprise me.' He snickered again.

Chris felt hot lava erupt in his stomach, and clamped down hard so his voice remained even as he said, 'Sir, the Chinese are interested in the regional resources, but the Russians are exploiting the unrest caused by the Islamists, promising muscle to governments in exchange for the rights to exploit the region for its minerals and other...'

Elgar held up his hand again. 'Don't want to hear any more speculation about Africa, but you'll be pleased to know you'll be getting a posting. The minister wants a team set up in Jakarta. It seems, a fairly sophisticated people smuggling outfit has set up new operations. The team in Sri Lanka got wind of it. Run by an American so they believe, but so far the criminals have avoided detection. It seems the network includes Thailand and Malaysia and who knows where else. Setting up the team will get you out of the way of the Chinese. Especially after... well, you know. Anyway, you will get your transfer after all, and if you don't blot your copybook again, we may forget your little Beijing indiscretion, in time.'

Chris's hands bunched into fists. My indiscretion! Uncovering the source of leaked classified information, an indiscretion. Fuck that. In an abrupt tone he said, 'I don't speak Malay or Bahasa.'

'You speak Arabic. Lots of the migrants speak Arabic.'

Chris drew in a breath, noticing Elgar didn't use the term refugees. A fat lot of good speaking Arabic would do if he wanted to find the criminals in charge of the people smuggling and disrupt their operations. It was pointless arguing with the man and at least he would be out of the office. He could learn the languages. Zoe had said they were similar and relatively easy. Then another thought struck him.

'Sir, you will need to speak to the chief. He has given me another assignment.'

Chris had been reluctant when the chief mentioned Sydney. How the hell was he to prevent the next attack on western democracy and innocent people, by chasing around Sydney after some rich aristocrat in a fancy hotel. Now both assignments didn't seem so bad. Anywhere away from this half-wit.

'It will have to wait. The minister's needs come first.'

'I'll leave that with you to sort out with the chief. Will that be all, sir?'

'Yes. Get the hell out of my office.'

Chris reached to take his report, but Elgar scooped it into his desk drawer.

Chris walked out of the office. If the report was so bad, why keep it. If he hadn't been given another job to do, he might be tempted to resign, but at least that dickhead didn't run the show. Thank Christ. He took the lift to the floor above and asked Anna Thompson, the chief's executive officer, if he could have a word.

She smiled. 'Go on in. He's expecting you.'

Not for this reason. Chris pushed open the chief's door.

'Come in Mr. Davis. I haven't yet sorted out the desk situation. It might have to wait until the morning...'

'It's not about that, sir. I have just come from Dr. Elgar's office, and he tells me I am to take up a post in Jakarta. I explained you had another job for me, but he said it would have to wait as this request was from the minister. I just wanted you to have the heads up.'

The chief sat back in his chair, and Chris wished he knew what went on in the man's head. Elgar, he could read like a book, but when it mattered, the chief had absolute control over his emotions, barely a tell anywhere.

'Thank you for bringing this to my attention, Mr Davis. You'll have a desk on this floor by tomorrow morning. Just come straight up and report to Anna. She'll show you where you'll be, but in the interim, you can take over my conference room while you acquaint yourself with the contents of the file. Once you have absorbed it, we'll talk further.'

Chris edged closer to the lip of the void. 'So, will I be going to Jakarta?'

'Mr Davis, I decide how to deploy my staff. You concentrate on your job, and I'll focus on mine. Does that answer your question?'

Chris grinned. 'Yes, sir.'

5. A Police Investigation

Susan Ainsworth examined her daughter's frowning face. Boudica the warrior she should have been named not Cassandra, the ravishing daughter of Troy, who was said to have entangled men. She was pretty enough to have the name but only if she would make the most of herself, instead of this modern career-woman attempt at sexlessness. No wonder no one wanted to marry her. Dowdy grey suit and white shirt, like a man's. Beautiful dark curls scraped back from her make-up-less face. Shoes like a policeman's beat boots made for kicking in doors. 'Cassie dear, it's alright. I know you couldn't get away, but I sorted out the issue, so don't worry.'

'What was the problem?'

'Oh, um, a leak. Mason fixed it.'

'Mum, you called me for a plumbing problem!'

Susan sighed. 'I was so worried. I thought the Chief Justice's bathroom was going to flood and he would sue me. I know I shouldn't have called you, but... Well, he likes you, doesn't he?' She glanced down at her shoes.

Lying was becoming easy, even to her daughter. She had never lied before Martin abandoned her—never felt the need. But now, just to stay afloat in this business, she lied all the time. *Oh, no problem sir... Madam, you look so well...* Even to the staff. *Well done, everyone, sterling job. I couldn't have done it better myself.* On and on. Lie after lie. She hardly blushed anymore.

When Martin died suddenly of a heart attack, just before the divorce came through, she even lied that she was grieving. Fat chance of that. The floozy who had thought she could snaffle him, along with his money, was left not only at the proverbial altar but also penniless. He hadn't had time to alter his will. Susan had had the last laugh, but she didn't show it—pretended empathy for the poor woman's loss. Ha! That gave her the utmost pleasure.

Cassie pulled a wry face. 'I think the Chief Justice has better things to do with his time, even though he is an old crab pot. Suing you over a toilet flooding surely doesn't constitute the proper use of the Court's time.'

Susan pulled back from her reverie. 'What was that dear?' To her relief a knock on the door interrupted the conversation's thread. She called out, 'come in.'

Mason Bronson, Bancroft House's majordomo, poked his head in. 'The police are here. They have requested a meeting with the general manager. I have put them in the manager's office.'

Susan rolled her eyes. 'Cassie darling, can you be the manager's legal representative? He's not here right now.'

'Oh Mum. This is the police. You can't fob them off like you can with the guests. This charade is so unnecessary. What do they want, Mason?'

Mason shook his head. 'Not sure, madam.'

'Please, don't call me madam. How long have you known me? I'm Cassie, okay, like since I was a baby.'

Susan said, 'Please darling, you know how nervous I get.'

Cassie sighed. 'Why can't you deal with them, Mason?'

'Gracious me. Not my purview, madam... Cassie.'

'Where is he meant to be, then? This phantom manager.'

'He's on business in... London.'

'When is he coming back?'

'Two weeks.'

'Okay. I'll find out what they want, but that's all I am doing. Mason, you'll need to come with me in case they ask questions for which I don't have the answers.'

When Cassie and Mason had left, Susan turned on a screen and, using a mouse, focussed a hidden camera on the manager's office. A woman in police uniform waited with a man in a suit. A detective. Ice shrunk Susan's entrails.

The door into the office opened and Mason entered, standing to one side to allow Cassie to pass.

Susan's eyes narrowed. Something in the detective's face changed, like a light had sprung from within.

He said, 'Cassie, what are you doing here?'

'Alistair.' Cassie looked like a startled fawn, ready to flee.

Susan sighed. Her daughter had never been any good at lying. That naked face of hers gave everything away.

The detective addressed the woman in uniform, 'Sergeant Ryan, Cassie is an old friend. Daughter of the late heart surgeon, Martin Lewis. Cassie this is my colleague, Sara Ryan. But I thought you worked for some swanky legal firm...'

'I do.' Cassie interrupted. 'I'm only here as a favour. The manager is a friend, and he's away, so I said I would call in and check on things once in a while.'

Susan could see the pink flush in her daughter's cheeks, but Cassie was braving it out.

'It's just a coincidence you caught me here. How can I help?'

Susan applauded quietly. Her daughter could do it when needed. But who was Alistair? He seemed really pleased to see Cassie. A suitor, perhaps. One could live in the hope of grandchildren.

Alistair said, 'We are just here to ascertain if a certain Harvey Kashton was a guest here?'

Cassie said, 'The billionaire?'

Alistair nodded.

Cassie raised her eyebrow at Mason.

Mason stepped forward. 'I am not at liberty to say, sir.'

Susan clutched her hands together at her chin. Good old Mason. What a trooper. Just the right note.

Cassie frowned. 'Mason, that's nonsense.'

'House rules, madam.'

'This is the police wanting to know Mason, not some hoi polloi from off the street.'

'Well then, yes sir. Mr Kashton has been known to frequent this establishment.'

Alistair looked amused. Susan hoped he was a suitor. He was lovely. Medium tall and trim. Dark hair with a touch of grey at the temples. Nice facial bone structure. Athletic build, although it was hard to tell through the suit, but she could imagine.

Cassie said, 'What's this about, Alistair?'

Alistair glanced at a notepad in his hand. 'We are trying to ascertain Kashton's movements since last Thursday. His wife, ex-wife, reported him missing, last seen at a dinner function here on Wednesday night.'

Cassie turned to Mason; an eyebrow raised in silent query.

Mason nodded. 'There was a private dinner function last Wednesday. If my memory serves, he was in attendance. He stayed the night and checked out the following morning.'

'Do you know where he went?' Alistair asked.

Mason shook his head. 'No, sir. The guests rarely confide in me.'

Alistair continued as if he hadn't noticed Mason's jibe. 'How did he leave? In his own vehicle, taxi...'

Mason looked up at the ceiling, directly into the camera's lens hidden in the pressed metal scrollwork. Susan's breathing faltered but then he said, 'By sailing boat, I think, sir.'

Alistair scribbled something in his notepad before closing it. 'Can you show me?'

'Certainly sir. Please, follow me.'

The four of them filed out of the manager's office, and Susan switched off the screen. They hadn't found him yet. Was that possible? After depositing the man on his yacht, Mason had untied the mooring ropes and pushed the boat away from the jetty, but this was Sydney. There was water traffic everywhere. Surely the ketch would have been discovered by now. She walked over to the window.

Her rooms were at the top of the house, the place she referred to as the garret—servants' quarters in by-gone days—now converted. She and Mason lived in. Separate bedrooms and bathrooms, but a shared sitting room, kitchen and office space although Mason usually used the manager's office downstairs.

In a way, she supposed, he was the manager although she made the important decisions and always intimated to guests that the manager was someone else. Someone imposing and important, unlike Mason. He had always been good company, knowing when to be there and when to make himself scarce, but he was not management level material.

Most of the other staff had rooms in the old stables, converted into garages where Martin had kept his vintage car collection. After he'd died she had auctioned off the collection, taking a revenge-fuelled delight in the process, before converting the garages into staff quarters.

From her window, she could see out both sides of the hotel. From the north-east window she looked out over the gardens to the sea. From the other side, she looked down on the hotel's entry points. Her own personal lookout tower. She fingered the keys hanging from a hook connected to a loop on her belt as she watched Mason lead Cassie and the police across the garden to disappear down the steps to the beach.

The day was gloomy although the rain had stopped. She turned away. No point worrying. She would go downstairs. The work couldn't wait for a police investigation. Bancroft House was becoming quite the global destination and featured in some of the best travel magazines.

At the moment the rooms were almost at capacity. Aside from a smattering of Australians there were a number of international guests, with a new one arriving today from London. An officer in the British Royal Navy, no less. The Australian navy operated not too far from Bancroft House, which was why she supposed he was staying here, although she hadn't credited naval men with having the wherewithal.

The unfortunate demise of Mr Kashton, no matter how wealthy he was, would not derail Susan's ambitions. When she had first turned the place into an exclusive hotel, it was so she wouldn't have to sell it. Regardless of the fortune her husband had left, the upkeep costs were enormous, but Bancroft House had always been in her family, since the early days of the colony.

Of course, that was no longer something to brag about. Colonial times were now considered opprobrious, which Susan found distressing, although she remained determined to hang on to her little corner of the past. She didn't know what would happen to the lovely old building if Cassie chose not to have children, but while she was in charge, the house would stay in the family, no matter what she had to do to maintain it.

***

When the four returned from the jetty, Mason excused himself and Cassie accompanied Alistair and Sara Ryan through the hotel and out to the front door.

Alistair stopped at the front entrance and said to Sara. 'Go ahead. I'll just be a minute.' He watched her walk towards the unmarked car before he turned to Cassie. 'Maybe we could catch up—get a drink after work or have dinner when you have time.'

Cassie gazed at him, mouth pursed, before she said, 'Nice try, but you still have a wife, don't you, Alistair?'

'You know she hates me, Cassie. Come for a drink tomorrow night. Or if you like, I can come here—just friends.'

She shook her head. 'We were never friends and nor could we be. To be friends, you need to have more in common than raging hormones.'

'Promise I'll behave. I'll meet you at the bar at seven.'

Cassie didn't reply. Instead, she said, 'Excuse me. That looks like a guest arriving and having the police around, even dressed in a suit, is not good for business.' She turned and walked back inside.

6. Crossed Paths

Chris Davis hoisted his overnight bag from the boot of his car, a flash Mercedes-Maybach S-Class. It was a rental, but he was here as a man of means with interests in naval combat system integration. His legend was that of a consultant, retired Navy, ostensibly here for discussions with Lockheed Martin Australia, regarding the Australian Government's deal with France to deliver state-of-the art naval capability.

A man and a woman stood at the top of the steps. The man looked familiar. At that moment, the woman turned and disappeared inside the hotel, and the man walked down the entrance steps.

As the two men crossed paths, Chris turned his face away. Damn. What were the odds? Too late.

The man stopped, and said, 'Chris? Chris Davis?'

Chris gave up. He turned to the man; an expectant look plastered across his face.

Alistair said, 'As I live and breathe. Chris Davis from Darwin High. What the hell are you doing here?'

Chris smiled. 'Alistair McMahon. Might ask you the same question. It's been a long time—barely recognised you.'

'You haven't changed a bit. Except for the plummy accent, although if I correctly recall, you always had that tendency. How the hell are you?' He glanced across to the Maybach. 'You've done well for yourself. Or is that a hot Merc I see?' He laughed. 'I remember back in the day we all had you pegged as a budding criminal with the way you always hung out with that Larrakia mob.'

Chris said in a level voice, 'You mean my friends?'

'Is that what they were? Strange mob for a pom to hang with, but then you were always in a scrap somewhere. So, what did you get up to after school? I heard you went back to the UK.'

'I did, and you must have joined the local constabulary.' Chris glanced across at Sergeant Ryan waiting by the car. 'Your colleague I take it.'

'Yeah.' Ryan made a hurry up gesture and Alistair grimaced. 'Guess I should be off. But we should catch up. Have a drink or something. I can come back when I'm off duty. They have a good bar here and the food is special; pricy but good. It just so happens that I know someone involved in the running of this joint and I am meeting her tomorrow evening. If you are staying here, we could catch up beforehand. What do you say? Fuck, it's good to see you again. Blast from the past. I sometimes miss Darwin and the old mob.'

Alistair hadn't seemed all that enamoured with Chris at school. In fact, he had led the gang of cool kids. Dumb bullies mostly. Chris had been their target, not their friend. But there was nothing he could do about it now, not even avoid the man.

'I'll only be here a couple of days.'

'Great. Keep tomorrow evening free. As I said, I'm over here to meet a friend, anyway. We can catch up over a drink in the bar.' He waved to his colleague, then turned back to Chris. 'Around six.' Alistair walked off, shaking his head, muttering, 'Chris Davis. Well, I'll be damned.'

Chris watched him go, waiting until Alistair got into the driver's seat before walking into the hotel. That was the trouble with Australia, vast spaces, small population. Running into someone you knew was always a possibility, although that could happen anywhere. He had once run into another school friend in London's St. James Park station. Although busy London tube stations were a tad different from antipodean five-star hotels.

Through a door leading to an office behind the reception, Chris could see the woman who had been talking to Alistair. She was now in conversation with an older woman, dressed in grey and white hotel livery.

From behind a reception desk, a younger woman in a similar uniform greeted him with a smile and a cheerful, 'Welcome to Bancroft House, sir.'

Chris glanced at her name badge. 'Good afternoon Mia. I am very glad to be here. Heard wonderful things about the place, especially its staff.'

Her cheeks turned pink.

While he filled in the register, she launched into what sounded like a regular instruction to guests delivered countless times in a cheerful voice.

'Now sir, this hotel is not like others. Here we like to ensure our guests feel as if this is a home away from home. Their own private club so to speak. We serve dinner from 7 pm to 9.30 p.m. Black tie preferred. Afterwards, guests may retire to one of two withdrawing rooms for desserts, coffee, tea or an after dinner digestif. There is a ladies' withdrawing room, which is separate from the gentleman's room. If you wish to either mix with the ladies or bring in guests, who are not staying in the hotel, there is a large and comfortable public lounge and cocktail bar available. The gentlemen's withdrawing room also has a humidor for your convenience, and a smoking area a step away along the terrace. The ladies withdrawing room shares the smoking garden with the gentlemen. After dinner, many gentlemen like to read the papers, play cards or chess with other guests, or just engage in conversation with the like-minded. If you require an introduction to any of our other guests, please don't hesitate to ask. Details are in the booklet in your room, but if there is something you require, which is not identified, please let Mr. Mason Bronson, the majordomo know. His pager number is also in the booklet.'

'I will be on my own this evening, and as I don't know anyone staying here, I would be very glad to meet up with any other guests so inclined. Particularly British guests if there are others in residence?'

'Of course. I will alert them to your arrival, and what time shall I say you will be available in the withdrawing room after dinner in case they are also available to meet?'

Ten minutes later Chris lay on his bed, hands behind his head, his mind combing through a mental list of people staying at the hotel. He knew who most of the staff were, including the owner of the hotel, who styled herself as housekeeper. An intriguing bit of information, but probably of no importance. He wasn't sure who the woman in the office was, the one speaking to Alistair when he arrived. It was possibly the housekeeper's daughter, Casandra Lewis, a well-regarded barrister in the city. Then there was the majordomo, an ex-copper, who was related to the housekeeper.

Chris had checked all the staff backgrounds before leaving Canberra and then gone through the guest list of the people staying here the same night as the dinner party with Myles Delahanty, the chair of the Foreign Investment Review Board. The dinner, which was also attended by the missing Harvey Kashton.

Kashton's disappearance wasn't why he was here, although it was tempting to get distracted by it. But that was a job for the police. Of course, that was the most likely reason for Alistair's presence. What Chris was interested in, was who else was here, and why MI6 might be interested in this little piece of the world. If indeed there was an operative or agent from British intelligence staying here at all.

Assume nothing, the chief had said. Just go for a visit, stay for a day or two, try to get into conversation with Walker Fitzsimmons. You and he should have a lot in common, and what you don't have, fake. Report back if you think further examination is warranted, but only if it is about foreign interference or a security threat. We don't want to step on ASIO or the AFP's insteps.

The issue that had brought the man's activities to the chief's notice came via Dr Sharapova, the Deputy Chair of the Foreign Investment Review Board's insistence there was an MI6 operative noising around.

Chris had already tracked the man down. The ex-naval commander, Walker Fitzsimmons, was the brother-in-law of a minor royal, and preferred to be called Fitz. He had worked in MI6 although the chief had explained that when he had contacted his counterpart in London, he'd learned Fitz had retired some years previously. Perhaps that was a euphemism because Chris had also unearthed some scandal relating to the hacking of Royal mobile phones.

If Fitz wasn't acting for MI6, what was he doing here? Myles Delahanty's concern was about foreign investments in a mining venture, but Fitzsimmons wasn't a mining tycoon, nor did he have any registered interests in mining, despite his inherited wealth. All the same, the chief wanted to be sure, which was why he chose Chris to inveigle his way into the man's personal space. Nothing like fellow patriots, shared service, common values, and the right political persuasion when building rapport.

Chris got up and looked out the window. It was a pretty special view. Sunset had cast an orange glow to the edge of the cyan sky, although he conceded the orange band was probably pollution. He walked out of his room and made his way to the garden. He would take a look around before dressing for dinner. It had been a while since he'd worn a tux, although formal occasions in Beijing often required dinner jackets, but it was unusual in Australia, especially at an hotel.

Yet despite Australia's claim to egalitarian standards and, judging by the guests engaged in various rituals of British tradition, this place aspired to retreat to the days of Empire. It was quaint, but obviously such traditions appealed to the mega-wealthy who stayed here. Afternoon tea in the garden, followed by cocktails on the veranda, followed by dinner, for which one dressed formally. Perhaps quaint was too mild a word. It didn't conjure the acrimony now invested in any flaunting of Australia's imperial past. Anachronism was probably more descriptive.

A thought struck him. Conceivably the wealthy scheduled their time so completely around these outdated traditions because it gave them a sense of who they were, and where they belonged, immigrants in the country of their birth. He understood that kind of displacement. He hadn't been born in Australia, but neither did he feel he belonged in Britian. There should be a passport for internationalists. People who felt they belonged nowhere, yet chose to move among people anywhere, all the while pretending to fit in.

He reached the end of the garden path and stood behind a railing at the cliff edge. To his right a set of steep stairs descended to a rocky shore, which boasted a narrow spit of sand occupied by gulls alone. Further along the beach was a jetty where a couple of yachts were moored. Beyond that lay bush. In front of him a white capped seascape undulated with undertones of deep blue, turquoise and purple.

A voice at his shoulder said, 'Wonderful view.'

Chris turned, recognising Fitzsimmons from photographs. He was mid-fifties, thinning fair hair of the almost translucent type, parted on the side and square cut. Average height, average build. Eyes, an indeterminate hazel with marked circles beneath as if he didn't sleep much or had a kidney problem. Nothing out of the ordinary. A man who wouldn't warrant a second glance. Just the right type. It seemed British intelligence was still recruiting Oxbridge types although to be fair, Fitz would have joined the service decades ago. Most intelligence agencies had broadened their horizons since then.

The Brit stuck out his hand. 'Heard a fellow naval man was in lodgings. 'Walker Fitzsimmons. Fitz to my friends. Commander, Royal Navy until the early eighties, probably exited at the time you were born.' He chuckled.

Chris took his hand. 'Chris Davis. You're right about the view. Brilliant weather—nothing like this back in Maulden.' The man would recognise the link between the village and the Lockheed Martin facility at nearby Ampthill in Bedfordshire.

'You are from Maulden?' Fitz's gaze flashed to Chris before returning to its languid embrace of the seascape.

'Well, London actually, but have been spending a bit of time lately in Maulden.'

Fitz said, 'Join us for dinner. We British chaps should stick together.'

'Us?'

'Yes, James Sinclair and me. We usually get in a game of billiards after dinner.'

Chris's brow cleared. 'Sinclair is also from London.'

'Of course. Are you here for the conference?'

'What conference is that?'

'Mining Futures. Several of the guests are here for it.'

Chris shook his head. 'You're in the mining game, then?'

'Opposite side of the fence, actually. Environmental concerns. WorldWatch, you may have heard of it. A group of American environmental scientists started the firm to raise global awareness of eco related vandalism in hidden corners of the world. I am speaking at the conference about Chinese interests in bauxite mining in Ghana. The Chinese appear to be intent on colonising Africa. Not that I will be approaching the subject in such a blunt way, but fundamentally I hope to get one of the Australian or British ventures interested. Much easier to pressure shareholders to do the right thing in a liberal democracy. Look, the barman here does rather a good G & T and the others will have gathered by now. What about it? Shall we join them?'

'Sounds good.' A glint of metal caught Chris's eye. The angle at which he was standing, and the setting sun, made what would otherwise have been difficult to see, obvious. 'Go ahead. I'll follow in a minute.' He walked down a few steps and, with the edge of his hotel keycard, dug out a cufflink. Gold, engraved with the initial H, off set with what looked like a cluster of emeralds. He dropped it into his pocket and followed Fitz along the pathway, back to the house.

Before heading to the bar, he left the cufflink at the reception asking for it to be delivered to the housekeeper as lost property. When he entered the cocktail lounge, Fitz was at a table on which sweated two tall glasses, a curled slice of lemon hooked over each rim. He was alone.

A WILDERNESS OF MIRRORS

As Chris sat down Fitz said, 'Just time for one before dinner. Charming notion in this day and age, expecting guests to dress for dinner—like time stood still in the colonies. I admit, I find it reassuringly nostalgic.'

***

The other men didn't join them until after dinner, by which time Chris and Fitz were playing a game of British billiards. When they did arrive, there was not one man but three of them. Sir Hamish White, a naturalised Australian and racehorse breeder from the Southern Tablelands, spoke with a Scottish brogue through a clipped, nicotine-coloured moustache. By his own account, he fancied himself a ladies' man, although he claimed to abhor the hotel's policy of segregated withdrawing rooms.

Probably to save women from just this sort of fate, Chris thought as he shook the man's hand.

Sir Hamish then introduced Chris to Robert Carlisle, Chair of the Australian Mineral Council. He was Australian by birth. A bulldog with few words, and with a nose that looked like it had been broken at least once.

The other Britisher, James Sinclair chalked a cue as Fitz introduced him as London's Blue Eagle Investment Bank.

Sinclair dropped the chalk into his pocket and stretched out a hand towards Chris. 'Bond trading, mergers, and acquisitions. I'm your man, old chap.'

Which left Chris wondering who here was acquiring or merging with what and for whom, but one didn't ask an Englishman his business over a game of billiards, not if one was feigning to be of the old boys' club.

He really needed to know more about the mining fraternity and how they operated, although he wasn't sure why? His job was to find out what Fitz was doing in this place. What he'd learned already might be a legend, but if it was, Fitz had played it well, and why wouldn't he? He had been trained by the best.

7. The Perseus Project

Devin Royce watched fury streak across Robin Elgar's face and disappear as quickly as it had sprung into life.

Elgar cleared his throat, fiddled with his tie, and shifted his weight in the chair. 'So where is he, may I ask?'

'I've asked him to carry out a small errand for me. Part of the Secretary's Perseus Project.'

'Yes. You said, but I don't understand what it is, or why he's not here. Or why you didn't see fit to consult me. After all, I am the man's direct supervisor.'

'Usually, you are, and normally, I would, but these are unusual circumstances. Not to worry, he'll be back in a couple of days. Was there something urgent?'

'Not so much urgent, but the minister thought my idea for the Perseus Project had legs. She wants him posted to Jakarta as soon as possible, thinks we should keep him out of the way for a while.'

'I wish you would both go through the proper channels.'

'You think I have a choice?' Elgar's voice rose an octave.

'Yes. I think the Act under which we all work, insists you do.' Devin's mouth remained in a thin line.

'You don't know my mother-in-law very well. Her greatest ambition is to abolish the public service, never mind asking her to comply with its bureaucratic systems. Besides, she's on the joint security committee and has the requisite clearance.'

Devin sighed. This wasn't the first time he and Elgar had discussed the minister's interference and his acquiescence, and it probably wouldn't be the last, but the politics of it were wearing him down. Elgar just didn't have what it took to stand up to the woman. 'Leave it with me. I'll speak to her.'

'What about the Perseus Project? What's it to be?'

'Still working on it, but in the meantime I have sent Davis on a goose chase. It really is a minor issue to check out a British visitor in Sydney, just to ensure MI6 is not carrying out operations on our shores without notifying us.'

'Why would the British be here?'

'I don't know that they are.'

'Why do you think they might be?'

'It was a tip-off. That's all. One I have little faith in, but Davis was available. He is one of our senior officers, so I thought I would give him the job, being a fellow Brit and all. Besides, I agree with the minister. We should get him out of the way for a while.'

'So, you are happy with his posting.'

'I didn't say that. Let me mull it over.'

'What do I say to the minister?'

'Let me deal with her.'

Elgar got up. 'That's all very well. You don't have to live with her daughter.'

'Perhaps we should get you a transfer to another department, just for a while.'

'Ha. You won't get rid of me that easily... Sir.' Elgar stood up.

Devin watched him leave the room. It was a pity. A transfer would have suited all of them. When the door clicked shut, Devin picked up the phone.

'How is it going? He asked when Chris answered.

'Good sir. Far as I can tell, it's a beat up. I am at HMAS Watson at the moment, but just about to head back. Unfortunately, I ran into someone I know and have to have a drink with him this evening.'

'Is that likely to compromise your legend?'

'No sir, but in any case, I am pretty sure our man is who he says he is. I can do more checks back at my desk, so returning tomorrow. Unless you have more for me to do here.'

'Right. Good job. Take the weekend and fill me in on Monday.'

Devin depressed the receiver and dialled again, this time to speak to the minister's office. He would have to speak to her about demarcation lines. If she wanted the Perseus Project set up in Java she would have to go through the departmental Secretary, but Devin was pretty sure the Secretary didn't want to involve foreign powers in the damned operation. He wished he could just refuse to do it. The whole thing was a dumb idea.

Later that same day, the Minister for Foreign Affairs, Marianna Laidley's driver stopped outside the house. She told him he could go home for the night but to be back at 7 am. Then she stomped up three steps to the open front door. When she reached the sitting room her husband, Brian Laidley was standing at the drinks cabinet sampling a bottle of Lark whisky, a Tasmanian take on a Scottish tradition.

He turned around. 'This isn't a bad drop.' He poured a hefty slug of the golden liquid into a cut crystal glass and held it up to the light. 'Want one?'

She shook her head. 'And you shouldn't either. They'll be here in a minute.' She took the whisky from his hand.

'Hey, you said you didn't want one.'

'Changed my mind. Had an awful day.'

'What happened?'

'Oh, you know... Sanctimonious public servants. Wish I could get rid of the time-wasting leeches.' She looked at her husband of thirty years. He was a handsome man despite some greying around his temples, but for a fifty-eight-year-old he was in good shape. It was his Chinese ancestry. The Chinese always managed to look younger than their years. It wasn't fair. Marianna was five years younger, but he looked like the younger party.'

Like so many Chinese Australians, Brian had been born in Hong Kong, the product of a liaison between a British administrator, Charles Laidley, and the daughter of a Chinese property developer. With the support of family connections, Brian's father had left the civil service and set about making his own fortune during the 1970s Hong Kong property boom.

As a nineteen-year-old, Brian had arrived in Australia to study engineering and had never returned to live in Hong Kong other than for short visits on business or to see family. In the following years, he had established a profitable business in property development in Sydney through links to his father's and grandfather's interests, as well as to the Chinese mainland manufacturing and supply chains.

On one of his trips a few years ago the Chinese government had detained him under a charge of corruption. He blamed the Chinese President, Xi Jinping who had changed the rules, suppressing the national sport of gratuity and compensation under a corruption crackdown. Xi's sudden zeal coincided with a bleak outlook for Sydney property in 2012. In turn, this lined up with some bad business decisions Brian had made after the 2008 financial debacle. Kept in detention for a few days, Brian quickly capitulated to threats and was released on the understanding that he knew where his loyalties now lay.

When he returned home, Marianna had threatened to divorce him if the news got out. They had managed to keep his detention quiet and out of the media and eventually his wealth and influence in business circles had persuaded her to give him a second chance. After all, Brian's money had got her into parliament, helped with the position she was in now, and she wasn't finished. She had set her sights on the PM's job.

Brian argued she needed to become the Treasurer first, show her financial credentials before toppling the PM, but Marianna had always been impatient.

She took a sip of the whisky. Mm it was good. Tasmanian peat. The best. Marianna had been born in Launceston, an aeon ago and into another life completely, one of hardship, brutality, and poverty. She would never go back, not even for good whisky.

Brian poured himself another couple of fingers. 'What can I do to help?'

'You can check that your young prodigy is organising the dinner to be on time, while I go and change.'

Brian smiled. Huang Jia-Qi's culinary skills were exceptional. The transaction had suited them both. Marianna wanted a cook, and Jia-Qi needed to leave China for a while. What better way than through a skilled migration visa, which with the right contacts hadn't taken long to arrange.

Now the bloke cooked all their meals, and looked after the house, wowing their guests, and leaving Marianna to entertain as often as she liked. Although tonight it was just a family gathering.

'Dinner will be fine. Aren't you excited? You are about to become a grandmother.'

'Don't. That's not funny.'

'What? Aren't you looking forward to cooing over your own grandchild?'

'What's there to look forward to? I'm already becoming the invisible woman.'

Brian frowned. 'You have everything a woman could want.'

'No, I don't.'

He walked over and placed his arms around her waist. 'What's missing my darling. Tell me and I will buy it for you.'

She turned away. 'You know perfectly well. It's all right for men. The greyer their hair, the more respected they become. Women just fade away until they disappear completely from society's gaze.'

He touched her dark curls. 'Well, you have no grey visible.'

'Thanks to my hairdresser.' The doorbell chimed. 'That'll be them now. No more talk and for goodness sake Brian, don't give Robin the third degree tonight.'

'I thought you wanted rid of all public servants.'

'I do, and soon Robin will be out also. He's angling for a spot with Democritus. That's how it should be. The private sector running projects funded by government.'

Brian raised his glass. 'Big money to be made.'

'Yes, but you know how it works. He just needs an introduction to the right people at the right time. But don't bait him tonight. He's not going to drop any national security secrets, no matter how much you encourage him. It's just tedious.'

8. A Distraction

It was six pm, Friday night, and guests filled the Bancroft House cocktail bar, spilling out onto the terrace. The evening was balmy, with just a light breeze fluttering skirts and putting a glow in complexions. There would be a full house for dinner. The Premier and his wife were dining with some members of the New South Wales cabinet. Susan clicked on one of the cameras, shifting her focus to the other public areas of the hotel.

The cameras had been Mason's idea, back in the beginning when she had complained of not being able to be everywhere at once, run off her short little legs checking the quality of service, food, drinks, and cleanliness. He had tried to persuade her to record what the cameras saw, but she was adamant that would be a breach of privacy. Her only reason for having them was to check on things without having to run hither and thither. Certainly, they came in handy for other reasons, like eavesdropping on the conversation with the police in the manager's office, but that was all. She had never intended her cameras to be invasive.

A view of the lobby caused her to stop scanning and peer closer. Was that her daughter all dressed up and heading for the bar? What was Cassie doing here again? She clicked on the cocktail lounge camera. Yes, there she was, walking over to a man sitting in the corner.

He stood as she approached. Listened, head to one side as Cassie gestured with her hands. At this distance Susan couldn't hear what Cassie said over the piano music and the buzz in the bar, but she could see the girl had never mastered the art of speaking while her hands were still. All Susan's efforts to turn her daughter into a lady had failed.

Cassie looked nice though. Hair loose around her shoulders. Clad in a fine charcoal cashmere shift and wearing heels, no less. There was hope for her daughter yet, but who was she meeting? Susan adjusted the camera's focus. Good lord, it was the British naval officer who had dropped off the cufflink. How on earth did Cassie know him?

The cufflink was still in the drawer. She hadn't dared do anything with it. What if it had fallen from Harvey Kashton as Mason lugged him down the stairs in that awkward fireman's lift? No-one else had reported losing a link.

She would just ignore it. But who was the man? Or rather, what was he doing here with her daughter?

***

Chris had chosen his seat well, arriving a little early to ensure he had everything arranged the way he liked. Full view of the room and out onto the terrace, solid corner at his back, and clear view of the lobby entrance. It usually made him feel relaxed, but tonight he was simply annoyed. It was already 18:15 hours and Alistair was late.

The woman he'd seen the previous day, made her way through the tables. He stood up as she arrived.

'Mr. Davis?' She asked.

'Yes—Chris...'

'Hi. I'm Cassie. Look, I'm really sorry, but Alistair's been delayed. He asked me to let you know, as he didn't have your phone number.'

Chris said, 'That's okay. I haven't seen the man for almost twenty years. A while longer won't hurt.'

Cassie tilted her head, a small frown furrowing her forehead. 'He insisted I buy you a drink and keep you here until he arrives. Do you mind?'

'Be my pleasure but let me do the honours. What will it be?'

'Thanks. I'd love a martini.' She sank into a chair opposite him.

Chris beckoned a waiter, made the order, and sat down. 'You look like you might be in need of a drink.'

'I am. Work was an absolute schmozzle, and no, I don't want to talk about it. Let's talk about you Mr. Davis. Alistair says he went to school with you.'

'Chris please, and yes. He went to school at the same time as I did my level best to avoid going.'

She laughed. 'I imagine he would have been an awful bully.'

Chris raised his eyes looking directly into hers. 'What makes you say that?'

'Well, he's getting better I suppose, but he's arrogant, oblivious to people's feelings, a little racist if you'll forgive my saying. He would have taken your accent and heritage as a personal affront.'

'Yet you choose to date him... Sorry, none of my business. I should not have said that.'

'No. You shouldn't, but I am most emphatically not dating him! Although...' she gave a rueful grin. 'I did once. Very foolish. He's married you know, but we are all allowed one mistake, aren't we? I only said I would meet him tonight for a drink... Well, I am not sure why except, it's been a while since I last dressed up and went anywhere nice. We are just friends now.'

The waiter brought her martini, and she took a long drink and sighed. Then said, 'He really was keen to catch up with you again, although I doubt he will make it tonight, despite his promises.'

'Do you know why he has stood us up?'

'It's a missing person's case he was working on. Apparently, a bloke's yacht sank in that storm we had last week, and they have been searching for him since. They just found him. Oh, you wouldn't have been here. I saw you arrive just yesterday.'

He smiled. She was the most uncomplicated person he'd ever met. Whatever went through her mind seemed to land on her lips without guile. He liked that. 'Just you and me for dinner then.'

'Goodness no. I don't expect you to take me to dinner. I'm just the messenger.'

'I'll be eating alone if you don't, and you will have dressed up for nothing. Perhaps we can be each other's consolation prize.'

She laughed. 'That's me.'

'I didn't mean...' Chris felt the heat rising up his neck.

'I'm only teasing.' She tilted her head to examine him. 'Okay, but let's get out of this joint and go somewhere less suffocating.'

'Suffocating.' He glanced around at the opulence; marble pillars, vaulted ceilings, and huge glass panels leading out to a veranda that might have been at home in Kenya during its colonial heyday.

She grimaced. 'Old memories. You don't want to know.'

'I'll have to get my keys, but otherwise, I am in your hands.'

She grinned. 'I can drive you know. Oh, no, never mind. I saw the car you arrived in. Let's go in yours.'

She walked with him to his room, and as he swiped the key card, he noticed someone had already opened the door. The small wad of paper he'd left in the crack had fallen to the floor. Now, who would have been in his room and why? He said nothing, pushed open the door and stopped.

Cassie peered around him. 'Mum! What are you doing in here?'

The housekeeper stood at the bathroom entrance next to the luggage rack, on which rested his suitcase. Her face registered guilt like a kid with forbidden sweets. In her arms was a pile of fluffy towels.

'I was just checking that the gentleman had clean towels. She glanced around as if looking for an escape.

'Oh.' Cassie turned to Chris. 'Sorry. This is my mum, Mrs. Ainsworth. She's the housekeeper here. Sorry... gosh...'

Chris walked into the room, hand outstretched. 'Nice to meet you, Mrs. Ainsworth. We just came to collect my car keys. Your daughter has kindly agreed to have dinner with me. And thanks, I have plenty of towels.'

'Dinner, but you don't need a car. You must have it here. I insist. Cassie darling Monsieur Lavigne will be so upset if you don't eat here.'

'He doesn't even know I am here.'

'Yes. He does. He saw you come in. Besides, you won't get a better meal in Sydney, especially if you haven't booked on a Friday night.'

Cassie sighed and rolled her eyes at Chris. 'It's true. Do you mind awfully?'

'Not at all. I ate in the dining room last night and the food was excellent. I am sure it will be tonight as well.'

The housekeeper recovered her composure. 'That's settled then. A bottle of Bolly on the house. You look lovely, my dear.' She rearranged Cassie's hair on her shoulder and walked out.

'Mum...'

But Susan Ainsworth was already on her way down the corridor.

Chris grinned. He hadn't been this entertained for a while. 'Your mother is an interesting woman.'

'Yes, sorry. I don't know what gets into her sometimes.' Cassie's mobile rang. She fished it from her handbag, glanced at the screen and said, 'It's him.' She thumbed the pickup button and said, 'yes Alistair.'

Chris watched her face while she listened. It showed every emotion that went through her mind as if there were no filter.

She said, 'That's okay. I'll let him know and give him your number.'

As she put her phone back in her bag, she said, 'I knew he wouldn't come, but he wants you to give him a ring tomorrow, if you can.'

He wondered if she was disappointed. If she was, it didn't show. 'No problem. Shall we head for the dining room or return to the bar?'

'Let's go to the dining room. I don't think I have ever scored a bottle of Bollinger out of my mother. It must have been because she was so embarrassed to be caught in the room of a guest. She prides herself on being the invisible housekeeper.'

Chris smiled. So, Cassie had bought her mother's story. Chris didn't, despite the towels in her arms. How did she know the chef had seen Cassy arrive? And why was she in his room? By the look of the smudged fingerprints on the brass locks, she had been trying to open his suitcase. Now, what was she after and why? Curiouser and curiouser.

***

That evening Susan watched the dining room through the monitor, or rather, watched her daughter and the Englishman. He had registered as Chris Davis, with a UK home address, and was checking out tomorrow. She had never seen Cassie like this, flicking her hair and laughing at just about everything the man said. She wondered if Cassie knew he was leaving tomorrow. This was clearly him just passing the time—using her daughter to do so.

Sadness engulfed her, although she didn't know why. Cassie had chosen a career over having a partner and children. Besides, having a husband wasn't what she had thought—a lasting partnership into old age. Martin was concrete evidence of that fact. She tried to chivvy herself out of sadness. Perhaps she should spend more time with Cassie. She would take the day off tomorrow. They might go shopping. It was Saturday and if she arrived early enough, Cassie couldn't fob her off.

***

The next morning, Chris awoke and glanced at his watch before he arose and went into the bathroom. Ten minutes later, he let himself out of the quiet hotel and loped down the driveway towards the gate. He would do a circuit and then head into the city to meet Alistair. He may yet need to work with him, if Kashton and Fitzsimmons were in any way connected. Although that wasn't the only reason he wanted to meet Alistair again. He'd had a good time last night with Cassie. She had persuaded him to stay one more night and suggested he meet her and Alistair for brunch this morning.

He told himself he could get more details from Alistair about the Kashton case and what the police had found. One never knew where such information might lead and he had found nothing to report about Fitzsimmons, although he would have to check out his claims once he was back in the office.

Of course, he recognised he was making excuses to see Cassie again. A dumb idea, he knew, but he hadn't met a woman with whom he had felt so comfortable since Jenna. Guilt rose from his stomach, and he put on speed as if to outrun his own memories.

9. Smoke and Mirrors

Alastair stepped over the sleeping dog, and kissed his wife's cheek, before he tousled his son's hair, and bent to hug his daughter. 'I might be late, don't wait for me.'

'Oh, Alistair, you promised.'

The dog opened its eyes and thumped its tail.

'I know Minty, but it's work. I wouldn't go in if I had a choice. Tell your mum I'll be there, next time.'

His dainty Chinese/Australian wife sighed. 'She no longer believes you.'

The dog closed his eyes with a sigh that echoed Minty's as Alister drew the front door closed behind him. None of them really cared if he was there or not. He suspected he was merely tolerated in his home and if he never returned, none of them would notice. Except the dog, perhaps. He was the only one who ever took it for a walk.

Alistair walked along the short path to his car parked at the curb. One day, he swore, he'd own a house with a garden big enough to park a car, at least in the yard if not in a private garage, but he'd almost given up hope. Sydney property prices were not coming down.

Still, he should be thankful for his foresight. If he hadn't hocked himself to the hilt fifteen years ago, when he first arrived from the north, he could not have afforded a house this close to work and the city. He'd be like all the other shmucks out in the burbs, battling traffic to get into town. Despite the noise from the airport, he was thankful, although he was determined to upgrade, but for that he needed to transfer to the financial squad. That was where there was real potential to learn how to make money. He was studying finance in the hope that a degree would get him to where he wanted to be.

His first port of call was Kafana Nebo, a Serbian-styled coffee house. He pulled up outside and went in. Milo was in the kitchen but came out when his daughter, a middle-aged woman with salt and pepper hair and an apron that swaddled most of her round body, called out.

Milo and Alastair's relationship went back to the early days when Alastair had moved to Sydney as a rookie Australian Federal Police Officer. He had rented a room above the café. That was before he had resigned from the AFP to join the NSW police force, but he and Milo continued their relationship, meeting weekly.

Milo was possibly Alastair's best informant for the neighbourhood as well as a conduit for further afield. This was the suburb where Alastair lived and raised his children, so he wanted to know all the gossip. He sat at the table in the farthest corner as Milo waddled over with a cup of coffee.

'I just made Gurabija. You want with your coffee?'

'Na. Coffee's good.'

'You on a diet?'

'Sod off. Do I look like I need to diet? Now you, for example...'

'You insult your elders now.'

Alastair grinned. 'I'm meeting someone for brunch.'

'Brunch. What is this word? You joined the yuppies.

'You're out of touch, old man. The term now is Yuccie—young urban creatives.'

'Malo sutra.' Milo shook his head in disbelief, placed the coffee in front of Alastair, and added, 'you want the paper?'

Alistair nodded and took a sip of the dark liquid.

Milo shuffled off behind the counter. A minute later he was back and laid the newspaper on the table next to Alistair. 'Enjoy,' he said and lumbered back to the kitchen.

Alistair pulled the paper towards him and read the headlines. There was a story about critics of the Russian president, Vladimir Putin, who had died in violent or suspicious ways. Fingers pointed at the GRU, one of the branches of Russian intelligence.

Thank Christ this kind of thing didn't happen in Australia. The bloody Triads were bad enough. Assassins for hire. Although, he paused his thought, was there any difference between the Triads, the GRU or even the Moscow billionaires club? Weren't they all organised crime gangs used for political purposes by their respective states?

Aside from their criminal activity, some Triad groups in Australia had long links back to the CCP - Chinese Communist Party - keeping control of the local Chinese population for the CCP. The police knew who they were and were having an effect on reducing their influence in the drug, sex, and slavery trade but stamping it out altogether was proving harder.

Immigrants to Australia should leave their past behind in Alistair's opinion, or at least their politics and allegiances to foreign powers. Look at the Triads, involved in Hong Kong's crackdown of the pro-democracy movement, muscle for hire by the CCP. Yet they wanted to live in democratic Australia. He shook his head.

Triad groups around the world were nothing if not expedient. Ideology be damned where there was money to be made, weapons, drugs, sex, slavery, democracy busting, nothing was beyond them. They looked after the CCP in the same way as the Russian billionaires looked after Putin in Moscow.

He supposed, in their own countries, it was a means to keep doing their business without too much government interference. Although the difference between the Chinese and the Russians was those same Hong Kong Triad groups had Australian chapters. From what Alistair knew, Russian oligarchs didn't much bother with Australia.

He read the article slowly, creating the impression he was just a man on his way to work stopping for a coffee and the early morning news. After a few minutes he carefully opened the paper to the racing pages and slid out the concealed envelope. His winnings and perhaps some new titbit of gangland information.

Alistair wasn't stupid. He never gambled with his own money, nor did he go in for shake downs, but a bit of gossip and gratitude, as quid pro quo, never went astray. He slid the envelope into his pocket, drained his coffee cup and left with a cursory nod towards Milo's dour daughter.

Half an hour later, he was at the morgue looking into the bloated and grossly disfigured face of Harvey Kashton. It hadn't taken long for the fish to find him. No matter how much money you have, we all end up decaying in death. That thought made him feel better. He looked across at the pathologist. 'Do you have the cause of death?'

The pathologist, a large dark-haired man in his early thirties, with soft white hands, shook his head. 'On the surface it looks like he died of natural causes, but toxicology isn't back yet. Do you have any reason to think this might be foul play? I mean, what am I looking at here? You're not usually involved in missing persons' cases or natural deaths.'

Alastair grimaced. The whole thing had been a waste of his time, but when his superiors told him to take the missing person case, what could he do? The bloke was a billionaire and friends with the Premier. That warranted a show of intense effort and feigned interest or at least one that his superiors could report to the Premier's office.

He said, 'The powers that be are nervous, but there are no suspicious circumstances as far as I can see.'

The pathologist pursed his lips. 'There were certainly no signs of a struggle, nor any significant bruising.'

'So, the bloke took off in his yacht in wild weather and drowned. The only thing I have to say is he may have been an idiot. Who sets sail in a gale, for Christ's sake?'

'He didn't drown.'

Alastair tilted his head. 'What then?'

'He was dead before he was immersed. There are signs of atherosclerosis and arrythmia. He also may have suffered some breathing difficulties, but it looks like actual death was brought on by myocardial infarction.'

Alistair said, 'That would account for why the boat capsized—no one attending to its direction. He was touted as being an experienced sailor.'

The pathologist nodded.

'Okay. Maybe not an idiot. At least no one can belittle his sailing ability. I guess that's important to some people. Find anything else unusual?'

'He was wearing one antique art nouveau cufflink, if that matters.' The pathologist pointed to a counter on which rested several bags of clothing, shoes and other paraphernalia taken from the body. 'The other link is missing. Probably not important given the yacht was immersed, but who knows. You might find its pair on the boat, or it might have been washed away. Each link is probably worth more than most people's weekly pay packets.'

'You thinking robbery?'

'Seems unlikely.' The pathologist shook his head. 'It might be an heirloom. The family may want it back.'

Alastair glanced at his watch. He was going to be late. 'How long before the tox report is back?'

'Basic analysis—four to six weeks. The lab's swamped. That's if they don't find anything odd. Otherwise longer.'

Alistair sighed. Bloody billionaires. There is no way in hell the ordinary man in the street would warrant this level of police interest.

He left and gunned his car through the traffic. Luckily it was Saturday, and the roads weren't the choked arteries Sydneysiders were forced to navigate on a weekday. He smiled, hearts and roads, both conduits of life and death.

***

The restaurant overlooked the harbour, and Alistair entered twenty minutes late. The first person he saw was Cassie, head back laughing, fingers touching Chris's arm. Alistair felt a surge of fury rush through him. Who the hell did the bloke think he was with his plummy accent, fancy cars and probably wads of cash? Another fucking rich waste of oxygen. Didn't belong in Australia, never had. He straightened his shoulders, donned a small sardonic smile, nodded at Chris, and bent to kiss Cassie's neck, before he sat in the vacant seat next to her.

Cassie said, 'Oh Alistair, my mum's sitting there. She's just in the ladies. Take the seat next to Chris.'

'Your mum?' What the hell... he shrugged. 'I'm sure your mother won't mind sitting next to Chris. I doubt he bites.'

Chris smiled. 'Hello Alistair. How's your missing person's case going?'

Alistair frowned. 'What do you know about my cases?'

'Isn't that why you were a no-show last night?'

'Ah yes. What are we having then?'

'We've ordered already,' Cassie said. 'You were late, so I wasn't sure you were coming. Sorry. Mum was starving and the place is so crowded.'

'Why is your mother here?'

'Oh, she showed up first thing this morning. Wanted to go shopping.' Cassie shrugged.

Chris stood up as Susan arrived back at the table. He pulled out his chair. 'Mrs. Ainsworth, please take my seat.'

Crawler. The old bat actually fluttered her eyelashes at him. Alistair felt another surge of volcanic rage and struggled to regain control.

Chris remained standing, glancing at Alistair. 'Tell me what you would like. I'll go up and place your order, tell them to link it with ours so they arrive at the same time.'

After Chris left to go up to the counter, Alistair leaned back in his chair. 'Mrs Ainsworth. I don't think I have had the pleasure.'

'Oh gosh. Sorry. I forgot you haven't met my mum. Mum this is Alistair McMahon. Um... he's an old friend. Alistair, my mother, Susan Ainsworth.'

'You were at the hotel yesterday.' Alistair's eyes narrowed.

'Yes.' Susan smiled at him. 'I'm the housekeeper at Bancroft House.'

Alistair lost interest and turned to Cassie. 'How was dinner with wonder-boy last night?'

***

Susan watched Alistair flirting with her daughter, attempting to gross her out with details of his visit to the morgue this morning. It was, he said, what had made him late. She had changed her mind about wishing Cassie might get into a relationship with either man.

Alistair was handsome, but a swaggering boar. Chris was charming, nice looking in an understated way, and kind but there was something unsettling about him. Never mind. Cassie clearly had Alistair's measure and Chris wouldn't be here long enough to do any damage, or at least she hoped not.

She watched Chris walk back from placing the order. He moved like a cat, with languid ease and a heightened awareness of his surroundings. Intuition told her he was lethal, and she drew in a breath. What on earth made her think that? He had been nothing but attentive and mannerly since she'd met him, but that façade hid something deeper, she was certain. Susan prided herself on knowing people and Chris wasn't what he seemed.

Alastair said something about the missing man, Harvey Kashton, and Susan focussed her attention away from Chris and back to Alistair.

'Kashton died of a heart attack on board his yacht. I'm no sailing expert but the sea was pretty rough and without someone guiding the boat it would have been easily swamped. The only odd thing about the whole case is a fancy cufflink, lost but not surprising in the circumstances. Otherwise, I think it's a pretty cut and dried case of misadventure.'

Chris arrived at the table and sat down, looking straight into Susan's eyes. She blushed and dug about in her handbag for a tissue. Had he heard Alistair? Did the look mean anything? If he did hear, why didn't he say something? Perhaps he hadn't heard, and anyway Kashton could have lost the cufflink on his way to his boat that same morning.

Silence was the better option. Mason always told her that. Never volunteer information. She could always claim the cufflink had slipped her mind. It would be what Alistair expected, judging by the way he treated her. That suited her just fine.

Sweat ran down his flanks, the stench of his own exertion in his nostrils. His muscles shivered with the ague of depletion as he bowed to his opponent across the mat. 'Next week,' he asked?

The bloke shook his head. 'Sorry mate, in Melbourne but the week after maybe. Same time?'

'Great. I'm Chris Davis by the way.' He held out his hand. 'That was some elaborate elbow-move you pulled.'

'Sorry. I also train in Krav Maga. Get my protocols mixed up when I'm under pressure. I haven't been put on the back foot like that for a while. Name's Alan Marshall.'

'I'll be seeing you then.' Chris picked up his towel and mopped his neck as he watched Alan walk across the gym to a woman waiting for him.

She smiled at Chris and took Alan's arm to walk away. There was something familiar about her. As he walked towards the changing room, Chris sent his mind on a journey through its catalogue of faces. It stopped at the file on Dr. Huma Sharapova, the woman whose identification of Fitzsimmons as MI6 had sent him off to Sydney.

He ran through what he knew about her. Ex service. Now lecturing at ANU. Deputy Chair of the Foreign Investment Review Board. Bumping into her at this gym wasn't so unusual. Canberra was a small place and most of the service personnel used this facility. But she had smiled at him. Did that mean she knew who he was?

If that was the case the only person who might have mentioned it to her was the chief and that was unlikely. Perhaps the smile was just politeness towards her partner's sparring opponent. He was becoming paranoid. When he got back to the office, he would check out both her and Alan Marshall.

He took his watch from the locker. There was just enough time to shower before he headed out to the firing range to get some practice. That was another area of his life he had neglected recently. When he'd returned from Sydney last weekend, Zoe Wilson, the recruit who sat in the desk near his, had said she'd heard he was pretty handy on the range and asked him to give her some pointers. He hadn't got in any practice for a while and had little else to fill in his free time, so he'd agreed.

Australian intelligence services didn't carry weapons as a matter of course. Not since the debacle in Melbourne and the Royal Commission in 1983 after a botched training exercise at the Sheraton Hotel.

There was talk about the government reviewing the legislation to allow limited use of weapons for training and self-defence with the approval of the minister, but in the meantime, Chris kept up his skills through the gun club. It meant complying with the stringent laws in Australia. Not a bad thing to his way of thinking although criminals always had access to weapons.

At the range, Chris discovered Zoe was a weapons enthusiast. No doubt about her. But then she seemed to have a zest for most things. Smart and eager to help, probably bored silly doing stuff beneath her mental ability, but that was bureaucracy for you.

She had transferred from defence after she had finalised her PhD. Yet no matter how qualified and clever she was, everyone had to do their time according to a certain standard. That was, until some juicy operation came along, and rank and longevity gave way to brains and creativity, at least until the job was done. Then back to the humdrum, but it was no different from his time in the Royal Navy. Hurry up and wait most of the time.

Yet in this context it was a humdrum he didn't fit into, and no one knew quite what to do with him. Zoe was the only person in the office who didn't treat him like some kind of leper they needed to keep at arm's length in case of contamination.

Poor kid was probably desperate to get her teeth into something vaguely meaningful even if it meant befriending a sorry-assed candidate like himself. He knew what that was like, and this latest project wasn't turning into a likely path out of limbo.

He'd spent the whole week researching the people he'd met in Sydney and hadn't come up with a damn thing about any of them, other than they were all involved with the sale of a bauxite mine in some way. Even the lecherous old Scottish accented Australian rogue, had land adjacent to the mine, but there was nothing there that had any implications for national security.

Walker Fitzsimmons also seemed to be just what he said he was. Although World Watch, the company he represented, had the whiff of CIA about it. That was interesting in itself but didn't detract from Fitz's story. Perhaps he should talk to the chief about the possible CIA connection. It was a long shot, but he had nothing else.

The only lead from the whole trip that came remotely close to cracking anything was the cufflink he'd found on the steps leading to the beach and the jetty. Mrs Ainsworth had studiously ignored Alistair's mention of its likely twin on Kashton's corpse, which had intrigued him.

She knew more than what she was letting on, that was for sure, but it wasn't his job to solve police investigations or do Alistair McMahon any favours. The man hadn't changed. Still after his own agenda. Chris had just tucked the information away in his vast mental filing cabinet until something else came along to make more sense of it. At least in relation to the job he was tasked with, although that looked to be at a dead-end.

***

Huma Sharapova started her BMW, backed out from the parking space, and put the car into drive. 'Your place or mine?' She grinned at the man sitting in the passenger seat.

'Mine. I need a shower before we hit Steve's barbecue. Not sure why you wanted to come to the gym with me today. We could have just met up at Steve's place.'

'I wanted to see you fight. It's a turn on.'

'Does that mean...?'

'What do you think?'

He sighed and settled back in the seat. 'Drive faster.'

She ran her hand along his leg. Alan Marshall was a good looking forty-year-old. Twice divorced. Two teenage kids he saw rarely. They lived with his first wife in Melbourne, the city in which he had been born. Short blond hair, 180 centimetres tall, not a gram of fat on his body despite his job sitting all day at a desk or in meetings. He ran his own information technology security firm, and increasingly worked on government contracts, which was why he had moved to Canberra.

Huma had met him a few weeks ago at Steve Nathan's place. Steve was a mutual friend, an executive with Democritus Australia, an armaments supplier to Defence. She had been keen on Steve at one point, but he had taken up with a woman to whom he had just become engaged. It was hard to find single men of her age who were remotely eligible, and Huma hadn't wasted anytime bewitching Alan Marshall the moment she had met him.

'Who was your sparring partner?'

Alan shrugged. 'Never met him before. Said his name is Chris Davis. Bloody good fighter. I guess we were paired because I complained last time that all the others they put me with were too easy.'

'Will you fight him again.'

'Yeah. In a couple of weeks.'

Huma pulled up outside Alan's place. 'I'd like to be there.'

He eyed her as he opened the car door. 'Good looking bloke like that—are you sure it's the sparring technique that gets you in?'

She laughed. 'Get showered and I'll show you.'

***

Just as Huma and Alan arrived at Steve's barbeque, Chris and Zoe were locking away their pistols.

'You shoot like a pro.' Chris said. 'Don't know why you needed my help.'

Zoe smiled. 'Just wanted a buddy I guess. Hate coming out here by myself and I wanted a chance to tell you something outside of the office.'

'Go on.' Chris appraised Zoe, a deceptively delicate looking woman with surprisingly frank green eyes, long, straight, dark hair, and the porcelain skin tone he guessed she had inherited from her Chinese grandmother. She had a trim figure but was about ten years younger than his thirty-eight years. She was definitely pretty but Chris didn't date women so much younger than him, and especially not colleagues.

'I know you were supposed to be in line for the project leader position in Jakarta, but I heard Brad Jefferies has it now?'

Chris's mouth twisted. 'I heard.'

'I applied for one of the positions in his team.' She looked at him with her bottom lip caught in her front teeth, a furrow between her anxious eyes.

'Congratulations.'

'I had hoped I'd be working for you.' She shrugged. 'Although I haven't got the job yet, but I just wanted to make sure you wouldn't mind...'

'Why would you think I would? It's your career. Just because mine's hit an IED doesn't mean yours should take a back seat.'

'What's he like?'

'Who?'

'Jefferies.'

'He's okay I guess. Career officer. When I started he was a graduate trainee. Bit of a butt snorkeler but competent. This is a promotion for him, but I haven't seen him in a project leadership role or in a supervisory capacity, so don't really know.'

'I heard he has a tendency to kick down.'

'You'll need to be on your metal then.'

'That's if I get the gig.'

They reached her car. She opened her door, and then, looking over the roof, said, 'Hey. What are you doing now?'

'Going home.'

'I've been invited to a party. It's a Democritus thing. I used to help manage one of their contracts when I was in Defence. The director loves to entertain and everyone whose anyone in town was invited. They'll all go too. When I say barbeque I mean flame grilled lobster and champagne kind of barbeque. You might like to share my pain.'

Chris hesitated. He didn't need any more complications in his life, but he pictured the cold empty flat waiting for him.

Zoe smiled as if she could read his mind. 'Just friends. Besides you never know who will be there. His parties are usually full of military and diplomatic personnel. Her hands came up to make speech marks in the air. You may uncover some juicy morsel of gossip. Come on, you'll be doing me another favour. I hate going to these things by myself.'

11. Gods of Mt Olympus

Across Canberra, Devin Royce stood in the sitting room of his comfortable home and gazed at his wife of twenty-nine years. Tilly or Matilda (a name she hated) was an intelligent and gregarious woman, who had sidelined her career in the foreign service to support his. A gift he could never repay but would spend his life trying.

She had brought up their two boys, often singlehandedly, while he was posted to places not conducive to family life. Both boys had left home although they weren't far away, working for the Public Services in Canberra like it was a dynastic requirement. But since then, Tilly had made up for lost time, heading up a charitable foundation, which she ran with admirable foresight, skill and efficiency. With the added advantage of her considerable diplomatic skills, she had recently taken the organisation global.

He supposed it was a silly question, but Devin had to ask, 'Are you sure you want to go?'

'Of course. Lots of deep pockets will be there. You know what Steve's parties are like. Every management consultant in town will be trying to ingratiate themselves. It's a networking opportunity.' She glanced at him, 'and not just for my Foundation. Your career might benefit too. You just need to make the effort. I know you are a spook, but you need to make yourself visible for us mere mortals occasionally.'

Devin frowned.

Tilly laughed. 'Besides, you said the minister will be there. She's one of Steve's fans. It will give you an opportunity to get into her good books.'

'I don't think she's speaking to me at the moment. She would much prefer Robin Elgar as chief.'

'Well, this is your moment to show her that you count.'

'Don't see how I can do that but never mind. Let's get on with it then.'

'You make it sound like going to the dentist.'

'Give me the dentist any day.'

'Oh you.' She fiddled with his shirt collar and stepped back. 'You look very handsome. I will have to beat off all the single women.'

He laughed, genuinely amused. At forty-nine women barely noticed him, let alone came on to him. In some things, Tilly gave him more credit than he deserved.

***

Chris stood, champagne in hand, back against a concrete column, supporting the two-storey house—the column that is, not his back. He smiled inwardly: Atlas holding up the world.

Across the pool area, Zoe walked easily among the guests. She was heading towards a fair-haired man she had said was her father. He was standing with a group who included, among others, the U.S. deputy Chef de Mission along with the bloke he had been sparring with earlier, and the woman, Dr Sharapova. Now that was interesting.

The connections in this antipodean Mt Olympus were intriguing in themselves. He would enjoy watching them play out, so long as he didn't have to join in the squalid Bacchanalia. These were people, who thought they owed nothing to humanity. Instead, they held aloft ideas of their own superiority, claiming individual liberty and freedom as a rallying flag to the ever-shifting power base of self-interest. Or perhaps he judged them unfairly.

Zoe kissed her father and greeted the others before taking his hand to drag him away from the group and towards Chris.

As they came closer Zoe said, 'Daddy this is my friend Chris. He and I work together. He's senior to me but he's been like a mentor showing me the ropes. He speaks Mandarin also. Chris this is my father, David Wilson, country director of Democritus Australia.'

'Afternoon sir. Nice to meet you.' Chris shook his hand, thinking, Jesus Christ she moves in hallowed company, but not a whiff of it before now.

Her father didn't look at all Chinese with his blue eyes, sandy skin, and fair hair. He must be where Zoe got her light eye colouring despite her grandmother's heritage.

'Glad to meet any friend of my daughter. So, you work for the Foreign Office also. Is it as boring as Zoe claims. I warned her not to leave Defence.'

'Most of the time sir, although like any job, not always.'

'Too many chiefs not enough Indians, is what I heard.'

Chris grimaced at the archaic and objectionable colloquialism. 'I wouldn't necessarily put it like that...'

But Wilson was no longer listening. 'Ah. I see your minister arriving.' He nodded towards a cluster of people entering the swimming enclosure via a gate from the garden.'

Chris's heart sank. One of the people with her was Elgar, who strode across the paving to claim the chairman of IPA, the Australian Institute of Public Affairs, an Australian Zeus. His empty flat began to look enticing.

'We've been at the gun club.' Zoe glanced at her father. 'Chris is an excellent marksman.'

'Is that so. Can you give my daughter a run for her money?'

'I tried sir, but she was too good.'

'Call me David, please.'

Zoe interjected. 'He's too modest. He actually scored higher than I did, which doesn't happen often.'

Chris glanced across at Zoe, wondering what she was playing at. Was she just another Dionysian acolyte. Had he misjudged her or was it simply his jaundiced view of the Canberra establishment.

As if by way of explanation she added, 'Daddy was an Olympic shooter in his day.'

For one moment Chris saw her father hefting a javelin in the sanctuary of Olympia. He shrugged off the image and focused his attention on Wilson who laughed with a practiced self-depreciating levity.

'My only attempt at the Olympics was a bloody disaster. Before your time. Moscow 1980—just after the Soviets invaded Afghanistan. In hindsight I shouldn't have gone, but there you go. All lost in the dust of history. Now the Russians are our friends, despite Tony Abbott's threat a few years ago to shirt-front Putin.'

Chris examined David Wilson with interest. The head of the biggest armament manufacturer in Australia started off as a sporting shooter. How did men, even one's with extraordinary sporting talent, climb to the top of a global enterprise like Democritus. Not by playing a straight bat, of that he was certain.

He hoped Zoe wasn't putting him in line for a job. There was no way he wanted to work for an armaments manufacturer. It wouldn't be the first time consultants had tried to lure him into their webs. They were everywhere—denuding the public service—but that was neoliberal ideology for you. Small government, big society; a euphemism for government's role changing from protecting its citizens, to one where they looked after the market by channelling fiat dollars straight into the pockets of the wealthy.'

And there it was. Wilson handed his card to Chris. 'If you ever fancy joining the private sector...'

Chris told Wilson what he'd told other recruiters. 'Thank you sir, but I am in the diplomatic business. Becomes tricky when billing by the hour gets in the way of preventing war and terrorism.'

Wilson glanced at his daughter with a mock rueful look, and said, 'Anytime you change your mind... Well, you kids enjoy the party. Nice to meet you Chris. I need a word with your minister if I can prize her out of the grasp of SinEnergy. Edwards has managed to waylay her before she even has a drink in her hand.'

Chris nodded. It was a long time since anyone had called him a kid. As her dad walked away he said, 'Zoe. Would you be offended if I left?'

'Why? We just got here, and we haven't even tasted the food. Is it my dad? Sorry I should have asked if you would like to meet him. He's okay really. But please don't go. I will be left alone...'

Chris smiled at her. 'Surely, I'm not your only friend here. You seem to know everyone.'

She sighed. 'I was raised in this company, but I hate it really. It's like work, you're always looking over your shoulder, assessing the situation for its potential.'

And yet you thought dragging me into it was a good idea, but Chris didn't give voice to his train of thought.

She grimaced. 'Look at my dad making a beeline for the minister so he can use his influence. I wonder if she believes in her own popularity. Does she recognise that once her office title is lost, after some election or cabinet reshuffle, no one will notice her, ever again?'

'The gods only exist because of human belief.'

'Pardon?'

'Nothing, sorry. Just agreeing with you.'

'At least you are real.' She gave him a pleading look.

He laughed despite his misgivings. 'I guess that's a compliment.'

'It is. Come, they are bringing the cooked stuff to the table.'

He looked over to where she pointed, seeing people carrying food trays in from the barbeque area.

Zoe wrinkled her nose. 'There is usually more caviar than anything else, although Steve's favourite meal is cocaine, but I guess that won't be on display.'

Chris followed her reluctantly. He didn't want to mix with these people outside of work, but as he approached the table he saw Alan Marshall placing a large crab claw on his plate. He could cope with Marshall.

Marshall turned and saw Chris. 'Ha. Chris Davis, we meet again. Sorry, I do have your name right, don't I?'

Chris nodded and shook the outstretched hand.

'Have you met my partner. Huma Sharapova? She was drooling over your Kyokushin technique, earlier.'

Huma smacked Alan on the arm. 'I was not. Don't listen to him. Nice to meet you Chris. Hi Zoe.'

Chris said, 'You know each other?'

Zoe nodded.

Huma said, 'My father worked for Democritus before he retired. I used to babysit Zoe for pocket money when I was at Uni. She was just a tiny little thing. Oh, is that showing my age?' She pulled down the corners of her mouth, and her eyes moistened. She placed an arm around Zoe and hugged her. 'After your poor mum passed away.'

Chris thought, Jesus, this town is an incestuous maze. He would have to watch his step.

A familiar voice cut through the emotion, and Chris turned to face his boss.

Elgar said, 'Good grief. Davis! What brings you here?'

His look told Chris he wasn't pleased to see him. Then his eyes widened as he saw Zoe. 'Oh, I see. Hello Zoe. I guess you're here with your dad. Nice to see you both enjoying this lovely autumn day.' Elgar busied himself by picking up a plate and loading food on to it.

Chris had just lost his appetite. Standing at the food table had been a mistake. He backed away as unobtrusively as he could, fading into what he hoped were the camouflaging shadows of overhanging shrubbery. It was one thing to navigate these sorts of events when one had an official role, but Chris felt like a gate crasher at this party. He rubbed his forehead as if the giveaway was there, writ large.

As he stepped back into the deep shade someone moved. A voice said, 'Mr Davis, I see you are as allergic to these kinds of events as am I.'

'Chief. I didn't see you there.'

'No, I am trying to hide from your boss and his mother-in-law. They are both furious with me.'

Chris laughed. 'You are the ranking officer, sir.'

'No fury like that of power thwarted, but I didn't realise you knew Dr. Sharapova.'

'I've just met her. Of course, I know who she is from the file, but this is the first time I have spoken to her. Zoe knows her well, though.'

The chief's phone rang, and he swore. 'Blasted thing.' He thumbed the green icon, put the phone to his ear and walked a few steps away. 'Devin Royce here.'

Chris took a sip of his champagne and watched the assembled crush of people. Zoe was still chatting to Huma. Another bloke wandered over towards the food table and Chris sucked in a breath. It was the Argentinian investment banker Elias Aguirre, who had been staying at Bancroft House. Chris hadn't spoken to him, but he'd seen him there. Now he was stopping to talk to the chair of SinEnergy.

What did an Argentine investment banker want with both a bauxite mine, and one of the biggest energy groups in Australia? Maybe something as straight forward as investments, but maybe something more. SinEnergy was mostly owned by Chinese interests and that always had alarm bells attached.

He couldn't let the man see him. Who knew if he would remember Chris from Bancroft House. Although being seen in this crowd probably would not blow his cover. Where else would an ex Royal Naval officer turned consultant hang out, but with armaments manufacturers and the people who bought them. Besides, this joint held the who's-who of the Canberra establishment. Why wouldn't he be here? The only person not in evidence was the Prime Minister and that was probably because she preferred living in Sydney to remaining in the Lodge in Canberra over the weekend.

If Chris were a terrorist this was the type of event he'd target. All these people had let down their guard, thinking they were among friends. Small chance of that. There were at least half a dozen intelligence officers here from a variety of foreign missions. Across the far side of the pool, he could see Liam Garcia, his CIA counterpart, talking to Liesel Fischer from the political section of the German mission. He had spoken to Liam last week to ask him what he knew about WorldWatch.

Liam had been evasive, leaving Chris convinced it was a CIA front. That meant Fitz was working with the CIA in some capacity.

The chief hung up the phone. 'Mr Davis, may I have a small word somewhere more private.'

Chris followed him around the side of the house.

Devin Royce stopped and looked around before he said, 'That phone call was from a colleague in the AFP. He has just had news that Myles Delahanty was found dead in his home in Sydney.'

'Chair of the FIRB sir?'

'The very one.'

'Dead. How sir?'

'First pass seems like a heart attack brought on by arrhythmia. There are apparently no suspicious circumstances, but I don't like this one little bit. As far as I was aware he had no prior health issues other than advancing years. His wife said he was ill with a bad cold before his heart went AWOL. She had been out playing golf and had left him tucked up in bed. When she returned she found him.' He grimaced. 'I don't understand it. He was a health nut—fittest fifty-eight-year-old I have seen in a long time.' He drew a breath. 'It's reminiscent of the Kashton death. Nothing wrong with the man then boom, dead from a heart attack. Kashton's drowning a mere distraction. Too many coincidences or maybe I'm just a suspicious old man.' He sighed.' I will have to inform the minister. While I do that, can you and Dr Wilson brief Dr Sharapova. A quiet word in her ear might be appreciated. Delahanty was her mentor, and she is his deputy. She should be one of the first to know, but I reckon she'll take it hard.'

'Sure. But before you do sir, you should know one of the parties interested in the bauxite mine is here. The Argentine banker, Elias Aguirre.'

'I remember the name. Which one is he?' Devin Royce walked to the corner of the house. 'Point him out to me.'

'The bloke talking to Christian Edwards, SinEnergy's Chair.'

'I see him. You think this is significant...'

'Not sure sir, but SinEnergy is mostly Chinese owned and there are some indications it has CCP links.'

'Jesus Christ. This becomes more and more interesting. Did you get to talk to Aguirre when you were in Sydney?'

'No sir. Not part of my mission. Just looked into Fitzsimmons' reasons for being in town.'

'Good man. Do a bit more digging and see what you can find. But it can wait. Talk to Huma... and Chris...'

'Sir.'

'Go gently on Huma. Show her the compassion I know you can fake so well.'

Chris grinned. He left his champagne glass on a window ledge and went off in search of Zoe. He would need her to pull Huma aside somewhere quiet.

A week after the party the chief called Chris into his office. 'Mr Davis, I would like to send you over to Treasury for a while.'

This was it! They were getting rid of him. Last week, it had begun to feel like he could have had his heart's desire, except for some reason it wasn't. First he'd been offered a job with Democritus, and later that day after seeing Huma home, Zoe had propositioned him. He hadn't felt good rejecting her. Even so, both offers had done his ego a power of good, but Zoe and a well-paying private sector job was not what he wanted. So, why did he still feel like such a failure?

What he did want was to get back into the intelligence game, preferably in some country where his particular skills-set might come in handy. But nothing in his life was panning out the way he'd planned. Now, instead of firing him, they would move him sideways where he'd drown under a load of dusty files in some financial archive.

He frowned. 'Sir?'

The chief smiled as if he could read Chris's mind. 'Don't worry Chris, It's in your current capacity with the Perseus Project, but you will need to work under their legislative framework. I have two reasons for doing so. The first is that Elgar is still intent upon sending you to Jakarta, where I think your talents will be wasted. I need to put him off for a while or he will manage to wear me down through political pressure. You won't be at the Treasury for long, and the good news is that I have a possible vacancy coming up where I think you might be useful given your languages and resourcefulness. That's restricted information at the moment and don't hold your breath. It may or may not happen. In the interim I want you to carry on with the FIRB matter, but this time to provide closer support to the new Chair. Dr Sharapova argues she can manage quiet well, but I am increasingly concerned for her wellbeing given the short history of the decision making regarding the bauxite mine's ownership.'

Chris nodded. 'Dignitary protection. Isn't that ASIO's job?'

'Consider it part of the Project Perseus. So, you are it.'

'What about a weapon, sir.'

'Not deemed necessary, Mr Davis. We don't think the risk of Huma being shot is high, given the way both Kashton and Delahanty died. Besides, your job is not protection. Huma refuses to be, in her words, babysat. Instead, you will be at her side when she requires. Otherwise, your job is to provide her with intelligence briefings on the suitability of the investment parties.'

Chris nodded. 'By the way sir, did the autopsy on Mr. Delahanty find anything?'

'No. Both Kashton and Delahanty's tox reports came back inconclusive, although Kashton had elevated levels of potassium, but the report claims it was not enough to kill him. I have asked for the results to be held back from public disclosure, just in case more information comes to light. At least until the decision is made on the bauxite mine, which the Treasurer says will be soon. The NSW coroner's office is unhappy, but they've agreed.'

'Sir. I am not sure how useful this information is, but there are a few things I should mention. They may be unrelated, but one never knows...'

'Go on.'

Chris explained how he'd found a cufflink at Bancroft House, which he had given to the housekeeper Susan Ainsworth. He then told the chief about her reaction to the police detective's information about a missing cufflink. 'It seemed odd behaviour at the time but as it had nothing to do with my mission I didn't follow up. Perhaps I should have.'

Devin Royce folded his arm across his chest, resting his elbow on it while he covered his mouth with his palm. After a moment he took his hand away and said', 'What do you suggest Mr Davis?

'I think Mrs Ainsworth knows more than she is letting on.'

'Do you think she had something to do with Kashton's death?'

'I doubt it sir, but she may know something.'

'What about the police? This is their province. We should bring them in.'

'I think that would be a mistake sir. If the police get wind of it they'll make too much noise, and then any intelligence we might have gleaned will be lost in the tramp of heavy boots. Or worse. Besides, I have my doubts about the detective in charge.'

'What do you have?'

'Nothing specific yet. Just a hunch.'

'This is most irregular. I am not sure we should be keeping information from the police or poking around in their business.'

'If I thought she had something to do with the murder I would be happy to go to the police, but Bancroft House is central to the puzzle, and alienating the owner won't help the police nor will it help us. She's in a prime position and a possible candidate for recruitment.'

'Recruitment! That's a tad left field and besides we are not in the business of surveilling our own population.'

Chris grinned. 'I would like to keep my options open. Most of her patrons are foreign movers and shakers and she has surveillance systems everywhere in the hotel, which I am sure she uses. If we channelled her activities we might learn some interesting information.'

'Such as?'

'It's in my report sir.'

'Tell me anyway.'

'Well, why is the CIA using a British asset within the WorldWatch organisation to attend a Sydney mining conference?'

'You think these issues are connected.'

'I don't know sir, but it's possible. WorldWatch is monitoring Chinese interests in bauxite mining in Ghana. They are concerned at the growing presence of Chinese involvement in the Sahel region. I personally think Russia is a bigger concern and wrote a report on a similar subject just recently. The Russian mercenary group supplying arms to the Central African Republic is of particular interest to the CIA and I wondered if Fitz wasn't here on a related matter...'

'I don't recall such a report.'

'No sir. I handed it into my director before I began this job.'

'And...'

'He didn't agree with my analysis, sir.'

The chief paused. 'All right Mr Davis. Go to Sydney but leave out the recruitment for now. Just talk to the housekeeper. See what you can find and send me a copy of the report you sent to Elgar.'

'There is another thing. A long shot I know but did the toxicology investigation look for poisons?'

'I imagine so. Why?'

'You wouldn't know which ones by any chance.'

Devin shook his head.

'It's just that Mr Delahanty's wife said she left her husband at home with a cold. It started me thinking, and then Zoe mentioned a Chinese medicine called fùzǐ. Her grandmother swore by it for colds and coughs. I looked it up and it's a species of the Aconitum genus, a purple flower that grows in China and Vietnam and its deadly in anything greater than the microscopic amounts. They add traces to some herbal medicines. I was just wondering if that kind of thing would show in a toxicology report.'

Devin's fingers beat a tattoo on his desk. 'Are you saying he was poisoned?'

Chris shrugged. 'I was just looking for an explanation for why a perfectly healthy man would suddenly develop arrythmia and drop dead. That plant will do it. It only requires a relatively small dose to kill a person instantly and it is not the first time it has happened, whether intentionally or accidentally.'

'And Kashton?'

'Don't know sir, but as far as I know he was also a fit man who up and died of a heart attack.'

'You do realise what you are suggesting Mr Davis?'

Chris nodded. 'I said it was a long shot, but there are significant Chinese interests in the bauxite mine and the plant is well known in China.'

'I thought there was only the one Chinese company. Besides, the Chinese are not in the habit of poisoning their competition. That's usually a Russian thing.'

'It's not so unusual for the Chinese, although they typically use other means. Besides, my investigations show there is more than one Chinese company interested.'

'Who else?'

'You remember the Argentine banker I pointed out at Steve Nathan's shindig?'

'Yes.'

'I did more digging, and it appears he and two of his colleagues resigned their directorships of the Argentine National Bank about seven years ago to go out on their own. They received their initial startup funding from the China Development Bank. Since then, they have done very well with the help of several large investments, which I have traced back to Chinese Government interests.'

Devin put his head in his hands. 'This is worse than I thought. Have you checked out the other investors?'

'Yes, sir. Rio has links with Rusal the biggest aluminium company in the world until it was taken over by the China Hongqiao Group. Ditto the XNT Group. Although none of it is surprising as Rusal and Hongqiao own most of the Aluminium interests worldwide. Hongqiao seems to own some of Cǎihóng shares. Cǎihóng is the other group interested in buying the bauxite company. The only one of the potential investors for whom I haven't found any links to the Chinese, is James Sinclair of Blue Eagle Investment Bank in London, but several of his clients include Russians. There is one in particular who has interests in aluminium. A Russian oligarch by the name of Misha Yelchin. I am still looking into his connections.'

'If they have most of the bauxite in the world under their control, what the hell do they want with an Australian mine? No, don't answer that. It's pretty obvious, especially after the Ebola outbreak in that part of the world.'

'That and the on-going civil unrest. Yes sir, they need a safe source.'

'What for? How much bauxite can a country use?

'President Xi is modernising his military capability and that takes a lot of aluminium.'

'Let's hope we are not seeing the kernel of a new arms race.'

Chris ran his palm down his cheek. 'Since their annexation of Crimea, Russia also seems to be gearing up. Their plans for significant military exercises with Mongolian and Chinese troops are scheduled for September. They may have something up their collective sleeves that we are not privy to sir, and I think we should be paying greater attention.'

'We are tasked by the government of the day, Mr Davis. We don't pick our own agenda, and at the moment the most significant threat is I.S., but I will raise the Vostok military manoeuvres with the minister and the National Security Committee. Perhaps they will agree, intelligence on Moscow requires beefing up.'

'I think IS are heading to the margins, sir.' Chris shrugged. 'They're a problem but are rapidly losing territorial control, especially now with Operation Inherent Resolve hammering them in Iraq and Syria.

'They won't go away.'

'No sir but we should not ignore other emerging threats because of IS.'

Devin raised his eyebrow. 'This is not about you getting a deployment to that part of the world, is it Mr Davis?' He paused before saying, 'never mind,' and changed the subject. 'I don't envy Huma's decision making. I wonder if she is happy with her appointment. It was touch and go for a while there. The retiring ambassador to Moscow was keen on the position.'

Chris hadn't missed the inference and hesitated before saying, 'I heard the minister also suggested Dr. Elgar for the job.'

'Is that a statement or a question?'

'Is it true sir?'

The chief moved his head from side to side, which told Chris nothing.

Then he said, 'With all this, it's even more important for you to provide support for Huma. Working with Treasury will allow you to act in a legitimate and unremarkable role, providing her with all this information so that the board can make a decision. Remember she was once one of us and can be trusted with sensitive information. She still has high security clearance with her current role. You will also remain close and keep an eye on her. The Chinese Communist Party weren't that keen on her in the first place. Her appointment will have them frothing at the mouth.'

'Sir?'

Devin Royce tapped his forehead with his index finger. 'Of course, you don't know. I'll have to get you cleared to read her personnel file before you move over.'

Chris frowned. 'The job with Treasury is just for the duration of the FIRB review and the Treasurer's decision on the bauxite mine, isn't it sir?'

'Yes Mr Davis. You'll be back in a few weeks no doubt. Unless you prefer it over there. You never know I might have to fight to get you back.' He laughed.

'Chief, I wonder if, while I am in Sydney talking to the Bancroft House owner, I can get further information on the toxicology of both Kashton and Mr Delahanty. I know the detective in charge of the Kashton case, and I could keep the query low key, only telling him what he needs to know. Also, I would like to visit Mrs Delahanty; ask about medicines her husband might have consumed.'

'Do what you have to do for us to get to the bottom of this but do it quickly and quietly. Huma takes up her new role next week and I am worried she is in danger.'

'I won't be stepping on other agency toes, will I, sir? I could pull together an interagency briefing.'

'No. The heads of the other agencies are in agreement. Until we find the source of the intelligence leaks, the project is eyes only. Besides, if Kashton and Delahanty were poisoned because of FIRB business decisions, it will set a new bar. I don't want anything like it getting an airing before we know for sure. Jesus, the international fall out would be horrendous, let alone what would happen to our relationship with our biggest trading partner. If we knocked China's nose out of joint they may stop trade. That would have the National Party snacking on our organs. Do what you have to do, but do it quietly, Mr Davis.'

13. Defection

Captain Mèng Yichen opened the door of the white Nissan Dualis and looked around before lowering himself into the driver's seat. He couldn't help the feeling of eyes following him, but that was fanciful. How could anyone know? He hadn't breathed a word, not even to his parents, and he was certain he had left no incriminating trail.

He worried about his parents, but they were old and sick. A man couldn't put his whole life on hold for people who would be dead within a year or two. Besides, Lieutenant General Liu knew them well and would not blame Mèng's parents for what he was about to do although it might be better if he could persuade them he was dead. Even so, as long as he played it right and didn't create the slightest ripple in an otherwise unblemished career, his actions would fly under the radar until it was too late for them to stop him.

He started the engine and put the car into reverse. Another car passed behind him, the driver appearing to study Mèng. Was he watching? Mèng shook his head. He had done this run every morning since the Lieutenant General had arrived.

Mèng had been assigned to the Lieutenant General as his aide while he was in Australia, which was only for the time it might take to ensure Cǎihóng's chairman, David Cho, was successful in his bid for the bauxite company. The Chinese government was keen to gain a majority share, if not outright ownership, and had sent Lieutenant General Liu Aiguo to make sure Cho didn't stuff up the deal.

The job had given Mèng a freedom he hadn't experienced before General Liu's arrival. The reason was Liu's love of cream cakes. Every morning Mèng took this same car to the bakery that made the best eclairs, horns, doughnuts, slices, and gateaux in Canberra. All made with fresh cream. He would select an assortment and take back a box for his boss. The cakes would be offered to his guests, who seldom took one, and that suited Liu just fine. The man was beginning to look like a bull frog.

Mèng reversed into the road and headed west on Coronation Drive before exiting onto Flynn and taking a right onto the State Circuit, going the long way around parliament. Then he turned right into Sydney Ave and left at John McEwen Crescent before he spotted his quarry riding a bicycle. The tension rushed from his shoulders.

He had been watching the man for weeks; certain this was the right person. But the past few days Chris Davis had not taken his usual route to work. Mèng had panicked, thinking Davis might have been posted elsewhere. He had been back from Beijing for two months. Surely another posting was on the cards. That was the nature of this kind of work although he had heard the Australians didn't direct their staff to work overseas but asked only for volunteers. He wasn't sure he believed it.

Regardless, Mèng would need to act soon, or he might lose the opportunity. He had tried to avoid making the move while General Liu was in the country, but he couldn't leave it any longer. How could he approach the Australian? It was not as if they moved in the same circles. Mèng could not pull up the car and accost Davis. That would be a dead giveaway, stopping in an area inhabited by federal police and spies. Mèng sped up and did a U-turn at the next intersection, driving slowly north.

He passed Davis again cycling along King George Terrace, entering the section between the Senate Gardens and the National Rose Garden. Mèng increased pressure on the accelerator, overtaking the cyclist before turning into Parkes Place West.

On impulse he pulled up and got out of his car. Other vehicles passed, all going to work. Bad place—bad timing—he was a fool. The Chinese Embassy was a few city blocks away. Anyone might see him. Mèng swung back into his vehicle and closed the car door just as Davis turned the corner. Mèng Yichen froze in the driver's seat.

***

Chris saw the same white Nissan drive past. This time the driver made no effort to hide his interest. A few minutes later, he passed Chris again as he rode past the Aboriginal Tent Embassy, before turning into Parkes Place and stopping.

What the hell. This was new. The hairs on his neck prickled as the man jumped out of his car. Adrenalin surged through Chris's body, but the man seemed to hesitate as if changing his mind. Then he turned back and climbed into his car.

Chris pulled up next to the vehicle. 'Are you looking for me, mate?'

The man glanced up the road and back again before winding down his window. Chris appraised him. Sweating forehead, jumpy as a tom thumb. Up close he looked vaguely familiar, and Chris tried again in Mandarin. 'Can I help you with something?'

'Mr. Davis?' The man responded in English.

'Chris, please.' He grinned at the poor bloke, feeling some empathy. This was obviously not his home turf.

'Please act like you are giving me directions.'

'Sure.' Chris turned and pointed down the road, curved his hand towards the right and made a few other inane gestures, which might be taken for street directions. 'What is it?'

'I need to talk with you, but not here, not now.'

'Where? When?'

'Tomorrow morning at 7.30 am. Pâtisserie de Solène in Civic. Do you know it?'

'I'll find it. What's your name?'

'Tomorrow.'

'Unacceptable. You know my name.'

'All right. Yichen Mèng.' He said it in the European way, placing his surname last. 'I am with the Chinese Embassy, but please Mr Davis, my life depends on your discretion.'

'Understood.' Chris held up his hand as if in farewell and rode off towards the Treasury building from where he was to operate in his new role as Dr Sharapova's liaison. Questions burned in his brain. What did Mèng want? He hadn't immediately recognised the man, but he knew the name. Mèng was assigned to Lieutenant General Liu as aide-de-camp.

Liu was a stalwart of the Communist Party, here with the Cǎihóng chairman, but his real boss was Mèng Li Jie, the highest-ranking diplomat of the People's Republic of China. Mèng was a relatively common name, but what if Yichen was a relative. Christ. He had to speak to the chief.

He turned at the entrance to the Treasury building and dismounted as Mèng drove past, eyes fixed ahead. Chris chuckled. Poor bloke must be wondering what the hell Chris was doing at the Treasury building instead of his usual workplace. That would be the question he would ask if he were in Mèng's shoes.

14. A Return to The Trade

The next morning, Chris ordered breakfast and coffee at Pâtisserie de Solène. At 7:15 am the place was already filling with patrons catching a quick take-away or stopping for a breakfast meeting on their way to work. The room was foggy with the cosy aromas of baking vanilla pastry, coffee, and humanity's breath.

Chris took the last vacant table. From his vantage point, opposite the cash register, he could see who came in through the door. He opened his phone to a news app, pretending to read while he carefully assessed the scene. This was an unlikely venue for a meeting, although he gave Mèng credit; it was probably a good one. The bakery was near the museum and art gallery in an area more dedicated to arts and law than politics and skulduggery, although the Chinese Visa Office wasn't too many blocks away. Conveniently, it wasn't far from the Australian University campus, where Chris was meeting Sharapova at 8 am, so he had plenty of time.

One thing he hadn't done was tell anyone about the meeting. He should have reported it to his director, but something told him that would be a mistake. Elgar would most likely stand him down and take the meeting himself, or hand it off to someone else. He could have gone to the chief given the connection between the bauxite mine and Lui's likely reason for being in Australia, but Devin Royce was at some function in Sydney with the Prime Minister.

Chris had decided having a croissant and espresso in a place that was on his way to the appointment with Dr Sharapova was a good reason to be here. The rest might be coincidence. Alternatively, he may have nothing to report. Mèng hadn't looked happy at having been sprung by Chris yesterday. With 20/20 hindsight it had been a dumb move. Too risky, still it livened up an otherwise uneventful day.

He took a sip of espresso. It was good, full bodied, strong, and smooth. Beans roasted to perfection. The door opened and in walked Mèng. He was greeted at the counter as if he was a regular. Chris watched him point to half a dozen different pastries and cakes. Once he had paid for the box of pastries he turned back towards the door, catching Chris's eye before he walked out.

Damn. Chris left his uneaten croissant and the remains of his coffee on the table and got up. He sauntered outside, pausing to zip his jacket against the biting wind. Russet leaves piled up against the curb and storm clouds gathered on the horizon. He should have brought a raincoat.

Mèng crossed the road and disappeared around the corner of the Museum. By the time Chris caught up, Mèng was standing in the entrance foyer of the, still closed, museum and gallery, examining a poster about a photographic exhibition of Aboriginal and Torres Strait Islander people. It was a good spot for a brief exchange as they were alone and hidden from the street.

Chris stood behind and to the left of Mèng, wary but intrigued. 'You like pastry I see.'

Mèng didn't turn around. 'They are not for me.'

'Who are they for, then?'

'My boss.'

'Who is that?'

'General Liu?'

Chris raised his eyebrows at Mèng's honesty. 'Okay. So, you wanted to talk.'

'I have information.'

'Go on.'

'I must have guarantees.'

Chris remained silent.

'I have information to make it worth your while, but the Australian government must promise to protect me.'

'I think you have the wrong bloke.'

'I have the right person.'

'How is that?'

'You were in Beijing.'

'Yeah. I worked for the foreign office.'

'You work for the Australian intelligence service. I have watched you ride to work every morning.'

Chris smiled. 'Then you will have observed I am now with the Treasury department. A lowly financial analyst.'

Mèng shook his head. 'You have the same rank as a colonel.'

'What?' That did surprise Chris.

'I know about you Mr. Davis. The level of your public service job is the equivalent to an army colonel. '

'First I heard, but okay if you say so. What can I do for you?'

'I want you to speak to your counterpart in the CIA. Tell him I am an Australian asset and to leave me alone.'

Chris's mind shrieked with questions, but his voice remained neutral. 'I thought you wanted to defect.'

'Yes. But I understand I must first provide value, or you will not help me. Now, I must go. We are too exposed here. One thing. Do not tell anyone of our meeting other than Mr. Devin Royce.

'Why him?'

'You have a leak in your service, which is how I know about you.' 'He shoved an envelope at Chris and said, my first instalment. I will contact you with more. Lock your bike to the rail running outside the bakery. I have created a dead drop. Just unscrew the rail end. When I have something, I will leave this tag on the wall across the road. The one with all the graffiti. He showed Chris a chevron design on a piece of paper. But remember this is what you would call an arrangement of quid pro quo, and I need protection.'

With a faraway look on his face, Chris watched Mèng scurry down the street towards the car park. The man had obviously done this before.

***

At 8 am Chris made his way through the grounds of the ANU, memories of his own time at the university uppermost. When he found the right place he knocked on a door labelled A/Professor H. Sharapova. The door swung open. Huma was dressed stylishly in high heels, tight black three-quarter length pants with a matching jacket and a cream silk shirt.

Chris said, 'Good morning Dr Sharapova. He glanced at the door, 'or should I call you Professor?'

'Huma will do fine. You're Chris Davis from Treasury and also Zoe's friend. You were kind when Miles died. I remember.' She held out her hand and smiled at him, the creases around her eyes deepening. 'May I call you Chris, or would you prefer more formality.'

'Chris is fine.' He was drawn into her web of warmth immediately. 'I hope I can be of service.'

'You will be. I am sure of that. Come in. Take a pew over here.' She walked to a seating area, her movements lithe and svelte. 'Would you like coffee or tea, something to eat?'

'I'm fine thanks.'

'Is that the information I need?' She pointed to the backpack he held in his hand.

'It's a start. I can take you through it now if you have time.'

'Just give me the highlights. I have pretty much been over most of the information with Miles.' Huma's eyes glistened and she took a tissue from a box to wipe her nose.

She must be missing the man who had been her mentor for so long. Once Chris had been given clearance, he had read Huma's file. An interesting human being. He wondered if her relationship with Miles had been purely work related, lovers, or perhaps he had been a kind of father figure.

She sniffed. 'Sorry. Realisation he's gone, catches me unawares sometimes. You'll think I'm a baby.'

'You knew him a long time.'

She lifted her head. 'I did. He was like a father to me.'

Chris thought that answers that question then.

She changed the subject. 'Did you know, I used to do your job. Your real job I mean not this one you are doing now.'

Chris kept his features neutral. She knew what his job was. Well, she probably had the clearance, and she and the chief seemed to be old friends, but it left him with some discomfort. Too many people seemed to know who he was and what he did for a living. This was not how the game was supposed to be played. He said, 'Yes. I read your file. Your track record in the agency was pretty impressive.'

Her mouth twisted. 'Not good enough though. Give the Chinese an ounce of leverage and they will ruin a person's chances. But you already know that don't you? I understand you have been compromised too.'

She really did know a whole lot about him.

'Devon said he'd given my file to you.' She grimaced. 'Poor man, you must have been bored to tears.'

'On the contrary. You've led a remarkable life.'

She smiled. 'I have rather, haven't I, and I am not complaining. I love my job here training the next generation. It's changing though.'

'What is?'

'The whole intelligence game. Humint is dying, while cyber is in the ascent. The community is in danger of losing its soul.'

'Not sure our community has a soul.' Although he would have argued human intelligence was still valuable. His meeting with Mèng earlier was testament to that, but he said nothing, just opened his backpack and pulled out a file.

Huma sat on the sofa next to him as he took her through the intelligence he had on each of the investment candidates. A faint scent of vanilla rose with her every movement, distracting him.

When he reached the end she said, 'Seems like James Sinclair is the last man standing. What else do you know about him?'

Chris thought about Sinclair for a minute. He recalled the moment Fitz had introduced them, and his first thought had been, entitled arrogance but all he said was, 'James Reginald Sinclair, born 12 March 1972 in Radley, Oxfordshire (formerly in Berkshire prior to county boundary changes in 1974). He attended Radley College, formally St Peter's College, an independent boy's only boarding school. Was a keen sailor and scuba diver. Read economics at Oxford. Joined his father's private bank, Blue Eagle Investing, which he took over at the age of 30 after his father died of liver cancer. Married briefly to Inga Peskova, a Latvian model, who had taken the London fashion industry by storm in 2012.' Chris visualised the woman's photo with her willowy and pale elfin looks. 'She divorced Sinclair last year, no children.' He drew a breath and continued. 'Prior to the GFC there was some scandal, unproven and now forgotten, regarding insider trading and the sale of debt. He has current membership of White's, London, and is on friendly terms with the British PM and numerous other members of the conservative party. I found nothing of significance regarding Sinclair to raise concerns over national security.'

What Chris didn't say was Sinclair was not who concerned him. A major client of Blue Eagle Investments was a Russian oligarch by the name of Misha Yelchin. Yelchin was a billionaire and Russian industrialist, founder of

Elemental, a global company with investments in energy, metals and mining, machinery, financial services, agriculture, construction, and aviation. He was also a shareholder in Russian Aluminium manufacturing as well as one of Blue Eagle's largest investors and one of Sinclair's close friends.

Chris had raised the issue with the Treasurer, but the politician had told him it wasn't relevant, saying bankers couldn't help their clients. Chris didn't agree. But he conceded Yelchin was also in deep with Glendening, a global mining company that had investments all over Australia.

Yelchin was also a close ally of President Putin and currently the FBI's main candidate under suspicion of running interference in the American presidential campaign last year. Not to mention allegations of influence in policy through his mates in the British government. There were also fears he was funnelling weapons to various paramilitary and revolutionary forces in north Africa.

The Treasurer had insisted Chris should not go into that with Huma, saying the stories were speculation and gossip and Yelchin was not on the list of investors for the bauxite mine. Since the fall of the Soviet Union, Russian billionaires had infested the London financial markets. It was not really surprising that Sinclair had some of them investing in his enterprises.

Huma seemed to recognise some hesitance in Chris's statement. She cocked her head and tucked a strand of streaked blonde hair behind her ears. 'Is there something else?'

He looked directly into her dark eyes. 'That's all.'

Her eyes narrowed for a second before she said, 'It was Miles decision to clear the way for both Harvey Kashton and Blue Eagle to make investments in the bauxite mine, with a caveat that the aluminium should be processed in Australia. Creates jobs you know. If there are no issues with Sinclair, I cannot see why I would change Miles's decision.'

'I didn't know he had made a decision.'

'Oh yes, although it wasn't official. We had been scheduled to meet with the board one more time to be assured of their agreement before providing advice to the Treasurer. It was all decided after our meeting with Harvey Kashton, before he died... I was thinking another meeting with the board could take place next week. Perhaps I'll have another investor-get-together at

Bancroft House, give the board a final look at the players. Miles loved that venue. 'You'll attend won't you?'

Chris hesitated. How could he go back in a public service capacity after posing as a wealthy consultant? Fitz, Sinclair and their cronies would be a little put out to say the least. 'I am not sure that will be necessary.'

The frown on Huma's face cleared. 'Of course. How forgetful of me. You were there before, checking out Walker Fitzsimons.'

It seemed there was nothing she didn't know about him. The chief must trust her.

She ran her hand down her neck and under the collar of her silk blouse, giving Chris a glimpse of the swell of a breast.

He raised his eyes to her face.

She said, 'I can see being there with me might send them into a spin.' She paused. 'You will just have to be there in your previous capacity. What was it?'

There seemed no reason not to tell her. 'Consultant to Lockheed Martin.'

'Well, you will have to retain your cover. You can also be there representing a client interested in investing in the mine.'

Chris laughed. 'They'll turn themselves inside out wanting to know who this late comer might be. Could Lockheed Martin be contemplating investing in a bauxite mine?'

'It wouldn't be their first foray into mining investments. But you can prevaricate over naming your client. It's what they would expect, and it will make them nervous.' She laughed. A joyous sound and placed her hand on his.

He looked down. 'If it's okay with the Treasurer.'

'Of course it will be. I'll talk to him and Devin. Now, enough boring investment chatter. I am so glad you were assigned to me. I saw you fight my friend you know. I would much rather talk about that. It's become my favourite keep-fit exercise. I used to do barre, but martial arts are so much more exciting. I haven't trained since I left the service. I decided to take it up again and have been taking lessons for almost a year. I would love some pointers.'

'I haven't seen you training.'

'No. It's a secret. My plan is to challenge Alan when I am confident enough. I avoid the club but have enrolled in a new gym called Basic Promise.'

'That's a Karv Maga club isn't it?'

She looked at Chris from under her eyelashes, a suppressed smile on her lips. 'It's more street-style defensive moves I am looking for, rather than ballet.'

'Ballet! Kyokushin?'

She gave him a sideways look. 'All those high leaps and kicks. It's like an animated barre without the bar.'

He stared at her fingers as they danced, twisting and kicking across the back of his hand.

Her phone pinged and she glanced at the screen before turning it over and getting up. 'You should give Karv Maga a go.'

He stood up too. 'Thank you for your time Professor.'

'Huma please. And it is I who should thank you. We will be friends, I know it.' She leaned in to brush his shoulder as if dusting off lint. 'One moment. Let me get you the details of the club. I'll give you a ring and perhaps you might be able to make time to attend a training session with me. Zoe told me what a patient tutor you are.'

Chris frowned. 'I am sure Alan would be a better tutor than I would.'

She took his arm to walk him to the door. 'Then it wouldn't be a surprise. Devin said you would be my protector until the end of this business so I think you would be the perfect self-defence tutor. Now I have a class to attend. Forgive me if I rush you out.'

Outside in the hallway, Chris stopped as the door clicked shut behind him. 'How the hell had he got into this? She was definitely flirting with him and that wasn't a good thing. She was his assignment not a date. How was he going to get out of training with her? The decision on the bauxite mine needed to be done and dusted as soon as possible.

Another thought struck him. Why was she coming on to him? She was gorgeous, sexy and at the top of her profession. He could easily lose himself in her but vice versa was odd. Chris had no illusions about his own appeal. He was a pretty ordinary kind of bloke in a mid-level public service job and had nothing to offer by way of influence or assets.

This was especially so as she was dating Alan Marshall, a good looking and well-known entrepreneur with oodles of assets and influence. If he wasn't yet in the billionaire's club he was heading that way judging by his company profile and the circles in which he moved. The last government contract that fell his way was worth millions.

Chris shook his head and walked from the building to retrieve his bike. Perhaps it was wishful thinking. Maybe he had misinterpreted her behaviour. He glanced at the sky. Clouds were building.

Before heading back to the Treasury building Chris took a short detour to his apartment to collect a raincoat. Again, he contemplated buying a car. He hadn't planned on being in Australia this long and if he was overseas, a car in Canberra would just sit in a garage, one thing he didn't have. Besides, most of the time riding a bike gave him exercise he didn't get sitting at a desk, but winter was on the horizon, and he didn't fancy riding home soaked to the skin in the freezing cold of a Canberra winter.

He rode north through the university grounds and cut through Central Canberra, past Civic and on into Reid. He pulled up outside his apartment block and left his bike downstairs locked to a convenient down pipe. He wouldn't be gone long, and the place was deserted during the day, with most of the tenants at work. This was not a family-oriented apartment block.

He ran up the stairs to the second floor, backpack thumping against his back. At the top of the stairs, he stopped abruptly. The apartment door was open a crack and he was damn sure he hadn't left it like that this morning. He glanced around for a weapon, but the hallway and stairs gave up nothing. Maybe his backpack would do the trick, but it held his laptop. It would be a last resort. He didn't want it damaged.

At his push the door swung back showing a narrow entrance hall, empty. On one side was the bathroom and on the other his bedroom. At the end was the kitchen and living room which led out to a narrow balcony, all sparsely furnished.

A sound came from the bedroom and Chris eased in through the doorway and crept toward the door. A figure, dressed entirely in black with a balaclava pulled over his face, walked out of the bedroom and saw him.

Chris said, 'Can I help you, mate?' The smell of sandalwood cologne wafted into his senses.

The figure's hand snaked behind his back.

Chris took a step closer, preparing for a physical confrontation. Instead, he looked into the barrel of a Ruger Max-9. He stopped, assessing his chance of disarming the bloke. The figure took several steps backwards, still with the gun trained on Chris, before turning to race out to the balcony, where he swung over the railing and disappeared.

Chris sprinted to the balcony and looked over the edge.

The intruder was on his knees, gun lying half a metre away in a garden bed. He leaped up, grabbed the gun, and dodged around the side of the building.

Chris turned, ran back through his flat, down the stairs and outside, but there was no sign of the intruder. He walked around the corner of the building to the garden bed and calculated the drop from the balcony. It wasn't that high he supposed although he wouldn't like to try it. The soft ground showed the bloke's footprints. They were relatively small for his height.

If indeed it was a man. He cast his mind back to the image in his memory. It might have been a tall and slender woman although one without curves. He didn't think it looked like a woman's body but that might have been his ego playing mind tricks.

Couldn't be bested by a woman, eh? He asked himself. No, that wasn't it. Being bested by women had been his experience throughout his life, starting with his mother. She had always been two steps ahead of him. He walked back around the building, trudged up to his flat and through the open front door, before gazing around his bedroom as he tried to see it from an intruder's point of view.

There was a double bed in its centre and a chest of drawers against the far wall. All the drawers were pulled out. A wardrobe, built into the opposite wall, was also standing open. Nothing of interest and there was certainly nothing of value in his flat. His laptop was in his backpack and his phone in his pocket. The only thing he owned of real value was a one carat diamond engagement ring, worth a few grand, but that wasn't why he kept it. It was the only thing he had left of Jenna. He walked over to the top drawer and found it still in its box.

So, this was not a burglary. He moved into the living area. Television still in place, although the unit drawers were open. Nothing to find in there except the TV manual and an old Xbox. He switched on the TV and opened the app for the hidden security camera that monitored the front door.

Definitely a pro who took less than five seconds to break in. He gazed around looking for anything else that might have been displaced. All the drawers and cupboards in the kitchenette were open, including the fridge and oven doors. He went about methodically shutting them. The intruder must have been disappointed with the contents. Chris didn't do much more than, shower, sleep, or occasionally watch the telly in his flat.

In the bathroom, cabinet doors and drawers were also open. What the hell was the intruder looking for? At least, Chris hoped he was looking for something and not bugging the place. He'd have to have his flat swept, but a cursory look showed nothing obvious. Curiouser and curiouser. He opened the toilet cistern. No little surprises left in there. Presumably no one had planted packages of incriminating evidence.

Chris walked back to the kitchenette and pulled a folding step ladder from behind the fridge. He took it back to the bathroom and climbed up to a small trapdoor cut into the ceiling. It was too dark to see much beyond the rim, but the dust hadn't been disturbed. He supposed he should make a report to the police although that would mean he would have to make a statement.

None of it would make a difference anyway and he needed to head on back to work. A quick glance at his watch told him the chief would be getting back from Canberra within the next hour. Chris wanted to report back to the Treasurer and then go and speak to Devin about Captain Mèng's desired defection, and Huma's request he attend the Bancroft House dinner.

He closed the trapdoor, locked the balcony door, went back to his bedroom to find a rain cape, before heading out. He checked the lock on the front door. It was undamaged. This was a professional job, but what the hell had they been looking for? Could it have been the file on the investors still in his backpack? Then he remembered the envelope Mèng had given him. It was also in his backpack. Jesus, could they be onto Mèng already? He walked back inside, took off his backpack and unzipped it, taking out the folder.

The document was a copy of a classified ministerial report, sent from Dr Elgar to the minister's office outlining the contingencies the department had put in place to stop information being leaked to the Chinese. The report was dated a week after the ministerial policy officer had been 'let go'. This was definite evidence of another leak, most likely in the ministerial office. Or was it the same leak and had Chris targeted the wrong suspect? Shit!

He replaced the file in his pack and walked out, locking the door behind him. This was bad. Very bad. No matter how he looked at it there were no positives. Not only was the leak confirmed and narrowed down to somewhere between the agency and the ministerial office, but he may have accused the wrong person.

No. He was certain the evidence pointed directly at her. This new leak may be an accomplice. Yet aside from the issue of who, was the question of why Mèng would do this. What was his story? Time to talk to Liam Garcia.

15. A Fateful Offer

There was no way out. Alistair McMahon had tried every tactic to get out of going, but this was it. A day with Nan and Pops. Nan and Pops, for Christ sake. It sounded like something from a kid's reader, rather than the united nations making up the Chin family under Nan's penetrating gaze. Nothing, but nothing, got past her.

It was one of the reasons why Alistair hated going to Sunday yum cha. She would grill him about money, ambition, his sense of duty to family, and demand to know when they would have more children. Fuck that. Additionally, all the stodge and pastry of the yum cha left him with indigestion. It was impossible to refuse. She would push and push until, to stop her, he would eat the bloody things, boiled pastry and all, then suffer all week.

He had tried; told Minty he had to go out and tell the people at Bancroft House that the case had been closed. Death by misadventure. He didn't really have to go but he wanted to see Cassie again. She often spent Sundays with her mum, but he had also read in the paper that Sir Hamish White had taken her on to represent him. The bauxite deposit from the mine next door ran under his land and he had seen a way to cash in. Cassie would be bound to spend time with him, and according to the papers, Sir Hamish was still in residence at the hotel.

Minty would have none of his pleas that he had to work. She had the hide to tell him if he didn't go to the family celebration of her brother's engagement today, it was the end. He wasn't sure she meant it but with Minty he couldn't take the chance. She and her family were a resolute lot, and the older brother Henry was a scary fucker with nebulous interests in the horse racing industry. He often placed bets for Alistair, ones his wife and her mother knew nothing about, and in exchange Alistair gave him the odd tipoff that the coppers were interested in some aspect of the business, but that was where their relationship ended.

Alistair didn't probe into Minty's family business interests either. Her father had started life in Australia as an importer of goods from China and went on to dabble in property development. How much money he had made

Alistair didn't know, but their home and assets indicated it was a substantial amount.

Minty's younger brother Ed had joined his father's firm. Recently, Alistair had begun to suspect Ed had made some pretty hairy connections to a gambling mob, who had moved their operations from Hong Kong to Sydney after the crackdown by the CCP. Gambling was still legal over there, but it wasn't easy to get a license. Australia was an easier bet.

The problem was, Ed wanted to talk to Alistair today, and that activated his self-preservation antennae, especially as Ed Chin had invited his new friends to his engagement party. Maybe he could get away after lunch. Nan and Pop's home wasn't far from Bancroft House.

**

When Alistair, Minty and the kids arrived, Nan's house was overflowing with relatives and friends. The decibel level was high enough to have neighbours complaining, despite the distance between houses. The kids raced off to find their cousins, and Alistair followed Minty inside. She went off with her mother and sister. Alistair helped himself to a beer, stopping to survey the room as he took a deep draught.

The sitting room was cluttered with rosewood furniture along with black, red, and gold soft furnishings. Cliché, but his mother-in-law was a firm believer in the power of fen Shui.

Ed approached, and Alistair raised his beer. 'Congratulations. When do I get to meet the poor girl.'

'Funny.' Ed grinned. 'Now, if you like. She's over there.' He nodded in the direction of a group of women. Minty was one of them. They were examining a blonde woman's hand or presumably a ring on the hand.

Alastair glanced at Ed in surprise. He thought Minty had told him the fiancée was Chinese, but apparently not. Ed was taking a leaf from his older siblings and marrying a gwailou. Why not. This was Australia, one of the great melting pots of the world. Pretty soon its inhabitants would become a café au lait blend. Something that worried Alistair. He had recently read about the great replacement theory, but Minty had scoffed at that, saying it was just a conspiracy theory propagated by right-wing nutters.

What if it wasn't? He had fallen for Minty, and he loved his kids, but he didn't want to lose the Australian culture he loved. The one that said white, working-class men ruled, and fuck the establishment, all while swigging back the next beer.

Still, skin wasn't culture was it? Besides, Ed's skin was lighter than Alistair's. A sort of ivory compared with his tan, and Ed certainly wasn't what anyone could call working class. Not with the money his family had. Perhaps the old concepts of social echelons no longer worked.

'I wanted to have a word.' Ed said.

'Yes. Minty passed on the message. But if it's anything to do with your mates from Hong Kong, I don't want to know.'

Ed frowned. 'Why not?'

'They have background. Look,' Alistair nodded towards Minty and the fiancée, 'the crowd around her is thinning. Maybe now is a good time to meet her.'

His brother-in-law placed his hand on Alistair's arm. 'One minute Bro. My friends are legit. They've bought a stake in the Lightening Entertainment Group and are looking for security.'

'The new casino?' Alistair's eyebrows rose.

'Yep. And besides,' he glanced at Alistair slyly, 'you don't seem too fussy when it comes to helping out my brother.'

A shiver crawled across Alistair's shoulders. How the hell did Ed know about his deal with Henry? It was supposed to be a secret between the two of them. 'Different league man.'

'All gambling though. My friends have interests in the Hong Kong racing industry too. But I hear you also have a side gig with the Serbians, who, unlike my friends, don't have a licence for their gambling clubs. You're spreading yourself thin mate.'

The bloke had him. Where the hell was he getting his information? Alistair sighed. 'What kind of security are they looking for?'

'That's my man. I'll leave them to discuss the details, but let me tell you Bro, they pay really well for loyalty. You won't need to bother with your other sidelines. Come on over. I'll introduce you to Jessica. You had better say nice things, and for the sake of happiness, admire the ring. It cost a fortune.'

• • • •

A few hours later, Alistair left the party to make a quick visit to Bancroft House. He had told Minty he'd be back to take her and the kids home.

She'd relented. At least he'd stayed for lunch, she said, and the kids were happy playing with their cousins.

He strode down the steps to the driveway where he'd parked the car, pointed the key fob, and pressed the button to open the car door. The lights blinked at him, and he hurried towards it, his heart rate accelerating at the thought of seeing Cassie again.

As he reached the car, three men stepped out from the side of the house. One of them waved and called. 'Alistair McMahon!'

Alistair nodded, but he didn't have time to stop and chat now.

With a quick skip the bloke was at his car door, preventing Alistair from opening it. He thrust out a manicured hand. 'Mike Leong. It's good to meet you. Ed said you were interested in talking.'

Mike was taller than Alistair by a good few centimetres, and sender. His shoulders were broad as if he lifted weights although it was difficult to tell with the suit covering his body. It was a good suit too, grey raw silk by the look of it, with a black shirt unbuttoned at the neck and no tie. Sharp jaw line in an oval face. Hair brushed back, from a high forehead, but loose like it had some kind of styling lotion to give it body and keep it in place. In any case, it wasn't greasy. The man looked like a movie star. He had style; Alistair gave him that. Minty would call him handsome.

Alistair shook his head. 'I have another appointment.'

'I'll drive you.'

'I'll take my own wheels, thanks.'

'And you a law-abiding police officer...'

'What the hell does that mean?'

'I counted at least three beers...' Mike held up a hand and clicked his fingers.

'A dark blue Range Rover eased along the driveway and stopped. One of the other men, opened the back door and stood aside.

'Come on mate. A ride can't hurt, and we can talk on the way. I'll make sure you get back okay.'

Alistair figured he didn't have much choice. He relocked his own car and climbed into the backseat of the Range Rover. Leather recliners, console with champagne cooling on ice. Glasses. He said, 'Nice wheels.'

Mike got into the back with Alistair. The other bloke shut the door and got into the front passenger seat next to the driver. The third man walked over to a black Suzuki Hayabusa, pulled on a helmet, climbed onto the motorcycle, and followed them.

'Where are you heading.'

'Bancroft House.'

Mike nodded. 'Fancy place.'

Alistair raised an eyebrow. 'You know it?'

'Sure, visit often. Good food.'

The driver had obviously heard because he seemed to know where he was going.

'So, what did you want to discuss?' Alistair asked.

But Mike seemed in no hurry. 'What's at Bancroft House?'

'None of your business, mate. Look the hotel is five minutes away. We don't have long. If you have something to say, get on with it.'

Mike smiled. 'My old grandmother used to say, with time and patience the mulberry leaf becomes a silk gown.'

Alastair shot back. 'My mother-in-law says the man who waits for roast duck to fly into his mouth must wait a very long time.

This time Mike laughed. 'A good proverb to live by. You like the finer things in life, Alistair?'

'Who doesn't? But I also like to keep my head on my shoulders and out of gaol.'

'I can understand that. It is my sentiment too. Ed told you our business is legitimate. The Lightening Entertainment Group is licensed. We do not seek to fall foul of the Australian law. We are immigrants after all, and do not wish to be sent back to Hong Kong. It is becoming increasingly difficult to do business over there if you are not a party member.'

'If the communist government doesn't grant you a licence, you mean.'

'It is the same thing.'

'Okay. What is it you want from me?'

Mike held up a hand. 'Perhaps a drink first. There is champagne but we also have spirits. No beer, I'm afraid.'

'No, I don't want a drink. What I want, is for you to get to the point.'

'Alright then. I am fairly new in Australia and must learn the culture. You are all in a hurry, is that not right?'

'You speak English well.'

'My dear Alistair, I was born in a dependent territory of the British Empire. One of my grandfather's was from Yorkshire and came from a lineage of capitalist and marauders, back as far as the Vikings, I believe. My own father was from Scotland. It is the maternal side which carries the Chinese heritage. Of course, I speak English. It was all but my native tongue when I was a child. That is the legacy of colonialism. None of us remain unsullied by its insidious reach. For our ethnicity we must either chose a side or have it chosen for us. I have chosen my paternal heritage, although my brother has chosen to follow our matrilineal culture. This you will understand Alistair. You too have been required to choose.'

'No mate I am Irish to the core. Never colonised anywhere.'

'Really Alistair? I thought you were Australian.'

'Well of course, but with Irish heritage.'

'When did your ancestors arrive on these shores.'

Alistair laughed. 'They were brought here and dumped by the bloody English, somewhere early in the 1800s.'

So, you choose to call yourself Irish. This means that you have chosen the Irish aspect of your heritage, but not even the Irish are pure. Surely your Irish ancestors did not only marry Irish women. By the look of your dark eyes and olive skin tones you have some Spanish or perhaps French blood. Both settled in Ireland, along with Vikings and other plunderers. It wasn't just the English. Or perhaps you have blood from this part of the world running through your veins. Can you be sure you have not?'

'That's bullshit. Blood is blood, with just a type, A or O or B, or some such. It doesn't have a nationality. But never mind all that. We are nearly at the hotel. I don't have much time, so can we get to the point?'

'Right. What I need is for someone, who knows and understands the nuances of the law in this state, to keep us from making any mistakes. I understand ignorance is no excuse before the law.'

Alistair grimaced. 'Only lawyers can get away with that.'

Mike raised his eyebrows but said, 'We do not wish to inadvertently find we have made some mistake. We would like to offer you a generous retainer and if you managed to warn us, say for example of an impending mistake, one that might bring consequences, you would receive a bonus for your trouble.'

They turned into the driveway leading to Bancroft House.

Alistair frowned, 'I am not sure how that would work, but it sounds pretty benign. Let me finish my business here, and we can talk on the way back. I assume you will wait for me.'

'Certainly. Although we might wait inside. I have friends staying here, and the bar has a good assortment of fine whisky.'

Mike accompanied Alistair into the hotel, his two men trailing a step behind. He peeled off, heading to the bar, while Alistair walked to the reception counter.

Alistair asked to speak to the housekeeper.

'May I explain your business with Mrs Ainsworth. It is her day off and she may not be available.'

Alistair placed his card on the counter. 'Just let her know it is police business.'

The woman picked up the card and then put through a call.

Alistair walked away, his policeman's eyes scanning the foyer while he waited.

The receptionist walked around the counter and approached him. 'Detective McMahon, Mrs Ainsworth will see you shortly. If you would like to wait in the manager's office.'

She indicated the office behind the reception. The one where he had first seen Cassie again. He nodded and walked around the counter and into the office. The office window looked out over the garden. Shrubs crowded around the window affording privacy from a curious guest's gaze.

A few minutes later, Mrs Ainsworth came in and shut the door.

'Good afternoon, Detective. What can I do for you?'

'Please, Mrs Ainsworth, call me Alistair. Your daughter and I go back a long way. Is she here by the way?'

Susan Ainsworth shook her head. 'She's working, snowed under.'

'Is this not her office?'

'Good lord no. Whatever gave you that idea?'

'It was where she was working when I first came here.'

Susan bit her lip. She'd forgotten. 'Oh no, she was just covering for the manager who was away at the time.'

'So where is the manager today?'

'Golfing, I think. It's his day off.'

Alistair blinked. This phantom manager business was odd, but that wasn't why he was here. 'I just dropped in to let you know that the missing person's case is now resolved.'

'Yes. I knew you had found him. It was in the papers, and I was at the café when you told Cassie and that lovely friend of yours about it.' She paused before saying, 'He's coming back, you know?'

'Who?'

'Your friend, Mr Davis. He's booked in for next weekend. I thought you would want to know. Give you an opportunity to catch up again. Cassie really liked him.'

Blood rushed into Alistair's head. 'What's he back for? Does Cassie know?'

'Gosh, I don't know. I will have to make sure she does.'

Susan gave a small triumphant smiled, and at that moment, Alistair would have enjoyed strangling her. He pulled back his shoulders, wishing he hadn't told the stupid bitch the case was closed. He would have liked to terrify her a little, just so she might recognise who was in charge here. He added, 'You will remain available in the event we need any further evidence.'

'Oh, I thought the case was closed.'

'Cases are never closed completely. New evidence has a way of reopening them.'

Susan nodded, remaining silent but gazing at him as if waiting for him to speak.

The silence lengthened.

He said, 'Well, I'll be going then. If you know of any other information, you will call me or ask Cassie to do it. I'll leave my card.' He took another card from his pocket and placed it on the desk, before stomping out of the office.

At the bar entrance he saw Mike talking to two other men, both Chinese. He stopped and waited until he caught Mike's eye, then raised a finger and walked out to the car. He wasn't going to be seen drinking in a public place with the likes of Mike and his cronies. And fuck Davies. What the hell did he want coming back here? He glanced at his watch. The whole episode had taken fifteen minutes. He still had time up his sleeve.

When Mike got into the car, Alistair said, 'I have one more stop before we return to the Chin's.'

Mike said, 'Sure. What's the address. He poured a glass of champagne and handed it to Alastair. 'Looks like you could use it. Business didn't go as well as planned?'

Alistair took the glass absently, while he told the driver Cassie's address, then sat back and drank deeply. He would have preferred a shot of bourbon, but this would do.

16. Manipulation

As soon as Alistair left the office, Susan turned on her camera system, focussing on the lobby monitor so she could watch Alistair leave. He walked towards the bar and signalled to someone. Who? She switched monitors to scan the cocktail bar. The two Chinese guests, Mr Cho and General Liu, were there. They were with a man, who raised his hand to Alistair, but didn't move. She switched back to the lobby and saw Alistair leaving through the front entrance. She switched again and the forecourt monitor showed him walking towards a dark blue car. It didn't look like a police car, but what did she know about such things?

The man from the bar and two others came into the scope of the monitor. One of the men got onto a motorcycle and the others got into the car with Alistair. Both vehicles eased from the parking lot and drove off.

Susan was glad he hadn't decided to hang around. Cassie had told her the man was married. Married men had no business chasing after single women. She knew the results from bitter experience, and she was pleased Cassie had refused to fall into the trap of becoming the other woman.

Alistair, unlike Martin, would never leave his wife. He just wanted a bit on the side to suit his narcissistic image of the sophisticated man about town, with a clever and attractive barrister on his arm. It would give him a status he didn't deserve. She sighed and went back to her sitting room at the top of the house to tell Cassie she had got rid of the man.

In the service lift, she felt a sudden lightness as if she could breathe easier. The Kashton affair was behind her.

When she entered her sitting room, Cassie was curled up in the chair, an open file on her lap, her eyes closed. Susan gently removed the file and placed a mohair throw across her daughter. It was chilly and one always feels so much cooler when one falls asleep. Then she went to the little kitchenette to boil a kettle for tea.

The door opened and Mason came in.

Susan held up her hand in a silencing gesture and pointed to Cassie.

He nodded and walked towards their shared office.

Susan followed him in and shut the door.

Mason's face was wretched with worry. He was a stocky man, with a solid squarish frame, salt and pepper hair receding at the forehead but remaining thick at the back. He was a man easily overlooked, but loyal to a fault. Susan's dog, strong, hardworking, obsequious, and silent. They were traits that made him the perfect type for the multitude of tasks he undertook, not only for her but also for the guests.

'She whispered, 'What's up. I thought you were supervising dinner arrangements.'

'I was, but I just had the most peculiar conversation.' For a moment he looked bewildered.

Susan said, 'What's wrong, Mason dear?'

'I am not sure.'

'For goodness sake Mason. Just tell me.'

'That woman with Mr Sinclair... Who is she?'

'You mean Ms Carmichael? She's his assistant.'

'Yes.' He shook his head. 'Not sure if I imagined it but I think she was coming on to me.'

'What?'

He shuddered. 'It was bizarre. She collared me in the service lift and slipped a wad of notes into my pocket. Look.' He pulled out a roll of fifties. 'She said she was counting on me to look after her.'

Susan tried to hide her smile. 'And you thought she wanted to buy your body.'

Mason shrugged. 'She kind of pressed against me, counting my buttons with her fingers while she spoke, leaned into me and whispered in my ear, while her hand sort of trailed across here.' He indicated his crotch.

Susan noticed the base of his neck had turned a dark maroon. 'What else did she say?'

'I don't know. I was in too much of a panic to listen. Something to do with the bauxite mine. What shall I do with the money? Can you return it?' He shuddered again and ran his palm across his face. 'I feel weird. I think I need a shower.'

Susan raised her eyes to look at the ceiling. If Ms. Carmichael was not trying to buy Mason's body, what did she want from him? Information was the most obvious reason to pay the man. All these billionaires and multinational companies were vying for the same thing. That's why they were here, to outbid their competitors for the bauxite mine. Cassie had told her the dinner next weekend was D. Day. Surely she and Mason could capitalise on it in some way.

'Keep the money, Mason dear. I think I have an idea, but it will require installing a few more discrete cameras. Leave me to work it out.'

'In the meantime, what do I tell her?'

'You can tell her that the Chinese bidders for the bauxite mine were in deep conversation with another man who is friendly with a NSW police detective. They are probably interested in the FIRB decision. Tell them that's all you have for the moment. She patted his arm and opened the door. The kettle was boiling. 'You'll feel better after a cup of tea.'

A few days after Mason's unsettling experience, Chris pulled into the forecourt of Bancroft House, driving the same Maybach he'd hired previously. Nothing much had changed since his last visit except this time the sun was shining, although the breeze was chilly.

He had arrived early for the FIRB dinner with the investors tomorrow night, hoping to carry out a spot of recognisance beforehand. He just wanted the decision made, and made in Australia's interests, but without Harvey Kashton in the mix, all the investors had foreign interests. He had never seen power or profits take a backseat to humanity's welfare, let alone when those interests were foreign. At least, not unless coerced. With the players involved, that wasn't going to be easy.

Dr Sharapova was due to arrive tomorrow evening in time for the dinner. In the meantime, he had an appointment with Mrs. Delahanty. He also wanted to speak with Mrs. Ainsworth, and it would give him an opportunity to catch up with Captain Mèng, who was also here, accompanying General Liu and the chairman of the Cǎihóng Group, David Cho. Liu and Cho were expected to attend the dinner as potential investors.

He had a few questions for Mèng. After their last meeting Chris had spoken to Liam Garcia, his CIA counterpart, and discovered the Captain was up to his chin in money laundering. Liam had told Chris that Mèng was a heartbeat away from the CCP charging him. The only reason it hadn't yet happened was that Mèng's had a relative who was a senior member of the party apparatus in Beijing. The Americans had held their knowledge of his nefarious activities over his head and recruited Mèng, but he was considered a bit-player, mostly trying to avoid being caught by the Chinese government's drive to stem corruption.

The gang Mèng had been using to launder his money, were involved in a circular economy scam, funnelling cash transactions in Chinese currency to finance South American drug cartels, who in turn imported the raw ingredients to make Fentanyl, from China. They then sold the drug on US streets.

A WILDERNESS OF MIRRORS

The Americans had forced Mèng to cut off the supply of cash, while at the same time they had extracted all the information he had to give. Once Mèng had exhausted what he knew about the drug cartel, the CIA began squeezing him for intelligence on China and the Communist Party.

The Americans played hard but soon found that Mèng was too low on the bureaucratic pole to warrant special consideration. They kept him on the hook but barely bothered with him otherwise. The man had no bargaining power, which was possibly why he had approached Chris. Liam had readily agreed to Chris's proposal to take over handling Mèng, so long as he shared any information.

Now that Mèng's motivation was clearer, it would be easier to place some pressure on the man. If he had been laundering the Yuan into American dollars, the CIA had foiled that, but Chris speculated that Mèng was now doing the same thing in Australia.

There was another unofficial reason for Chris arriving early. He had arranged to meet Cassie at a Spanish tapas bar in the city, and he was looking forward to it with an uncommon sense of optimism. Before it was time to head into the city, he would check in, make a time to speak to Mrs Ainsworth and then do a dash out to Mrs Delahanty's home in Balgowlah, and find out what medication her husband had taken for his cold.

As he took his bag out and locked the car, his thoughts on Zoe. Yesterday he had dropped into the office morning tea to farewell her before she left to take up her three-month post in Jakarta. He had forced himself to choke back a surge of longing, tinged with envy, to focus instead on how happy she had been. When he shook her hand she had turned a dull shade of pink, stepping in and hugging him a little too long, tears wetting his neck as she said a muffled goodbye, before giggling and apologising to everyone in the office at her emotional display.

She asked if he would water her plants. He would only have to go there once a week maybe even less as it was coming into winter, and she lived just a few streets away from his flat. He didn't ask her how she knew where he lived but agreed. After the morning tea, he had gone with her to see where she lived and learn the technicalities of plant watering.

Her place was much bigger than his, and homier, with good furnishings, rugs, and the kind of knickknacks he'd never had the time or inclination to collect. There were framed photos, family he supposed, hanging on the walls along with large-framed prints of either an abstract nature or prints of Aboriginal art. His mother would have loved it.

When he saw the plants, he understood her concern about the technicality of watering them. These were bonsais, old and gnarled, that she said her grandmother had started. When her grandmother had died her father wanted to get rid of them, so Zoe had taken them on. She didn't trust her father to look after them. She said she trusted him, then gave him her keys offering her car, parked in the garage, if he needed to use it. She added, in fact, make yourself at home anytime you like. I am really grateful to you for doing this.

Chris had shaken his head saying I won't need to but thanks. And I will endeavour to keep your plants alive for a few months, but I am a bit terrified I might do something wrong.

She had laughed, saying my grandmother would tell you that if your heart is good, the plants will thrive.

Which left him thinking, in that case they may not survive. He realised he would miss her in the office. She was a good colleague. It had been her insight that had suggested Miles Delahanty's death may have resulted from some obscure medication. It was a long shot, but Chris still didn't believe Delahanty had died of natural causes, no matter what the autopsy suggested. Going to see Mrs Delahanty, might throw more light on her husband's final hours.

Chris climbed the steps and entered the hotel's lobby. The same young receptionist greeted him warmly and presented him with a small, gift-wrapped box as a gesture of the hotel's appreciation for a returning guest.

He smiled at her and dropped the package it into his pocket. No point getting excited. No matter what it was, he would have to hand it in when he returned to the office. 'Could you ask the housekeeper to come to my room as soon as she has a moment?'

'Certainly Sir. What shall I tell her is the issue?'

He shrugged. 'A wardrobe malfunction. Just ask her to come to my room. I will be here for the next half hour.'

'I can't guarantee she will be free within the next half hour sir. If you let me have the offending article, I will see she takes care of it immediately.'

'No need. I am sure she can find a minute or two in her busy schedule. Just let her know it is to do with a cufflink.'

The receptionist frowned. 'A cufflink, sir?'

'Yes. You know the little holes in the shirt cuffs that take the links... Perhaps a stich is all that's needed.' He made a fiddly gesture at his wrist.

Her face cleared. 'Certainly sir.'

Chris had barely finished unpacking the few items he had into the wardrobe before he heard a knock on the door. He opened it to find Susan Ainsworth with an anxious look on her face, and a sewing basket in her hands.

'Thank you for coming so promptly Mrs Ainsworth.'

'I was told you needed some mending done.'

'I hope you will forgive the subterfuge, but I wanted to speak to you in private.'

He stood back to let her in. 'Please sit down Mrs Ainsworth. What I wished to discuss will take a few minutes.'

'It's about the cufflink you found.' She plonked down into the chair, sewing basket on her lap, eyes avoiding contact although they darted repeatedly to a framed print above the bed.

An impressionist seascape in a painted wooden art deco frame, featuring curlicues and glass bubbles, hung on the wall. He couldn't make out the artists name and wasn't familiar with the work, but it was standard fare for an upmarket hotel. He returned his attention to what she was saying.

'I know you are friendly with Alistair, but I didn't connect the dots right away. I'm sorry, the lost cufflink completely slipped my mind. By the time I had worked it out I felt too foolish to mention it... I should have, but...'

It is difficult to tell when a person is lying. All the usual wisdom about evasiveness, sweating, hesitation, lack of eye contact, etcetera, is the fable of crime novels, although at this moment Susan managed to display them all. Some people swear they can tell, but according to science, there is less than a 50/50 chance of getting it right, even with polygraphs. Those kinds of odds are as random as coincidence, but Chris didn't need to know if Susan was lying. Nor did he care. What he wanted was her on the backfoot and ready to work for him.

'That's all right. It is an easy thing to overlook. In any case even if the cufflink you have, had matched the one on Harvey Kashton's corpse, it would not have proved he had died in the hotel.'

Susan sucked in a breath, her hands twisting the tortoiseshell styled handle of the sewing basket until it looked in danger of snapping.

Chris watched her. It had been a long shot but what else would motivate the woman to avoid mentioning evidence in her possession, other than trying to cover up her knowledge of his death. Either she had killed him, or she had moved his body. Chris opted for the latter.

He said, 'It's all right. I am not going to say anything. I wouldn't want you to get into trouble for withholding evidence in a murder enquiry.'

'Murder!' She shook her head. 'No. He died of a heart attack.'

'How do you know?' Chris was pretty sure the autopsy results weren't yet public knowledge.

'I...um Alistair... the police detective, said so, you remember at the restaurant...' Her mouth pursed, and she shook her head.

Chris hadn't heard that, but he didn't doubt her sincerity. 'If he died of natural causes, why did you move the body?' It was a gamble and Chris was curious, but he could see his questioning was terrifying the poor woman. Her hands had started shaking and her nose had turned pink. She raised her eyes to look at him, and they were filled with unshed tears.

'Who are you?'

'I don't want you to worry, but I need to know what I'm getting into here. My clients are a global enterprise who can't afford a scandal...'

She sat forward, her face brightening. 'But you see... That's why I did it.'

He paused, gazing at her with deep curiosity. 'Why?'

'To prevent a scandal. I didn't want my guests to feel uncomfortable. I was better if he died on his yacht. I didn't know it would sink.' She put her hands over her eyes. 'Are you going to report me?'

He remained silent until she took her hands away from her face. Then he said, 'What? So, you found him dead and put him on his yacht...'

Tears spilled from her faded blue eyes as she nodded.

'Mason Bronson helped you.'

Her mouth compressed into a line.

'Okay, that explains it then.' He paused watching her with his head tilted to one side. 'Look, I need your help.'

'Yes.' Her voice was eager, and she lowered her hands to the sewing basket.

'I'm here on behalf of my clients. You are arranging a dinner for us to gather with the Treasurer and the Foreign Investment Review Board. I need to win that contest for the security of western democracy.' He paused wondering if he had overestimated her patriotism.

'Of course. You don't want the Chinese getting their hands on it. I told Cassie that only yesterday. She said it didn't matter who won it...'

Chris frowned. 'Cassie?'

'Oh yes. She is representing Sir Hamish's claim that the bauxite deposit runs under his land, and he should be recompensed. Didn't you know that?'

Chris shook his head. He should have known but this was another complication in an already overly complicated deal, although it was most probably another distraction. 'What else can you tell me?'

'Well, between you and me I think Sir Hamish is just greedy. He's hoping he can capitalise on the deal in some way because his land is becoming useless. It's in a dry spot you see, and his place is perpetually in drought with the exception of La Nina weather events.'

'Thank you. I will be sure to inform my clients of his intentions.'

Her hand flew to her mouth. 'Oh, you won't tell Cassie, will you? She'll be ever so angry with me.'

He smiled. 'If you hear anything more, you won't forget to pass it on to me, will you? You will be doing your bit to protect the free and democratic world and to support Australian interests. My clients will show their gratitude.'

'How?'

Again, Chris was taken aback by this meek little woman with what appeared to be a backbone of titanium. 'What would you like?'

'I just want my hotel to remain relevant and retain its growing reputation.'

'I don't think that will pose any sort of problem?'

'When your clients come to Australia, will they stay here?'

'If you like.'

'I do.' She stood up, the basket clutched to her stomach. 'I am aware of who your clients are and if you can make sure they patronise my hotel, I will make sure you hear anything that might help you to invest in the mine.'

'And perhaps anything else relevant to our ongoing freedom and democracy.'

Her eyes slitted with suspicion.

She relaxed when he said, 'Just listen to the two of us saving Australian assets from falling into the wrong hands. Now, I must also make a confession if you promise not to let on.'

She eyed him sharply.

He grinned. 'If you don't object I have a date with your lovely daughter tonight. I didn't want you to hear from someone else or you might think I had broken your trust.'

Susan nodded. 'I have a concern about it, but only because you live in England. I don't want Cassie to be hurt.'

'I am thinking of moving here, especially if the investment materialises.'

'Then, I'm glad. Cassie really liked you.'

He sighed as Susan shut the door behind her. So far so good. He didn't feel good lying to the woman, but he didn't think he could trust Mrs Ainsworth in a pinch. She hadn't admitted it, but her majordomo must have been in on the body shifting. There was no way she could have managed to move Kashton on her own.

He turned to pick up his keys. He would head on out to see if Mrs Delahanty could shed any light on her husband's demise. Then he remembered the painting above his bed. It was worth further investigation. Mrs Ainsworth's eyes were too often drawn to it.

He sat down, holding his phone to his ear and talking to an imaginary client on the other end. As he spoke he gazed at the painting, methodically scanning each square centimetre from top left to bottom right. And yes, there it was. One of the glass bubbles. The old biddy was spying on him, and he wondered why. Or did she spy on all her guests as a matter of routine? He would check later, but for now he had a few appointments to keep, although knowing about the cameras made meeting with Mèng in his room difficult.

He left the hotel and, taking the Maybach, headed out to meet Mrs. Delahanty.

18. Old Habits

Huma opened the gate to the Sydney town house before walking up a short pathway recently lined with white standard roses. She smiled. Who would have thought her dad would take up gardening in his old age. He had never shown the slightest interest, but then the house, from which he'd moved, was not one that allowed pottering. His departed wife had had gardeners to take care of that sort of thing.

When she had succumbed to a stroke, Huma's dad had found living in the big house in Bowral too much for his peasant origins. He had found this little unrenovated house near the university and lived modestly, although his wife had left him millions.

Not that Alex Sharapova needed any more money. He had made his own fortune in armaments sales before he had retired. He still dabbled for favours, occasionally.

She found the house key on her car key fob and pushed it into the yale lock. The door swung open, and she stepped inside.

'Dad.' She put her suitcase down, hung her bag on a row of coat hooks by the door and took off her coat. 'Dad. Are you home?'

The house creaked as she walked along the hallway and stood at the base of the stairs. Perhaps he was up there sleeping, although that wasn't like him. She had told him her time of arrival, for he didn't like surprises. She looked at her watch.

From the landing above a net fell with a slight whoosh of displaced air. It landed and slid over her head, shrouding her entire body before it closed in at her ankles with a jerk.

She fell, cracking a knee then her hip against the floor. A jolt and she tipped forward as the net rose. She struggled but she was already suspended a metre off the floor, her legs at an uncomfortable angle.

A chuckle came from above.

'Dad, it's not funny. Let me down!' Why, oh why, had she let her guard down?

'You are becoming soft.' He looked over the balustrade at the top of the stairs as he lowered her to the ground and released the net.

'For Christ's sake! How old are you.' Huma loosened the rope at her feet, ripped the net over her head, and adjusted her clothing and her hair. 'I thought you were too old for this kind of nonsense. What if it was someone else? What if I had brought someone home with me?'

'But you didn't. I watched you arrive.'

'That's not the point... Oh, forget it.' She stomped back to the door and picked up her suitcase. Then marched back to the stairs and began to ascend. It was her own fault. She had grown complacent, and she had been distracted by the possibility of him gardening. Little chance of that.

Her father stood on the landing and held out his arms. 'Come. My little Solnyshkuh. Kiss your old father.'

'Speak English, Dad.'

'There is no one here. I think you become...'

'Don't!' Huma held up a warning finger. 'Just don't.'

Her father grinned. At sixty-nine, he was still a good-looking man, tall, and silver haired. His eyes, an indeterminate hazel, were as gleeful as a boy's.

He grasped her shoulders and kissed her three times. 'You must get rid of Mikhail.' He whispered in her ear before standing back and taking the suitcase from her hand.

'Why?'

'He owes allegiance to too many masters.' Alex took her case into her room and came out. 'Come I have made tea for you.'

'Michael has already explained that. He doesn't have a choice.'

'The Chinese are one thing. The police are another. Get rid of him. You have come too far to blow it all by using a nayemnik.'

'He's not a mercenary. He's a criminal.'

'Criminals are like mercenaries. They work for money and are loyal only to the highest bidder.'

She smiled. 'Or the ones who can do them most damage.'

'You?' He shook his head. 'No. For him, the police are the danger. If he is deported back to Hong Kong the 14 K will kill him.'

'Not me. You.'

He shook his head.

Huma frowned. 'Anyway, what police are you talking about?'

'He was with a detective at the Bancroft.'

'How do you know? You didn't go there, did you? I don't want you interfering in my job, Dad.'

Alex shook his head. 'I have friends who talk to me, but we can find someone else. Come the tea is getting cold and I have made honey cake. It is in the kitchen. The afternoon sun comes in and makes the room warm.'

He walked towards the rear of the house. Huma scowled at his retreating back, frustrated by her father's meddling. All the same she followed him just as she had always done. Why change the habits of a lifetime?

19. Venial Distractions

Sixteen kilometres north of where Huma and Alex ate honey cake and drank tea from a samovar, Chris said goodbye to Mrs Delahanty and drove back into the city. His trip had been a waste of time. After introducing himself as a Treasury staff member, who had worked for Mr Delahanty, he had offered his condolences. But when he had asked her if her husband had been taking cough medicine, she had become deeply suspicious.

First, she had denied it, then she agreed perhaps he had, but she would have thrown the bottle away, and she had no idea what it was called or where he had purchased it. She was visibly agitated and told him she wanted him to leave. When she threatened to call her lawyer, he heard a voice, deep and masculine, coming from somewhere inside the house, asking if everything was alright.

She shut the door in Chris's face.

As he drove back into the city, he reflected on her behaviour. Who was the man? A lover? Could she have wanted her husband out the way? Had she bought the cough medicine for her husband? Surely not. Mrs. Delahanty didn't seem the murdering type, not even for the sake of a lover. Divorce would have been easier if she had wanted shot of him.

Who else would have benefited from her husband's death? More people than he could count on two hands. For a start, there were the numerous bauxite mine investors, who would have known Delahanty's views on foreigners investing in Australian assets. They would also have been glad to see Kashton out of the way. Who else? Huma Sharapova had taken Delahanty's place as chair. Could that be a reason? Unlikely. The chair position held some prestige, but she had that in spades and through her own merit. Killing your boss and long-time mentor for his job seemed a tad extreme.

Perhaps he was chasing shadows. Both Delahanty and Kashton had supposedly died from natural causes. There was no evidence either man had been murdered, other than his gut feel.

Again, he reminded himself, murder was not his mission, and he had to let it go, intuition or not. The chief would tell him to focus on the job at hand. Get the bloody bauxite sale done in the national interest. Keep information from getting into Chinese government hands and get back to Canberra with Huma alive and in one piece. The rest was a distraction. Still, it niggled.

Chris found a place to leave the car in a parking basement, and walked to the restaurant, putting work aside in anticipation of meeting Cassie again.

Earlier, she had texted him with a change to the venue, apologising in advance for the presence of some uninvited guests. It seemed she had thought it her ethical duty to inform her client, Sir Hamish White, of her conflict of interest, whereby she was having dinner with another potential investor in the same mining venture.

When White had heard who she was having dinner with, he had decided to make it a party, inviting himself and James Sinclair along.

Chris had been looking forward to the evening with her and while he could cope with the two men, he couldn't say he was happy about them crashing the dinner. Although it might turn out to be a good thing. The dinner was intended as a casual get to know you. Cassie's mother had made Chris wary of investing too much in the daughter. Yet her declaration of a possible conflict of interest to her client, indicated Cassie's moral compass was more firmly fixed than her mother's might be.

Of course, Chris was well aware that people shouldn't be judged by their family members. He'd learned that early. His own mother was an antiestablishment rebel, anarchic and vocal about individual freedoms. If he was to have been judged by her character he would have been in trouble long ago, particularly with the career choices he had made.

He spotted Cassie sitting at a table with four others, two men and two women. So, White and Sinclair had brought their wives. No. Sir Hamish's wife was almost as old as he was and the woman sitting with him didn't look much older than thirty. The other woman wasn't James's model ex-wife either. Chris had seen photos of her.

He pulled up at the table and greeted Cassie before turning to White and Sinclair.

Cassie, with a sideways glance at Chris, introduced the two women. 'Vikki Carmichael is Mr Sinclair's personal assistant and Maria Arvato works for Sir Hamish.

A waiter arrived with menus, and the rest of the evening went by pleasantly. The only mention of the bauxite mine was via a few cracks from Sinclair about Chris's supposed armament firm of investors, and what a sly dog he'd been when they had first met by not letting on about his interest.

At the end of the evening Chris drove Cassie back to her apartment. There were few vacant parking spaces, and he pulled up some distance from the building.

'I'll see you to your door.'

Cassie smiled. 'Come in for a nightcap.'

Chris was tempted. 'Can I take a raincheck on that. I have a lot of documents to get through before tomorrow evening.'

She wrinkled her nose. 'Don't work too hard then, but you don't need to walk me to my door. This is a fairly safe suburb.'

Chris walked around the car to open her door but by the time he got there she had let herself out the car.

She laughed. 'Crickey, you are a gentleman. I thought chivalry had died somewhere back in the fifties.'

'Sorry, bad habit. Don't know why I do it. It's not as if you aren't perfectly capable of fending for yourself. I guess it's a reaction against everything my mother believed in.'

They walked together along the pavement.

Cassie glanced across at Chris. 'Tell me about your mother.'

He grinned. 'It's a long story. I'll tell you when I get to know you better and we have more time. We can swap memories of our childhood.'

From the corner of his eye, he noticed a man in the driver's seat of a sedan. Across the road, six cars back, a dark SUV showed the shadowy outline of a driver and passenger, both unmoving. The hair on his neck lifted.

He turned to Cassie. 'Do you have coffee?'

'Of course.'

'Can I change my mind?'

'Coffee it is.'

Cassie's flat was on the second floor overlooking the road, and while she made coffee Chris parted the curtains a fraction.

The sedan had moved and was now passing the entrance, heading south towards the next block. The driver looked up as if staring at Cassie's window, the one in which Chris was concealed behind the curtain. The light from a streetlamp illuminated the man's face. Alastair!

What the hell was Alistair doing watching Cassie's place? If that was what he was doing. Chris watched him cruise across the intersection. The SUV pulled out of its parking space and followed in the same direction, its lights off.

'See anything interesting?' Cassie walked in with a tray, which she placed on a coffee table in front of a sofa. She sat down. 'Sugar? Milk?'

Chris left the window and sat next to her. 'Just black. Thanks. This should keep me awake long enough to read the prospectus.'

He really didn't have time to hang around now that the watchers outside had moved off, although he wondered if Alistair's presence was official surveillance or if he had been waiting for her to come home. Most likely the latter.

He took a sip of the coffee and then smiled at her. 'Sorry I can't stay longer but perhaps we can catch up again after tomorrow night. Maybe we could do something on Sunday?'

She nodded and poured milk into her cup.

He asked, 'Were you expecting to see Alistair tonight?'

Some of the milk slopped over the lip as she placed the jug back on the tray. 'No. Why?'

Chris shook his head. 'I thought I saw him drive past a minute ago.'

'I doubt it was Alistair. He lives on the other side of the city.'

20. Photographic Evidence

Half an hour after leaving Cassie's flat, Chris cruised to a stop outside Bancroft House and switched off the Maybach's engine. He sat silently watching the building before glancing at his watch. 02:30 hours. He had better get a move on.

When he got to his room, he took off his jacket and kicked off his shoes before sitting with his back to the camera in the picture frame above the headboard. He opened his laptop blocking the screen from the camera's view with his body. The first thing he needed was to have a look at the set-up Mrs Ainsworth was using.

Ten minutes later he had gained access and began to catalogue which camera focused on which area of the hotel. His room wasn't the only one with spyware, although not all rooms were rigged. He went through each one.

The first was focussed on the living area of a suite, now empty. The second, on a room in darkness. It looked like there was a person in the bed, asleep. The third was an office, dark and empty and the fourth, a room like his. Someone was up and about, also engaged in doing something on a laptop, his back to the camera. It was Mèng. Good he was alone, but Chris could not go to his room to meet him if there was a camera in the room.

He leaned back in his chair. These cameras were a problem, especially as he couldn't find the recording function. If he interfered, Ainsworth would know, but if he walked about the hotel now, Ainsworth would also know. All he could do was assume she was asleep right now, but any recording of his movements would be a dead giveaway, unless he could record over the track after he had finished.

He sat forward and continued scrolling through each camera angle. Most of them were focussed on the public areas of the hotel, but there were another three that focused on empty sitting rooms belonging to suites. He had no idea if the suites were occupied. Presumably the guests would be asleep in their bedrooms by now.

Cassie's mother was proving to be a cunning spy, without the moral scruples her daughter harboured. She was certainly not the retiring housekeeper she pretended to be, and it didn't bode well for progressing any relationship with her daughter. It was a shame because he liked Cassie, but her mother was a potential threat. Perhaps going to dinner hadn't been a wise move. He would probably need to abandon his plans to meet her on Sunday. He swallowed what seemed like a pebble stuck in his throat.

To hell with it. He switched off the cameras. Who could Ainsworth complain to? She shouldn't have cameras in guests' rooms in any case. He would turn them back on when he had finished. He got up and took a black sweatshirt from his bag, swapping it for the dress shirt he'd worn out with Cassie. He pulled on a pair of black sneakers and let himself out from the room.

***

Mèng let him into the room and looked each way along the hallway before closing the door. 'Did you see anyone?'

Chris shook his head. 'What do you have for me?'

Mèng said, 'Did Mr Royce agree with my proposal?'

'Depends on what you have to offer.'

'You spoke to Liam Garcia and told him to back off.'

Chris nodded.

'Good. You are my handler now.'

Again, Chris nodded. 'If you can tell us where the leak is coming from, then sure.'

'No. This I do not know. It is above my level of clearance.'

'Then what use are you?'

'I have other information.'

'Go on.'

'A Hong Kong Triad group is running a money laundering operation here in Sydney.'

Chris frowned. 'Not sure if money laundering is my bailiwick, mate. You should be taking to AUSTRAC.'

'I thought you might be interested because a friend of yours is involved.' Mèng raised himself onto his toes and back down. His face took on a crafty look as if he'd found Chris's Achilles heel.

Chris's face remained deadpan. 'You must be mistaking me for someone with friends.'

Mèng's brow furrowed. 'I don't understand. The policeman Alistair McMahon, he was at school with you.'

'You seem to think you know a lot about me.'

'I told you; I have been researching you for a long time. It is only so that I can know to trust you. You would do the same.'

'True. So, what about Alistair McMahon and this Triad group?'

'They are related to the same enterprise that set up money laundering by funnelling money for drugs into America. Your associate Liam Garcia would have told you I was involved in a small way, but all I was trying to do was to get money out of China, so I could get out myself. Now I have an opportunity to do the same thing here. I can find out more about their operations in Sydney if you will support me.'

Chris would have to pass this on to the AFP, but it wasn't why he was here. 'I'll have to take this on notice mate, but what else do you have for me? Any further bits of paperwork you shouldn't have?'

Mèng shrugged. 'I was lucky.'

'You'll have to do more than wait for luck to strike.' He noticed the camera on Mèng's desk. It was plugged into his laptop. 'Keen on photography are you?'

'It is my hobby.'

'Nothing to do with work. No Australian installations then?'

'I like to photograph people, but it is for my use only.'

Mèng was full of surprises. Corruption, graft, and a self-serving opportunist, but Chris hadn't figured he was also a blackmailer. 'So, you have photos of Alistair McMahon with the Triads.'

He shook his head. I saw him only, but they were at a distance from each other.'

'Pity. How do you know he is in cahoots with them then?'

Mèng shifted his gaze and moved his weight to his other foot but said nothing.

'Come on Mèng. This is about exchange. You give us what we want to know, and if it's good enough we give you what you want. A nice safe life in Australia.'

'I will never be safe, even if you do help me.'

'Not my problem mate.' Chris glanced at his watch. He'd been in the room too long already. 'So, far you have given me nothing of use as a trade. Let me know when you want to get serious.' He turned to go.

'Wait.'

Chris turned back.

'I have something else.'

'Go on.'

'My superior has been using the Triad group to spy on Dr Sharapova.'

Chris's breath stilled. 'Go on.'

'My government is keen for China to win the contract for the Bauxite mine, and they have been trying to find leverage to gain Dr Sharapova's favour.'

That was interesting. Chris thought they already had leverage through her Uyghur relatives. But all he said was, 'Did the Triads have anything to do with the death of Harvey Kashton?'

Mèng shook his head. 'I don't know.'

'You don't know much, do you? What about the former FIRB Chairman, Mr Delahanty?'

Again, Mèng shook his head. 'I am not given such information.'

'But you are not ruling it out.'

'I am telling you Mr Davis, I don't know.'

'What do you know?'

'The Triad gang leader is Michael Leung, and he is wanted in Hong Kong on charges of conspiracy to commit criminal intimidation. He worked for a Triad group whose boss was arrested in 2015 on suspicion of laundering more than HK$100 million.'

An allegation is not a conviction, and it certainly doesn't mean he is committing any offence in this country. Even if he has, I am not sure that's enough of a bargaining chip.' Seemed Liam Garcia was right. The man was a waste of time. Then Chris had an idea. 'Where were you in 2015?'

'I was in Beijing, as were you?'

'Did your hobby include taking photos of formal diplomatic occasions?'

'Sometimes.' Mèng took a step towards his camera as if wary Chris might steal it.

Chris pressed home what he saw was an advantage. 'Listen, I want you to go through your photos and find any with Australians in them. You can leave the copies on a USB in the dead drop, but make sure the photos include details of time taken, place and names.'

'Then you will help me defect.'

'Maybe. If the information is of any use.'

'I will do it as soon as I return to Canberra.'

Chris let himself out of Mèng's room. It seemed the bloke wasn't going to be any help in finding the mole. He would speak to the chief about handing him over to the AFP to deal with the money laundering issue. It wouldn't surprise Chris to find Mèng was already laundering his Chinese yuan. The bloke was nothing more than a crook and a venial one at that. It could be the police were already on to it. Perhaps that was why Alistair was hanging around. Although it didn't explain why he was loitering outside Cassie's apartment block, or who might have followed him when he took off.

He reached his room and glanced at his watch. Just time to turn on Mrs Ainsworth's cameras and catch a couple of hours sleep.

Sherry was served before the formal dinner in an anteroom to a private dining room. Chris was offered a glass as he entered the room. He took it without thinking and walked towards the milling guests clustered around the Treasurer.

Ms Carmichael, James Sinclair's personal assistant, whom he'd met at dinner last night, stepped into his path.

She said, 'Sherry! Can you believe it, and only one glass per person before dinner.' She smiled at him and raised her glass.

'Ms Carmichael. Nice to see you again.' He glanced at his glass. 'What's the significance?'

'Vikki, please Mr Davis.'

'If you call me Chris.' He grinned at her. 'I am afraid the significance of the sherry is beyond me.'

'It's an old colonial custom. One aperitif before dinner to demonstrate restraint and to show this is not a vulgar American cocktail party. It wouldn't surprise me to find that there is no smoking before the loyal toast. This whole place is an anachronism.'

'No smoking anywhere inside nowadays.'

'True. Do you smoke Mr Davis... Ah, Chris?'

'No, but I don't mind if you do.'

'We will have to go out to the smoker's area. Will you accompany me?'

'Sure.' He followed her out to the terrace, placed his untouched sherry on a table, and took the lighter from her to light her cigarette.

She exhaled, a long thin stream of smoke, towards him, and he tried not to blink or turn away. This was a game, and he wanted to know how it would play out. He handed back her lighter and turned to face the dark garden.

'Tell me, who are you working for Chris?'

'I thought you knew. Your boss seems well aware, judging by his cracks last night.'

'Yes, but it's not true is it?'

Chris turned to face her. 'Which bit?'

'You don't work for Lockheed Martin, do you?'

He smiled. 'Depends on what you mean by work for.'

She took another drag of her cigarette.' I have a friend in the company executive, and he's never heard of you.'

'What's his name?'

'Gary Fromisher.'

'Okay. I don't personally know Fromisher but then he's in the Space Division based in Colorado. I haven't been there, at least not yet. Did you ask him if he knows all the contractors in the UK's Integrated Systems section? Besides, just because I do occasional contractual work for Lockheed doesn't mean it's an exclusive gig. My clients prefer privacy.'

She looked uncertain and drew hard on her cigarette before stubbing it out in an ashtray. 'You haven't touched your sherry.'

He looked across at his glass. 'Showing good British restraint.'

She laughed. 'Come on. We had better go in. People will begin to talk. You know—Lockheed Martin and Blue Eagle ganging up.'

'Winner takes all.' He followed her back inside.

Huma was in a dark corner, head tilted as James Sinclair spoke to her in what seemed like an intimate tête-à-tête, but then that seemed to be Huma's modus operandi. The Treasurer was still in his element, surrounded by sycophants. Two of the board members looked uncomfortable, caught in the unrelenting grip of the Chinese contingent, with Mèng hovering on the margins. Another group of board members clustered together, keeping the supplicants at bay while they nursed their empty sherry glasses. And then the gong went for dinner. A collective lift of faces as chins pointed towards the dining room doors.

Chris followed the rush and found each place setting on the table was accompanied by a name, ensuring that the right people were placed side by side. He was placed next to Huma with the XNT chair on her other side. That would send a signal. The fictious bid from Lockheed Martin was on the short list. He wondered if his placing had been allocated by Huma or Mrs Ainsworth.

James Sinclair sat on the Treasurer's right and the Argentinian Investment banker Elias Aguirre sat on his other side. David Cho and General Aiguo Liu glowered among the other board members along with some of the other bidders. Mèng and Vikki Carmichael had both disappeared. Too low on the greasy pole to attend dinner or perhaps they had other business to attend to for their bosses.

***

The next morning, Chris rang Cassie to apologise for having to stand her up. He made the excuse that he had an urgent meeting to attend in Canberra. She was so nice about it he felt his neck getting hot with shame. He had really liked her, thought there might have been a future in their relationship. Too bad. Sometimes that was the nature of the game.

Still, he had acted like a jerk, and he didn't want her seeing him as such. Dumb really, given he was unlikely to see her again. So why did he feel so bad about it. It wasn't like he had a dearth of offers. Last night by the end of the dinner Huma had been flirting with him again. He had walked her to her car, and she had suggested they meet up in Canberra after the project was over.

Remember you promised to give me some sparing tips, she had said.

He hadn't said anything of the kind. It had been her suggestion but once again he didn't contradict her. His job was to provide her with intelligence and see her safe to the end of the project, then be on his way. She was returning to Canberra this morning and so was he, but there was no way he wanted further involvement with her. Mixing work with pleasure was always problematic although his role in the project was almost done.

As he drove back to Canberra he thought about his report. It would be one of failure which-ever-way he spun it. He supposed he had seen Huma through the process safely, although his part in her safety was debatable, and she seemed to know as much as he did about the backgrounds of the various candidates.

The next phase of the process was for the final board meeting, a report advising the Treasurer and then the public announcement of the decision, none of which he would have a part in. It was all academic anyway. Clearly Huma and the Treasurer were in firm agreement about the winning candidate. The rest was fairy floss, designed to placate criticism or political blow back.

The only thing he had to show for his involvement was a lot of supposition. He made a mental list of his intelligence cache. There was an inkling that WorldWatch was a CIA operation with an ex-MI6 operative on its books, but what were they really doing here? Was it what Fitz claimed? Then there was Mèng, a petty consular official with sticky fingers and relatives in high places, who may or may not be useful. Although to be fair, he had shown a concrete possibility of a mole in the service, or where else had the memo, he had produced, come from. And Alistair... He may or may not be involved with some money laundering operation involving Triads. Then there was Mrs. Ainsworth, who claimed she was interested only in the success of her hotel. She seemed prepared to go to extraordinary lengths to ensure Bancroft House's anachronistic triumph.

All he had to show for the whole waste of time was a possible mole, a defection, and a lead into a money laundering operation. None of which he had been tasked with, and even then he had no evidence, just the word of a corrupt foreign diplomat who needed Chris on side.

He hadn't found a single clue as to who had killed Kashton or Delahanty, if indeed they were murdered and didn't die of natural causes. Not that that was his mission, just his conviction. He hadn't found out, who might be leaking classified information to the Chinese. He had wounded the most decent and likable woman he'd met in a long time all because of her mother's dubious moral compass. A woman, if given a chance, with whom he could have found a meaningful relationship.

All in all, the project might be considered a dismal waste of government funding, and his time. Although what else he would do if he had the same project again, he didn't know. If Elgar got to read his report, he'd never hear the end of his criticism. If that happened, he really would have to resign and find another job.

Hopefully it would remain eyes only for the chief. The man was a thoroughly decent bloke although he'd drawn a dud when he gave Chris the mission. Perhaps someone else would have found out what Fitz and WorldWatch were up to.

22.Stepping into Quicksand

Alistair McMahon was at his desk when the call came through. His heart pounded and his breathing became difficult as an AFP officer introduced herself as Janice Burton. She explained that she had received a referral regarding a Sydney money laundering operation from AUSTRAC. She understood Alistair might be already working on the case.

'Yes.' He said without thinking. 'No, not really,' he added.

She paused and he could feel her frown down the phone. Christ, he was an idiot.

'Well, are you involved or not?'

'What do you mean by involved?'

'Detective McMahon, I was told you may be investigating a man named Michael Leung, who I understand is suspected of money laundering.'

Alistair glanced across his desk at his colleague and lowered his voice. 'Yes, I know what you mean. It's just not that simple. I was not officially investigating him. It was just... I was... I mean, I thought there might be something. It was a hunch, but I had no evidence, so I didn't pursue it.'

'How did you come by the knowledge?'

'A tip off.'

'Who was your source?'

'Ah... an informant.'

'Can you give us a name?'

Alistair fell silent.

'Come on Detective. You know how these things work.'

'Yeah, but I don't want you scaring him off.'

'We'll handle him with kid gloves.'

Alistair gave her the name of an old meth-head who hung around the Cross, and who had given him a few tips some time ago. The bloke's brain would be well and truly fried by now.

'Okay thanks. We'll find him. Do you have a file on Leung?'

'No. I didn't get that far. Christ, I had a look and there was nothing I could see, so I let it go. That was all.'

'Are you okay, Detective?'

'Yes. No. Look I am swamped at the moment. Can we make another time to talk about this.'

'Okay, sure. How about tomorrow morning, say 9:30 am. I can come to you, or you can come here.'

'I'll come to you.'

'Do you know where to...?'

'Of course.'

'That's right. You used to be AFP, didn't you. Before you joined the NSW force.'

'Look, I really don't have time to chat at the moment.'

'Right! I'll let you get on with it, then. Anything you can think of will help. I'll see you tomorrow.'

Alistair fumbled the phone back into its cradle and leaned back in his chair. Shit, he knew this was a bad idea. He ran his forefinger across his forehead. It was wet. He leaned forward and ripped a couple of tissues from the box on his desk, wiping his face then blowing his noise.

His colleague looked up. 'You okay mate?' She peered at Alistair. 'You look pretty pale. Are you ill?'

Alistair nodded. 'Yeah, I think I must be coming down with something. I might just check out of here before I pass on any bugs. I haven't anything pressing today, nothing that can't wait anyway.'

Twenty minutes later Alistair pulled his car into a side road and stopped in an empty parking space next to the curb. He took an unused phone from his glove box and rang the number Mike had programmed into the phone. It was picked up immediately.

'We have to meet. It's urgent.' He listened for a moment before hanging up. Then he took the Sim card out of the phone, broke it half and chucked it out the window before pulling out into the road and heading for Manley.

When he arrived at his destination, he slowed to crawl as he passed the building. This was prime real estate on a road that ran along the shoreline. Yet the plate glass windows on the ground floor were opaque as if not wanting window shoppers to take too much interest. It seemed odd that the ground floor had vacant shops facing the sea.

He scanned the street; certain no one had followed or was watching him. At the end of the building and the city block, he turned left up a narrow one-way street, passed the building entrance Mike had described, and then turned left again into a basement parking. He parked and walked back up to the narrow street and turned towards the entrance.

From a lobby inside the entrance, stairs led up to a door at first floor level. Stairs also descended to what looked like the basement he had just parked in. He could have come up that way, but he hadn't noticed the stairs. Alistair walked up to the first floor and knocked. The door swung open, showing a large reception room with several exits.

He knocked on the open door again before stepping inside. Expensive joint. Carved wooden Chinese motif furniture was interspersed with soft European styled sofas, armchairs, and push carpets. Framed paintings hung on the walls. Alastair knew nothing about art, but he guessed these were worth a bit, like everything else in the room.

Mike appeared in one of the doorways on the other side of the room. 'Ah Alistair. Welcome to my office. Good to see you my friend. You look well. What can I get you to drink? Please take a seat. Are you hungry? I can arrange some food...'

Alistair shook his head. 'What is this place? Why are all the windows downstairs boarded up?'

Mike smiled. 'We are carrying out renovations on our restaurant. Afterall, Alistair what else would Chinese people do in Australia, other than open a restaurant. But of course, this one will be very upmarket.'

'Are you taking the piss? If that hadn't come from you, I would think you were being racist.'

Mike laughed. 'Isn't that what all you Aussies think of us?'

'Bullshit.'

'I am serious Alistair. It is a restaurant. My group bought it, but it needs renovation, so it remains boarded up for no other reason.'

A man arrived through a different entrance. Mike spoke to him using a language Alistair didn't understand, although that wasn't surprising as Alistair's only language was English, and Aussie English at that.

The bloke bowed his head and walked out.

Mike turned back to Alistair and said by way of explanation. 'My assistant.'

The assistant was a strange looking dude, hairless, ageless although his face was leathery, tall, and thin, and dressed in a three-piece suit with tie, replete with gold tiepin. The word bloodless came to mind, with those pale eyes and yellowish skin. Not the pale alabaster skin of Mike's Chinese heritage, but like he had liver disease. Yet the two men bore a familial resemblance.

Alistair sat down in one of the chairs that Mike indicated. He was nervous and couldn't figure out why. Sure, he was concerned about the Feds, but it was Mike he found intimidating. The bloke was way to suave. That was it. Never trust anyone that polished.

Alistair took a breath. 'We have a problem.'

'Yes, I gathered. Can you be more specific?'

'The Feds are interested in you in relation to money laundering.'

Mike's eyes narrowed. 'Tell me more.'

'I just got a call. Someone must know something. They thought I might be investigating you.'

'And are you?'

'What! Don't be stupid.'

'The last thing I am, Alistair, is stupid.'

'Sorry. Didn't mean... It's just a saying.'

Mike's eyes didn't move off Alistair's face.

Alistair fidgeted and felt his armpits let go despite the anti-perspirant his wife made him wear. 'The Feds got a referral from AUSTRAC. They are the agency...'

'I know who they are Alistair. What I don't understand is what AUSTRAC knows or how they found out.'

'They track banking transactions and other data bases, like those in the Australian Tax Office. Any reporting you do to any agency, in this or other countries, is data matched against numerous records. You must have made some data entry that triggered their algorithms. They would then have handed the case to the AFP to take a closer look.'

'We are aware of the data matching capabilities of AUSTRAC and take great care our activities do not trigger anything. I would know if they did. My guess is that you have made a terrible mistake Alistair.'

'No! I swear, I have said nothing to no one.'

Mike nodded. 'A double negative. Either ignorance or a lie.'

'No, it's not a lie. Sorry, I misspoke but I swear I have said nothing to anyone. And I have carried out my end of the deal by warning you. Just as you asked.'

Mike smiled. 'If this is true. You should be rewarded, not questioned. Forgive me. In this business... Well, one becomes suspicious.' He stood up. 'I'll see you out my friend. Thank you for the warning. This is exactly why we retain your security services.'

Alistair got up and pumped Mike's outstretched hand, perhaps a little forcefully, but the weight that had lifted from his shoulders at Mike's amiable attitude, filled him with gratitude.

***

When Alistair had gone, Mike called his assistant back into the room. 'Did you hear all of that?'

His assistant nodded.

'Follow him. I want a team of men on the job. Don't let him out of your sight. I want to know everyone he sees and everything he does. Put a tracker on his car and see if you can get a tap on his phone and in his house.'

The assistant bowed and left the room.

Mike walked over to the window that overlooked the side street. He remained motionless, staring outside for several minutes, before he took out a small flip phone and pressed a number.

When the number was answered he said, 'They know. Find out what, who, and how. I want the information today.'

He hung up, prised off the back of the phone to retrieve the sim card, and with pressure from his thumb nail broke the tiny square of technology, before walking out of the door.

23. Betrayal

A few evenings after leaving Sydney, and at the end of a workday, Huma let herself into her Canberra apartment. It was in a recently completed development and cost more than she could afford on her salary alone. She owned it outright, thanks to her dad. The best thing about it was it was close to work, walking distance in fact although her car was parked in one of two spaces allotted to the unit.

She walked into her study, really a converted second bedroom, and placed her bag on the desk before switching on the PC. Beyond the light from the study, the flat was darker than usual even though winter brought on an early dusk. Odd... The curtains in the sitting room were closed. She thought she had drawn them back this morning. They were serious blackout curtains that allowed her to watch movies in comfort on her giant television screen, but they made the room too dark for normal use. She felt for the switch and the room flooded with light from rows of ceiling inserted LED globes.

A man was sitting, still as a painting, in a chair across the room. She stared in shock. Her phone rang. She held up a finger at the man before spinning about to go back to the study to pick up the ringing mobile. 'Dad?'

'They have just announced Devin Royce will head up the Office of National Security. He is to take up the role a couple of months, and then...'

'Dad, I can't talk right now. Let me ring you back, okay.'

'This is urgent. Make sure that you do...'

Huma hung up and laid her phone back on the desk, her mind spinning. She took a breath and walked back into the living room. 'What the hell are you doing here? I told you never to come to my home.'

'No one saw me. Besides I am at a party in Sydney right now. I have witnesses who will swear to it.'

Huma sighed. 'Do you want a drink?'

'Whisky please.'

She poured herself a glass of wine and him a whisky and then sat on the sofa facing him. 'So why are you here?'

'You told me you work in the intelligence field.'

'No. I lecture in security. That is vastly different.'

He shook his head. 'So, you teach security to people in the intelligence field, but I think you also work for intelligence.'

She stared at him, her features unmoving.

He added, 'And you have expensive tastes.' He gazed around the room. 'Doesn't everyone.'

'Yet somehow you, a lecturer, can afford this and my fees.'

She nodded. 'You are expensive, but my employers are generous.'

He leaned forward. 'I can become a friend rather than a contractor.'

'Why would I want that?'

'Friends don't charge, or at least not so much, and you can rely on friends to watch your back.'

'What would this friendship cost me.'

He leaned back and took a sip of his whisky. 'Some information.'

'Go on.'

'I have it on good authority that someone in the intelligence service has knowledge about my operations, and I want to know the name of this person.'

Huma blinked. 'That's all you've got! How the hell do you think I can put a name to such a sweepingly broad description—go around asking my students if they know someone, who knows someone, who knows about you?' She laughed, amused by the image. 'You clearly don't know how these things work. For a start, which intel service are we talking about. In this country all operations are need-to-know only. They don't share information.'

He shrugged and finished off his whisky. 'I doubt that is true, but you are capable. I am sure you can find out, otherwise...'

'Otherwise, what?' She stood up, hands on her hips. 'I think you should leave.'

'Otherwise, I am in deep water.'

'Oh.' The air went out of her, and she sat down again.

'You think I would threaten you? We are friends now after all.'

'Tell me what you know?'

He explained that a police detective, Alistair McMahon, had warned him, and his source in AUSTRAC confirmed, there was an investigation into his operations. It had started as a referral from an intelligence agency. 'I had McMahon followed, and my people saw him going into the AFP offices. He is implicated, but I think someone else in an intelligence office knows something, and I need to know who.'

'You know the information could have come from any one of several agencies.'

He stood up. 'This I leave up to you. I know you will do your best, if only to protect me and the contractual arrangements we have.'

'You shit. You are threatening me.'

He shook his head. 'No. This is merely a fact. A threat would mean physical harm to you or those you love. Friends do not harm each other, but they can be useful allies as you well know.'

She saw an opportunity. 'You can begin our friendship with some information in exchange.'

'Yes.'

'What were you discussing with Cho and Liu at Bancroft house while you were waiting for the police detective?'

'McMahon told you that?'

'Never mind my sources. Is it true?'

'A contract. That was all.'

'What contract?'

Mike sighed. 'They want me to follow you and find out how they can compromise you, so you view them favourably in the FIRB decision.'

She laughed. 'What did you tell them?'

'We followed you but found nothing.' He came closer and touched her arm. 'Now I will get out of your hair, so you can unwind after a hard day. Find the source of the information to AUSTRAC and I will ensure the CCP learn nothing from me.'

She stared at him for a moment, wondering if she should part with a small titbit she had picked up a while back from a contact in the CIA. 'Perhaps they should learn that Lui's aide is selling secrets.'

'To you?'

She smiled and shook her head. 'The Americans.'

'Thank you.'

'Remember where your loyalty lies.'

'Always my friend.'

Huma watched the door close behind him. Did she believe him? She hadn't asked how he had got into what was supposed to be a secure building. That was blindingly obvious. Michael Leung and his crowd didn't let small deterrents stand in their way. Fuck! Her father was right. She sculled her wine and poured another. She should call her father back, but he was going to say he told her so. She needed a cigarette.

It was only just after 6 pm, clear, cold, and with the faint tang of wood smoke in the air. A tendril of her own exhaled smoke hung in the stillness as she sat down on one of the chairs from her balcony's outdoor setting and picked up her second glass of wine.

She stared out at the lights blinking on. How the hell could she find out who knew about what? Devin might know if it was something from his agency, but that seemed unlikely and, in any case, how could she ask him? What would they be doing with intel on a Sydney drug and money laundering operation? Sure, they may have come across it in the course of other duties and forwarded it on, but that seemed unlikely.

Unless... oh Jesus Christ. It was there in front of her... Chris fucking Davis was in Sydney with her recently. How the hell he might have come across Michael's enterprise still stretched the imagination, but it wasn't out of the question? What other spies might have been hanging around Sydney recently. She slumped. The possibilities were endless, including that ex-MI6 bloke, Walker Fitzsimmons. Although she was pretty sure he had gone back home weeks ago. But there could be a dozen others about whom she knew nothing. Spies were like Indian Myna birds; the feral bastards were everywhere.

She also knew the name Alistair McMahon, but from where? She relaxed, let her mind run free as she took another drag of her cigarette. It would come if she let her mind do its job. Clear her head of all thoughts. Focus on breathing in, hold, out.

And there it was on the report. McMahon was the name of the detective investigating Kashton's death. He had come up with nothing conclusive, and the cause of death was determined to be natural.

She smiled and flicked her cigarette in an arc over the balcony; watched its glowing line until it disappeared. An act of rebellion. You never knew where the wind might blow. In moments of fantasy, she imagined it falling onto a lower balcony, rolling in through an open door, setting fire to the curtains, consuming the building. She alone would escape the inferno. In her imagination, she always did.

Wine in hand she went back inside to call her father, but at least now she had a place to begin. After ringing her dad, she would give Davis a call.

***

Chris's mobile rang, and he looked at the number. Few people had his private number, and this caller display said, number withheld. He hung up and turned his attention back to the news broadcast on the television. A minute later a text message pinged into his phone. He glanced at it and sat forward. Then the phone rang again. He answered. 'Sorry I didn't know it was you.'

Huma's voice chuckled in his ear. 'Thanks for taking my call. I got your number from Zoe. I know I have your other number, but this is not work and I didn't think it was proper to call you on a work phone. After all, you couldn't hang up on me then.'

'Dr Sharapova.'

'Huma please Chris. I told you this is not work, but personal.'

'Okay.' Chris frowned. 'Huma. What can I do for you?'

She laughed again. 'Are you always so serious? Where are you now?'

'At home.'

'Where is home?'

'Reid. A block of units.'

'Ah, not far from me.'

Chris remained silent.

Huma drew a breath. 'Look, remember I asked you to give me some pointers so I can challenge Alan.'

Chris nodded and made an ah-hum noise.

'Is tonight too soon? It's only six-thirty and we could get some dinner afterwards, my shout. Oh, you may have eaten already.'

Chris didn't have anything on, hadn't thought as far as dinner, probably would open a can of baked beans, or go to bed without. Winter evenings in Canberra weren't conducive to riding around on a bike although tonight was fine.

She said, 'Tell me your address. I'll pick you up.'

'It was as though she had read his mind.'

'Okay,' he said and gave her his address.

'I'll be there in ten. Is that okay?'

'Yeah sure.' He hung up, switched off the telly and got up to go and change, all the while quashing the misgivings shrieking at him.

To hell with it. What was the harm? Since the job on the sale of the bauxite mine was done, Chris had been at a loose end. When the chief's promotion was announced Chris dreaded to think what it meant for his career. Elgar was the definite favourite to take over.

The chief had promised Chris he would be okay. A vacancy had opened up at the Cairo station. By September, he would be out of the country. But somehow Chris knew Elgar would scupper his chances of taking up the Cairo role, even though he fitted the criteria perfectly.

Ten minutes later he was in Huma's BMW, seat warming his bum as they drove toward her gym, *Basic Promise*. The route Huma took, ran past the dead drop he had arranged with Mèng. Chris saw the chevron chalk mark at the end of the wall. It wasn't that obvious unless you knew where to look, but Chris's spirits lifted. Finally, Mèng had something although, whatever it was, would have to wait until tomorrow.

They arrived at the gym, a much newer and flashier place than the gym at which he usually trained.

Once inside, Huma signed a book on the counter listing Chris as her guest.

While she did that, Chris stood a little behind her.

The man behind the counter watched her. His arms were folded, legs spread, a red MAGA cap on his head covering short blond hair. He caught Chris's eye and took a step forward.

'Where are you from?'

Chris said the name of his gym.

The bloke shook his head. 'No. Where are you really from?'

'Sorry.' Chris frowned at the bloke's tone. 'Not sure what you mean mate.'

'You're an immigrant, right? Where are you from.'

'I grew up in Australia, but you are right. I am originally from the UK.'

'Bullshit. What country are you really from?'

Huma looked up. 'Ah Jake don't start. This is Chris Davis. My friend, all right. Just leave him alone.'

Chris eyed the bloke for a moment before saying, 'I don't mind answering your question. I'm actually an Iraqi refugee, and I'm Muslim. Is that a problem?'

Jake glanced at Huma, then looked down at his feet and muttered. 'He should fucking go back to his own country.'

Huma giggled and took Chris's arm to drag him away.

Chris glanced back at the man. 'Doesn't that offend you?'

She leaned into him and said, 'Ignore Jake. He's a simple soul. He did the same to me when I first came in here. Once he knows you, he's fine.'

Chris glanced at her, his pulse rate up a beat. The bloke was a racist dick, but he didn't say anything more. Afterall, it was her call.

Huma was an accomplished fighter. She didn't need any pointers from him although his size and strength gave him the advantage. He held back, merely blocking her rather than making quick work with a knock-out blow as he had been taught. Fights according to Masutatsu Oyama, the founding father, shouldn't take longer than three minutes, unless sparring.

He asked her about some of her Krav Maga moves and tried them out. Thereafter, the session consisted of her giving him pointers, rather than the other way about. And she was right, this was street fighting at its meanest, similar to the Russian Spetznaz systema training he'd tried when he was in the Royal Navy. Not his style but useful if a fight was life or death.

He'd never been in one of those, at least not outside a Wildcat helicopter, equipped with Sting Ray torpedoes, a door-mounted 0.5-inch heavy machine gun, and Anti-Surface guided weapons missiles. Or at the very least, with a personal SA80 and a 9mm to hand.

Afterwards, she said, 'I'm too sweaty to go out for dinner. Why don't we get an Uber eats at my place. We can have a shower and chill. I have wine and whatever else takes your fancy.'

He hesitated.

'Come on.' She grabbed his hand. 'I don't want to eat alone, and I am sure I can find you something clean and decent to wear after you shower.'

She always seemed one step ahead as though she was reading his mind. And what the hell, they were both adults even if she was seeing Marshall.

That was her affair, not his. He was a free man. A twinge caught in his throat as he thought of Cassie, but she was history and Mèng's message could wait until morning.

Back at her apartment, he came out of the guest bathroom clad in a track suit, which she said belonged to her father. It was a little short in the arms and legs but otherwise comfortable and quite presentable.

She was setting the table, also wearing tracksuit pants and a long-sleeved tee shirt, her hair still wet from the shower. The door chime sounded, and she said, 'Make yourself at home. I'll just get the food.'

Before he could say anything she was gone. He looked around the living room, noticing a cut-crystal glass on the coffee table, and a wine glass on the kitchen bench. He picked up the glass from the table and sniffed. Definitely whisky. Had she had a visitor before she called him?

He ambled over to the window and looked out over the lights of Canberra. This was a spacious apartment, modern, warm, comfortable, and new. Unlike his daggy relic of a building. Still, hopefully it wasn't for much longer and then he'd be in sunny Egypt.

He turned as she came back in. 'Can I do anything?'

'Pour us a drink. There is a white wine in the fridge next to a couple of beers, red wine in the cupboard and spirits in the cabinet over there.' She gestured with her chin as she took cardboard boxes from a paper bag.

'What do you drink?' he asked.

'White wine before dinner, whisky after.'

'Exclusively?' He smiled.

'Pretty much.'

'You have a well-stocked array for an exclusive white wine and whisky drinker.'

'You never know who you will be entertaining.'

'I can see that.' He poured her a glass of wine and took a beer from the fridge. 'I feel I should contribute.'

'Your turn next time.'

'Okay deal.'

His stomach churned. So, there was to be a next time. Interesting. He wondered for a moment what had happened to Alan Marshall, then dismissed the intrusion.

They sat down to eat and afterwards moved to the lounge chairs. By which time Chris noticed the whisky glass had gone. He hadn't even seen her move it.

She said, 'Would you like another drink?'

'Ah, no thanks. I should be going soon.'

'Stay a while.' She got up then came back with two full glasses of pale amber liquid and placed them and the bottle on the coffee table before sitting on the sofa next to him.

'That's a large whisky.' If he hadn't known better, he might think she was trying to get him drunk and seduce him. He smiled at his presumption. Small chance of that happening. He took a sip. It didn't taste of much, but he was no connoisseur.

She raised her glass to him before knocking back half the contents. 'Tell me about your life?'

'There's not much to tell. What about you? You've had a much more interesting life. Went to school in America, didn't you?'

Her eyes became serious. 'Yes. It was really awful. When I got there I couldn't speak a word of English and well I guess I was traumatised from things that had happened earlier. You know the story. You read my file.'

He nodded. 'You were just ten? It would have been hard.'

'We were stateless people.'

'But your father was born in Lithuania, wasn't he? It was your mother who was a Meskhetian Turk. She would have been Muslim, I guess.'

'My father too. He converted for her. But the Soviets didn't care. He was from Lithuania, working in the oil fields in the Fergana valley, near Namangan in Uzbekistan, when we were all caught in the Uzbek nationalist violence. No one cared about ethnic subtleties. You were either Uzbek or you weren't.'

'You no longer practice your faith.'

'Not since my mother died. My father was never a committed Muslim. He just went along so he could marry my mother.'

'And you mother's relatives? They ended up in Xinjiang. How are they faring?'

She took a breath. 'What is this? The third degree.'

'Sorry. Didn't mean to pry but I read in your file that the Chinese Government tried to blackmail you using your relatives as collateral.'

'The bastards locked them up when I resigned. I haven't heard anything since. My guess is they are all dead. But I was so young when I last saw any of them, so I didn't really know them.' She skulled the rest of her drink.

He drank his whisky and changed the subject. 'Do you miss it. The service I mean.'

She nodded. 'I often wonder if they would have me back. The Chinese government can't touch me now. They have done their worst, and it didn't work.'

That was interesting, especially after Mèng's comment that the Chinese were having her followed, trying to get some leverage on her to make the FIRB decision in their favour. It clearly hadn't worked, but he told her none of that. Mèng was not information he could share. Instead, he said, 'I am sure the chief would have you back in a heartbeat.'

She smiled. 'Do you want to sound him out? I could be your agent. Infiltrate some unfriendly country and pass its secrets back to you.'

He laughed. 'I reckon you could come back for real. They are looking to recruit officers at all levels. With your experience and profile, you could go for the top job. I'd have you in place of my director, any day. Although maybe you could apply for the chief's job. He's being promoted you know.'

'I heard. Heading up the revamped Office of National Intelligence.'

She gave him a wry smile. 'Tell me Chris, what do you do when you are not on Her Majesty's business? Do you have friends, a lover?'

Chris's eyebrows went up. 'I never thought about it like that. I guess we are still on the Queen's business, even in Australia, at least until either she dies, or we become a republic.'

She eyed him for a moment before leaning forward to run her finger down his cheek. 'You are a handsome man you know.'

His neck became hot, but he maintained eye contact. 'And you are a beautiful woman.' Christ, what a dumb thing to say. Shit. His eyes burned.

'You didn't answer my question.' She got up. 'Do you smoke Chris?'

He shook his head.

'Have you ever tried.'

He laughed. 'Sure, when I was a kid, but it didn't do much for my fitness.'

'Let me pour you another and we can go out to the balcony while I smoke. You don't mind do you. I don't smoke indoors. Makes the place stink. Besides I like annoying the neighbours when the smoke drifts onto their balcony.'

He didn't much like the smell of cigarette smoke either, but he was prepared to endure it for her. He picked up his refilled glass and followed her to the balcony. 'It's bloody freezing out here.'

She smiled. 'Toughen you up.' She lit up and blew out smoke before saying, 'So...'

He tilted his head. 'So... what?'

'What do you do in your spare time if you don't have a lover?'

He shrugged. 'The usual I guess. Keep fit. Play cricket occasionally.'

'You fly with the RAAF reserves.'

'Yeah that too. I also read, sometimes play video games, chess against the machine mostly. He smiled. I also watch movies, oh and I have just recently taken up figure drawing, or at least I took my first class. I tried pottery but I was no good at it.' He laughed self-consciously. 'Not sure I should go back. I wasn't much good at figure drawing either. How about you?'

'I also like to keep fit, but I don't have much free time. Too many student essays to mark and this last FIRB decision took a lot of my spare time. What do you like to read?'

Chris ran his hand over his mouth and glanced across at her. 'You'll laugh.'

'I won't.'

'Okay. I'm right into John le Carré at the moment.'

She laughed.

'You said you wouldn't.'

'Sorry, but that is such a cliché.'

He gazed out into the night.

She placed her hand on his leg. 'Is it anything like the real thing?'

'A bit. Lots of time where nothing happens except walking about, drinking coffee, office gossip, and politics. But you know. You used to do this job.'

She raised her eyebrows in acknowledgement. 'I spent most of my time overseas, often in war zones. But I did read a spy novel once. It was an

American novel, all action and violence. The spy was a superhero. Unbelievable. I didn't finish it.'

He laughed. 'I quite enjoy those too, but you are right. There are few who can fight like that.'

'None!'

'Yeah. There are two guys who come to mind.'

'Who?'

'A Japanese bloke, Yamoaka Tesshu, took on a hundred consecutive opponents with a bamboo sword and won. And the founder of Kyokushin, Mas Oyama, went three hundred consecutive rounds against his best students and won them all.'

'Well, I don't think the hero of the novel was of quite the same calibre. He was a CIA analyst for Christ's sake. A desk jockey.'

'I don't think the CIA is much different from us, do you? All just pen pushers at heart. When it comes to the rough stuff they either use paramilitary units or the military's special forces.'

'Mostly private contractors now-a-days. You were in the Royal Navy, weren't you?'

'Yeah, a glorified bus driver.'

'Weren't you a pilot?'

'Same thing.'

'I think you are a hard man to get to know Chris Davis. Everything is understated or redirected.'

'Sorry. It's a bad habit.'

'It's a spy's habit.'

Chris yawned. 'Sorry. I am really tired. Must be the whisky. I'm not used to it. Jesus!' He blinked and stood up. 'I should go.'

'Hm, more redirection.'

'No, seriously. I'll call an Uber.'

'Stay with me. Come.' She flicked her cigarette away and took his hand.

By the time they reached the bedroom, Chris was almost falling over with tiredness. He couldn't understand it and sank onto the accommodating mattress gratefully. A second later he felt her hands running over his body, and then nothing, oblivion.

***

Huma sat on the bed before she touched Chris, lightly and seductively at first, running her hands under his clothing, feeling the smooth outline of long muscles under the tracksuit. When he didn't move she went about searching him with more purpose. His phone and house keys were in his pocket. The house keys were no use. He didn't keep anything of interest at his home, she already knew that, but the phone might give her some clues. She eased it out and awoke the screen. It required a thumb print. That was easy.

Then she walked over to an armchair by the window, switched on a reading lamp, and opened his message app. Nothing. Canny fellow. There were no social media apps either and this was his personal phone. Strange dude. She scrolled through his contacts and recent calls list. This was more like it. Yes. And there was Alistair McMahon's phone number. Michael's instincts were right. She would let him know but not right now. Let him sweat for a while.

Although she would have to warn him to stay away from Chris. It was one thing knowing who your enemy was, but another thing letting them know you knew. Chris Davis was no pushover and if anything happened to him the agency would become involved. She would have to warn Michael to stay clear.

Huma returned Chris's phone to his pocket, then stood back to gaze in admiration at him. He really was dishy in an understated kind of way. Perhaps she should have slept with him before knocking him out. So long as she hadn't given him too much of the stuff. It was always difficult to get the dosage exactly right. She couldn't have him waking up while she was riffling through his pockets, but by the same token she also didn't want him sleeping in her bed for the next 20 hours.

If that happened, he would definitely work out that his tiredness was not merely due to two large glasses of neat whisky after a beer. He hadn't cottoned on that the whisky was well and truly watered down or she would be falling over by now, too. If she had got the dosage right, he would wake up at his usual time with nothing more than a headache, which hopefully would be put down to a hangover. She walked out of the room and went to check her emails.

24. Incrimination.

The next morning Chris locked his bike to a rail outside the Pâtisserie de Solène. He walked along the pavement to the glass doors, pushed them open and joined the queue at the expresso machine. As he inched forward, he opened the news app on the phone, occasionally glancing up and around, memorising the faces, figure outlines, and patterns, looking for signs, things amiss, but he wasn't on his metal today.

She was up and gone before he had awoken this morning, a note left on her pillow to say how much she had enjoyed last night, and he should make himself at home. But he could recall little of the night before. It was a fuzzy blur. That damned whisky had crept up on him. The glasses Huma poured must have been the equivalent of four standard drinks each. Two glasses on top of a beer. Why had he drunk them?

Although he was pretty sure she had matched him, drink for drink. She must have one hell of a tolerance. He had a vague memory of her hands inside his pants. Still, he was sure he had passed out before anything happened between them. Inwardly, he cringed. Her note was an exercise in manners. That was all.

When he got up he had found his clothes from the night before in the bathroom, sniffed them, grimaced then put them on in exchange for the tracksuit. He ran the four kilometres back to his flat, pushing himself beyond the pain, hoping to shake off the hangover.

At home he showered, swallowed some headache pills, changed into work clothes, and rode his bike to the bakery. On his way he spotted the new chalk mark, a chevron on the end of the graffiti covered wall bordering the car park. Two birds. He needed coffee and food, and he could check the drop.

He took off his backpack and puffer jacket and sat at a table, drank the coffee, ate a cheese and ham croissant, and got up to leave, backpack over his shoulder, jacket slung over his arm. When he reached his bike, he hung both jacket and backpack over the end of the rail and bent to unlock his bike. At the same time, he shielded the dead drop with his body, while he unscrewed the steel cap from the end of the rail and withdrew a small plastic box. After replacing the cap, he stuffed the jacket, along with the box, into his backpack which he slung onto his back. He then clipped the U-lock into its mount on the bike's seat tube, mounted and steered his bike towards the road.

Fifteen minutes later he was at his desk, half an hour late but he was still using the desk the chief had arranged, and nobody seemed interested in his comings and goings. It had got around he was working on a special project and although the gossip and speculation had gone through the roof, the chief had decided Chris needed to stay where he was, reporting only to him, until they could ascertain how much use Mèng might be.

Devon Royce had tasked Chris with finding out who had leaked the document that Mèng had given him as a priority, but so far Mèng had not proved much use. The man was a flunky and knew very little. Chris suspected he had the attaché role to General Liu purely because he had a father with influence.

He opened the small box and inside was a flash drive. Damn! An A plug. Why did his laptop only have a C port. He rummaged in his drawer for a converter. Once he had the drive opened, he discovered it contained folders labelled 2012 through to 2016. Inside each folder, were dozens of files all dated and labelled with street or building names, all in Beijing. Mèng had come through although what use the photos might be, was anyone's guess.

Chris drew a breath. This would take a while. He began scrolling, not knowing what he was looking for but convinced this was a treasure trove of information. The faces needed names but here, Mèng had failed him. Some of the more notable people in the files had names attached when Chris hovered the mouse over them, but most didn't.

Some of the photos were of large gatherings, some merely one or two people, some in groups at a function, some depicted as lone European figures on the streets. A few men with European women, possibly Chinese kompromat. No doubt Mèng had kept the more risqué photos out of this collection although Chris had asked for all photographs with Australians in the mix.

He opened the 2014 file and scrolled through before stopping to peer at a photo. He had been at this function, recognised it, and it took him back three years. This was one of many events surrounding the negotiations of the

Free Trade Agreement, but this had been his first. It had made an impact because he had only recently arrived.

The event was held in The Beijing International Convention Centre. He enlarged the photo, searching through the crowd. It was his practice to avoid showing his face when there were cameras around, so he doubted he would feature in the photo, but he could see the ambassador. And there he was, standing a little way behind her, his face turned away, although he was probably not aware of the camera at the time. A few photos on, and there he was again. This time with name and job title attached. So, this was when Mèng had targeted him. So much for avoiding being photographed.

This photo had been taken at the reception for the ministerial visit. That was when Chris had discovered his Chinese counterpart knew more than he should about some of Australia's strategic interests. More disconcertingly, the man already knew what the minister's speech would cover and warned Chris that she would be overstepping diplomacy's threshold unless she altered some critical parts.

Chris suspected a leak from the Australian contingent or how else had the man known what might be in the minister's speech. But from where? He asked his counterpart directly.

The bloke had just grinned and said, it was an educated guess. Chris didn't believe him, although he supposed it was plausible. He'd made guesses of a similar nature, and any evidence to the contrary was so tenuous he hadn't passed it on. He should have, but he wanted more concrete evidence.

He examined the photo more carefully, enlarging it to maximum capacity without losing too much of the photo's pixilation. The minister's policy officer was in a corner with a man. The man looked as if he could be a Chinese national, but he had his back to the camera and Chris couldn't make out who he was.

There was something familiar about him. Did he work for the Embassy? There were more photos of the event and Chris found the man again. No wonder he looked familiar. The man in the photo with the policy officer was none other than Brian Laidley, the minister's husband.

Chris grimaced. He was jumping at shadows. He went back to the photo where Laidley was talking to the policy officer. There was another man with them, but his face was almost hidden from view by a large flower arrangement. He kept scrolling and after reviewing a few more photos he found the bloke or, at least, the clothing was the same. The minister, her husband and the policy officer were in a group, and the bloke stood a few meters away, watching them.

He enlarged the photo and took a screen shot. Then he ringed the face in the original photo and placed the screen shot and a copy of the ringed photo in another folder before he carried on scrolling.

Before he finished for the day Chris added a few more photos to his file and downloaded them onto a flash drive. Along with a few question, he would leave the drive in the dead drop tomorrow morning.

He sat back in his chair and stared into space. It was a shame there was no safe mechanism to share the files online with Mèng but after the Chinese had hacked into the CIA secure database and exposed all the American agents in China a few years ago, Chris wasn't about to trust any technological comms to get this job done, even though it took longer and was more of an inconvenience.

Maybe Mèng would come up with something he could use. Even so, he would need more than a photo to get permission to carry out any surveillance on an Australian citizen especially the minister's husband. He would just have to do it the old-fashioned way. Maybe he should speak to the chief. Last time he had left his suspicions until he had proof and look where that had got him. They blamed him for not coming forward before more material was leaked. All but arrested him as her accomplice, but Jesus, this was the minister's husband. He had to have something more than his gut worms grumbling.

If he knew who the other bloke was, it would be better. It wouldn't do to discover he was an assigned ministerial driver or some such. More likely he was an employee of that sprawling mass of human intrigue called the Ministry of State Security. Although he wasn't someone Chris had come across before. Yet that meant little. The Ministry employed many thousands of people. He just hoped Mèng might give him something to settle his intestinal intuition.

He also needed a car but not an agency vehicle. He could use Zoe's car. She had given him the keys, but he didn't want to take advantage of her good nature. Instead, he used an alternative driver's licence, one not on the books, to hire a small vehicle that looked like a delivery van.

That night he parked on a street that led off diagonally across the road from the minister's house. It gave him a good view of the driveway and a corner section of the attached garage and a couple of upstairs windows. Then he waited. The minister was in London, but her husband had remained in Australia.

Chris had no idea what he might learn by watching the house, but it seemed a place to start. Brian Laidley arrived home at 6:30 pm. He left his Audi in the driveway and went into the house. Perhaps that meant he was going out again. Chris was prepared to follow him if that was the case. Maybe he would notice something, a pattern if nothing else.

He was disappointed, the man didn't come out of the house again although Chris could see a silhouette occasionally passing a lighted window. By 11 pm the house was in complete darkness. At 1 pm Chris went home to sleep. He still had to work in the morning, and Brian Laidley was not moving. He would just have to return tonight. He hated this kind of mind-numbing surveillance but sometimes it bore fruit.

On his way to the office the next morning, Chris left a chalk mark at the other end of the carpark wall, crossed the road, locked his bike to the rail while he inserted the flash drive in the dead drop space. Then he went into the bakery and bought coffee and a croissant.

While he drank his coffee and ate, he watched the rail, but Mèng did not appear. Perhaps he had missed him. At any rate Mèng would pick up the drive tomorrow morning on his usual run to pick up General Liu's pastries. If things went to plan, Chris might have some answers by the end of the week.

25. Paranoid Floundering.

Someone was following Alistair, and he suspected the AFP. Who else could it be? He had made a mess of things that was for sure. When he had gone to see Janice Burton, she had told him his source denied passing on any information and, in fact, swore he hadn't seen Alistair for at least a year.

Turned out, the source had found God and cleaned up his act before any meth-related dementia had a chance to set in. Alistair knew he was screwed. He had told Janice he'd made a mistake. Said the wrong name, but he had been under the pump over another case and wasn't thinking straight.

He gave her another name, insisting this time the name of the informant was the correct one. Then he went to check that the bloke was still on meth, gave him an 8 ball and had a conversation, where he mentioned the last time they had spoken about a month back.

The bloke couldn't remember. Neither could he remember telling Alistair about overhearing some Triads in an alley behind the casino discussing money laundering. That was despite Alistair telling him it was so, and if he wanted another 8 ball he would do well to remember next time he was asked.

He didn't know if he had got away with all the bullshit he'd told Janice, and he was pretty sure the addict would screw up the message, but at least it might sow doubt. That's if he wasn't dead from an overdose by the time the AFP found him. But Alistair didn't have that kind of luck.

Now, he was definitely being followed, and by professionals. He had seen the same person, wearing different clothing, three times in as many days. The bloke was Asian but that meant nothing. The AFP, particularly in Sydney, were awash with Asian heritage Australian officers, and would use them on a case like this.

It wasn't definitive proof but added to that were other signs, like fleeting glimpses of vehicles in a holding pattern behind traffic, only to reappear wherever he turned. Then there was the abrupt about turn of a woman on the other side of the street. She was a looker in a mini skirt and Alistair had been admiring her legs before he realised she was taking a bit too much interest in him.

Nearby a bloke was gazing into shop window that held a display of the latest best sellers, and he didn't look the bookish type. The woman stopped next to him and eased off her shoe as if there was something irritating her. She didn't look at the bloke examining the books, but Alister was sure her mouth had moved.

More than anything it was intuition, but Alistair became increasingly paranoid, and he was too afraid to contact Mike Leung in case he led the AFP to him. He thought of going to see Ed Chin and getting him to pass on a message, but Minty wouldn't thank him for embroiling her family.

There was nothing else to do but carry on with his working day, although he avoided all his usual haunts and hung around the office more than was usual for him. He also went straight home from work, which caused his wife to make some caustic comments. You would think she'd be grateful.

Alistair didn't know what to do until he decided he would go and see Cassie. She might be able to give him some ideas, although he guessed it all depended on how much he could tell her. Still the more he thought about visiting her, the more he wanted to, and not just for lawyerly advice. He took the dog out for a walk.

Once he was out of the house and far away from Minty's Xray vision and pointy ears, he rang Cassie and left a message that he had something urgent to discuss—said he'd call in to her place the following evening at 6:30 pm. He half expected to get a text back saying she would be out.

The following evening, when Cassie opened the door to him, he couldn't think how to approach the subject. She poured him a beer and sat down opposite him, glass of wine in hand.

'What's so urgent?' she asked.

'Did I say urgent?'

'You did. Alistair, I hope this is not just a ruse.'

He grinned. 'It would have worked.'

'No, it wouldn't.' She stood up. 'You can leave now.'

'Don't chuck me out. It wasn't a ruse. I really need your advice.'

'Why?'

He blurted out before he could stop himself. 'I think the AFP is following me.'

'Holy dooly! Why?'

'Not sure but I think it's about a case I was working on. They seem to have the wrong end of the stick about my role in it.'

Her eyes narrowed. 'That makes no sense.'

He realised he was making a hash of it. Cassie was nobody's fool. She was a bloody Queen's counsel for crying out loud, not some bimbo in a club. He wouldn't be able to fool her easily. Perhaps it had been a mistake coming here.

'Come on Alistair. Tell me what's going on. You asked for my help. Now I know you are lying to me.'

'How do you know?' He was actually interested in her answer.

'What?'

'How do you know when I am lying? You always seem to be able to see through me.'

'What is this? I thought you wanted advice but instead you are playing some stupid game.'

'It's all the same thing. I can't tell you Cassie unless you agree to represent me.'

'Well, two things. I am not going to represent you if I don't know what the problem is, and in any case our past relationship would get in the way. Any opposition worth their salt would uncover it in a heartbeat and use it against both of us. So, as a friend I am asking, are you in trouble with the law?' She laughed. 'Sorry, that sounded so pompous.'

He sighed. 'If I tell you, are you going to dob me in?'

Cassie pressed her lips into a thin line. 'Depends. I might be subpoenaed if the AFP think I know something. I won't be accused of concealing evidence if that's what worries you. Come on Alistair. This is not America with attorney client privilege. You know how it works.'

He nodded. Then leaned forward, picked up his beer and drained it.

She raised her eyebrows. 'Do you want another?'

'I'd prefer something harder.'

'I've only got wine. Oh, I have some cooking brandy left over from last Christmas when I tried making a cake.'

'That'll do.'

'Are you driving, Alistair?'

He pulled a face. 'Yeah, but one won't hurt.'

'Okay, but maybe I should order an uber eats to go with it. Pasta do you?'

He shrugged.

She poured him a small brandy and then ordered the food while Alistair sat winding logic through different scenarios.

Eventually he asked, 'If I tell you and they don't summons you, you'll keep it to yourself, or at least not volunteer the information.'

She paused. 'So long as it's not a child, or a murder, okay.'

'It's money laundering.'

'Okay, that doesn't immediately set off any moral dilemmas. Tell me.'

He told her a slicker version of the story he had told Janice Burton and watched her carefully to see how she reacted. He didn't expect advice, but she was smart and would spot holes in his story. That way at least he would be ready if Janice hauled him in again.

She did pick holes, 'What was the case, you were working on?'

'A drug syndicate,' he said. 'Can't specify the details...'

'And that flustered you?'

'No, it wasn't the case... it was the pressure to wrap it up. You know...'

'Okay, so how did the meth addict know the men he had overheard were Triads?'

'I didn't ask him...'

She pursed her mouth. 'I don't understand why you think the AFP don't believe you...'

Was that sarcasm in her tone? 'I don't fucking know do I. That's why I came to you.'

'Jeez, calm down Alistair. From what you've told me, they have no reason to follow you unless they think you are involved or covering up. Could that be it Alistair? Are you hiding something or are you just being a tad paranoid?'

'I'm doing nothing, and I don't think it's paranoia!'

'Well, then why...?'

'I told you. I don't fucking know, and it's doing my head in.' He ran his hand through his hair and looked up at her.

Cassie's face had gone pale.

'Alistair, I can see you are scared, but don't shout at me, okay.'

'I'm not scared.'

'What is it then? I can't work out what your problem is. Maybe the AFP is not following you and...'

'Then who is?'

She drew back and took a sip of her wine. The doorbell chimed and she got up. 'I'll just get the food. Try to chill a bit Alistair. You can have something to eat to soak up the alcohol, then you have to go.'

While she was gone, Alistair got up and poured himself another brandy. A large one, filling the tumbler. Maybe she was right. Maybe it wasn't the AFP following him. But who else. Unless... He supposed it might be Mike keeping an eye on him.

The air left his lungs in a whoosh. Mike said he'd look after him when he told him about the AFP. Maybe that was it. Thank Christ. Did he say that? No, he said he should be rewarded. Was that the same thing? Maybe he should ask Mike, but if the AFP were following him, they would have tapped his phone. He had a burner to contact Mike, and the Feds couldn't know about that yet, surely. But it all came back to the big question: was it the Feds following him or not? Shit! Maybe he just needed a holiday. That was it. He would take Minty and the kids away. Byron Bay, Cairns, somewhere warm and just forget about it.

He heard Cassie open the front door and downed the brandy.

She came into the room with a brown paper bag in her hands.

'Thanks Cassie. I feel much better. You are right. It's probably my imagination. Look, sorry but I should go. My wife is expecting me for dinner. But thanks, you've been a great help.' He grabbed her shoulder and kissed her before pulling back to gaze into her face. 'That is unless you have changed your mind and still want to sleep with me.'

'Fuck off Alistair. What about the food I ordered.'

'Take a rain check Cassie. Have to go, really. I'll be in touch.'

***

Cassie stood stock still as he walked out. She would never learn. The man was a nightmare. Well, at least she would get a good dinner. Her earlier plans had centred on something like a toasted cheese sandwich. She placed the paper bag on the table and went to the kitchen to get a plate and cutlery, refilling her wine glass on the way.

Why she bothered with men, she didn't know. They were always a letdown, Alistair, and now Chris. There were others she had dated but none of them stacked up. Mostly she hadn't found them interesting. She still didn't know why Chris had run away, but she didn't want to think about him.

The thing Alistair said about money laundering just didn't stack up either. He was probably up to his oxters in some racket that he should not have anything to do with. He wouldn't be the first copper to get sucked in by the money and glitz of casinos but surely he wasn't doing anything illegal. At least she hoped not, but then this was Alistair. He couldn't lie straight in bed if his life depended on it.

Squealing tires and a loud bang sounded from the street outside. Cassie frowned and moved to the balcony door. She opened the curtains and then unlocked the door before stepping out onto the balcony.

It was freezing outside, and a thin mist reflected the light from the streetlamps as it wrapped tendrils around the bare limbs of trees that lined the street. She peered over the railing and saw a body lying in the road. Her hand flew to her mouth. 'Oh my God, Alistair.'

Cassie raced from her flat, took the stairs down to the lobby and ran out onto the pavement. A car had stopped in the middle of the road with a man standing next to it, his phone to his ear. Five metres ahead, Alistair lay crumpled across the white centre-marking.

Cassie stepped towards him and heard a groan. 'Oh, thank God, he's alive.' She looked up and down the street and knelt next to him. 'Alistair. Can you hear me?'

No response.

She glanced up at the man who was now standing a metre away looking on. 'Did you call an ambulance?'

He nodded. 'Is he okay?'

'I don't know. Do you know any first aid?'

The man shook his head. 'Sorry.'

Neither did Cassie. All she knew was that she shouldn't move him in case something was broken. 'How long before they get here?'

'They said they were on the way.'

The sound of an ambulance siren came to her as she sat on the road next to him.

The man said, 'You probably shouldn't sit there. You might get run over.'

'I can't leave him here by himself. You redirect any traffic.'

'I have to go. I have an appointment.'

'You can't go. You are the only witness.'

'I didn't see anything. He was lying in the road, and I stopped.'

'You must have. It happened seconds before I got here, and you were already on the phone.'

The man sighed. 'I didn't see much. I was looking at the apartment for sale sign over there when it happened.'

'You must have seen the car that hit him.'

He shook his head. 'You would have seen something. You arrived just after I did.'

'No. I heard the thunk from my flat.'

'If you didn't see anything, how do you know a car hit him?'

She raised her finger and tilted her head. 'Ah, Alistair, I can hear the ambulance. You will be alright now.'

A minute after the ambulance pulled up, a police car arrived, and Cassie left Alistair to the ministration of the paramedics while she walked over to the patrol car to give her details.

'Two police officers got out.'

'Hit and run?' one of them asked.

Cassie nodded. 'I think so, but I didn't see it.' She pointed to the witness. 'He did. He called triple zero. The victim's name is Alistair McMahan. He's one of your mob, a detective.'

The police officers looked at each other. One went back to the car, while the other took out his notebook. 'What can you tell me?'

Afterwards, Cassie went back to her apartment. She realised she was trembling and plonked down on a chair next to the now cold food. Was the hit and run deliberate? Maybe Alistair wasn't paranoid, after all. But it wouldn't have been the AFP following him. Someone seemed to be after him and Cassie suspected the money laundering crowd Alistair had mentioned. She should probably call the AFP, but what if Alistair was implicated in some way. He wouldn't thank her for interfering. Oh God, she didn't know what to do.

26. Surveillance

Tonight, Thursday was the fourth night Chris had parked outside Brain Laidley's house and seen nothing untoward. Aside from going to and from work, Brian had gone out twice and both times Chris had followed him. The first time he had gone to the bottle shop, the second to attend a business dinner function at the National Convention Centre.

Nothing was going Chris's way. He had not heard from Mèng, and the dead drop hadn't been visited. The flash drive was still inside the rail cavity. Now, his stake-out was a wash-out, and tomorrow Marianna Laidley would be arriving home. There would be no more covert surveillance. The AFP were more vigilant regarding cars parked around the minister's home when she was in residence.

Tonight, was his last chance. Besides the vehicle hire was costing a fortune. He sighed and opened a sandwich he'd bought at a Seven Eleven somewhere between work and here. He sniffed it. The bread was a bit stale but otherwise it would plug a hole.

Then movement. Someone came around from the back of the house wheeling a motorcycle. The man had on a helmet. It wasn't Brian. This helmeted man was smaller. Chris laid the sandwich on the passenger seat and waited until the motorbike rider took off before he keyed the van's ignition to follow him.

The man pulled up outside a grocery store, removed his helmet and walked towards the entrance. Chis couldn't see his face but assumed this was another dead end. Just a man shopping. Nevertheless, he parked and waited until the man had gone inside before he got out and sauntered over to the store.

It was one of those expensive boutique places that sold luxury goods as well as normal food at eye watering prices. Chris held open the glass door as a woman in her fifties walked out, hugging a brown paper grocery bag with what looked like celery leaves poking out the top. As she passed the peppery scent of the leaves confirmed it.

He walked into the store and stopped at a display of cheese, ignoring the instant clamour from his stomach. A glance around the shop showed the bike rider browsing in the first isle, a shopping basket over one arm, holding up a can as he read its label.

Chris picked up a basket from near the counter and sauntered along the second isle before turning into the first. The rider looked directly at him, but Chris avoided his gaze and moved sideways to pass. At the same time, he realised he had seen the man's face before. It answered a lot of questions, or did it? He would have to be sure.

He picked a small, tinned item off the shelf and went to the counter to pay for it, replacing his basket with the stack of others while the salesperson rang up the purchase.

'Seventy-five dollars.' She said.

Chris almost choked but he couldn't back out now, or he would draw attention to himself.

'Do you want a bag? They're 25 cents.' The salesperson stared at him, hostility rising from her like a vapour, while he fumbled for his credit card.

He shook his head, paid for the small green and gold can, and walked out wondering what the hell he had just bought. It wasn't until he was in the car that he examined the can. Goose foie gras. He had bought a can of pâté for $75. What an idiot. He chucked the can onto the seat next to his now curling sandwich, took his phone from his pocket, zoomed the camera app in on the door to the shop, and waited. He had to be sure it was the same bloke.

When the man came out, he carried a full, 25 cent shopping bag in his arms, but Chris managed to get some good photos of his face. He would check the shots against Mèng's photos back at the office. He followed the man back to the house and settled in to wait.

It was almost midnight before Chris gave up. The house was in darkness and Brian hadn't shown himself. When Chris arrived home, he parked the van outside his block of units, chucked his uneaten sandwich in a public bin, and walked up the stairs to his flat.

He reached the top of the steps and stopped, adrenalin surging through his body. In the dim light from a low wattage globe in the stairwell, Chris made out a figure slumped in his doorway. The body stirred and stood up.

'What the hell, mate.' Chris kept his voice low.

Mèng said, 'I am in trouble.'

'Shit!' Chris unlocked the flat door and pushed Mèng inside. He shut the door and raced through to the living room to shut the blinds. Mèng placed a backpack on the kitchen counter, and said, 'I need somewhere to hide.'

'And you thought coming here was a good idea. How the hell do you know where I live?'

'I followed you for a long time before even I met you. You must protect me now.'

Chris sighed. 'It's not up to me mate.' He ran a hand through his hair. 'What happened?'

Mèng slumped down on the sofa. 'I am hungry. 'Do you have some food for me to eat?'

'Sorry mate. Ah, there's a $75 can of pâté in the car, but I don't have anything in here except beer. I guess I can order something from Uber eats. What do you want, Thai, pizza, Indian, Chinese? He smiled at the last label. Chinese food in restaurants here barely resembled any like the provincial food differences of China.

Mèng shrugged. 'Pizza is good.'

Chris placed the order then said, 'So tell me what happened.'

'I was being watched. I couldn't open the dead drop, even though I went to the bakery every day. I was followed.'

'Are you certain? How do you know?'

'They are not subtle if they want to frighten you.'

'Okay, go on.'

'This morning, I was informed I was to return home.'

'That doesn't sound too bad.'

'It is bad, very bad. A significant loss of face. But the worst thing is that it most likely means they will arrest me when I get back.'

'What for?'

'I have told you this already.'

'Yes, but you haven't been carrying on while you've been in Australia, surely. Not since you spoke to me.'

'I had no choice. Once you start you can't just back out.'

'Jesus!' Chris wiped his hand across his mouth.

'When I heard that, I went to see General Liu to beg him to keep me here in Australia. He wasn't in his office, and I saw an opportunity to copy a report that was lying on his desk. It will be enough I think to give me asylum.'

'What's the report say?'

'It is what you call a draft policy paper examining how China should conduct foreign relations into the future. Xi Jinping wants us to present as equals to the Americans, standing up to, rather than appeasing the West. It is a good time now. Western hegemonic influence is in the decline.'

'What do you mean, in decline?'

'The west is tired of democracy and fighting amongst itself. Liberalism is dying. The British Brexit, the election of Donald Trump, the reemergence and rise of fascist-style populism in Europe are just some of those indicators. Now, we will make strategic alliance with Russia and other countries. This will give us the power and leverage to take on the west at its own game. You have heard of wolf warrior diplomacy...?'

Chris nodded. He had heard the term used, but only recently. Maybe Mèng really did have something useful to trade.

The door buzzer sounded. He checked the security camera, but it was just the arrival of the pizza. He told Mèng to hide in the bathroom, while he collected the delivery. When he came back inside, he chucked the pizza box on the counter.

Mèng came out the bathroom and went straight to the box. 'I love pizza.' He grinned, sank his teeth into a slice and tore off a mouthful. 'This is another reason why I must stay. You must help me.'

Chris handed Mèng a beer. 'There is nothing we can do now but you can sleep on the sofa tonight and I'll sort something out tomorrow. How did you get here? You weren't followed, were you?'

'I took many busses, and I am sure I was not followed. I have good trade craft.'

Obviously better than his. He'd become lazy. 'Okay.' Chris went to the cupboard, took out a sleeping bag, and chucked it on the sofa. 'Get some sleep and we'll deal with it in the morning.'

Mèng said, 'I forgot. I also have photo of another memorandum from your government.'

'Why didn't you say?

He shrugged. 'The draft policy document I think is more important.'

'Maybe. Let me see the photo.'

Mèng opened his phone to his photo app.

Chris took the phone and enlarged the photo. It was a memo from Elgar to the minister's office. He would have to read it on a larger screen, but it looked like Elgar was relaying the details of Chris's first visit to Sydney and his subsequent assignment to Treasury. He hadn't even known that Elgar knew about the project.

The chief had said Chris's report was for his eyes only. Jesus the leak was either in Elgar's office, or in the minister's office. He had to talk to Devin Royce, but it was after one in the morning. He hesitated. Maybe the leak was coming from the minister's own household. He was pretty sure the bloke at the market this evening was the same bloke in the photo with the minister's husband in Beijing. He had planned to check in the morning, but Mèng was here now. He opened the photos he had taken outside the grocery store. 'Do you know this bloke?'

Mèng screwed up his eyes before wiping his hands on his jeans and taking Chris's phone to enlarge the picture. 'Where did you take this?'

'Just answer the question.'

'I don't know. He looks a little like a man I have seen before, but this man is in Beijing, not here.'

'Does he have a name?'

Mèng shrugged. 'I don't know his name, but he was often at diplomatic events in Beijing. At one time I thought he was following me, but he was more interested in foreign nationals. I assumed he was from the Ministry of State Security, but I didn't want to draw attention to myself, so I didn't ask.'

Chris took a slug of beer then helped himself to a slice of pizza. Could the minister have a spy working in her house and not even know about it? At least now he would have more evidence to offer the chief, but it was going to be tricky accusing anyone, let alone the Minister of Foreign Affairs, without solid evidence.

Chris shuddered at the memories after his previous accusation of the ministerial policy officer: two AFP officers escorting him on his return from Beijing to Australia; being stood aside while the investigation progressed. At first they had accused him of being her accomplice before he was cleared to resume duty.

If Elgar and the minister didn't like him then, they were going to go ballistic when they found out he'd been spying on them, and without authorisation. He would be finished. Although if the minister and Elgar were implicated in the leak... That didn't bare thinking about. Jesus, had his dealings with Mèng been leaked? He put the pizza and beer down.

'Come on mate, I'm taking you to a more secure location. Grab your bag.'

***

Chris drove around with Mèng hidden in the back of the van for an hour, making sure there was no tail before he headed for Zoe's flat. He left Mèng there with strict instructions about keeping hidden, staying off any form of communication device, and more particularly not touching anything, including Zoe's precious collection of bonsais. He just hoped Zoe would forgive him, but leaving Mèng at his own flat was not a safe option.

From Zoe's place, Chris drove back to his flat and checked the security camera before he collected his bike, put it in the back of the van, and drove into work. It was 4:30 am when he let himself into the office. At 7:30 am, with a file full of notes and photos along with the two document's Mèng had given him, he sat outside the chief's office and waited for him to arrive.

27. Suddenly it's Serious

Devin Royce was late for work. He hated arriving once everyone else was already there although he might be forgiven the odd tardy day given the hours he usually worked. But being late set a bad example. Of course, the reason he was late was Huma's unexpected telephone call to congratulate him on his promotion.

The call came through just as he was about to leave home and instead of getting into the car, he ducked into the privacy of his study. He had enjoyed talking to her. They hadn't had such an intimate conversation for some time, and it occurred to him that she most likely wanted something from him. Still, he had found the banter exciting, more than he probably should as a married man.

She said she hoped to see him at the mid-winter ball.

He had hoped he wouldn't have to go, but his wife had insisted. Now, it might be okay. Talking to her took him back, and, as he hung up, nostalgia threatened to swamp him. He should be looking forward to his new role heading up the Office of National Intelligence, but on occasion, he hankered for the old days. The whole time he had been talking to her his mind was back in the war zone where everything, including human relationships, sharpened into a life affirming high.

When he kissed his wife goodbye for the second time that morning, he didn't mention the call was from Huma, although she asked who it was.

'Just work dear. You know...'

She pursed her lips. 'Honestly! Couldn't they have waited until you got there?'

When Devin arrived at work his personal assistant, Anna Thompson, held her finger to her lips and then grinned, pointing at the slumped body on the chair in the lobby area outside his office.

Devin frowned. 'Mr. Davis...'

Chris started and leaped up. 'Morning sir.'

His eyes had the glazed look of a man not yet awake.

'Apologies sir. I think I might have dozed off, but I need to speak to you urgently.'

'You had better come in then. Anna can you bring in a good strong pot of coffee. Thank you. After you Mr Davis...'

Once inside the office, Devin took off his coat and hung it on a peg before turning to Chris. 'Sit down Mr Davis and explain what is so important that you had to sleep on my doorstep.'

'Sorry about that sir, I didn't mean to fall asleep, but I've been awake all night. No excuse I know...'

Devin waved the explanation aside. 'Get to your purpose please Mr Davis.'

Chris rubbed his face. 'Last night when I got home I found Captain Mèng on my doorstep. He said he has defected and wanted my protection. I explained it wasn't up to me but...'

'I thought the man was just a criminal trying to evade Chinese justice for corruption.'

'Well, yes I think he is, but he has traded something worthwhile I think, which he took at some risk to his life. Besides, he's in serious trouble already for absconding. I couldn't just turn my back.'

'So where is he now?'

'I have him holed up until I spoke to you.'

Devin placed his arm across his chest, resting the elbow of the other arm on it, while his hand covered his mouth. 'There must be more... Ah, Anna thank you. Have a cup of coffee Chris and we will try this again.'

'Thank you sir.'

After Anna had poured the coffee and left the office Devin said, 'Right, explain from the beginning, please.'

Chris ran his hand through his hair, took a gulp of the coffee, placed the folder on the desk and said, 'It's a bit of a convoluted story sir, but Mèng's defection is only part of it. I also think I have found the leak.'

***

Chris followed the chief into the Ben Chifley building. It was his first visit, and he looked at the endless glass, and forest of pillars as they entered. Inside were long corridors, and doors. Lots of doors.

This morning, after Chris had explained what he'd found, the chief made a couple of calls, got up and requested Chris tag along to a hastily convened meeting, to answer questions. The situation with both Mèng's defection and the potential spy in the minister's household was really ASIO and AFP territory—Australian home security, rather than foreign surveillance.

As they were shepherded into a secure meeting room, it flashed into his head that he might never leave the place given his crude and unauthorised reconnaissance, but if he hadn't done it they would still be scratching their heads over the leaks. At least now they knew it wasn't in one of their agencies. That had got to be a relief.

Eight people sat around a table, most in civilian dress but some in AFP uniform. That was a lot of people, all about to become privy to what only Chris, and now the chief, knew. He wasn't comfortable with that, but he supposed it wasn't his call any longer, and he was right. After he had finished his briefing, the file on Mèng was purloined.

The meeting broke up with a decision to set up a document trail that would provide admissible evidence for an arrest warrant for the minister's cook, a necessary check on whether Elgar, the minister or the minister's husband had any knowledge of the household spy's activities, and to ascertain the cook's method of passing information to the Chinese. In the meantime, Elgar and the minister were not to be informed. Any knowledge outside of the room might be a giveaway allowing the cook to bolt.

A woman in uniform asked Chris where Mèng was. 'Will he be able to shed light on the cook's role?'

Chris shook his head. 'I'm pretty sure he's told me all he knows.'

'Where is he now?'

'Mèng?'

'Yes.'

'I'll bring him in.'

'No need. We just need an address.'

Chris didn't want heavy boots tromping all over Zoe's flat. 'He'll bolt if he so much as catches a whiff of you guys coming for him.'

'He'll be better off in a safe house,' she said.

Chris shook his head and appealed to the chief. 'I really need to bring him in. Just tell me where?' Privately he acknowledged it was his innate mistrust of coppers rather than concern over their methods. He really should get over it. He smiled at the woman. 'You can do your thing, and I'll make sure Mèng knows he can trust you. If he is sure he is to be protected, he'll give you everything he knows. For him its transactional. Information in exchange for safety. The bloke has no ideology.'

Finally, they agreed to go together, but Chris would go up to Zoe's flat and speak to Mèng before handing him over to the AFP. Another day on the van rental. Maybe the chief would cover the cost as a legitimate expense now Chris had uncovered the source of the leak.

The following day, Chris was at his desk, pleased it had all gone well. The chief had agreed to his expense claims, including the bloody tin of $75 pâté, about which he laughed himself silly. Mèng was off his hands, in a safe house being interrogated by ASIO officers. Zoe's flat was none the worse for its experience, and Chris had managed to water the bonsais and tidy up after they had taken Mèng away.

He presumed the trap being set for the cook was in motion although what it was, he didn't know or want to know, and he was just finalising his report on the mission to find the leak and manage Mèng's defection. Two tasks successfully completed. Perhaps it was more than two.

The chief had initially only tasked him with finding out what Fitzsimmons's was doing in Australia and then with ensuring Huma Sharapova remained safe while the FIRB decision was made. Project Perseus kept expanding.

In reality, Mèng and the agency leaks were just a bonus arising from a chain of interrelated events. It was the kind of thing that happened often in his world. It was all interrelated. So long as there were nation states with national border to protect and the means to uncover other nations' secrets, he would have work to do.

Yet, despite these lucky breaks, he had never got to the bottom of why Fitzsimmons was really here. It left a hole in the project. He sat back and gazed at the report on his screen. He should give it a final once-over and send it to the chief—failures, inconsistencies and all. Then the project would be well and truly finished. He would have to return to his desk downstairs, and Elgar. His elation deflated. Maybe the chief would bring the posting to Cairo, forward. September, he had said, but that was still two months away.

The phone on his desk rang. 'Davis speaking.'

'Chris Davis?'

'Yes.'

It was a woman's voice. 'I'm with the AFP, Sydney office. My name is Janice Burton. I have been trying to contact you for a few days.'

'And how can I help you, Officer Burton?'

'Janice, please.'

'Okay, how can I help Janice?'

'I have a referral here from AUSTRAC, about a money laundering operation in Sydney. I understand the intel came from you or a source you have.'

Chris frowned. 'How did you get my name?'

'It wasn't easy I can tell you, but I would like to meet and discuss what you know about the case.'

'This is not really my area. Why don't you ask the NSW police?'

'The detective you—or at least the AUSTRAC referral—said was involved in the case is unavailable at the moment, and his colleagues and superiors don't know anything about an investigation. Look, can we meet.'

'Why is the detective unavailable?'

'He's in hospital, intensive care and is not yet conscious. I did speak to him before the accident, and he gave me the name of his source but...'

'What accident, what hospital?'

'Look if we can meet I'll explain it all, but I am getting nowhere at the moment. Too many barriers and I have no evidence to make a request for surveillance.'

Chris paused for a moment, his thumb drumming against the edge of the desk. 'Okay. Where?'

'Are you in Sydney anytime soon?'

'No... Ah, maybe. Give me your number and I'll get back to you.' Perhaps this was the stay of execution he was desperately seeking before he had to return to his desk downstairs. He would take it to the chief and ask.

He said, 'By the way, do you know anything more than what I said in my referral.'

She drew a breath before saying, 'I spoke to my Chinese counterpart in the Chinese Ministry of Public. We have a Joint Agency Agreement with them. Anyway, he said the Triad leader here, Michael Leung, has prior form in Hong Kong. He promised cooperation, but I haven't been able to contact him again. I also know that Detective McMahon gave us two false leads for his sources. Oh, and there is a friend of his, Barrister Cassandra Lewis. I hoped she might be able to give us some information. McMahon had just left Ms. Lewis's apartment when he was involved in a hit and run incident. He may have told her something before he was run over.'

'What did Cassie say?'

'You know Ms. Lewis?'

Chris nodded and then realised he was on the phone, and his hand was hurting with the force he had used to grip the receiver. He relaxed. 'Yes. I met her through Detective McMahon. I went to school with Alistair and bumped into him when I was in Sydney. He introduced us.'

'So, he told you he had suspicions about Mike Leung.'

'No. Look, give me your number and I will call you back.'

Chris wrote down the number and the officer's name and then folded his arms on his desk to cushion his forehead. Jesus. Was nothing simple? Janice Burton should ask around her own agency about the source of the information. Although Mèng probably only knew as much as his own money laundering activities allowed. Had he known about Alistair's involvement? Maybe he hadn't told Chris everything, but then money laundering wasn't exactly front of mind when Chris had questioned him. Perhaps that was an omission for which he would pay.

He would just have to go back and speak to Mèng again, and that might take a bit of string pulling, but did he want to get involved? Not with Cassie and Alistair in the mix. Or was it just Cassie? Maybe his report wasn't yet finished.

He closed his laptop, got up and walked along the corridor to Anna Thompson's desk. 'Anna, can I have a word with the chief?'

She smiled and picked up her phone. A minute later she said, 'Go on in Chris.'

28. Interference

Chris was back at Bancroft House. It didn't matter what or who he was attempting to track down, all missions seemed to boomerang back to this place. After meeting with Officer Janice Burton and with a bit of leverage from the chief, Chris had managed to interview Mèng again.

The AFP had put him in a private house. Some safe house, but the AFP officers looking after him had shrugged off Chris's concerns. They were short of places. Their usual rooms at the top of their building were all full, and he had a 24/7 watch assigned. Chris could see multiple security issues, but the saving grace so far seemed that the Chinese Embassy hadn't a clue about his disappearance, or if they had they weren't making a fuss. Maybe they were glad to be shot of him.

Mèng was pathetically grateful to see him, and Chris had listened to his complaints, promising he would pass them on to a higher authority although privately he thought Mèng had little to complain about. He was safe, living in relative comfort, fed decent food, and interrogated not tortured. He should be so lucky. He could be back in China in gaol awaiting prosecution for corruption. Really the bloke had nothing to grumble about.

Still, Chris feigned sympathy, if for no other reason than to let him vent so he could clear his mind to recall what he knew about the money laundering venture in Sydney. By the time he'd finished, Mèng had given him little more than he already knew.

The only detail that differed between the accounts was that Mèng had seen Alistair and Leung at Bancroft House and skipped to the wrong conclusions. He hadn't even seen the two men together—just saw Alistair at the door of the cocktail bar and thought he had nodded in Leung's direction. The connections he had made about Alistair knowing something or being involved in some way were pure speculation.

Chris knew he should have found this out before now. He had sent the information to AUSTRAC without delving into how Mèng had come by the information. He had also included his own assumptions that Alistair might be investigating the case, without checking for evidence. Chris hadn't seen it as his role. A side issue. In other words, shoddy work. It was his own fault.

When Mèng had told him about Alistair and Leung, he had been too focused on trying to find a lead into who was leaking secret intelligence to the Chinese and had dismissed the stuff about the Triad money laundering operation. It wasn't until Mèng had said they were using the same gang to spy on Huma, that he had paid attention.

Yet, whatever they had done hadn't worked. Huma had told him the leverage they once had over her, through her Uyghur relatives, had most likely died with those same relatives. Besides, the Chinese bid for the bauxite mine had failed, so it was no longer an issue.

He was at a dead-end. Meng seemed to know nothing more than he had already told Chris and there was no way to know what Alister knew until he came out of the coma. Then Chris recalled the cameras. Perhaps any recordings would shed light on whether Alistair and Leung were connected.

He hacked into Susan Ainsworth's secret camera network again, but he could not find any recordings. Ainsworth would have to give up the information of her own accord. With that in mind he had gone to the chief, suggesting he go back to Sydney to pay her a visit.

Janice insisted she accompany him. She claimed her police powers might be required in case of some procedural issue such as an arrest, if one was warranted. Besides, she maintained, this was her case.

If that was how she wanted to play this, she could go without him, or she would blow his cover.

Devin Royce scuppered Chris's objections saying his cover was no longer required and Chris needed to operate in a more collegiate manner.

Not his style but what choice did he have?

So, now he was here with Janice whether he wanted to be or not. Janice approached the reception. Chris hung back wondering how he was going to tell Susan Ainsworth he wasn't a wealthy armaments contractor. All he wanted was to get a posting overseas, somewhere where work remained in the shadows, deep, deep, shadows. The endless paperwork and delays, while he waded through interagency protocols and turf demarcation lines was doing his head in.

Janice flashed her credentials and was shown into the manager's office behind the counter. He followed and the receptionist asked them to wait. It was a different receptionist from the one he'd met previously and for that he was relieved.

Chris gazed around the room looking for the camera he was certain was centred on him right this moment. He spotted a tiny dark area set back in the centre of a floral design in the pressed metal ceiling panels. That would be it. He walked over to gaze out the window.

29. Another Problem

Ten kilometres west of Bancroft House, Cassie sat on a chair next to Alistair's hospital bed. Wires and tubes snaked toward a machine that bleeped away to itself, monitoring the unconscious man's vitals.

This was her first visit since the night of the accident. She had waited, hoping the family would have left his bedside by now. The last thing she wanted was to bump into Alistair's wife. Not that there was anything for her to be ashamed of. It was Alistair's behaviour that was questionable, but she didn't want to add to the woman's pain.

On her arrival, the duty nurse suggested she talk to Alistair even though he remained in an induced coma. She said, he might be able to hear. Cassie doubted it. He had never listened when he was awake. Why would he start now? But she said nothing to shock the nurse.

What he had told her before the accident weighed heavily, and she had come in the hope he might have woken up by now. She needed his clearance. The AFP had asked to speak with her, but what the hell was she going to tell them?

She glanced around to make sure she was alone and despite her misgivings she spoke or rather hissed at him. 'What am I supposed to say to them Alistair? I wish you hadn't told me, you bastard. It's just like you to put me in this predicament. Why can't you wake up and tell them yourself. I'm going to have to say something, if for no other reason than so they can catch the people who did this to you.'

She put her head in her hands. She would have to tell the AFP what he'd said, but it sounded mad even to her ears. After all Alistair had thought it was the Feds following him. Yet he had also said he had told the AFP officer everything he knew, including how he had found out about the Triad money laundering operations through an informant. So why had he wanted her to keep it secret when they already knew? Because he had lied to her again. She should have known. But then she hadn't had much time to think clearly since the whole thing had happened.

It was pointless sitting here. She stood up to go as a woman accompanied by a man arrived. Cassie lowered her eyes and walked out of the room. Thank

God, the woman was not Alistair's wife. This woman was a blonde Caucasian with blue eyes that showed the puffy redness that excessive crying brought on. She barely noticed Cassie, but the man blocked her exit.

'Who are you?' He asked.

'A friend. His lawyer actually,' she lied and then supposed she was committed now. 'And you, who are you?'

'I'm family. Why does he need a lawyer?'

The bloke's tone was aggressive, and Cassie's chin went up. 'I am afraid that is a question for Detective McMahon. Now please excuse me.' She pushed past, but behind him was another man. He stood in the door frame but stepped aside as she approached. Cassie didn't look at him but felt his eyes drilling into her.

Once in the corridor she quickened her step, and as she exited the hospital, she raised her face to the weak winter sunshine, glad to be out of there. Her phone rang and she fished it out of her handbag. 'Mum?' She listened for a moment, before saying. 'Don't say anything. Not a word. Tell them to wait until your lawyer gets there. I am on my way.'

***

Chris glanced at his watch and then at Janice. She was scrolling through screens on her phone, unperturbed as the minutes ticked by without Mrs Ainsworth appearing. Chris glanced at the camera before he said, 'I might get some air while we wait.'

Janice looked up. 'She'll be here in a minute.'

Chris shook his head. 'I doubt it.'

Janice frowned.' Why?'

Chris moved his head sideways indicating she should follow him, but Janice didn't get the message.

'Do you know something?'

Chris gave up and opened the office door to walk outside.

Janice leaped up. 'Wait.'

Chris carried on walking until he was outside of the building on the concrete apron that led to the front stairs. He turned around to wait for her to catch up.

'What the hell do you think you are doing?' She stomped down the stairs towards him.

When she stood in front of him he said, 'There is a camera monitoring us, which is why I signalled for you to follow me outside.'

'Oh, I didn't realise...'

'Doesn't matter. I don't think Mrs Ainsworth is coming.'

'Why?'

'Her daughter is a barrister...'

'I know. I have sent her a request for a meeting with regard to what she knows about Detective McMahon's accident.'

'When?'

'The other day.'

'I mean, when is your meeting?'

'Tomorrow. What's this got to do with Mrs Ainsworth coming to speak with us?'

'I reckon she is waiting for Cassie to get here. She'll want a lawyer present. We are wasting our time.'

What he didn't say was that if he'd come by himself, he'd have the answer already, but this heavy-handed approach had turned the whole thing into a lawyer's picnic. Susan Ainsworth would stand behind her right to silence, and her daughter would make sure it held.

Janice had no evidence of illegal hidden cameras to persuade any judge to sign a search warrant. Cameras in public areas were not illegal, and Susan would use the intervening time to get rid of any evidence of hidden cameras in private rooms. Now they would never get hold of the film he needed. Unless...

A white EV glided up the driveway and pulled up in a parking spot near to where Chris and Janice stood.

It was Cassie.

Chris turned to Janice. 'Let me do the talking.'

'Why?'

'I know her.'

'I told you this is my case.'

'Yes but a friendly approach might do better than an official one.'

177

'Are you sure it's not because you are a man and can do things better than everyone else?'

Chris frowned. Was that how he came across?

Cassie strode towards them her face flushed, her dark curls springing loose from their confines like errant children and she the avenging mother. 'What are you doing here Chris?'

'Hello Cassie. How are you. I'm sorry I haven't been in touch before now. I heard about Alistair. It's awful. How is he?'

She grimaced. 'I understand you are harassing my mother.' She turned on Janice. 'Who are you?'

'Ms Lewis. I am Officer Burton. We spoke on the phone.'

Chris watched the flash of concern in Cassie's eyes and knew she knew something. He stepped closer. 'Can we have a word in private. We have a request to make of your mum. Maybe you can help.'

Janice scowled but he ignored her, holding out his hand as if to usher Cassie into the building before him.

When they were in the manager's office, Chris glanced at the camera lens and said, 'Officer Burton is here to speak to your mother about any camera footage she has stored for the public bar area, around about the time of the FIRB dinner with the Treasurer. It would be immensely helpful for a case she is working on. I understand Alistair was also involved in the case at the time. Do you think your mother might be able to supply her with that film. If it's too much trouble to run through it all I would be happy to do the slog work on her behalf.

Cassie was staring at him, a strange look on her face. 'Two things. How do you know my mother might have film footage of anything, and who the hell are you? Are you with the AFP?'

Chris laughed. 'Do I look like a police officer? I am just trying to help, and I can see there is a camera covering the reception. Most hotels have cameras covering public places. Nothing wrong with that. I just thought it likely.'

Cassie pursed her lips. 'Okay I will ask. Wait here.' She walked out the room.

Janice opened her mouth but before she could say anything Chris suggested it was such a beautiful day. Maybe they should wait outside.

Janice shut her mouth and followed him out.

When they got outside Janice said, 'You didn't tell me you were so pally with the woman.'

'Pally. I haven't heard that word in a while.'

A dark SUV pulled up in a car park at the far edge of the parking spaces. Chris noticed no one got out the vehicle, but then Cassie came back before he could mention it.

'My mother says she doesn't have what you want. Apparently the cameras are there more for show than anything else. She doesn't record anything.'

'Do they work?' Janice asked.

'Yes I think so. She said she initially had them installed so she could make sure everything was working well, but she seldom uses them now.'

Janice looked unconvinced. 'I would still like to speak with your mother.'

'I don't think that will be necessary. She is a busy woman, and your visit is upsetting her.'

'Why?' Janice said, 'If she has nothing to hide she has nothing to worry about.'

Chris groaned inwardly as he saw the glint light up Cassie's eyes.

'Officer, I would choose your words with more care. That statement sounds as if you are accusing my mother of something, which may turn out to be defamatory.'

Janice glanced from Cassie to him and back again as if Chris might be in collusion with Cassie, but she was dealing with a barrister who was protecting her mum, for crying out loud.

He intervened. 'Look, no one is accusing anyone. Tell your mum, we are grateful for her time. I know she is concerned about the reputation of the hotel, and we are probably making the place look untidy.' His gaze lingered on Janice's uniform. 'We'll get out of your hair. Really nice to see you again Cassie and give Alistair my best when you next speak to him.'

'Why don't you go and see him yourself?' Cassie said.

'I understood he was in an induced coma.'

'He is, but the nurse said he can hear you.' Cassie bit her lip. 'Are you staying here?'

He shook his head. 'Not this time.'

'Where are you staying then?'

He glanced at Janice. 'A place in the city.'

'I'll take you to see him.' Pink suffused Cassie's cheeks and she looked down.

This was not a conversation to have with Janice watching on and Chris said, 'I'll wait until he's conscious.' He turned away and walked towards the car before Cassie could say anything more, but not before he had witnessed the hurt in her eyes.

As the AFP vehicle reversed onto the apron, Cassie felt the pressure building behind dry eyes. Arrogant arsehole, but the whole thing was just weird. Since when did an armaments consultant run around helping the AFP? Nothing in his behaviour gelled. There was something odd going on and it was linked to Alistair's accident, she was certain.

A dark blue SUV reversed from its parking and momentarily blocked her view of the retreating AFP vehicle. She swung on her heel to go back inside. Her mum had some questions to answer.

When Cassie walked into Susan's sitting room, her mum was talking to Mason, but she stopped mid-sentence.

'Oh, Cassie dear. Thank you for coming so quickly and chasing them away. Why do the police think they must stand at the front door of my hotel as if they own the place, and in those dreadful uniforms. It's an embarrassment. I am going to make a complaint to the Chief Justice.'

'Mum they were AFP, federal police, or at least she was. I have no idea who he is. The Chief Justice is state not federal so he can't do anything. Besides they were not doing anything wrong. Their request was quite reasonable and when you said there were no recordings they accepted it and went away. It was true that you don't record, wasn't it? I must admit, I didn't even notice you had cameras around the place but then I suppose I never looked. What's the point of them?'

Susan said, 'What do you mean you have no idea who he is? He's that man you had dinner with here. That friend of Alistair's... I think he's dangerous. How is Alistair, by the way?'

Cassie sighed and pulled the elastic band from her hair, smoothing the curls with her hands before replacing the tie, errant strands once more under control. 'He's still unconscious. They are waiting for the swelling in his brain to reduce before they bring him out. What do you mean he's dangerous?'

'What dear?' Her mother had become vague again.

'You said Chris was dangerous.'

'Did I?'

'You know you did.'

'It's just intuition.'

'How though?'

'Oh, I don't know. Mason,' Susan turned away, 'you will take care of what we discussed immediately, won't you?'

'Mason nodded and excused himself.'

Cassie wasn't going to let her mother off the hook. 'Mum what do you know about Chris Davis?'

'I don't think you can trust him, dear.'

'You said you liked him.'

'Well, he is charming when he wants to be, but there always seems to be something threatening about him, don't you think?'

'That makes no sense. How?'

'Oh, I don't know, but he's always turning up unexpectedly.'

Cassie paused. That was true enough.

'Cup of tea dear.'

'No Mum. I have to go back to chambers.'

'Not in court today, then.'

'No.' Cassie sighed. 'Thank goodness. I feel exhausted. I think I need a holiday.'

'You should take one. Come and stay here. You can be a guest on holiday. Another month or so and the weather will be warming up. If it's fine you will be able to paddle in the sea, take out the skiff, lie on the beach. You loved that when you were a child. And I won't bother you, I promise.'

'You don't know how appealing that sounds.' Cassie kissed her mother. 'Take care. I'll come and see you on Sunday, okay.'

31. Poking Bears

Janice drove with concentrated fury and Chris felt his foot pressing against the floor on the passenger side of the car as she narrowly missed the car they had just overtaken.

'Are you sure you wouldn't like me to drive,' he said as the tyres squealed around a corner?

'Why? Because you are a man?'

'Ah no. Because you seem angry.'

'I am fucking angry. Has anyone ever mentioned what an arrogant arsehole you are?'

Chris pressed his mouth together. 'A few times, yes.'

Janice made a noise that sounded like a grunt. 'When were you going to tell me you are sweet on that woman? What the hell was that about, back there. You made me look a fool and your fucking girlfriend threatening me with legal action.'

Chris glanced in the wing mirror. 'Look, can we discuss this later...'

'No, we fucking can't. You just wasted my time, and we got nothing with your stupid games... You let them both off the hook.'

'Neither of them was on any hooks as far as I could see and there was nothing to get. She doesn't use the cameras to record. At least we know that now.' His eyes remained focussed on the wing mirror.

'You are just going to take their word for it are you? Criminals telling the truth. Ha!'

'Assuming any of them are criminals. And yes, I think they are telling the truth.'

Janice made that same grunting sound.

Chris didn't explain that the information they had learned through the visit accorded with his inability to find any recording devices when he had hacked into Mrs. Ainsworth's camera system. Somehow he didn't think Janice would be happy, especially as he didn't have authorisation for the surveillance. But then that required the minister's sign-off, and the ministerial offices weren't safe. Besides, his get-in-and-take-a-peek-around method sure as hell got things done quicker than Janice's crash-and-tackle approach.

Janice turned into the road leading to the office and Chris said, 'I think we are being followed.

'What?'

'Check out the car three places behind us. The dark blue SUV.'

'What of it.'

'Didn't you see it pull into the hotel behind Cassie earlier, and now it's following us.'

'Maybe a hotel guest on their way into town. Don't try and change the subject.'

'Seriously. I'm sorry if my tactics upset you but I think this is important. Can you check the plate.'

'Read it to me.'

'Too far back. Can you slow down...? Damn. It turned off. Can you follow.?

'Nowhere to turn here.'

'Okay, never mind.'

'Back to what I was saying... This is my case, in the event you may have forgotten, and you will need to follow my lead... We can't go off again at tangents, following hunches that go nowhere. Okay.'

Chris sighed. 'Sure. How ever you want to play this.'

'Right. Our first job will be to establish what Detective McMahon knows about the Triad operation, otherwise we have got nothing. AUSTRAC hasn't found anything out of the ordinary in the casino operations although they are looking into some high roller games at the moment.'

'What about drugs?'

'Drugs. What the fuck Chris, haven't you listened to anything?'

'I mean if we can't get into their operations via the casino maybe we can through their drug operations.'

'What drug operations?'

'I told you about the American money laundering syndicate and how financing the supply of Fentanyl ingredients from China to South American cartels was a part of it.'

'Yeah but that was in America. We don't have the same Fentanyl problems here, nor do we have South American cartels to worry about, or none of significance. Our people are on the ball when it comes to knowing the drug trade here, and it is mostly middle eastern stuff.'

'You don't think it's all linked, the whole global criminal enterprise. I mean Triads, south America cartels, middle eastern gangs or European mafia will trade if there is money in it... You don't think they are doing the same, or similar, here. I'm not a copper but it just makes sense. Global supply lines need...'

'You are an intelligence analyst so leave the policing to those who have a clue.'

Chris raised his eyebrows but leaned back in his seat and looked out the window. Perhaps she was right. What did he know about policing except he always managed to rub them up the wrong way.

***

Later that day, Chris stood in the hallway outside Cassie's apartment hoping she was home. The lights were on. He had seen that from the street below, while he was trying to avoid being seen by anyone watching the place. That black van down the street with the dark blue SUV behind it; just for example. But there had been no sound since he'd rung her buzzer. He rang again and this time her voice came to him through the closed door.

'What do you want?'

He looked at the small glass centre of the peephole. 'Can we talk?'

'No, go away.'

'Please Cassie.'

The sound of a click and he pushed the door. It yielded.

She stood with her arms folded, one leg in front of the other as if ready to chuck him out.

'This better be good.'

He nodded and squeezed past her into the flat. 'Do you know anyone with a dark blue SUV?'

'No.' A scowl scrunched her face. It cleared. 'I saw one follow you out of the hotel grounds today.'

'You saw that did you?'

'I did. So what.' She left the door open with her hand pointing outside into the corridor, indicating he should leave.

'I think it's downstairs right now.'

Her face crumpled. 'What do you mean.' She left the door and took a step towards him.

'Well, it's why I asked. I am not sure if they, whoever they are, is following you, me or maybe both of us. Neither do I know why and that's unsettling.'

'Oh my God.' She put her hands over her eyes.

He took a step closer. 'What's wrong?'

She lowered her hands and stared at him. 'What's wrong? You are an idiot, you know that. A complete and utter fuck wit.'

'Jesus.' He took a step back.

'Show me.' She walked towards the balcony.

He grabbed her arm. 'Cassie wait. Let's think about this.'

'There is nothing to think about.' She wrenched away from him and opened the door to the balcony. 'There is either a blue car out there or there isn't, and you are a liar... I can't see it.' She stepped back inside.

'Trust me.' Resignation crept into his voice. 'It's out there, but maybe a bit of subtlety is needed. They may not know which flat is yours and showing yourself will just help them. Maybe you should shut your front door.'

She swung on him. 'Trust you. Why should I trust you? One minute you are here making me think... Next you are gone, and I don't see you again until you turn up with the Feds, interrogating my mum.'

He smiled. 'Hardly an interrogation but you are right. I'm sorry.'

'Who are you Chris? You are not a contractor to Lockheed Martin are you?'

Chris shook his head. 'No.'

'So, are you going to tell me?'

He shook his head again. 'I don't want to lie to you again Cassie, but I really can't be specific. I work in Canberra, just a public servant. That's all.'

'Then you are with the AFP.'

He shook his head again, before he paused and nodded. 'I guess I am working with them.'

'You're lying again.'

'No. I'm really not.'

A noise behind him and Cassie's eyes widened.

Chris swung around. Four men, all with pistols in their hands. Fuck.

A man in a three-piece suit, bald and jaundiced, an almost bloodless looking creature, bared tobacco-coloured teeth. 'Answer the lady, Mr Davis.'

Cassie shouted. 'Who the hell are you?'

And how do you know my name? Chris thought but said nothing.

The man raised his gloved hand with its pistol pointing at her.

Chris noted the pistol was a Ruger Max-9. He glanced down at the bloke's feet. Neat, maybe size 7. Yet he was as tall as Chris whose shoe size was 12. The build was familiar too. So, this was the dude riffling around in his flat. Chinese State Security perhaps?

Cassie took a step back, her face blanching at the sight of the gun.

The man waved his hand. 'My name is not important, and this man is not a police officer but a spy. You didn't know that Ms Lewis?'

Cassie shook her head. Her face had drained to an unhealthy pallor and Chris put his arm around her shoulders.

She shrugged him away and stepped to the side.

The man smiled, a terrifying grimace in a face of wrinkled parchment. 'You are a friend of Alistair McMahon's. His barrister.'

Cassie nodded.

'Perhaps you can tell me why Detective McMahon came to visit you before his accident.'

Cassie seemed to recover some of her colour. 'It was you who ran him over.'

The man pulled in his chin. 'Please Ms Lewis... We are not barbarians.'

'Well, who did then? He said someone was following him and then he was run over. Now you are following me and... And you have guns. And you are pointing them at me. If that is not a barbarous act, I don't know what is.'

The man muttered again, 'Not barbarians.' He scowled and lowered his gun.

Chris hid a smile. Cassie. Brave as they come but a bit reckless. Chris sized up the situation. Four guns were hard to beat, and Cassie might get shot in the process, besides there was something odd about the man. Like he was playing a role he couldn't quite get right. This was not State Security. Maybe the Triad group.

Chris wanted to see this through, and find out where it was going, hopefully without violence at least none involving Cassie. He would try to engage the man. You never knew when you might learn something from an adversary's grandstanding.

He stepped closer. 'You are Michael Leung, are you not?'

'Very good Mr Davis but you are misinformed.'

The scent of sandalwood. The man's cologne was expensive.

Chris asked, 'What is it you want?'

'I would like to know who your source was for the AUSTRAC referral.'

How the hell did he know about the referral to AUSTRAC. Chris said, 'I think you must be mistaken mate.'

Cassie said, 'He's a Federal Police Officer and you are all in serious trouble.'

'No Ms. Lewis. As I already mentioned, Mr Davis is a spy. The lowest form of life, would you not agree.'

Cassie took a step away from Chris, staring at him as though he were an alien life form. He felt his throat constrict.

'How do you know?' She moved further away.

The man stared, his pale eyes directed towards Cassie, whose pupils were wide with fear.

He placed his pistol behind his back, held out his hands palm up, and took a couple of steps towards her. 'I do not wish to hurt you Ms Lewis. I came to invite you to a small drinks party, but you must believe me, I didn't expect to find this man here, which is why we require weapons. They are not for you, but for him. He is dangerous.' He nodded his head at Chris. 'Although it is fortuitous that he is here for we did wish to ask him some questions about the spies he runs, traitors to both their country and their friends.'

Chris stared at the man. What the hell did he mean? Surely, they didn't know about Mèng...

The man chuckled and took another step toward Cassie. 'Like Detective McMahon, one man's spy is another man's traitor. Is that not so Mr Davis?'

Chris realised what the man was doing with his incremental movements. 'Cassie don't...' But he was too late.

The man took another step closer and grabbed Cassie's hand, whipping her around to stand in front of him, his gun reemerging to thrust into her side.

'Perhaps Ms Lewis can tell us a bit more about these sources or traitors and what they have divulged to her.'

'She doesn't know anything. If you want information about sources, I'm your man. Leave Ms Lewis alone.'

The man jerked his head, and the three men surrounded Chris. 'While my boss had asked me to invite Ms Lewis to meet him, I am sure he will be pleased to entertain you both.' He paused. 'Of course, if you try anything heroic Mr. Davis, she will die.'

32. Ministerial Circles.

The meeting to inform the Prime Minister and Attorney General was held in a secure room in Ben Chifley Building. The subject was Devin Royce's minister, Mariann Laidley, and her domestic servant or cook, Huang Jia-Qi. It was Devin's agency that had uncovered the intelligence, or specifically one man, Chris Davis. But this wasn't Devin's sting. He sat back and let the others do the talking. At the moment the man doing the speaking was the Director General of ASIO.

This briefing session was providing the Prime Minister with the information gleaned from an operation using ASIS, ASIO and AFP officers working in collaboration. They had sought and received approval to conduct the operation from the Attorney-General. Two days ago, the AFP had picked up the suspect Huang Jia-Qi carrying incriminating evidence, which had been planted by ASIO officers. Once in custody, Huang had admitted working for a foreign power, namely Chinese intelligence.

It was now up to the Prime Minister to decide where they went from there. The people around the table fell silent as she thought through the issues they had presented. 'Where did ASIS get this evidence?' She asked.

Devin sat forward. 'From a defector Prime Minister. He is now in ASIO's care.'

The Prime Minister raised an eyebrow. 'Strange choice of words. But never mind that. Is Minister Laidley implicated?' She stared at the ASIO director general.

He shook his head. 'It seems not Prime Minister. Huang Jia-Qi, the man we have in custody says not.'

'What about the defector?'

'He says he doesn't know.'

'What? He knew about this bloke Huang Jia-Qi but not about the minister. Doesn't that strike you as odd. What's his name, this defector?'

'Captain Yichen Mèng.'

'Good grief. Not...' The Secretary of the Department of Foreign Affairs and Trade, sitting opposite, sucked in a breath, and glared at Devin. 'We'll have to send him back.'

Devin intervened. 'We can't do that. No one will ever trust us again.'

The Secretary said. 'This is a diplomatic nightmare. Why wasn't I informed earlier?'

The Prime Minister asked. 'Do they know we have him?'

Devin said, 'There have been no representations. So far, we believe not. He was ordered home, and he didn't want to go. My information is they are still looking for him.'

'It must remain so or there will be repercussions.' She paused before saying, 'On one hand, we have to stand up to them. Show them we are not afraid to confront them. On the other, if the media get hold of this, it would be extremely embarrassing for my government.' She lapsed back into silence. After a few minutes she said, 'What chance Marianne or Brian Laidley are involved?'

Heads shook and Devin's colleague spoke up. 'We have no evidence as yet, but we are still looking.'

The PM said, 'They are personal friends. This is terrible.' She pursed her lips and looked at Devin. 'Doesn't Marianna's son-in-law work for you?'

Devin said, 'Yes, Prime Minister. His section covers the Islamic terror networks, and potentially associated people smuggling operations into Australia.'

'Nothing to do with China. Does he know about this?'

Devin shook his head. 'We have no reason to suspect Dr Elgar knew any of this. Regardless, we have kept him in the dark about these events to date.'

'Still, it's embarrassing for you.'

Devin didn't feel the slightest embarrassment, but he could see the PM needed company, so he nodded.

The PM frowned. 'The man will have to go of course.'

Devin ran his hand over his mouth. Go? Go where, and why for pity's sake, but all he said was, 'Do you mean transferred, Prime Minister.'

'Whatever you think necessary.'

Devin hadn't thought carrying out retaliatory measures on any of his staff was necessary, but he said nothing. He understood the PM had a difficult task. It was easier to go for low hanging fruit than make the big decisions.

The PM placed her hands on the desk and pushed herself up. 'Thank you, Gentlemen, Ladies. Attorney-General, a word in private please. I will speak to the minister involved. I believe we can keep a lid on this—a quick resignation for health or family obligations—or the like. It will require a by-election which is unfortunate. We are only one year into this term of government. It will not look good, although not as bad as if this information were to find its way into the public domain. She glared at the people around the table. 'I will hold you all responsible for ensuring it doesn't.'

After the PM had left with the Attorney-General, Devin looked at his colleagues and asked aloud. 'Anyone know the legal or constitutional ramifications?'

The director general shrugged. 'Ours is not to reason why... We work for the government of the day.'

'The AFP commissioner said, 'Pretty sure we can find something that will cover this case under the National Security Information Act.'

Devin frowned. 'Those are two different takes on our role here, but neither fit my view. My understanding is that our job is to provide frank and fearless advice rather than blindly following orders. A subtle distinction, I know, but...'

The departmental Secretary, Devin's boss, interrupted, 'My concern is Chinese retaliation. They already feel under siege. Now they will claim persecution. We have two of their men for goodness' sake. This is not going to end well.'

They all looked at the Secretary.

The Commissioner put his elbows on the table. 'Which is precisely why the PM wants it hushed up. The whole thing could lead to a shit storm of a magnitude that renders Devin's linguistic subtly, purely philosophical. What we need here is a bit of pragmatism.'

Devin sighed. This was spoiling to become another political brouhaha, but all he said was, 'I don't agree. I think we need to play a straight bat. Don't forget the lessons from the Timor debacle.'

A WILDERNESS OF MIRRORS

***

By the time Devin got home that evening, his head was aching and all he wanted was a quiet whisky and bed, but he had forgotten what tonight was. When he opened the front door he was confronted by his wife in all her finery.

'You are so late darling. Hurry now and change. You won't have time for a shower, just use some bottled stink.

'Do I have to go?'

'Yes. Of course you do. I can't very well turn up on my own and you know how important this is for my Foundation. We are the Charity du jour and your absence will be noticed.'

An hour later Devin and his wife walked into the marble foyer, and he attempted to disappear beneath his wife's glamourous shadow.

Almost immediately he spotted Huma with the Treasurer, the Prime Minister and the Attorney General. Interesting. Huma never did anything for no purpose. The company she was keeping tonight held some significance. The question was what, and did it relate to her phone call the other day?

They had chatted, and flirted for so long, he had forgotten why she had phoned. But of course. It was to congratulate him on his promotion. Add that bit of intel to what Davis had told him about Huma wanting to come back to the service, and he might speculate she was after his job. It hadn't even been advertised yet.

Tilly elbowed him. 'What are you smiling at?'

'Ah, was I smiling. I didn't realise.'

'You were. So, what was it about?'

'You never let me off the hook, do you my dear?'

'I know you too well. Fess up.'

'I was thinking how lovely you look. You cast all the other women into the shade.'

'Rubbish.' She smiled and took his arm. 'Come on, I want you to introduce me to the Editor-in-chief over there.'

'What makes you think I know him?'

'Darling, you know everyone, and if you don't, they want to know you. Talking to the spy-in-chief is the closest thing they will ever come to the ultimate in salacious gossip.'

'I wish you wouldn't say things like that.'

'But it's true isn't it. People are either terrified or fascinated. Either way...'

'Looks like you are too late. He's heading into the Great Hall.'

'You are not going to get away with it that easily.'

Devin took his wife's arm and walked towards the hall, glancing back to see Huma on the Treasurer's arm. The man was a bachelor, so why not? Lucky bloke. But Huma was definitely up to something.

33. Kidnapped

Chris had no idea where they were. Underground somewhere he guessed. From Cassie's apartment they had been taken downstairs in the lift, pushed into a van, and stripped of all possessions such as his phone, before driving for some time to this destination.

The van had opened to let them out into an underground parking garage. For a moment he thought he could smell the sea. Then they had been ushered along a corridor and into this room. A storage room with empty shelves, no windows, a single light bulb hanging beneath an opaque plastic shade, might come in handy, and a heavy-duty door. It wasn't particularly clean either. Litter on the floor. Dust on the inbuilt shelving and what looked like spilled spices of some kind. That gave him an idea.

At least their hands weren't bound, and they were free to move, although it wasn't much use as there was no way out. He had checked. Air vents high in the wall allowed air flow but they were too small to be an option for escape. He needed to think about the best way through this, to get the most from his visit here. Who was their captor and more importantly who did he work for?

Chris assumed the Triad gang and Michael Leung, but he could be a Chinese agent. No, the latter was unlikely. This was a criminal gang. Any intelligence service worth their salt would not have locked them, unbound, in a storage room. Intelligence agencies knew how to create a heightened sense of terror in a captive. Yet, their surroundings did not instil fear, and they had been left unconstrained, which made it too easy to escape. The puzzling thing was that if they weren't affiliated with the Chinese intelligence services, how did they know who Chris was?

He recalled Mèng saying the Chinese used the Triad gang to spy on Huma. So, the CCP and the Triad gang were occasionally in some kind of partnership. Although it seemed more likely that this abduction was related to the Triad's criminal activities, for they were more interested in what Alistair had told Cassie.

Then again, their information was faulty, specifically thinking he was running Alistair as some kind of agent. That was an interesting, if unlikely, proposition too. He wondered how much Cassie knew about Alistair's activities.

She sat on the floor her back to a blank wall between shelving. Her face was pale and pinched with what looked like anxiety.

Chris crouched down next to her. 'Are you okay?'

'No. Idiot. I am not okay. I am angry.'

'Angry.' He repeated the word. It wasn't what he was expecting but it was better than anxiety.

'Yes, fucking angry.'

'Okay. With anyone in particular?'

'Yes. You, Alistair, that arsehole out there, whoever he is. Me for being such an idiot. This is all about you and has nothing whatever to do with me. How did I manage to get caught up in it? First Alistair now you.'

'Tell me how Alistair is involved.' He picked off a bit of rubbish that had stuck to her skirt, a label of some kind. He glanced at the Mandarin characters before he placed it in his pocket.

'No. You tell me what's going on. Are you really a spy?'

Chris pressed his mouth together. 'Look, I am sorry I lied and told you I was a contractor. I am really just a Treasury analyst, advising on foreign investment in the country. It was my role to advise the FIRB chair on the players who wanted to invest in the bauxite mine.'

'Same thing. A spy.'

He smiled. 'I don't think Treasury employs spies. They prefer the term financial analysts. Spies are part of a network providing information for intelligence analysis, but they are usually foreign actors or contracted agents, not public servants.'

'Oh my God, now you are mansplaining! You'll understand why I don't believe you?'

'Sorry, didn't mean to patronise.' He stood up. 'But it doesn't matter if you believe me or not. A more pressing issue to work out, is how we get out of here, or indeed if we want to get out of here.'

'Now I know you are mad. Of course we want to get out of here. Do you even know where we are or who those people are? You said a name.'

'Yes, but I was wrong.'

She looked at him sideways. 'Can you stop prevaricating and just tell me straight. What's going on?'

He ran his hand through his hair. 'I'm not sure. If you can tell me what you know, maybe something Alistair told you, perhaps I can piece it together.'

'You first.'

'Okay. I think these people are part of a money laundering racket that Alistair may have been either investigating or involved with. They came after you because, as his lawyer, they think Alistair has told you something. They think he is either a plant or a traitor. They didn't expect to find me there. Since I was at your place, they now think Alistair was a plant placed there by some agency like the Serious Financial Crime Taskforce.'

'Who are they?'

'Tax Office, Feds, Criminal Intelligence Commission.'

'Is that who you work for?'

'Sort of...' He looked into her worried eyes. 'No, not really. Look, I can't tell you the details, okay. You will just have to trust me.'

She laughed, a bitter sound filled with derision then sobered and said, 'But they know who you are.'

He shrugged.

'Chris, how do they know?'

'I have been asking myself the same question?'

'Maybe Alistair.'

'Maybe.' But Chris didn't think so. For a start Alistair didn't know what Chris did. So, none of it made sense, but all he said was, 'now your turn.'

'Okay. I will tell you, although Alistair didn't want me to tell anyone. I think he was afraid and didn't know where to turn so he came to me. He asked me to represent him, but I refused although I told your friend, that AFP woman, that I did represent him. So, I guess I do now. But he was your friend, and I am sure he would tell you himself.'

Hardly a friend but Chris remained silent.

Her hand flew to her mouth. 'Oh my God. I have an appointment with her tomorrow.'

'If you are late, I am sure she will understand.' Chris said it dryly, wishing she would get on with it. How much time they had before the man came back for them, he had no idea.

Cassie scowled at him. 'You are all kindness and sympathy aren't you?'

He sighed. 'Please Cassie, just tell me. I don't know how much time we have.'

'Okay.' She laced her fingers. 'But I warn you it doesn't make any sense... Alistair came around to my place the night of his accident. He was scared. I could tell that. He said he was working on a case, a money laundering case, and that the AFP had got involved. They wanted to know where he had got the information. Apparently, it had come from some meth-head, and he gave the Feds the wrong lead. He said he was under pressure from another case and had just made a mistake.' She shook her head. 'The weird thing about it was that he thought the AFP were following him, maybe because they thought he had lied... I don't know. Anyway, he left and was hit by a car downstairs from my flat. That's all I really know.'

Chris sat down next to her. 'You are right. It doesn't make sense.'

'Alistair has always been a liar, Chris. You must have realised that by now, although I must admit it took me a while...'

Chris lapsed into silence until Cassie said, 'What are you thinking?'

He glanced at her. 'I'm in a quandary.'

'What the hell does that mean?'

'It means that my preferred course of action is to play this through to find out who these people are, what they know, and what they are up to, but I also realise, I should get you out of here before you get hurt.'

'Well, you will be pleased to note that the debate is moot. No matter how omniscient and powerful you might think you are, there is a locked door between us and freedom.'

He laughed. 'Do you want me to get you out of here, or not?'

'Of course, but as you can see, it's not exactly possible.'

'I think it is. This is how we can do it, but it's dangerous and might not work. We can only do it if you are willing to take the risk.'

'How much of a risk?'

'Cassie, these are not nice people.'

'No kidding, Sherlock.'

'They have guns, which are usually enough to intimidate. If we are not intimidated we might just have the advantage.'

'How much of a risk is it?'

'Honestly?'

'Yes.'

'I think it's a risk between taking a chance at life or going meekly to the slaughter. They can't afford to let us go now.'

'Right, risk it is. What do you want me to do?'

'How good are you at painting?'

***

Across the other side of Sydney, was an apartment overlooking the harbour. Michael Leung had just returned home from a trip to Canberra. He moved back and forth across the glass fronted living room, fingers tingling, knees bouncing. The whole thing was fucked. He turned on Roland. 'This is a disaster.'

The bloodless man bowed, but his lined face remained serene. 'Brother you said you wanted the intelligence officer dead.'

'You fool. That was just a turn of phrase not an order. Besides he's not dead. He's locked in the fucking pantry in the restaurant basement, with a barrister. Do you think it will go unnoticed that these two people are missing? This is Australia. These sorts of things do not happen here. If you want to do away with people you make it look like an accident. You do not shoot them.' He paused and his voice became thoughtful. 'that is, not unless they are other gangsters... Then no one cares, at least not the establishment but if you shoot their own... Fuck.' He put his head between his hands and screamed. Then he turned on his brother. 'If we are caught, we are deported, and you know what that means.'

'You said to bring the woman. The man was with her. I had no choice, but they are unharmed.'

'I said, ask the woman to meet with me. An invitation. I would have given her a drink and had a chat, but instead you go in with guns and kidnap her.'

'I am sorry brother. I did not expect that man to be there, and he gave me a fright.'

'A fright! You moron. And for fuck's sake, stop calling me brother.'

Roland Leung cringed. 'You must not call me bad names. Father said, and you are my brother. He told me it was so, and you have to look after me.'

Michael sighed, turned around and picked up his keys from the entrance hall table where he had placed them just moments ago. His brother was right. Poor Roland was loyal to a fault and carried out each task he was given, usually with meticulous precision, but instructions had to be clear.

Really Michael blamed himself. He hadn't given clear instructions. Although to be fair he had been distracted by the woman from the embassy. The one who called herself Zheng Pingru. What a joke. The woman hardly resembled the beautiful and brave socialite, who had been executed during the Second Sino-Japanese War for her attempt to assassinate the security chief of the puppet government the Japanese had installed in China.

Maybe the whole debacle was Zheng's fault. She had Michael ambushed from all sides, telling him to eradicate a traitor, or she would expose his activities. When he had gone to the address, a house with a walled garden in a leafy suburb near the city, to scope out how Roland might carry out the contract, there were Feds crawling all over the place.

He had told Zheng it was impossible, but she wouldn't have any excuses. She outlined his activities with alarming accuracy, not just the drug imports, assassins for hire and money laundering but she also implied she had evidence he was involved in gun running. That wasn't his gig, although he had helped set up the operation. How the hell had she so much information on him?

On the drive back from Canberra, he had racked his brain but couldn't figure out a way to get past the AFP at the house. Now he had to come back to this: an Australian Intelligence Officer and a Queen's Council locked up in the restaurant pantry. All because Michael wasn't concentrating and had given his brother instructions on the phone. A mistake, given how the instructions were always necessarily cryptic on the phone in case anyone was listening.

Roland wasn't stupid, but he had always harboured grandiose ideas, and if left to his own devices tended to act in the way he'd seen gangsters behave in films. When he was given precise instructions, his ability to carry them out was faultless.

It really wasn't his fault. Roland had been born different. Westerners called it, being on-the-spectrum, but there was also a strong streak of narcissism that ran through him. A personality trait or his father's bullying, Michael didn't know, but it made his brother a dangerous but fragile being, who, since he was a boy, had enjoyed inflicting pain and death on living things.

All Michael's life he had been responsible for his older brother, a burden he loathed until he found a way of turning it into financial success. And Michael was a financial genius. Besides his other enterprises these contract killings had added a layer of honey to his bank accounts. But now the CCP were demanding favours. In return they would turn a blind eye to his other business activities in Australia, but only if the laundering service excluded the Yuan. They clearly didn't yet know about the vast sums Mèng funnelled through Michael's businesses. That would hurt, but maybe he and Sharapova could team up as a replacement for Mèng.

Wasn't that what Alex was doing for the Australians? Perhaps all security agencies were the same. He supposed he would have to talk to Huma about Roland's cock up, but he wasn't driving all the way back to Canberra. He was loathe to put himself in her debt again. She would extract more than she gave although he had little choice.

He opened his phone to call her. Thought better of it and took a burner from his pocket. He would call on Alex for advice. He preferred dealing with him in any case and Alex still owed him. Huma was way too demanding, and Alex had a way of moderating his daughter's reactions although it was only fair that Alex knew Zhang was onto the export business.

Funny how business ran in families, his in crime, which he'd learned as an apprentice to his Anglo/Cantonese father. Huma as apprentice to Alex. It was like families needed the continuity to get it right through the second generation. Second chances so to speak. Perhaps he would get another go at fixing this current round of problems. Another boat accident was a possibility for the pantry pair.

Now he was thinking clearly. He would speak to Alex and arrange a boat... He smiled. That was it, and it had a bit of symmetry. That last boat-themed job had got him out of having to answer any nosy questions, even though he hadn't planned it. Although he was still mystified as to how Kashton had managed to get from the house to his yacht. Roland assured him he had left him dead in a chair inside the house.

The distraction had suited them, and Alistair McMahon hadn't found anything other than what was expected. Kashton had died of a heart attack. It was a brilliant strategy, even if he hadn't thought it up himself. He would use it again, but not on Mèng. Not unless Roland could get near the man, otherwise it might need to be a sniper bullet. Perhaps Alex would help. He was a fine marksman.

Before he left the house, he said. 'Roland, make sure my guests in the pantry are comfortable. Take them food and water. I will decide what to do when I get back.' But he already knew. They would both have to die. The decision now was how to make it look like a boating accident and keep Huma off his case.

Cassie finished painting Chris's neck and cheeks with the spilled grains of turmeric, paprika and coriander seed powder. The place smelled like a curry, and he looked like a corpse in a horror movie. Dark circles around his eyes, and in the creases of his mouth, and nose, fading out to red and yellow. Yellow/red on his neck, forearms and hands, red/brown behind his ears.

Chris blended a bit more paprika and turmeric into her forehead. The ghastly colours should at least make anyone coming through the door hesitate. If they lay still it might fool their captors into a moment of complacency, which was all he needed. Afterall, if he was right about the label he'd picked off Cassie's skirt, these people understood poisons.

He told her where to lie down, arranging her limbs into a foetal position as if hugging her stomach in pain before he lay down at an angle to her, closer to the door. But nobody came near the pantry.

Sometime during the night, Cassie snuggled closer, for warmth only, she said as she laid her head on his arm. He dosed fitfully, his arm supporting Cassie's sleeping head. When he awoke his watch showed it was 6 am and Chris was sure someone would come this morning, if for no other reason than to check on them. He eased his arm out from under her and grimaced at the instant pins and needles. He sat up, waiting for the tingling to subside.

Cassie stretched and said, 'What now?'

'Now we wait,' Chris said. 'Take up your position.'

'What if they don't come?'

'They'll come but remember when the door opens make sure you have your eyes closed, and don't open them for anything, okay. For absolutely nothing, Cassie I mean it. Doesn't matter what happens. Keep your eyes closed and stay relaxed like you are unconscious, until I tell you otherwise.'

'What are you going to do?'

'Depends on what he does.' Chris lay down a metre away from Cassie. 'Quiet now. I think I hear something.'

A minute or so later, the door opened.

Chris relaxed, eyes closed, breathing shallow, hoping Cassie was doing the same. No sounds, but the door stood open. He could feel the draft.

Then an intake of breath. Someone had bought the ruse. Steps, hesitant and soft, approached. One man. Who else was there? No way to find out. Weapons? No way to know.

The steps stopped. He could feel the man's presence—fleeting body warmth—the scent of sandalwood. Their captor. Right-handed. If there was a weapon...

Chris's mind turned the world into a slow-motion play of essentials, while adrenaline raced through his arteries. He opened his eyes, and his legs shot out to scissor the man's legs, forcefully knocking him off balance.

As their captor fell, a pistol shot sounded loud in the confined space. It thudded into the ceiling sending a cascade of plaster down like confetti. Sloppy and dangerous.

The man rose but Chris was already on his feet, hand deflecting the pistol, pushing it to point away from where Cassie lay. Another round buried itself in the wall. He drove a knee strike into the captor's liver—a weak area judging by man's jaundiced skin.

The captor's scream was involuntary. He staggered and fell to his knees, retching.

Chris pulled him into chokehold until he slumped, but he could hear heavy footfalls slapping the floor, coming towards him. With one arm around the captor's neck, he wrenched the pistol from his hand just as a man rounded the corner. He pointed and fired. The man staggered, a red mark in the centre of his forehead.

Their captor spun out of the loosened hold and came at Chris.

Chris's left hand delivered a palm strike to face. He followed with his right hand stilling holding the gun. His knuckles slammed into the captors throat. Clumsy but effective. The captor lay on the floor convulsing for air.

More sounds of running. One man only. Chris fired and a third man went down. Four rounds used. Any more coming?

Silence.

Shout, 'Now. Cassie quick.'

Too sluggish. Haul her up. Take her hand. Pull. Run.

Chris raced along the corridor, dragging Cassie along with him, their captor's pistol in his hand. There was no way of knowing how many rounds he had left. These subcompacts usually had capacity for 12 + 1. The man had fired two. Chris had fired off two more. No knowing how many to begin with, but possibly, if the magazine was full, he had eight bullets left, or nine if one round was in the chamber. Fool if it wasn't. More than enough, he hoped.

They reached the underground garage. Four vehicles and one motorbike, a black Suzuki Hayabusa. Closest to Chris was the van that had brought them here, alongside the dark Blue SUV, then an Audi A4 Sedan and on the other side of the basement what looked like a vehicle covered by a tarp.

At that moment a yellow Porsche Boxster convertible roared down the entrance ramp. The driver saw them and screeched to a stop in the middle of the parking zone. A man leaped out. Their captor? Impossible. Someone of similar build, but not him. He crouched behind the car door, gun in hand.

A round zinged past and buried itself in the wall behind them. Chris pushed Cassie behind a pillar and raised the pistol.

The man was gone, nowhere to be seen. Another round in the wall above his head. Too close. Came from directly across the basement parking, behind the tarp covered vehicle, and near what looked like another exit with stairs ascending.

He touched Cassie's arm and whispered, 'When I shoot, run to that pillar over there. Stay low, head down. Keep behind the cars. Try to get to the exit but wait until I fire to cover you.'

She nodded, eyes glittering in their spice darkened orbs.

Chris turned back, scanning the garage in the dim light. Where was the Porsche driver? He fired a double tap into the tarpaulin and Cassie ran.

Returning fire hit the Blue SUV, and then she was safe behind the next pillar.

A noise behind him, and his captor staggered out of the corridor, holding his throat. With the pistol hampering the throat strike, Chris hadn't done a good enough job of putting him out of action. Now he had to contend with two men.

He fired.

Their captor fell and once again there was one.

A hail of angry bullets sent splinters of plaster and brick flying around him. A sting in his neck. Not a bullet. Blood. How bad? No time to worry. The fire was definitely coming from behind the tarpaulin. Bad angle. He fired, ducked, and raced to the next pillar. Cassie was halfway up the ramp, out of the line of fire.

Bullets thudded into the walls above him. He fired again, and more rounds pockmarked the walls and cars around him. Definitely coming from behind the tarp. He ran, firing at the spot until the magazine was empty, but the tarp was no longer in view and there was no further returned fire.

He paused out of the line of sight.

Then two pfffs, and two more. Sensation along his arm. Fuck. There were two shooters after all. One with a silenced gun. He dropped the empty pistol and raced up the ramp until he found sunshine.

Cassie was on the street to his right about twenty metres away, bent double, her backside pressed against a large, dark crimson vehicle, skewed sideways across the pavement. She retched into the gutter and wiped her mouth with the back of her hand.

Chris glanced back to the parking area. It seemed no one was following. He hurried towards her, noting the four by four was a Cadillac Escalade, and memorised the number.

'We had better move.'

'Your neck is bleeding.'

'It's nothing.' He took her hand in his left hand and hurried along the road before turning a corner heading towards the sea. They crossed the road to the foreshore.

'Rub you face to get rid of some of the spice.' He dropped her hand and tentatively explored the wound on his neck. Lots of blood, maybe a shard of brick or plaster. He left it alone.

They walked on rapidly, trying to put enough distance between them and the gunmen. Whose car was on the pavement at the side entrance to the building? Was it coincidence or related? Did the Caddie's owner have a gun with a silencer?

Chris glanced at his dangling right hand. It dripped blood onto the street. He tried to bend the arm and winced as muscles spasmed.

The man, who had arrived in the Porsche, had shot at Chris with an unsilenced gun, but Chris was sure the shot that had got him was from a silenced gun. It hadn't come from the tarpaulin, which was out of his line of sight when the round hit him. There had to have been a second person, maybe located somewhere near the stairs. There was no other cover.

He glanced around. At least no one had followed them. Not as far as he could tell. He needed to get to a phone. But if he went into a shop with his face like this people would freak out. Not only did he not have a phone, but he also had no money and no ID. The bastards had taken it all.

He wondered if he could go back and retrieve it. At least he could take one of their cars and drive to the AFP building. Get Janice to do her job. Although getting into the federal police building without ID might be difficult especially with the blood and his face and neck looking like he had some horrible disease. They would more likely arrest him.

He stopped. 'Cassie are you okay?'

Tears steaked her cheeks making runnels in the red and yellow spices.

'Of course I'm not, you idiot.'

An elderly couple out for a stroll took a wide berth around them.

Chris stepped closer to Cassie and pulled her into an embrace. 'You were magnificent in there, but you are safe now.'

She pushed him away and wiped her arm across her face. 'Fuck off Chris. Is that supposed to make me feel better? You nearly got me killed and you are hurt. You need a hospital.'

'Not yet. There is a bench over there. I think we should sit down for a bit.' They sat and after a moment he said, 'If you wait here, I'll go back and take a look around.'

The sounds of shooting hadn't alerted anyone. Maybe because it was in the underground parking.

'You can't go back they'll kill you. We have to call the police and an ambulance for you and for those men.'

He shook his head. 'No phone.'

'We can ask someone. Look there...'

He grabbed her arm. 'No Cassie! No police, no ambulance. Not yet. Look, I won't be long. You'll be okay here, and I'll get a car to take you home. I'll try to explain once we are out of here and safe, okay but until then, just stay here. Don't call anyone. You don't know who is listening or who will come after us.'

She was staring at him in horror. 'You are not leaving me here. Not on your nelly buster.'

He hid a smile. 'Okay. I am going back. If you want to come with me, I am pretty sure it'll be safe now.'

'Why? Because you killed them all.' Her voice dripped with sarcasm.

He ignored the jibe. 'Not all of them. I think someone else might have killed the bloke in the yellow Porsche. Either that or he ran out of ammo, but anyone left is unlikely to stick around waiting for the police to arrive.'

She shook her head. 'Doesn't it bother you that you have just killed several men.'

He glanced at her askance. 'They were trying to kill us. Would you rather they had succeeded.'

'Of course not, but this isn't new to you is it?'

He stared at her for a moment, seeing himself through her eyes.

She added, 'Don't get me wrong. I am grateful you got us out of there. But not only did you murder several men, you killed one with your bare hands.'

He battled down the anger that arose at her criticism, wanting to say, actually, I didn't kill him. Turns out, I had to shoot the bastard to get him to lie down, but instead he said, 'I'm sorry you got mixed up in it.' Adrenaline still buzzed through his arteries, and he knew he had to move away from her. 'Look, I'm going back to the building.'

'What about your neck...'

'Later. Come, or wait for me here. It'll take a few minutes to find my things, get a car. I'll sort the police and everything else out, after I drop you home.'

He didn't wait for her reply, but stomped back to the driveway, passing the other entrance to the building, which no longer had the Cadillac blocking it. He looked along the road, a one-way street heading away from the waterfront. The Caddie was turning left a city block away. He'd memorised the number, but the car was most likely stolen. Still, if there was a camera in the area they might be lucky and get an image that showed the driver's face.

He walked more cautiously as he headed down the driveway, searching for their captor's pistol. The one he'd commandeered and then chucked when it was out of rounds. There was no sign of it. Neither was there any sound coming from the parking lot below. He moved on, rounding the corner before scouting around; moving from one vehicle to the next until he came to the tarpaulin covered vehicle.

There was the driver of the Porsche sprawled on the ground. Two bullet holes. One in the side of his head, the other in his neck. Small calibre but accurate enough to kill a man instantly. No weapon to be found. No bullets casing left lying about. He found a wallet in the dead man's jacket. The driver's licence showed he was Michael Leung.

He walked up the stairs to the lobby that serviced the building's side entrance. Glass doors to the street, locked. Bolts thrust into the floor on the inside. Odd. No shells or evidence of another gunman, but he was obviously there for he had placed those neat holes in Michael Leung's neck and head and then had shot at Chris.

He walked down the stairs, crossed the parking area, and found the dead captor, sprawled across the concrete where he had fallen. Chris searched and located his wallet. No drivers licence, but a Medicare card, a credit card and several other membership and loyalty cards, all in the name of Roland Leung. Hence the passing resemblance to Michael, except where one was handsome the other was certainly not. A kind of portrait of Dorian Grey.

Inside, was a similar story. Dead men. No evidence of weapons or bullet casings. He walked back to the parking garage and riffled through the van for his phone and wallet. Nothing. He returned to the stairs. Presumably they led up to some living quarters or an office. He passed the lobby with the glass doors leading out to the pavement and climbed to the next landing.

Double doors standing open. Inside, the room had been ransacked. Recently. On a table, a vase of flowers lay on its side. Water still dripped onto an Aubusson carpet. Maybe the Caddie owner. Turf warfare, or something else.

Chris glanced around the room, strode towards a red lacquered sideboard, and looked through the open drawers and doors. It didn't take long to find his phone and wallet. If the Caddie driver was looking for something it wasn't burglary. There was a cache of $100 notes in one drawer and the paintings on the wall would have fetched a tidy sum, let alone the art objects and furniture.

Whatever else Michael was into, his businesses made money. Chris was sure the AFP would find it was not just money laundering but also drug money. He searched the rest of the place, walking from room to room, offices, locked filing cabinets. The AFP could sort that out.

He moved on to what looked like a communal room with table-tennis table, television, and gaming console. Behind was a kitchen and a stocked pantry. He did a quick search across the shelves, but nothing stood out. To the side, was a bathroom. He walked back to the room he had first entered. It looked like a sort of reception parlour. Another door led off it. He walked through. Another office and another bathroom, and what looked like a walk-in wardrobe. Maybe some clues in there.

He opened the double sliding doors and stopped. In front of him was a shrine with candles burning in glass holders. He stepped inside and blew them out. Couldn't have the joint burning down before the AFP arrived.

A frown flickered across his face. Not just a shrine, an assassin's room with victims' photos on the wall. Five of them in a row with red lines across all. Three of the victims were unfamiliar to Chris, although he knew the other two. So, Kashton and Delahunty were not deaths by natural causes. Two drawing pins without photos continued the line. Scraps of photographic paper still attached. Removed hastily. Red Caddie driver, maybe.

Nothing too unusual about an assassin with a trophy wall. It was the shrine that was weird. Every god known to humanity seemed to be represented. He recognised Thor, Norse god of thunder and lightning, and to his left Höðr who had killed his brother with the poison from a mistletoe arrow. A crucifix hung on the wall. Statues to Buddhist and Shinto gods, along with the Norse gods and Indian deities, stood alongside Greek and Roman gods, but in pride of place were an assortment of Chinese gods.

Chris had always been interested in mythology and had taken an interest in Chinese gods when he'd lived in Beijing. He thought these figurines represented King Yan, god of death; Dian Mu mother of lightening; Yu Shi, god of rain, along with dragon Shenlong, master of storms. What the hell did this assortment of gods mean?

At least he now knew who had killed Kashton and Delahanty. What he didn't yet know was why, other than speculation. This joint would need a forensic psychiatrist to untangle the motivation behind the killer's behaviour, but he suspected the whole thing was down to Roland. He had known there was something wrong with the bloke, but this. This was the product of a completely deranged mind.

He opened a wardrobe. Sandalwood cologne mixed with body odour wafted out from several black outfits, all like the one worn by the intruder who had searched Chris's flat. That was weird too. It seemed the Triads knew about Chris before he had even heard of them from Mèng. Although maybe it wasn't Roland in his flat but someone like him from the Chinese embassy. Same small feet and narrow body, same cologne, same pistol. Seemed unlikely it was anyone other than Roland. Maybe the Triads were following Mèng after all. Or could there be another reason why Roland was in his flat?

His attention shifted to a sideboard on which was spread out what looked like a small chemistry lab. Droppers, scales, beakers, and a gas Bunsen. More bottles and equipment in a cupboard below. Another job for the AFP. A glass cabinet on the wall displayed a selection of Chinese bladed weapons and several firearms. The AFP would have a field day.

He was taking too long. Cassie would be freaking out. He went back downstairs and contemplated taking the Porsche but decided it was too flashy. The Porsche was blocking in the van and the SUV, so they were out of the question. The motorbike would have been nice in traffic, but not with his arm like it was or with Cassie. He climbed into the Audi and pushed the starter button. If the keys were anywhere in the car, it would work. It did. He pulled down the visor, and a key fob fell out.

Then he hit Janice's number, put the phone on hands free, did up his seat belt and reversed out of the parking. Janice answered as he drove up the driveway to the street. He explained where he was and what had happened as he headed off to find Cassie.

Janice listened for a few second before cutting him off with instructions to drive straight to her office and bring Cassie. She would send some officers to secure the building. It was now a crime scene.

He said, 'Not a chance. Cassie will want a shower first. I suggest you meet us at her place.'

He drove around the block to the seafront where he had left Cassie, all the while half listening to Janice's instructions and thinking Cassie would just have to put up with him a bit longer. He pulled into the curb and hung up the phone before Janice could demand anything more. Then he lowered the window to call out to Cassie.

When she got into the car she said, 'I saw him.'

'Who?'

'The man driving the red Cadillac. He drove down that way.' She pointed north.

'Did you get a look at his face?'

She shook her head. 'He wore a hat, and it was pulled down low on his face, but he was middle aged or older I'm sure.'

Chris frowned. 'How do you know?'

Grey hair poking out and a weathered neck. I'm sure he wasn't Chinese.

'How could you tell?'

'I don't know. He just looked European.'

'But you didn't see his face...'

'No, but you can tell, can't you?'

'I don't know. Can you?'

She glared at him and turned to stare out of the window.

Still, it was something. He'd tell Janice to get any camera footage along the road Cassie had indicated. They might be lucky.

Janice was waiting outside Cassie's flat when Chris pulled up in the Audi.

Cassie got out of the car and confronted her. 'Go away and take this man with you. I never want to see either of you again.'

Janice's pushed her lips together before she said, 'You will need to come downtown and give a statement.'

Cassie walked away. 'I am not going anywhere until I have had a shower, but you should probably take him to the hospital before he bleeds to death.'

Janice glanced at Chris and muttered, 'What's wrong with you?'

Chris got out of the car and Janice saw his bloody arm and neck.

'Jesus Christ!'

'It looks worse than it is.'

Janice shrugged. 'Your own fault. If you hadn't gone off chasing skirt in the first place, it would never have occurred.'

Chris snapped back, 'If I hadn't been here, Cassie would have copped it alone. And then what would have happened?'

Cassie spun around on them. 'For goodness sake. You are squabbling like children. Chris needs to go to the hospital.'

***

It wasn't until Chris got back to his hotel later that night and took off his clothes to shower that he remembered the label he had picked off Cassie's skirt when they were locked in the pantry. He had put it into the pocket of his now ruined jacket. He went to find the bag the hospital had put it in before they gave it back to him.

He found it and smoothed out the label. The first character was ◈ or Fū. It had many meanings, maybe attached, or complex or compound. He also thought it sometimes meant good luck or vice but that depended on the tone and other characters. The second character was ◈ making the sound Zi which could have been a surname or an honorific, even a reference to an offspring, or seed. It made sense. Zoe had called the medicine made from the poisonous Aconitum Carmichaelii, fùzǐ, which used these characters to mean daughter root.

Traditional Mandarin was the basis of the standard version of Chinese taught across China, a complex language, requiring tonal nuance and context above everything. His ability to read its characters was rudimentary, there were just so many to remember. If there was more context it might be easier to decipher.

He took a photo of the label and sent it to Zoe's mobile number asking for her advice. She was probably asleep now, but perhaps she would respond in the morning. He could have asked the expert at work, but he reckoned contacting Zoe, who knew about Chris's concerns, might be quicker. Besides the mode of Kashton and Delahanty's assassinations was still just guess-work. Janice might find something more when the AFP searched the building.

After his shower, he gave some attention to the stiches in his neck. It was an unlucky bit of shrapnel that had cause the gash, but it hadn't done too much damage. He couldn't see the stiches in his arm because of the plaster covering them. The bullet had rifled through the flesh but at least it hadn't lodged in his arm, nor broken any bones.

He lay down in the hotel's large, comfortable bed. Last night the concrete floor of the pantry hadn't made sleeping easy, and he was dog-tired. Tomorrow, he would persuade the chief to get the coroner to reassess the toxicology on Kashton and Delahanty. Roland had killed both of them, he was certain, but they would still need evidence for how the killings were carried out.

He was pretty sure he had that evidence but needed unassailable connections. Why had Roland done it, for whom, and how had he administered it? Was it because the Chinese wanted the competition out of the way in the bauxite sale? Although if they had, wouldn't they have killed Sinclair as well? And none of it accounted for Delahanty's death, but then, why else would Leung kill Kashton and Delahanty unless under instruction from the CCP?

He recalled that the Leung brothers had claimed on their entry visas' to be refugees from the Chinese government. So, working for the CCP made no sense although it wouldn't be unknown for the CCP to blackmail the Leung brothers into doing their bidding.

Yet no matter which way he looked at it, if this was Chinese interference in an Australian government decision it was serious, even though they hadn't won the bid. There was clearly a significant piece of the puzzle still missing, and he was clutching at fragments.

Who was represented by the missing photos on the shrine wall, and who owned the red Caddy? He had given the Cadillac's plate number to Janice, although he was not sure if she would tell him what she found. She had been pretty pissed off with him.

Somehow the women in his life all seemed to end up hating him. Cassie had seemed concerned enough about him to insist he visit the hospital. Yet, when he had left she had asked him to stay away. In fact, she had said, she never wanted to lay eyes on him again. Too bad. He really liked her. She was as brave and honest as they came. He closed his eyes and was soon asleep.

The Foreign Minister's retirement, with immediate effect, was all over the news, her photo on the front page of national papers, her name headlining radio and television broadcast. The twitterati speculated at the suddenness of her resignation. Breakfast show hosts flailed about for more spice to add to the story. News analysts offered motivation, and commentators opined she had been given a better offer. Defenders asserted she had a right to privacy, while she spent time with her newly delivered granddaughter, a difficult birth by all accounts.

Then a week later she once more made the headlines with her appointment as ambassador to Ireland. Chris hadn't realised he was still shockable, but as he read the news broadcast he felt his pulse rate increase and wanted to put his fist through something. There was no evidence that she or her husband was complicit. Not yet at any rate, but surely the whiff of treachery would render greater caution. Apparently jobs for mates were more important than national security.

The chief had told him to let it go. Deals happened in politics and there was no real national security risk to Australia through the appointment. He said he would make sure any sensitive information didn't reach her ears. What kind of lame duck ambassador would that make?

On the bright side, the office was also shot of Dr Elgar, who had gone over to the private consulting world with Democritus. Chris picked at the plaster on his neck, loosening its pull on his skin. Both wounds were healing and were as itchy as if he'd been covered by a swarm of caterpillars. Was swarm the right terminology? No, that was butterflies—army of caterpillars. He pressed the plaster over the wound in his arm, trying to will the itch away, and reread the report he had written.

The chief was becoming impatient, but Chris hesitated to finalise the account, kept thinking of new things to add, and worrying about missing pieces of the puzzle. Like, who had driven the Cadillac?

Janice had said the vehicle was reported as stolen, but the driver should still be found. He had questions to answer, such as, did he fire the silenced weapon that killed Michael Leung and why? The bullets that had killed

Michael were from a Russian made weapon. A PB or pistolet besshumnyy. In English, a Silent Pistol; a GRAU index 6P9, built by the Soviets and issued to the Spetsnaz units in the KGB. The pistol was still made and used by Russian special forces and intelligence units today.

Chris wanted to know if the Caddy driver was the owner of the 6P9. He also wanted to know how Roland Leung had known the AUSTRAC referral had come from Chris.

Janice had calmed down after seeing the haul Chris had found in the apartment and had promised that if she came across anything she would let him know—*if* being the operative word.

Chris also wanted to talk to Alistair. He had been brought out from his coma, but Janice wouldn't allow Chris an interview until the AFP were done with him. They had searched Alistair's home and found cash hidden beneath floorboards, but he had claimed the money came from a gambling addiction, which he was keeping from his wife and employers. His brother-in-law, a local horse racing bookie, had backed up his story.

Janice said she was still looking into it, but she didn't think Alistair was central to cracking the case. If anything, he was a bit player on the margins. She insisted that the fact the Triads had run Alistair down gave his story some credibility. The worst thing about that conversation had been Janice gloating they had found the hit and run vehicle, hidden under a tarpaulin in the Triad basement. Chris should have seen it.

None of it satisfied him, but once again the chief told him to move on. Not every detail required squaring away. His job was national security not venial crimes. Chris conceded, but by the same token he hated not knowing, not finishing the job, leaving lose ends.

Anna Thompson poked her head around the door. 'Finished yet?'

Chris sighed. 'Not really but it's all I've got.'

The chief wants you in his office now to run through it with him. He's got to brief the new minister.

***

After Chris had taken the chief through the contents of the report, answering what questions he could, he asked, 'Do you think the policy officer was in on it sir?'

'The one we let go... Of course. You have doubts?'

'Not really but it seems odd. I mean the cook was a Chinese intelligence officer. Did he tee up the deal with the policy officer? I think there is more to the story. In the photos I received from Mèng she looked way too cosy with the minister - ex-minister's -husband. I would like to speak to Captain Mèng about it, if I can get permission, sir.'

'You think Brian Laidley was behind it, don't you?'

'I do. I had a look into his background and there is something odd about a period a few years ago, where he seemed to have had an extra-long stay in China. There is nothing on any official files, no consular assistance required or that sort of thing. But all his other trips to the Chinese mainland were short. If he stayed longer it was usually in Hong Kong. Yet after the one extended stay, the only trips he made to China were the ones where he accompanied the minister.'

'Stay away from it Chris. I'll make sure neither of them are a threat to national security, but it's not only the Prime Minister who doesn't want a scandal. If Ireland found out we suspected the spouse of a diplomate of being a spy for a foreign power, our credibility on the global stage would be finished. Besides, all you have is a hunch, based on nothing?'

'It's more than a hunch. It's a change in pattern. People don't like changes in the patterns of their lives unless there is a reason. I would feel easier if I knew that reason. And another thing. I still don't know how the Triads knew I had made the referral to AUSTRAC.'

'Did they know?'

'Yes.' Chris paused. 'Yes they did. The question is who told them?'

'Maybe the Chinese, though the cook's spying efforts?'

Chris shook his head, then shrugged. 'Maybe, but the whole deal between the Chinese government and the Triads is weird. The Leung brothers came here as refugees, running away from the CCP.'

'It's not unknown for the CCP to blackmail people into doing their bidding. In this case, it appears as if they tasked the Triads with contract killings of two key players in the bauxite investment so one of their bids might win.'

'But why Delahanty? According to Dr Sharapova, he had already made the decision in favour of Kashton and James Sinclair. Why not target Sinclair along with Kashton. Why go for the decision maker and one candidate, rather than both candidates in the competition. The assassin's work was wasted because Sinclair got the go ahead and whoever ordered the killing missed out. Yet Sinclair was never in any danger. Or not that we know about.' Chris paused frowning. 'I think I need to talk to Mrs Delahanty again sir. If I can get her to speak to me and if you can persuade ASIO. I would also like a word with Mèng about...'

Devin shook his head. 'Take a few days off Chris. Go and lie on a beach somewhere warm and clear your mind. You deserve a break and time to let your arm heal.'

'It's not much more than a scratch.'

'Sounded like more than that. Janice said, 'Twenty-five stiches.'

'She exaggerates, sir...' Chris grinned.

The chief grimaced. 'Oh, almost forgot. You know your director's position has become vacant?'

Chris looked at the ceiling before he responded. 'Can't say I'm not relieved, sir.'

'I would like you to put in an application in for the position.'

Chris frowned. 'Not sure about that.'

'May I ask why?'

'It's a desk job.'

'It will get you into the executive service and allow you a shot at a third or second secretary position abroad. I'd advise you to do it. The service is changing. The PM wants to rejig intelligence. These sorts of Machinery of Government reshuffles can be brutal. She's intent on moving ASIO under the Home Affairs portfolio and who knows what else will eventuate. You know how keen they are to outsource to the private sector... Besides my colleague in ASIO wants you transferred over there.'

'Not keen on that.'

'Exactly.'

Chris asked, 'Who will be taking your job, sir?'

Devin gazed at him for a minute before he said, 'That is still very much under wraps. But hell, I can trust you not to mention it, can't I?'

'Of course.'

'Well, if it helps your decision regarding the director's position, it seems Huma has the front running. The Treasurer is keen and so is the AG.' He marshalled his features into seriousness. 'But that's confidential Mr Davis. I should not really have told you although you will be please to know you'll be in good company.'

'That's a relief. Thanks for letting me know.' Chris fell silent but he didn't move.

Devin said, 'Is there something else Chris?'

Chris jerked his head. 'Ah, no sir. Thank you. I will wrap up a few things here and then maybe take a couple of weeks leave as you suggested.'

Devin said, 'Right. By the way, thank you. First class job. I know you are not satisfied, but the FIRB issues were all you were tasked with. You found a leak, for the second time, and got the FIRB chair through the decision-making process without Huma being murdered. That's a job well done in my book. Not to mention bringing in Mèng and saving Ms. Lewis's life.'

That was odd. Devin had not mentioned the Project Persius, the initial assignment he was given to find out what Walker Fitzsimmons was doing in Australia. An assignment he had failed to bring home. Maybe it was an oversight. Besides it had turned up little of any worth. He said, 'Thanks sir.' But Chris wasn't satisfied, and he had a shoulder-sagging presentiment that the job wasn't over yet.

36. Insanity Plea.

Cassie shut the front door and locked it. Her apartment no longer seemed to be in a safe part of Sydney. She had contemplated moving, but then to where? Nowhere felt safe any longer. The AFP officer, who had conducted her debrief, said it was natural to feel like that after what she had been through. With time, the feeling would ease and perhaps she should consider trauma counselling.

Yet, rationally, she no longer needed to be afraid. The assailants were all dead, not murdered but killed in self-defence according to her debriefer, and could no longer pose a threat. So why didn't that make her feel any better? She wasn't a criminal lawyer, but the self-defence claim seemed absurd.

Isn't self-defence supposed to be proportionate, she had asked her debriefer?

The debriefer, a woman of about her age, had looked at her askance and said, there were several armed assailants against two unarmed abductees. In my book the response was proportionate, or you would be dead. She had paused then spluttered. Sorry I should not have said that.

Still, Cassie didn't see it like that. The debriefer hadn't been there. Armed criminals or not those men hadn't stood a chance. The whole thing had been terrifying, and she didn't want to think about it.

She placed her handbag on the sideboard and kicked off her shoes. The cold tiles under her feet were sharp and refreshing after a tiring day in court, and she padded to the fridge to pour a glass of wine, which she took out to the balcony.

Spring was almost here. The bare tree branches already hosted a wash of green even though it was still officially winter, but that was climate change for you. Perhaps, if the weather stayed nice, she would take up her mother's offer to take a holiday at Bancroft House as a guest. She had to get her head back into normal space without ducking every time there was a loud bang.

She had been blaming Chris, but she recognised it was Alistair who had led the criminals to her door. When he had been brought out of his coma, he had asked to see her. She had refused, saying she was a corporate litigator, not a criminal lawyer.

Then his wife rang and asked if she would represent him. Despite what she had told the AFP, she'd refused and had given the wife the name of a colleague. She hadn't heard from Alistair again, but she figured that was because she had blocked his number. Any contact with him was dodgy, if not outright dangerous. She should have learned that lesson a long time ago.

It was just bad luck that she had run into him at Bancroft House after managing to avoid him for years. That was her mother's fault, with her fixation on having a phantom manager. Why she couldn't just admit she owned the place was beyond Cassie. Susan insisted it was a means of garnering credibility with the establishment, claiming a private equity firm owned the place, and all the staff were mere employees.

Perhaps she had a point. Women had a hard job making headway in this world. All the same, renewing her acquaintance with Alistair was sheer stupidity. If she had just refused categorically, when he'd said they should have a drink for old time's sake, none of this would have happened, at least not to her.

She paused. But then she wouldn't have met Chris. If Alister had led those men to her door, would she have been killed if Chris hadn't been there when they arrived? No. She had gone full circle and was back thinking about it again. Besides, Chris was past tense. She hadn't heard from him since the incident, probably her own doing given she had told him never to come near her again. But perhaps blaming others for her problems wasn't fair.

As usual, her choice in men was at the root of the issue and Chris was just another dodgy bloke in a string of terrible relationships. Not that they had ever had a relationship... Besides he was a liar and a killer. How did someone kill people like that and then act as if it was not a momentous event? A voice in her head said, but he saved you, didn't he? She shut it down. If it wasn't for men she wouldn't have needed saving. Why on earth would she even think of him?

She went back inside, sat down on the sofa, took a deep drink of the cool wine, and picked up the remote. Maybe she would watch the evening news, although why she bothered she didn't know. It was probably just more disaster and mayhem. Her phone rang and she got up to retrieve it from her handbag.

'Sir Hamish. How are you?' As she listened she grimaced at her reflection in the wall mirror hanging above the sideboard. 'Yes, your land sale to the Blue Eagle Bank has been approved by the FIRB. You can go ahead anytime you like.' She paused before saying, 'That's really not necessary Sir Hamish although it's kind of you to think of me... Oh, all right then. When? No, it will be just me. No partner... Gosh no... I haven't seen him for some time. I understand he may have gone back... Back home... Lovely, thank you. I'll see you on Friday evening then.'

Cassie let out a sigh. A celebratory dinner with Sir Hamish was the last thing in the world she wanted, but she would have to go. He was one of her firm's major clients. At least it was to be at Bancroft House. She would ask her mum if she could stay overnight, maybe spend the weekend. She would take a few days off and make it a mini holiday. She paused. Was it odd that Sir Hamish had asked if she wanted to bring Chris?

The last time she had gone to dinner with Sir Hamish, Chris had accompanied her, but at that time they'd all thought he was a competitor bidding on behalf of Lockheed Martin. Of course, she knew different now, but Sir Hamish wouldn't know that, would he? So why would Sir Hamish think that she might want to bring along a onetime competitor to a dinner celebrating the sale of his land to Blue Eagle?

Did he want to rub Chris's nose in the Blue Eagle victory? That didn't make sense. Surely, he didn't think she and Chris were an item after one dinner date. Was she becoming paranoid? She refilled her wine glass, heartly sick of the lot of them, but the nagging feeling that something was just not right stayed with her throughout the night.

***

The next morning, just as Cassie had finished dressing for work, her mobile rang. The screen told her it was her mother. She glanced at her watch and thumbed the pickup icon. 'Hi Mum.'

'Cassie darling, I need you to come out to the house.'

Cassie took a breath. 'Can't Mum, I'm in court today. Can it wait until tomorrow? I'll be out there for dinner with Sir Hamish anyway. I'll come a bit earlier to talk to you.'

Her mother's intake of breath concerned Cassie. 'What's wrong Mum?'

'Why are you having dinner with him?'

'Mum, it's my job. He's a major client.'

'If you can't come now, can you come this evening? Please darling I wouldn't ask unless it was important.'

Cassie rolled her eyes. Sure, like the last time you rang wanting me to come out urgently for a leak in the Chief Justice's bathroom, but she didn't say what she was thinking. Besides, she didn't have much on tomorrow. 'Okay. I'll come out tonight and take the day off tomorrow. I was thinking of taking you up on the offer of a holiday. Is now a good time? I can take a few days leave and stay into next week, if you have a spare room I can use.'

'Of course, darling. Thank you. I will see you tonight. What time?'

'Maybe 6.30 or 7. I will have to come home and pack a few things. Thanks Mum. See you later then. Must go now or I'll be late.'

Cassie hung up the phone, took a last look in the mirror to make sure nothing was out of place, grabbed her car keys and handbag and left the flat.

***

Susan hung up the phone and looked at Mason. 'She's coming this evening.'

Mason shook his head. 'I don't think we should involve her.'

'We have to. I don't know what to do and I'm scared, Mason.'

'Can't we just reverse the blackmail. If Ms Carmichael makes us spy on the Premier, we can report her as a foreign agent or something.'

'She's English. That's not foreign.' Susan placed her hand across her mouth for a moment before saying, 'But we shouldn't have taken her money. That makes us look as if we were complicit in something nefarious.'

Mason frowned. 'We were, and I think the English do count as foreign but don't forget, I did ask you to give the money back. We should have done that in the first place before the whole mess escalated. I never trusted that woman. Can't you refuse the payments arriving in the hotel account? It makes the whole debacle look worse than it is.'

'I don't know. That's why we need Cassie. If we do anything rash, we might expose ourselves. How much do you think Carmichael knows?'

He shrugged. 'I don't know. She said she had photos, but how? There was a gale blowing and I am sure she wasn't even out of bed until after breakfast. I had to take a tray to her room because she woke up so late. What she does know is the information you gave me to give to her.'

'Well, that was hardly earth shattering. Just two prospective investors in the bauxite mine in conversation with their visitor in the bar?'

'One of them was a General in the Chinese military.'

'They were all Chinese men.'

'Exactly. Maybe they are all with the Government of China. We don't really know who their guests were. Also don't forget the bit about the police detective, Cassie's friend, the one in hospital now. Do you think his accident was because of what I told Ms Carmichael.' Mason's eyes squeezed shut and he ran his hand across his face.

'No. I don't and never refer to him as Cassie's friend again. He's not a nice man.'

Mason nodded. 'Oh yeah... Ms Carmichael was also interested in information about that Lockheed Martin consultant.'

'Like what?'

'Who he was seeing, his sexual proclivities, any drinking, gambling, or drugs, and so on, but I said I didn't know anything about him, and he hadn't made any requests like that.'

Susan blew out a breath. 'Well, we have to put a stop to this. I don't mind spying on the Chinese, but I am not going to spy on the Premier for Ms Carmichael. That's one step to far.'

***

That evening when Susan said something similar to Cassie about not minding spying on the Chinese, Cassie was aghast, but it got worse. Hearing her mother's confession was like peeling an onion. With each layer came more tears. First, Susan's fears and justifications, then Cassie's horror at the depth of her mother's deceit. Who was this woman? She thought she knew her but clearly she had no idea, and neither did she know how to help.

She was used to upholding the law and arguing her clients were doing just that. But her mother hadn't let small legal details deter her, never mind

Ms Carmichael's attempts at blackmail. Her mother and Mason would end up in gaol. No one had asked her to remove a dead man from the scene of the crime. No one blackmailed her into placing cameras in people's bedrooms. And from what she had said, she had spied on the Chinese guests' conversation. At least one had diplomatic status. It just got worse and worse.

The cameras! Oh my God. Chris had been on to it. He knew about the cameras. That was why he had come with Officer Burton to find the film footage. No. He was only after the public cameras. Did he know about the others? Surely he would have said... What did he expect to find on the camera film? 'Mum, do your cameras record?'

'No dear. I already told you that. They can but I have not bothered with it. Besides after the AFP and that man came looking, Mason removed most of the cameras.'

'That man? You mean Chris Davis?'

'Yes, if that's really his name.'

Cassie blinked. 'What?'

'He's not what he seems you know darling. You are well shot of him.'

'How do you know?' Again, she thought, he saved my life but said nothing. Cassie had made up her mind not to tell her mother about her abduction. The AFP had asked her not to speak about the details, but she had already decided she did not wish to be defined by the event and anyway, her mother's fussing would drive her barmy.

Susan compressed her lips. 'Take my word for it dear. He's not who he says he is.'

'What do you know about him, Mum?'

And then her mother told Cassie about the cufflink and how Chris had said nothing after Alistair had found its matching partner on Harvey Kashton's corpse.

'Oh my God. Mum, whatever were you thinking?'

***

That night Cassie could not sleep. How was she going to help her mother? Ethically she should not help her at all. But Susan was her mother, and no matter what she had done, Cassie had to find a way to save her from herself, even if it involved her mother being charged. Could she mount a defence of idiocy.

If it pleases the court my mother is a complete fool. She thought that moving a dead body was necessary because she didn't want a scandal. I beg your pardon. I will reiterate that first statement and add an addendum.

If it pleases the court my mother is a complete fool, and a racist. She installed cameras in guests rooms to spy on her guests. She was paid for intelligence by a British woman working for a competitor in an investment of national interest and justified her treachery by noting the people involved were Chinese, at least one of whom was a diplomat. My mother thought that she knew better that the FIRB process and had decided the Chinese should not be allowed to buy Australian assets.

She thought it was okay for the English to buy them because she can't understand the sovereignty issues distinguishing Britain from Australia. If it pleases your Honour, my mother still thinks Australia is a dependency of the British Empire.

For crying out loud. She kicked off the bedcovers and got out of bed to stand by the window, looking out over the moonlight gardens to the sea. Her mother was an idiot, an intolerable snob, and an opinionated sneak, as well as being a racist. More than that... She had got herself involved in espionage involving foreign nationals.

What had Chris said about spies? They were assets used to gather intelligence for analysts, who he claimed were usually public servants. Who the hell was Vikki Carmichael then? She had been introduced as James Sinclair's personal assistant, but what did that mean? Did she work for the British? Is that why she had recruited Susan to spy on her behalf?

No. More likely Vikki was spying on behalf of Blue Eagle Bank. Corporations used spies all the time to dig up dirt on their competitors. She expected, as Vikki was in residence, she would see her tomorrow at

Sir Hamish's celebratory dinner. Perhaps then she could find out more. Although knowing that wasn't going to help her mother or Mason. They were both in serious trouble.

Maybe she could ask Chris's advice. He seemed to know more about these things than she did, although she wasn't sure how to contact him. She wasn't even certain he was a Treasury analyst. Yet if she asked him, wouldn't she be exposing her mother's secret. Chris would tell Officer Burton. Or would he? He didn't seem to like Officer Burton much, and the AFP officer was certainly angry with him.

That was another strange thing. Officer Burton hadn't seemed concerned about the men Chris had killed. Wouldn't that require some sort of inquiry. They did that when the police shot someone. But Burton was more concerned that Chris had gone around to see Cassie without first telling the AFP what he was doing. She had called it *chasing skirt*, like it was a sexual thing rather than something official, and she was really mad with him.

She didn't even care that Chris was bleeding all over the place. If Cassie hadn't insisted he go to the hospital, she didn't think Burton would have cared if he had died. Maybe they had history. Or perhaps this was normal in their line of work. She grimaced. Anyway, she had no way of contacting Chris. She didn't have his phone number, and she was not about to ask Burton for it.

Yet, having come up with the solution of asking for Chris's advice, she now couldn't get it out of her head, despite the risks. Whichever way she examined the problem, on her own she couldn't figure out how to help her mother. If she asked Chris, and he reported Susan... Well, it might be a risk she would have to take. He was the only person who might know what she could do, and he hadn't dobbed-in her mother for hiding the cufflink from Alistair. Nor had he reported her for having cameras in private rooms, although Cassie wasn't sure if he knew about those.

The next morning, she rang the switchboard at Treasury and asked to speak to Chris Davis, an analyst in the Corporate and Foreign Investment section. She was put through to one person after another. Each time she asked, there was a short silence on the phone before she was put through to someone else. Eventually she spoke to a woman in the Investment Review

Branch. The woman took down Cassie's details and asked why she wished to speak with Mr Davis.

Cassie replied, 'Its personal.'

The woman breathed deeply and said, 'I am sorry to tell you that we do not have anyone by that name working here. I think you may have the wrong number.' She hung up.

Cassie stared at the phone. 'Liar,' she said softly and put down the phone with a sense of relief tinged with disappointment. It had been a bout of midnight madness to think calling Chris was a good idea. She would just need to find a way to save her mother from herself, on her own.

Chris stood in the middle of the room gazing at Mèng's lifeless body. Poor bastard. He hadn't deserved this but how much did anyone care. In this game caring was a luxury.

An AFP officer came into the room. 'The doctor said most likely sudden cardiac death. Blood has gone for tests but there will need to be an autopsy.'

It was Iain Ridley. Chris had met him before.

Ridley added, 'Sorry mate, but we got him here as soon as we found him this morning.'

Chris gazed at Ridley for a minute before he said, 'Tell me exactly what happened.'

Ridley gave an exasperated sigh and said, 'Look, I know you think the place wasn't secure, but we've used it before and never had any problems. He was fine last night and went to bed as usual. This morning when his breakfast arrived, I went in to wake him up and found him barely conscious. We got him here fast, but he was dead by the time we arrived. The doctor couldn't revive him.'

'And the security detail...'

'Same as before.'

'What about other staff.'

'Nothing's changed except the ASIO blokes have finished questioning Mèng, at least for now. It was just a matter of a new identity, a new location, and he would have been sent on his journey through the Witness Protection Program.'

'How did they get to him?'

Ridley shrugged.

'What about cameras?'

'Blanked out.'

'Shit. Any others in the area?'

'We're going through that now.'

'Okay. This needs to be locked down. No one leaking anything. I need a list of people who know.'

Ridley shook his head. 'It's just me and my partner outside the door. Oh, plus the security and my boss, and the doctor, maybe a few other medical staff, but they don't know who he is.'

'Get me a list. And I want copies of any camera footage you find within a five-block radius.' Chris put his phone to his ear and walked away. 'Chief. Bad news. They couldn't revive him.'

'Assassination?'

'Don't know but most likely.'

'I thought the assassins were all dead.'

Chris laughed. 'Like the Triad group were the only assassins for hire in the world, sir. But I have an idea...' He explained to Devon that an autopsy would have to be conducted to find out what killed him, with a focus on possible aconitine poisoning, but in the interim Mèng should be found in a motel in another city. Just another victim of a drug overdose. That way Devin might contact the Chinese Embassy to report the death of one of their nationals.

Chris said, 'With any luck sir, they won't know we had him. And if they did know and they assassinated him as a result, you might pick up some indication when you meet with them. They will likely demand his body back before an autopsy, especially if they did it. But whatever happens we can't permit it to be seen as something we allowed under our protection. A drug overdose will save the Prime Minister the embarrassment and avoid a national incident with the Chinese.'

'ASIO can take care of all that. I'll speak to the DG and the Secretary now. Sorry about your holiday Chris, but there is another thing...'

'What's that sir?'

'Cassandra Lewis.'

Chris held his breath.

Devin said, 'What do you know about her?'

Chris breathed out. 'Nothing that is not in my reports. Why. Has something happened to her?'

'She rang Treasury first thing this morning looking for you.'

'What for?'

'That's what I was hoping you could tell me.'

Chris shook his head. 'No clue sir. What did she say?'

'She said it was a private matter. Are you sure you have no idea? I only ask because Officer Burton suggested you might be sweet on her...'

'Doesn't alter anything sir. I deliberately didn't give her my number, and I didn't think, after the kidnapping, that she would speak to me again. At least that is what she said.'

'I think you had better go and find out what she wants. It might be important.'

'I'll give her a ring when I'm back in the office.'

'Go to Sydney Chris. Take her to dinner, romance her a little if you like, but find out what she wants and what she knows. It will be official business so rack it up to us. I'll approve it. Take a few days. The least I can do after cancelling your leave.'

'Can I take the Merc again sir?'

A sharp grunt, or maybe it was a snort, came through the speaker before the chief said, 'I think you have blown your legend with Ms Lewis. You can take a pool vehicle.'

'Worth a try, sir. But what if it's nothing, and she just wants a friendly catch up.'

'Then we will have wasted time and money. Not the worst outcome, and lucky for you, but it maybe something. I understand the call was traced back to Bancroft House, and it's my understanding that the successful investors are having a celebratory dinner there tonight. Huma was invited but of course she had to decline given her role in the decision making. I am guessing it is why Ms Lewis is at the hotel.'

'You want me to see if I can score an invite?'

'Not sure how?'

'Maybe Ms Lewis phoned to invite me.' Chris laughed.

'For a minute I thought you were being serious. But I imagine the nature of Ms Lewis's call has something to do with Detective McMahon. The AFP have just charged him.'

'For what, sir?'

'They found a financial transaction in his bank account, which they have traced back to the Lightening Entertainment Group. It implicates the Leung brothers who were shareholders. Apparently, McMahon couldn't explain it, or at least not to Officer Burton's satisfaction. They have charged him under section 400.6 of the Criminal Code Act. But its small beer. Eight grand I understand. If he has a good barrister, he'll likely get off with little more than a slap on the wrist, but his career in the force is over.'

'Is Ms Lewis going to represent him? You think that may be why she rang, to call me as a witness or something?'

'It's a long shot I know, but we won't find out by speculating.'

'Even if I knew anything, I can't be a witness for the defence.'

'You will have to impress that on her.'

'Shit. Sorry sir. I'm going to have to give her some idea why. I'll have to tell her who I work for.'

Now the sound of a chuckle. 'It's a mess I know. How much of a relationship are you likely to have with her?'

'None, if it's up to her sir.'

'And you.'

'I would like to get to know her better, but her mother is a challenge.'

'Okay. I have confidence you will sort it out without embarrassing the government and yes, I think you can say you work for Foreign Affairs and Trade. Accentuate the trade bit. That should do it, trade might explain your interest in the bauxite mine.'

Chris hung up. He didn't think she would buy it, but he could see the chief was enjoying his discomfort. Oh well, another trip to Sydney and a few days off. Not as good as lying on Noosa Beach as he had planned, but at least it was out of the office and the bonus was he would get to see Cassie again, even if she did hate him.

38. Breakthrough.

Cassie had agreed to meet Chris in a popular basement bar in the city. She had suggested Bancroft House, but he asked her to choose again, and this jazz bar was it. When she arrived, she paused at the base of the steps wondering if he would turn up, or if he had waited. She was late, having dithered over what to wear, eventually settling on jeans and a cashmere jumper.

She spotted him in the far corner. He stood up and she hurried towards him, then stopped short, not knowing how she should greet him.

He took a step towards her, and her breathing faltered, but all he did was hold out his hand. The formality seemed odd. They had spent the night together in a pantry, Cassie in terror, Chris as calm as ever, providing her with both comfort and warmth.

The pantry night had been an odd sort of intimacy but one he seemed to place at a distance by offering his hand, eschewing the ubiquitous hugs given to even the most short-term acquaintances. He asked after her health and what she would like to drink, even held her chair as she sat down before he went to the bar.

By the time he returned she had recovered her composure. After all she had asked him here to provide advice. When she was asked for legal advice she charged by the hour, and this was merely a business transaction.

That would be how she would address this meeting. Perhaps her choice of venue had been off. She should have chosen a more neutral setting. But never mind that now, she would still address him, and the issue, as if it was a legal transaction.

She took a sip of wine to fortify herself before she said, 'Thank you for coming and for the drink.'

His eyes searched hers and his grin disarmed her resolution to make this a business meeting, but all he said was, 'It's my pleasure although I must admit I was surprised after you said you never wanted to see me again.'

She bit back a retort and simply said, 'I need advice.' The glass of wine in front of her was almost empty. How had that happened?

For what seemed like an aeon, he said nothing but just as she was about to speak again, he broke the silence. 'Yes, you said it was urgent.'

His wine was untouched.

'It is... sort of...' Her gaze skimmed past him to rest on her hands now clenched on her lap. She had to pull herself together. 'Sorry. I don't know where to start or even if I can trust you with the information.'

Again, that grin, like he was enjoying her discomfort.

He said, 'Can I get you another glass of wine?'

She shook her head, took a breath, and said, 'It's about my mother...'

The smile faded and while it was a dimly lit room she swore his eyes darkened. He didn't say anything, just waited for her to speak again, but she couldn't think clearly. How could she tell this man about her mother's spying, the blackmail, the payments. Even to her own ears it sounded shocking—beyond belief that this seeming unprepossessing elderly woman was capable of so much conniving.

She stood up. 'I shouldn't have come. Sorry. Thanks for the drink.'

He stood too. 'Cassie, I know a lot about your mum already, so what you have to tell me won't come as a surprise. I think you need my help, and I can probably do something if I know what your particular concern is.'

Cassie blew out a breath. 'What do you know?'

He gazed at her steadily. 'A lot, but I also know she is not a bad person and what she's done was naïve, not wicked.'

'Under the law that doesn't matter.'

'No mitigating circumstances.' He smiled, this time with softer edges.

Cassie sighed. 'Not one that wouldn't require insanity as a plea.'

He laughed. 'Don't run away Cassie. I'll get another drink while you figure out what you can tell me.'

When he came back with her second glass of wine, she had made up her mind. 'You know about her cameras...'

'Yes.' He took a sip of his wine and leaned back in his chair.

'But the private room ones...'

He nodded. 'She had one in my room.'

Cassie sucked in a breath. 'Why didn't you arrest her?'

He shrugged. 'I neither have the power nor the inclination.'

Cassie blurted out, 'She's being blackmailed, and I don't know what to do.'

Chris tilted his head to the left and leaned in closer, a serious look in his eyes. 'Tell me everything Cassie.'

'I'm terrified of going to the police. She has broken more laws... well, they'll arrest her... Won't they? And I don't know how to protect her.'

Take a breath Cassie. 'Who is blackmailing her, and to do what?'

Cassie sucked in air and concentrated, her eyes fixed on Chris as if his features might steady her. 'Ms Carmichael, Vikki, you remember James Sinclair's personal assistant, has asked her to spy on the Premier and has threatened to expose her to the police if she doesn't do it.'

'Aside from the cameras, what else does Ms Carmichael have on your mum?'

Cassie pressed her lips together. What could she tell him? 'She says she has film of Mason doing something...' Cassie couldn't tell Chris about the body. What would he think or do? Cameras were one thing. Moving a dead man was so much worse but Chris was speaking. She tried to focus on what he was saying. 'Sorry. What?'

'I didn't say anything Cassie, but I can see you are in a bind. Would you like me to tell you?' He paused, she nodded, and he went on. 'I think you were about to tell me that Vikki saw Mason moving Harvey Kashton's corpse from the house to his yacht.'

'How did you know?' She could feel the hot tears pressing against the back of her eyes.

'I didn't know. I guessed. But she confirmed it when I asked her.'

'She didn't tell me that. When?'

'After I found Kashton's cufflink on the steps leading down to the beach and gave it to your mum. She kept quiet when Alistair said he had found its pair on the body. I asked her why she had said nothing, and she told me she was protecting the hotel's reputation, or words to that effect.'

'You knew about that, and the cameras and said nothing to anyone about her behaviour. Why?'

'It wasn't my mission, and it is not true that I have said nothing about this. My boss knows.'

Cassie stared at Chris with so many questions running through her head, most of which she knew he would not answer and then made up her mind to tell him everything. 'Vikki paid Mason to spy on the Chinese investors who were bidding for the bauxite mine. You remember?'

Chris nodded. 'What did he find out?'

'Nothing. I don't know.' Cassie gazed at the ceiling in awe at her own stupidity. Throughout all this, it had never occurred to her to ask her mother that question.

'Did she say anything about Alistair meeting with them?'

'Oh my God, was Alistair working with the Chinese Government?' Of course he was. The Triads are Chinese... But not the government. It was all so bloody confusing. She said, 'Mum didn't say... Was that who ran him down?'

'Cassie, stop a minute. Think hard. Are you sure you don't have any idea about the content your mum gave Vikki about the Chinese investors.'

She shook her head. 'She didn't tell me. All she said was that she didn't think spying on the Chinese was wrong because they should not be allowed to buy Australian assets. I am afraid my mother is also a racist as well as being a snob.'

'Right. Can you ask her?'

Cassie nodded. She wasn't much good at this stuff.

'Do you know why Vikki wants Mason to spy on the Premier?'

She shook her head. 'I can only guess. Sir Hamish told me about a land development application last night at dinner. The Blue Eagle Investment Bank want to use Sir Hamish's land to refine the bauxite to obtain alumina and then to smelt the alumina and produce aluminium in situ. That is why Vikki is still here with Sir Hamish. They won't settle the deal before they have the development approval, and Sir Hamish keeps badgering me to do something about it. Not that I can. Apparently, Blue Eagle are also planning some sort of manufacturing centre along with living quarters for the workers and they need the Premier's support. The land is in an environmentally sensitive area, and I know the development application won't get through the process without political intervention. When I heard Vikki wanted dirt on the Premier, his predilections etcetera, I put two and two together.'

Chris took another sip of his wine, his face unreadable and she said, as much to shock him into saying something as for any other reason, 'Vikki also asked Mason what your predilections were.'

Obviously shock tactics were wasted. Chris's expression didn't change.

He said, 'What did Mason say?'

Cassie shrugged. 'You don't have any apparently, or none they know about although my mother thinks you are dangerous...' It had been a cheap shot, and she didn't know why she had said it. Especially as he was being so nice about her mother.

Chris said, 'What else do you know Cassie?'

'Apparently they have been paying money into the hotel's bank account.'

'Who?'

'Blue Eagle, I think. But Vikki said it's a trail of proof that Mason has been working for them.'

He said, 'The money is meaningless. It does not go to motive.'

'Why?'

'Mason could say he understood the Blue Eagle payments were to retain rooms like offices or conference rooms in the hotel for their corporate convenience.'

'Of course.' She should have thought of that. Some lawyer she was. 'What should Mum and Mason do about the Premier? She is adamant she will not spy on him.'

Chris finished his wine. 'I might be able to help. For the moment they should do nothing, just go along with Vikki as if they will do her bidding.'

'You mean you can fix this.' A tear escaped and ran down Cassie's nose. She squashed it with her finger.

'I'm not sure but maybe.' Does your mother still have the cameras in place.'

'No, she was frightened after you came with that AFP officer, and she made Mason remove them.'

'Pity.' He glanced at his watch. 'Are you hungry? I made a dinner reservation at an Italian restaurant near my hotel. My boss rates the place. Perhaps you might keep me company?'

'I will if you tell me who your boss is.'

He laughed. 'I'll tell you after dinner.'

'Why after dinner?'

'You'll see.'

She pursed her lips. The man was infuriating but she hadn't felt this happy in ages and if he wanted to keep playing these mysterious games, well in every relationship there were compromises although that alone should send up a red flag. There was still the matter of dead bodies lying in his wake. She pushed the thought aside. It was self-defence.

Over dinner they didn't talk of business anymore. She drank too much red wine and talked about her childhood. The long days in summer, picnics on the beach, her mother's awful bridge parties, her father teaching her to paddle the skiff. Her father's affair. Her parents separation and shortly thereafter, her father's death, which came at the same time as her admission to the bar, leaving that whole decade of her life, a bittersweet legacy. He was a good listener, and she had talked herself out by the time they arrived at his hotel.

She found herself in his room, ripping off his clothes in her hast to feel his warm skin against hers, his arms around her waist, his mouth on hers and she couldn't get enough but cried out, demanding more, until slick with sweat she fell asleep in his arms and still, she didn't know who Chris's boss was.

***

Chris spent the weekend with Cassie. On the Saturday morning, she had woken up with a thumping headache, and he had insisted the only cure was either more alcohol or a big breakfast. Alcohol was a bad idea so coffee, bacon, eggs, hashbrowns, beans, mushrooms and tomatoes were his go to.

Cassie blanched in horror at the suggestion and dragged him off for an ice bath.

Never again, not if he could help it although he did admit it made him feel a lot better. Maybe he could learn to tolerate it.

After lunch he had gone out to Bancroft House with Cassie. She took him though the private entrance and up to her mother's quarters. He hadn't wanted to bump into any of the Blue Eagle hangers on although only Vikki was still in residence along with Sir Hamish. James Sinclair had gone back to London as soon as the deal was done.

After endless questioning, Chris hadn't got much more out of Susan than he already knew, although there was a little more colour within the picture's confines. She had seen Alistair get into a car with a man who had fitted Michael Leung's description. She confirmed Michael had met with the Căihóng chairman David Cho, and General Aiguo Liu, but she had not heard them talking, nor did she know what they might have discussed.

On the Saturday night, Cassie refused her mother's offer of dinner on the house, instead taking Chris to her favourite tapas bar. It was the place, she said, she had planned to take him the first time before she had been forced into having dinner with Sir Hamish, and his entourage.

The sherry that came with the Jamón Serrano took him straight back to the Basque country and hiking with Jenna. The ham stuck mid-way down his oesophagus, threatening to choke him. He gulped the Manzanilla as tears sprung into his eyes.

'Chris are you okay?' Cassie asked.

He nodded and filled up a water glass from the bottle on their table. 'Sorry.' For a moment he contemplated lying but decided she deserved the truth. If there was to be any future in their relationship, she had to know.

He pushed the ham to one side and said, 'I'm sorry Cassie. I should tell you about Jenna.'

Cassie face clouded, and he hated himself for causing that wary, defensive expression. He reached over to take her hand. 'I was engaged once to a woman called Jenna Debrett. We were going to be married. I loved her and I think in a funny sort of way I still do.'

'Why are you telling me this Chris?'

'I want to be truthful with you.'

'You have a fiancée, and you think telling me now is a good idea.'

He shook his head. 'I had a fiancée. She's dead.'

'Oh my God!' Cassie yanked her hand from his and held it to her mouth. 'You...'

'No. Christ, is that what you think of me? She died in a terrorist attack in London.' His eyes watered and he turned his face away.

Cassie's voice was soft now. 'What happened?'

He turned back to her. 'Do you remember the London terror attack in 2005. Maybe not. It was twelve years ago.'

'I remember. I was just starting out at my firm, and we were all horrified.'

He nodded. 'She died on her way to work near Russell Square. She had only just scored her dream job at the British Museum as a research assistant.

Then she was blown to bits by some fucking fundamentalist nut job...' He paused. 'Anyway, I'm only telling you, so you know.'

She took his hand back into hers. 'I'm so sorry Chris. Sorry for Jenna. Sorry I misunderstood you.' Her forehead creased. 'Does the food remind you... Oh no, I am so sorry.'

Chris said, 'We had just returned from a hiking holiday in Spain, where I had asked her to marry me. The food and wine brought it back. But it's okay. Look, I'm over it.' He put a piece of the ham into his mouth and swallowed a mouthful of sherry. 'Its fine. I was just reminded and thought I should tell you.'

'No, we will go somewhere else.'

She got up and went to the bar while Chris sat cursing himself. He had not had an emotion escape his control like that for a long time. He really needed to get Jemma's death out of his system. In a way he was glad he'd told Cassie. It was cathartic.

As they walked down the street in the direction of his hotel, he took her hand. 'You think I am a mass murderer, don't you?'

She pulled away. 'Of course I don't.'

'I think you do. You thought I had killed my fiancée, and it was something you were just waiting to discover about me. There was a latent expectation in your eyes that told me you believed that after sleeping with me, you would realise I was no good.'

She glanced at him. 'Am I that transparent?'

'Yes. And I love that about you.'

She changed the subject. 'You lied to me.'

'Yes.'

She glanced at him, surprised he admitted lying so easily. 'I mean last night. You said after dinner you would tell me who your boss is, and you didn't.'

'You fell asleep before I could.'

'Tell me now.'

'Okay. I work for DFAT in the trade section. My boss is the Secretary of the department.'

'Is that true.'

'Is what true? That I work for DFAT or that my boss is the Secretary.'

240

'Why wouldn't you tell me before?'

'I wasn't sleeping with you before.'

'If I hadn't slept with you last night...'

He shook his head. 'Then I wouldn't have told you anything.' He smiled but you did, and I have and its after dinner now, so I didn't really lie.'

'That was last night's dinner. We haven't had dinner tonight, or at least we haven't finished.'

'I didn't say when after dinner.'

'I give up. I don't actually care where you work so it doesn't matter, but I also happen to know that Australia's spy agency is buried somewhere in DFAT.' She held up her hand. Actually, I don't want to know, but I am hungry, so you had better find me something to eat before I ravish your body again.'

***

On the Sunday morning, he had an appointment with Mrs Delahanty. That had taken some persuasion after the last time he had tried to speak to her. Chris was determined this time to get her on side if he could get a foot inside her door. When he'd got nowhere with his efforts, he had asked the Chief to speak to her.

Cassie insisted on going with him. She said she would put the poor woman's mind at ease if Chris was accompanied by a woman, and he owed her.

Mrs Delahanty opened the door and invited them in.

Chris introduced Cassie as his assistant, ignoring the askance look she gave him.

She stepped forward and held out her hand to Mrs Delahanty. 'I'm actually his lover but he is worried you will think it strange my coming with him. You see, I insisted because I thought you might feel more comfortable speaking to a woman, and I too have a vested interest in finding out who killed your husband because I think the same people may have kidnapped me. Oh, and I am a Queens Council, not that my career choice has anything to do with today. It's just that I think it's always good to start with the truth, don't you?'

'*If* someone killed my husband... surely, it is still *if*... I understand there is no evidence yet or I would have been told. But thank you dear.' Mrs Delahanty smiled at Cassie. 'It is always good to know the truth, if truth exists outside one's agenda, but I am glad you have been frank with me. I really didn't know why the Treasury department keep hounding me over Miles's death. The NSW Police too, and the AFP. It's like they think I killed my husband; poisoned him or something. Come through. I have tea waiting and my solicitor.' She smiled again. 'You two might be able to chat about the law, while I talk to Mr Davis.'

Chris watched Cassie in action, building rapport with Mrs Delahanty like a trained professional, which in a way he supposed she was. Barristers needed to build rapport with all sorts of clients, judges and so on, and especially women barristers if they were to make any headway in a male-centric world.

He was glad she had accompanied him, although he had expected it to become a monumental disaster. But she was right. She had a stake in this game, not only to feel like she had retaken control over her life after the kidnapping, but also as a means of protecting her mother from people, who didn't let the law get in the way of their objectives.

They were introduced to the solicitor, Mr Rankin, an elderly balding man, shorter than average, who struggled to rise as they entered the room. Mrs Delahanty insisted they have tea before they launched into any questions.

Once everyone was settled with tea and a slice of sponge cake, she picked up an A4 spiral bound notebook and laid it on the coffee table in front of Chris. 'This is Miles's private diary or at least his deliberations and ramblings about his dilemma over making the right decision regarding the bauxite mine.'

Chris frowned. 'The AFP didn't take it with his other papers?'

'I said dear, it was his private ramblings. The AFP didn't know about it and as it was private I don't think he would have wanted it to be read by anyone without the right sort of attitude.'

'Yet you are giving it to me. Why?'

'Because Devin rang me and asked me to help you. Besides, Ms Lewis is honest and if she vouches for you, I believe Miles would have been happy for you to read his inner thoughts without misinterpreting them or worse, skewing them to your own ends. He always ran them by me you know, so I know that what he sometimes thought was not how he acted, especially if his views conflicted with his sworn duty. Duty came before everything, even life, in his opinion. Besides I am not giving you the notebook, I am allowing you to read it. That is all. Then you can tell me if you think he was murdered or not.'

Chris drank his tea and picked up the notebook to begin reading. 'This might take a while...'

'That's all right, dear. We will talk among ourselves if that won't disturb your concentration.'

Chris shook his head, and his eyes raced across the neat script. Most of the information wasn't new although it was put into different future scenarios for the country, along with pros and cons and discussions he'd had with the board members, mostly Huma.

It wasn't until he neared the end of the note pad, that an argument caught his eye, and he drew in a breath. He re-read the page to make sure he hadn't misunderstood, then went back and re-read the preceding pages. This was massive. He read the remainder of the notebook but only that one dispute stood out. He returned to it. Re-read it and sat back, staring at the page. Then he looked up.

The others had stopped talking and were watching him.

Mrs. Delahanty said, 'You found it.'

Chris nodded. 'I guess so. Did you know?'

She nodded. 'I thought it was strange. I had forgotten about it with everything else that had happened, but it was only after you called to make the appointment that I re-read the notebook and recalled his hesitation over the British Bank investing in the mine.'

'Why? Do you know?'

'Miles was uneasy about some Russian billionaire in London getting his hands on the mine, and although James Sinclair assured him it wouldn't happen he wasn't convinced.'

Chris ran his hand over his mouth and said, 'So, he was against the Blue Eagle Investment.'

'Absolutely. I was surprised when it was announced because I recalled his concern. As I said, Miles always placed duty first, so I thought perhaps this was another case of his particular form of moral reasoning.'

'Mrs Delahanty, I know you are not keen for this notebook to leave here, but would you mind if I photographed just these pages?'

'I suppose that would be all right.' She glanced at the solicitor.

Rankin shuffled forward on the chair and said, 'It wouldn't become a public document would it?'

'No, I would just like to show it to my boss. He knew your husband for many years.'

'Yes, I remember him well. I heard about his promotion, but then life moves on so quickly as one gets older, and I suppose all that time in war zones takes its toll on a person. I know that is why Miles got out. All right if that's all who will see it.'

'I give you my word.' Chris avoided Cassie's questioning gaze and took out his phone to photograph the relevant pages. 'I am very grateful Mrs Delahanty.'

'So, can you tell me if Miles was murdered.'

'Not for sure Mrs Delahanty, but if he was, I may have found the motivation for it.'

After they had left and Chris drove Cassie home she said, 'I thought the DFAT Secretary was a woman?'

Chris glanced across at her. 'She is.'

'Mrs Delahanty used the pronoun *he* when she referred to your boss and called him Devin.'

Chris sighed. 'You don't miss a thing do you. In the hierarchy of things, the Secretary is my ultimate boss, but I thought you didn't care.'

'I care if you lie to me.'

'Okay. Noted.'

39. Passing the Test.

Devin examined the man sitting in front of him, the desk creating a barrier between them, a folder stamped The Perseus Project *eyes only* in front of him. Chris was frowning in concentration as if he might have overlooked something in the report. He had given Devin a verbal briefing, but Devin had read the report last night and Chris had missed nothing.

If Devin had found Chris likable when he had first met him, he now admired him. In fact, he was a little awestruck by the man's intellectual and moral reasoning capability. The Secretary should have made an effort to get to know him, instead of reading reports written by Elgar, who had started off with and agenda and had ended with an axe to grind.

How could she not have seen how unreliable Elgar was before she had appointed him to the role? Although admittedly, Devin had made similar mistakes in his career, which was why he was never going to accept Elgar's assessment of Chris before evaluating him for himself.

Devin said, 'There is something else worrying you.'

Chris sighed. 'How can you tell sir.'

'You become silent and stare into the middle distance.'

'Good to know. I will have to work on that.'

'And you prevaricate, misdirect.'

Chris laughed. 'Just my usual behaviour I think sir.'

'What are you not telling me?'

'Nothing really, or maybe a couple of niggles that don't line-up.'

'Out with it then.'

Chris said, 'When I spoke to Dr Sharapova, she was adamant that Mr Delahanty had already decided on Kashton and Sinclair as the two winning investors.'

'I see, and the private diary entry you photographed shows that Sinclair wasn't on the favourites list for the very reason you advised against it.'

Chris nodded. 'Sinclair's biggest investor, Misha Yelchin was sanctioned by the U.S. over his involvement in the 2014 Crimean annexation by Russia. The Americans also suspect him of being involved in selling weapons to the Central Africa Republic against the United Nations arms embargo.'

'And you outlined your concerns to both Dr Sharapova and the Treasurer.'

'They said newspaper gossip about Yelchin had nothing to do with James Sinclair. In addition, Yelchin already has investments all over Australia, but that's not what concerns me sir.'

'So, what is it?'

'Why did Dr Sharapova claim Delahanty had made a decision in favour of Sinclair, when his diary doesn't support her assertion.'

Devin's gazed hardened. 'You are insinuating Huma lied and made the decision in favour of Sinclair, despite Miles's view.'

Chris shrugged.

'You know what you are saying, Chris, don't you...?'

'Yes sir.'

Devin placed his elbow on his other arm and put his hand over his mouth. 'What do you propose?'

Chris shrugged. 'We need to find out why, but it's two separate operations, sir.'

'How do you mean?'

'Well, we need to know what's going on with Blue Eagle Bank. Not that there is anything we can do about it now, except stop them from attempting to blackmail the NSW Premier into granting their development approval. That's a job for ASIO and the AFP. But James Sinclair can just deny all knowledge of what Ms Carmichael is doing. Nevertheless, it still needs to be exposed sir, and I have an idea for a joint operational sting.'

'And the second operation.'

'Ah, maybe there are three...'

'Get on with it Chris.'

'Well, we have to find out if and why Dr Sharapova went against Mr Delahanty's wishes. If she did it with intention, she has motive for his and Kashton's murders. We may have been chasing the Chinese all this time, but I am now beginning to wonder if we weren't sent on the wrong trail as a deliberate strategy.'

'What do you mean?'

'Well, if you wanted James Sinclair's bid accepted, you would need to get rid of Kashton. Plus, if you wanted to accept Sinclair's bid, you would have to get rid of the FIRB chair who was against it.'

Devin sighed. 'Not Huma. Look, you have to understand Huma's standing. She works for us—more than just teaching the craft to recruits. That's classified by the way. I am one of two who know any details. Now you, makes that three and as far as I am concerned that is one to many. Just forget I told you.'

'Told me what sir? But apologies, I knew she had once worked for us, and will again, but didn't know her role had continued on throughout.'

'It's on a piecemeal basis but glad you hadn't worked it out. Wouldn't say much for our security. Let's get back to who is playing us.'

'If James Sinclair is investing on behalf of Misha Yelchin, did he have Kashton and Delahanty killed?'

'We don't know that anyone killed them. All we have is an assassin's trophy wall with their photos.... By all accounts, Roland Leung was seriously disturbed, thinking he was in cahoots with the gods or some such nonsense. Oh, and wasn't there something Mèng said about the Chinese recruiting Leung to follow Dr Sharapova to get dirt on her so they might pressure her into making a decision in their favour.'

'Yes sir. At the time I thought it was odd, given they already had leverage through her relatives in Xinjiang. She alleviated my suspicions when she told me that all her Uyghur relatives were dead.'

'What are you saying Chris?'

'I don't know sir, but nothing adds up. We had been chasing the Chinese because of the leaks in the service. When Kashton and Delahanty died, or were murdered, I conflated my focus on the CCP mole with the Chinese interest in the bauxite mine and came up with the wrong conclusion. Mèng arrived at the same time. A coincidence and another red herring. While he didn't know anything useful, he was aide to the General who had been sent to ensure the investment went through.

All separate issues in themselves, but on the surface they seemed connected. But now, I have a horrible suspicion that Misha Yelchin, through James Sinclair and Vikki Carmichael, has played me.' Chris paused and looked at Devin.

'How the hell did you reach that conclusion?'

Chris didn't answer Devin's question but said instead, 'There are still issues unanswered. Fitzsimmons and WorldWatch. What was he really chasing? He sounded plausible, and he had retired as a SIS officer. Yet it is also possible that he was on a mission, and we were kept in the dark because both MI6 and CIA knew we had a leak and were by-passing us until we could sort it out.'

'All right, now you really are losing me. What the hell have they got to do with this?'

'Wasn't that what kicked off Project Perseus sir. The bauxite mine may be part of a bigger picture.'

'Like?'

Chris took a breath. 'Armaments smuggling.' He raced on before Devin could object. 'It occurred to me that Fitz may now be working for the CIA under the guise of WorldWatch. The CIA and MI6 have been tracking armament smuggling into Central Africa for some time, which may have been why Fitzsimmons was in Australia, looking into Sinclair's activities here?'

'That's a huge leap.'

'Not really, sir. Michael Leung was killed by a Russian made weapon.'

'Anyone can get hold of one of those on the black market.'

Chris pursed his mouth. 'Not that type, sir. It's not freely available outside the Russian military but I concede, it is possible.'

Devin was warming to his theme. If Chris had any idea why The Perseus Project had been started in the first place, none of his conclusions would make sense, but all he said was, 'Mèng explained the Triads worked for the Chinese, not the Russians. Mrs. Ainsworth said she saw them talking to General Liu, which backs up Mèng's story.'

Chris said, 'They were thugs for hire. They may have worked for both.'

Devin felt his blood pressure rise. 'If not the Chinese, who the hell killed Mèng? Why on earth would the Russians think it was a good idea to kill him. How would they even know we had him?'

Chris said, 'How did your meeting go at the embassy sir?'

Devin sighed and his heart rate returned to normal. 'Uneventful. The ambassador was unavailable, but I spoke to his first secretary. She thanked me for delivering the news in person and asked if she could have Mèng's body repatriated once the autopsy was done. Didn't get a glimmer of anything but genuine curtesy. She explained that Mèng had been ordered home and had disappeared on the way to the airport. Then apologised for not reporting a foreign national going missing, but she said they had hoped Mèng would come to his senses. In other words, they had their own out searching for him rather than coming to us. I was half inclined to think Mèng's demise had nothing to do with them, although... No, I just couldn't read enough to know what she knew or didn't know. And perhaps the Embassy staff had no idea.'

'Do you know the name of the officer?'

'Zheng Pingru.'

Chris blinked. 'Really sir.'

'You know her.'

Chris shook his head but said, 'I know about the historical Zheng Pingru, the Chinese spy who was executed by the Japanese during the Second World War. She's a Chinese folk hero.'

Devin put his head in his hands. 'I should study history I suppose. Never mind. So, she may or may not have been playing me. Does it matter? You already said, Mèng is a red herring.'

'I think so, or at least a separate matter.'

'Okay. Let's deal with these issues one by one. First, Vikki Carmichael and the NSW Premier.'

Chris said, 'I suggest ASIO devise a spy trap on that one sir, with the help and cooperation of Mrs Ainsworth and her majordomo. She'll cooperate so long as no one charges her for her earlier misdemeanours or brings her hotel into disrepute. I imagine her barrister daughter will want iron clad guarantees.'

Devin smiled. 'By the way, I didn't ask. Did you have a good weekend, Chris?'

Chris ignored him and Devin laughed. 'All right, agree to the iron clads. Next?'

'Can you speak to Dr Sharapova, sir. Find out why she went against Mr Delahanty's wishes.'

'You don't want to do it?'

'Better coming from you. Given her future role, she will see me as a subordinate.'

'Okay. What are you planning to do?'

'I would like to talk to our SIS colleagues about Blue Eagle and James Sinclair, and Liam Garcia about WorldWatch. He fobbed me off last time, but if I can explain to both services that we have uncovered the mole they might be more inclined to share.'

'It's too late to back out of the FIRB decision...'

'I know, and no legal reason why we should, but I just want to know if Sinclair's bank is a front for the Russians for future reference. By the way sir, did you hear any more on the toxicology results?'

The switch in subject matter wasn't lost on Devin. 'Ah yes. 'Drew a blank there I'm afraid. Apparently aconitine is very unstable and decomposes easily in the human body. Not only that but it can be absorbed through the skin so leaves no trace in the stomach contents. Not easy to detect and not routinely included in tox reports. They retested the samples but found nothing of note. We will have to accept that it is quite possible they weren't murdered?'

'Despite the assassin's trophy wall, and the label I found for the drug.'

Devin stared at him. 'I used to like you Chris, but Project Perseus is becoming a wilderness of mirrors and its doing my head in.' He smiled to take the sting from his words. 'I'll arrange a meeting with ASIO and the AFP again. I would like you to take the project lead.'

'Won't they object, sir?'

'Don't see how they can... But you will need to make sure the AFP particularly, can see the nuances you can see, and stop them going off on some tangent and arresting Mrs Ainsworth.' He laughed. I think Janice Burton still thinks she should be charged. Wait until she hears the woman is now our asset.'

'Gives me nightmares imagining just that scenario, while Vikki Carmichael wings her way back to London taking the real breach of national security story with her.'

After Chris had left his office, Devin sat staring out the window for a few minutes. Chris's last words reverberated in his head, *the real breach of national security*. The whole blasted project had been made up, for pity's sake! Project Perseus, a mission to seize a head of snakes, ones that never existed or that was what they had all thought.

Yet the implications of what Chris had told him had far reaching ramifications. The man was nothing if not thorough and had a huge mental capacity to hold all these disparate parts together. His willingness to admit being played and chasing the wrong trail was also a plus in Devin's book and his report to the Secretary would show it.

The man hadn't put a foot wrong so far. She should be pleased with the way the assessment had panned out, and yet what was meant to be a job assessment to ascertain Davis's suitability to remain in the service, after the perceived delay in exposing the policy officer as a Chinese asset, had morphed into something else.

Something unexpected, which had turned into a real issue. An entire wilderness of issues. Not only had he found a mole that until that point had been a hypothetical situation in order to watch the man perform, but he had also become involved with a home affairs national security breach. A breach that should have been picked up by any one of the agencies whose job it was.

His loyalty, analytic ability, and focus on the job was a lesson for them all. With Chris there was no getting side tracked by political agendas or victimhood. The service needed more of his type. Even when faced with unpalatable political decisions like the ex-minister's appointment as ambassador to the Republic of Ireland, he'd maintained his focus on his job rather than on the machinations of the politicians. The same applied when he was made to work with the AFP. He didn't like it, but he had also followed interagency protocols, even though Janice Burton admitted she had rather enjoyed riding him.

All the way through this project, he had used his head and got out of situations that could have blown up in all their faces. And still could. At least Chris hadn't fathomed Huma's role. Especially after she had searched his apartment. Devin paused. He had been furious with her for that. She had no authority to break into the man's private home. But there was a small discrepancy with that account too.

Chris had reported the incident and later had said it was Roland Leong who had broken into his apartment. He had recognised the man's pistol, his small feet, and his smell. Yet Huma had said she had done it herself and pulled a replica on Chris in order to get away. In his anger at her for taking matters into her own hands, Devin hadn't noticed the discrepancy before now. Besides, he'd been more worried about Huma telling him about Chris drinking too much and passing out on her bed.

At the time Devin thought Huma may have been too damn good at persuading him to take another drink. She was nothing if not convincing. Especially as Chris didn't seem to drink in excess at any other time, but he'd overlooked the small discrepancy between Chris's account and Huma's account of the apartment intrusion. How much of an issue was it?

It wasn't the first time Huma hadn't played a straight bat either. He would have to quiz her about the matter of approving James Sinclair's bid, seemingly against Miles's wishes. He was sure there was a perfectly reasonable explanation, but Chris was right. It was a question that should have an adequate answer, especially as she would be taking over Devin's job.

No one expected the assassinations, nor would they have known they were murders if it were not for Chris's persistence. After all the autopsy results hadn't come up with anything. It would have been a case of untimely death through natural causes, no matter what the odds. So, in fact no one would have been looking for the assassin. If that's what Roland Leung was. He may as easily have been a man with serious delusions.

Then again, if it hadn't been for Chris's tip off to AUSTRAC, no one would be looking for money laundering Triads either. Certainly, the NSW detective wasn't investigating them. Not according to Janice, although she was adamant he was criminally involved with them. The AFP was still trawling through the documents they'd found in Michael Leong's apartment and offices.

And who would have imagined Mèng's defection in this mix. The way he had handled that was another plus in Chris favour. He had brought the guy in, and it was no fault of his that Mèng had been presumed murdered although they were still waiting on the results of that autopsy. Chris had noted his complaints about the security of Mèng's lodging in his reports, but as he should, he had also known whose responsibility it was and left them to it.

Foreign spies, financial crimes, possible assassinations, moles, defections, and now this Russian oligarch's conspiracy, if that is what it was. Chris had found the evidence and dealt with each issue in a calm and rational manner. The more Devin thought about it the more amazed he became. The man deserved a bloody medal. But that wouldn't happen, instead the whole project would be locked down under a highly classified seal and Chris would never know the Perseus Project had begun as a means to get rid of him.

When the Secretary had given Devin this thankless task under instructions from the former minister, he had wanted to ignore it as best he could. But of course, Elgar had volunteered his own solution, trying to compromise Chris by setting him up via the phony project in Indonesia. When Devin had refused to involve another sovereign country in their dubious machinations, Elgar had still thought the project worthwhile and Devin, worn down with the arguments, had concurred.

The Indonesian project had turned up little of real value, a few low-level people smugglers, so it wasn't a complete waste of money. Maybe if Devin had agreed to Chris going to Indonesia, the minister might not have lost her job. Be careful what you wish for. Unless her motivation for getting Chris out of the country was because she knew about their domestic servant and didn't want Chris poking around. Now he was becoming truly paranoid.

Another thought popped into his mind. Huma's sighting of the ex-MI6 officer, Fitzsimmons, kicked off the pretext to get Chris on the trail. But maybe, as Chris had speculated, there was another reason Fitz was here. Devin hadn't really followed up with his colleagues in London, knowing Fitzsimmons had retired years ago.

Sloppy, but then when he had started out, the whole thing was a made-up project; one that Elgar had insisted on naming Project Perseus. Devin had to google the Perseus myth to understand it at all, and while he didn't see that the project had anything in common with a reckless chase after Medusa's head, he'd agreed it was as pointless a mission and put little effort in to thinking about it.

But this outcome.... He had never imagined or expected any of it. He wondered if any of the events uncovered would have occurred if Marianna Laidley hadn't wanted an excuse to fire Chris. Now, if it was his last act within the Department he would have Chris promoted.

He smiled and picked up the phone to ring his counterpart at ASIO. After the call, he would need to speak to Huma, maybe invite her for a drink, round the project off at the Commonwealth Club where Huma and Miles had given him the idea to set Chris off on a wild goose chase, or so he thought. At the very least, it would wrap the project in a nice symmetry.

40. Honey Trap

Chris spent the morning at the Ben Chifley Building, briefing, planning, and discussing tactics and operations with a group of ASIO techos, and AFP officers. They had decided to coincide the sting with a fund-raiser dinner the Premier was having at Bancroft House the following week. Once Chris was sure the plan was solid, he took a pool car, went home to pack an overnight bag, and drove to Sydney.

His briefing to the Premier was to the point. The man picked up his role quickly and without any fuss or puff, agreed that his wife would find something better to do on the night. Then Chris made his way to Cassie's apartment, where Susan, Mason and Cassie were waiting for him.

He explained their roles and had them all sign various forms. He explained Mason's role and made him repeat it back. Then he signed a document Cassie had prepared to protect her mother and Mason.

Now it was just a question of timing. Chris hoped he had done enough but it was a simple enough sting, although he could not take part. Vikki Carmichael knew him. Even if she knew him as a contractor, she had been suspicious of his cover. It was now up to Susan Ainsworth, Mason Bronson, and the Premier to put the plan into action. Then it was up to the techos from ASIO and officers from the AFP to nab her in the act.

***

Later that day a wired, in both senses of the word, Mason presented himself to Vikki. He explained about the fund-raiser, and that the Premier would be staying in residence that night. 'Is there anything in particular you would like me to do Ms Carmichael?'

She said, 'Can you get me and Sir Hamish on the guest list?'

He paused, frowning as if the request worried him. 'I am not sure, but I think all you need to do is stump up the party's plate fee. It's $5,000 per person. Then it will be easy enough to add two more names and two more place settings. Without the money, I couldn't just add the names. I'd be in a lot of trouble, probably lose my job.'

Vikki leaned into him and stroked his arm. 'Don't worry. We'll pay and we'll look after you.'

'Who's we? You and Sir Hamish?'

'No dear, Blue Eagle Investment Bank.'
,

'I could get into big trouble helping you.'

'Mason dear. I already explained. We look after our own and you have been a loyal soldier.'

Mason inhaled. 'I almost forgot. When the Premier stays here without his wife, he sometimes asks for a special companion.'

Vikki straightened her back, her eyes narrowing. 'You didn't tell me that before.'

'It has been a while since the last one.'

'Who was that? What was she like?'

Mason paused and licked his lips. Wordsmithing wasn't his forte, but he remembered Chris's instructions to describe a fictious woman in a way that might have been Vikki's twin. He said, 'She was medium, like not tall, not short, trim figure, dark hair to here.' He touched his shoulders and shrugged.

'What was her personality like?'

He grinned with what he hoped was a lasciviousness. 'Sexy,' he said, 'but clever. She was definitely clever and sort of winding.'

'What the hell does that mean?'

'Well, she winds the man around her fingers and gets what she wants.'

Vikki nodded. 'Anything else?'

He shrugged. 'I don't know. I think she will do anything for the right price.'

'Okay.' Vikki paused and gazed over Mason's shoulder as if thinking. 'What kind of clothes did she wear?'

He frowned. He didn't know what to say to this. 'I am not sure.' He settled for, 'sexy but conservative. I think her dress last time was red.'

It seemed to satisfy Vikki because as she turned away she said, 'Just get us on the list and if he asks for a companion, let me know.'

***

The night of the dinner arrived, and Susan oversaw the proceedings. Tables and rooms were set. Microphones in place. New cameras installed by the technicians.

No one knew what Vikki might do.

Chris had explained that she might try to compromise the Premier through photographic evidence of adultery, or she might offer campaign funding in exchange for his approval of the development permit. Either way they were ready. Cassie would also attend to ensure her mother and Mason were not compromised in some way, and Susan had told her to come early.

Now, in a nervous twitter, Susan dashed between the kitchen, the ballroom that had been set up for the dinner, and the anteroom where sherry would be served before dinner.

She made last minute changes to the décor. Rechecked the seating arrangements for dinner. Ensured the microphone worked at the lectern from where the party's president would give some opening remarks about issues close to the party's heart.

She had placed Vikki next to the Premier and hoped it wouldn't be commented upon, but then the Premier knew what was going to happen although no one else, outside federal officers, had any idea that this was anything other than an intimate and very expensive party fund-raiser.

Chris had said the operation was considered low risk. Vikki wanted the Premier's favour, not his life, so all would go off smoothly. They would get their photographic evidence and their video recordings, arrest Vikki and that would be the end of the sorry saga that Susan was sure, had aged her beyond her years.

Once this was over, she vowed never again. Her actions protecting the reputation of her hotel had almost blown-up that same reputation, and worse. If it hadn't been for Cassie she might have ended up in gaol.

She straightened a place setting and adjusted a name card, checked the flower arrangement on the Premier's table was just high enough to prevent easy conversation across the table. That way people would be forced to converse with those on either side. It might give Vikki an opportunity to present her case to the Premier, which then would be captured by the camera and microphone carefully concealed in the ornate scrolls of the pressed metal ceiling directly above the Premier's seat.

***

Cassie stopped for a red traffic light at the intersection. She was almost at the turn-off to the hotel and her stomach fluttered at the thought of what her mother was expected to do tonight. How had she never realised what her mum was up to all these years?

Yet Chris had known and never let on. She had left him at her flat, and as he saw her off he hovered, looking for assurances that she would be all right, saying, *remember, anything that isn't right call me, even if you are not sure. Promise me Cassie, anything...* She smiled. He hadn't wanted her involved but she was not going to miss out although she wanted him there when she got back tonight.

A vehicle pulled up next to her silent EV, its engine loud and irritating. The driver glanced at her, and her chin lifted as she chose to ignore him and his growling monstrosity. The lights turned green, and he engaged gears and roared off.

This time she did turn towards him, annoyance overcoming her lofty distain, but his car was already moving across the intersection and all she could make out was a profile. There was a familiarity about him. Someone she knew perhaps, although she didn't immediately recall from where.

Cassie turned into the private access driveway and parked near the staff quarters. The building had once housed her dad's vintage car collection. He would have known what kind of car that was at the traffic lights. She had no idea. It looked like something from last century, an American gas guzzling monster pick-up. For some reason, they had become popular in Australia although she couldn't see their appeal especially in the narrow confines of Sydney's road lanes.

She locked her car and walked along a concrete path to the staff entrance where she let herself into a brightly lit corridor. That was when it hit her. The man in the truck was the man in the maroon Cadillac. She was certain of it.

How was she so certain? She pulled herself together. After all, she had not seen the man's face previously. He'd had a hat pulled low and all she had seen was a chin, neck, and shoulders. She told herself she was imagining things.

She made her way along the corridor, but the idea of the man's familiarity stayed with her. What was it about him? Perhaps, he was a client. The man at the lights had been quite old, in his fifties or sixties she guessed. The man who had driven the red Cadillac couldn't have been that old. He had taken on the Triads and shot Chris.

Another thought struck her. If it was that man, what was he doing in this area? She stopped and fumbled in her evening bag for her phone. No. She stopped. That was just an excuse to call Chris. It could not be the same man.

She let her phone fall back into her bag and walked on, arriving at the staff elevators and the door that led into the guest section of the hotel. She pushed through the door and walked into the lobby from where she could see outside. The parking area was filled with cars but not the big American pick-up. Thank goodness.

She went up in the staff elevator to her mum's rooms and let herself in. The sitting room was empty. Mum would be downstairs supervising. This was an important event aside from all the skulduggery that went with it. Susan would leave nothing to chance.

Cassie walked over to the window that looked over the forecourt. Vehicle lights flashed briefly through the trees at the far edge of the property and disappeared. There was no road in that direction, just bush along rocky cliffs. She peered out into the dark night. Perhaps it wasn't a vehicle.

She returned downstairs. Her mum was at the reception desk.

'Hello darling, I didn't see you arrive.'

'I came in the staff entrance. Mum, can vehicles drive along the cliffs past the property?' Cassie pointed in the direction she had seen the lights.

Susan's eyes looked up towards the ceiling as if remembering. 'There was an old track along there years ago, when you were a child, but it's overgrown now and wouldn't be safe. Why do you ask?'

'I thought I saw lights...'

The lift opened and a voice boomed out. 'Ah my dear, you look good enough to eat.'

Cassie turned to Sir Hamish. 'That is a rather unappealing image Sir Hamish. Perhaps you might like to rephrase your greeting.'

Sir Hamish grinned. 'Always willing to do battle my dear, even though I know I will lose. Let me buy you a drink in reparation, eh.'

'I'll just have a word with Mrs. Ainsworth and join you in the bar in a few minutes.' She watched him go then turned to her mother. 'I am sure I just saw a vehicle down there. Do you think Mason should check it out.'

'He's busy dear but I'll ask him to do it when he has a moment.'

'Okay, thanks Mum.' She walked off to join Sir Hamish, who would most likely be with Vikki. Cassie wanted to see how those two would operate tonight.

She saw Vikki on the veranda talking on her mobile phone. Sir Hamish was at the bar talking to another man. Oh crickey, it was the man in the big American pick-up. How had he got here without her spotting his vehicle? Perhaps he'd arrived while she was upstairs or when she was talking to her mum.

Sir Hamish looked up and saw her. He waved her over.

She walked toward the two men, chiding herself for imagining things. As she drew closer she realised the man was even older than she had first thought and didn't look at all familiar. He must be in his late sixties, although a youthful late sixties. He was of medium height and slim with silvery hair. He wore his black evening jacket and bow tie with aplomb, right down to the silk pocket square. His was an old fashioned, expensive, and cultivated understatement to Sir Hamish's garish green tuxedo.

Sir Hamish called to the barman, 'One very dry gin martini for the lady, twist no olive.' Then he turned to her, 'my dear, may I introduce you to an old friend, Alex Sharapova. Alex meet my beautiful barrister, Ms Cassandra Lewis.'

Cassie held out her hand.

Instead of shaking it, Alex took it in both of his and squeezed, leaning over in slight bow. It was an antiquated gesture, but she found it pleasant, almost expecting him to click his heels like a 19th century Prussian officer.

'You are attending the dinner tonight Ms Lewis?' His voice held a hint of accent, Eastern European, perhaps.

'Yes.'

Sir Hamish said, 'I didn't know you were a party member Cassandra.'

'I'm not, but I did want to support the Premier.' She blushed as she spoke, feeling like the imposter she was. Are you attending Sir Hamish?'

'Naturally, and Alex is a party stalwart with very deep pockets.'

Alex picked up her martini and said, 'I will carry your drink through for you.'

'Where are we going?'

'We must adjourn to the Premier's reception, where we may have one sherry before he leads us into dinner. I am not sure if it is his preference or the way the hotel arranges things, but you have your gin and I have my vodka, which Hamish will carry with his whisky, and we will all survive the sherry crush.'

He laughed and turned with a bounce reminiscent of a younger man before holding out his right arm for Cassie, while he held her martini in his left hand. 'Now-a-days it does not matter, but in my day, a lady never carried her own drink from one room to another.'

Cassie found him quite charming—a bit eccentric but nevertheless, an old-fashioned gentleman. She gave a wry smile at recalling her fear at the traffic lights that he might be dangerous.

'You smile in secret,' he said.

'I was smiling at the quaint notions behind past manners. Why do you suppose a woman could not carry her own drink? Did men think she was helpless?'

'Never. Only a fool would label women helpless. I suppose men did it out of gallantry and respect. Or perhaps they were merely cognisant of the difficulties of navigation in high heels.'

She laughed. 'I have always thought that was why men offered us an arm to lean on. Perhaps, we are fools to wear high heels.'

The scandalous look he cast made her laugh again. She was still smiling when they entered the anteroom to the ballroom where dinner would be served and where wealthy donors gathered in a cluster around the Premier.

Alex handed Cassie her martini and said, 'Have you met the Premier?'

Cassie shook her head.

'Really? A well-connected woman such as yourself...' he tut tutted. 'Let me introduce you.'

Vikki was at the Premier side, and as Alex introduced Cassie, Vikki touched the Premier's arm and said, 'Cassandra and I are old friends.' She glanced around. 'but where is that handsome fellow you were dating.'

Cassie frowned. Why did they all ask about Chris? She said, 'You mean Chris Davis? He went back to England I believe.'

Vikki raised an eyebrow and glanced at Alex.

At that moment, Alex's mobile phone rang, and he excused himself, walking away as he answered it, leaving Cassie with Vikki and the Premier.

The night of the Premier's dinner in Sydney, Devin walked into the Commonwealth Club in Canberra and saw Huma already at the table with a drink in front of her. He smiled, waved, and made his way through the tables, nodding at acquaintances until he reached her.

She stood up and hugged him. Devin felt the taut lines of her body through the thin material of her dress, something silky, and inhaled her perfume, something subtle and spicy. He wondered, how many eyes on him now would soon be gazing into Tilly's sardonic smile as they confided in her that Devin had been seen out with another woman. Luckily he had told his wife why he would be late home tonight.

'Okay, what is this about?' She asked him after he had ordered a drink.

'Can't we catch up and socialise occasionally?'

'Since when did you last associate socially with an asset?'

'But you are no longer an asset, are you Huma? And even, then you only worked on an occasional favour basis. It would be better to say, with your job at the National Security College, we're close colleagues. Soon you will be the chief, and I will be sitting within call of the PM's office.'

'Night and day, I imagine.' She pulled a face.

Devin raised his eyebrows in acknowledgement.

She said, 'I would be happy to make this a social occasion, but I don't believe it for a minute. You never had eyes for anyone other than your wife.'

'Is that what you think?' Devin smiled at how many times he had dreamed otherwise. Huma might be surprised to find she was a most frequent target of his fantasy, but she was right in one way. He would never do anything to hurt Tilly. But then, neither had Huma ever alluded to her desire for a sexual liaison with him. This was new and he wondered why. Huma never did anything for no reason. That was one thing about her of which he was certain.

'So, come on Devin. What's this about?'

Devin sighed. 'All right. It's about Chris Davis.' Did he imagine it or had she gripped the stem of her wine glass tighter.

Her face was bland as she glanced at him. 'What's he done now?'

'Tell me what you thought of him.'

Huma took a sip of wine and placed the glass back on the table. 'I thought we'd had this discussion.'

'Yes I know, but its crunch time.'

'Really. The Perseus Project's finished.'

Devin raised his brows again in acknowledgment. 'I have to write a report for the Secretary, and I am in two minds.'

'How did he do?'

'Oh, you know, as expected. Found nothing of value, but then there was nothing much to find was there?'

'I know it was merely an exercise, but he seemed like a competent analyst to me. Gave me a through briefing on the investors, more than I expected in fact. Zoe also told me she had tried to compromise him twice, once sexually after a party, and once through dangling the carrot of a job with Democritus, but he bit neither time.'

'I wish you hadn't involved Zoe or had spoken to me before you did.'

'Relax. She thinks she was doing me a favour in her free time, by trialling one of my course assignments, trying to compromise a senior officer. She told me both that she had failed, and that it was a terrible idea to give students assignments like that. She said she felt as guilty as anything afterwards.'

'What if she had succeeded?'

'Then you would have known, wouldn't you. I did tell you right at the beginning, you can only really know a person's stripes if you observe them in action. Questionnaires, and interviews won't cut it. Too many confounding variables.'

'That's your professional assessment then.' Devin took a slug of his soda water. 'I detest this whole thing and wish I had never started it. If he ever found out, I hate to think what he would do.'

'He can't find out then.'

'Absolutely not.'

'Who else knows.'

'Just the agency heads involved. Oh, and Elgar. Too many people for my liking.'

'By the way, you didn't tell me the outcome of my tip off. The one that gave you the idea for the project, other than a quest to cut off the head of a fictious Chinese mole.'

'What tip-off?'

'Don't be dense Devin. It doesn't suit you. What was Fitzsimmons doing here?'

Devin waved his hand. 'Oh that. Nothing as it turns out. He retired years ago and was over here for some mining conference—interested in environmental concerns.'

'You believe that?'

'Yes, why, don't you?'

'What's not to believe. Who is Fitz working for now then?'

'Ah Huma, I can't remember. Some environment company, I believe. Why, are you keen to know?'

'Not really. Just curious to find out what SIS officers do when they are found with their hands in their employers' till, that's all.'

'Hang on. What are you saying?'

'Well, there was that scandal about Royal phone tapping or some such. Then all of a sudden the man retires. Convenient.'

'I don't know anything about that.'

'Liar.'

Devin laughed. 'All right. I had heard, but the whole project was a set up and Fitz is retired. I didn't pay much attention to Davis's reports on the matter.' He yawned.

'You could send him to London to find out.'

'I might just do that.' Actually, it was a good idea. Maybe there was more to Fitz's visit than met the eye, and Chris was unlikely to get it out of the local officers at their respective diplomatic missions, but all Devin said was, 'There was one thing that he wanted to clear up, made a point of it in his final report. It's about a discrepancy between a note he found that Miles had written, and the final outcome of the investment decision. It's most likely unimportant but I thought you might be able to clear it up.'

She had definitely stiffened. It wasn't so much a bodily movement—she was too good for tells to trip her up, but Devin knew Huma and he could almost sense her mood. What was she hiding. He watched her sip the wine and look around. That action meant her nicotine worms were biting. A sign of apprehension.

Sure enough, her next words were... 'I wish you could smoke in this joint. I might need to get some fresh air.'

Devin pushed back his chair. 'I'll walk with you.'

'Why don't we get out of here.'

'I thought you liked it here.'

'Yeah sometimes, but not tonight. Let's go to some divey bar and get drunk like in the old days.'

'Where would you suggest?'

Twenty minutes later they were seated in a dark corner of a wine bar, another white wine in front of Huma and a soda water in front of Devin. He wished it was a good stiff whisky, but he knew if he had a drink, Huma would run rings around him.

He raised his glass. 'Cheers.'

She smiled and picked up her own glass. 'Chin-chin. I always had a soft spot for you; you know that Devon.'

'That's interesting. I had no idea. Thought, in the old days you barely noticed me.'

'The other way around. You never saw me.'

'Yeah I did, still do, but what about an answer to my question.'

'What question?'

'The one about Chris finding a discrepancy between yours and Miles's accounts on the bauxite investment.'

'I cannot imagine what that might be.'

'Miles was against the Blue Eagle investment, wasn't he?'

She sighed. 'It was so tiresome. Eventually the Treasurer brought him around.'

'Chris says you insisted that, prior to his death, Miles had approved James Sinclair's Blue Eagle Bank.'

'How does he know that?'

'Apparently, you told him.'

'Did I? I don't remember, but it is true. Miles and I had some stand-up rows about it, but I didn't want to expose all the FIRB dirty linen to Chris.

Yet he is right, Miles was adamant, no foreigners, but when Kashton died, who else was there?

Devin nodded. 'So, it was only after Kashton's death that Miles agreed to Sinclair's investment proposal?'

Huma pursed her lips. 'I think so, although I couldn't swear to the timing. I know the list had been whittled down to Kashton and Sinclair, but when it all took place, I couldn't tell you exact times. Why is this important Devin?'

'Not important really. Just snipping off loose ends.' He watched her drink her wine, unsure whether to believe her or not. Her explanation sounded plausible and perhaps she didn't think it professional to discuss stand up rows or to explain to Chris that Miles had only agreed after some arguments and pressure from the Treasurer.

Huma's version fitted with Miles's dilemma over allowing a foreign investor into the mix. And it was true that none of the applicants were free of an agenda. As the Treasurer had pointed out to Chris, Blue Eagle bank was not Yelchin. The man was merely an investor. Perhaps there was nothing here. Chris would have to let this one through to the keeper.

Huma said, 'Where is he now?'

'Who?'

'Chris Davis of course.'

'On holiday. He has a girl in Sydney, I think... Bugger it.' Devin got up. 'I'm getting myself a whisky. Want another wine?'

She smiled. 'Still have this one. Maybe afterwards we can get something to eat, and I'll join you for a whisky.'

While Devin went to the bar, Huma made a phone call. He only knew because when he turned around she hung up, her face bland as he walked back towards her. He wondered who the call was too, but that would be easy enough to track down.

42. Collateral Damage

The Premier was surprisingly attentive for a politician engaging someone of relatively modest means and little influence, as Cassie considered herself to be by comparison with this illustrious company. But he soon drifted off, leaving a small crowd of hangers on standing in a semi-circle, holding empty sherry glasses, and wondering what they could say to each other.

Cassie took a gulp of her martini.

A woman in a lurid-green dress hissed, 'Where did you get that?'

She recognised Pamela Robson, a businesswoman prominent in the news for her assertive views on individual responsibility for one's status in life and smiled. 'A kind gentleman brought it in from the bar for me.' Cassie looked around, but Alex had disappeared. She shrugged and took another sip. 'It is rather good, and I much prefer a good martini to a sherry.'

Cassie looked around for someone else to talk to. This wasn't her usual crowd, and she really knew no one aside from Sir Hamish, Vikki and now Alex, who had vanished. She wished she hadn't been so determined to come here tonight.

She walked over to the wall; it might be required to prop her up as the martini was a double. The room was filled with people clustered in small groups. There must be a hundred and fifty, maybe two hundred people, which was hardly what she would have called an intimate dinner, and at $5000 a plate... That was an obscene amount of political money, but then what did she know about fund-raisers. She was glad she had not had to pay.

There was Vikki in a low backed scarlet mid-calf dress, now clinging to the Premier's arm and laughing up into his face. He looked smitten by her although he must know what she was up to. Perhaps he was just a good actor. Cassie searched for the Premier's security, but there didn't seem to be any, or at least none she could identify. Perhaps they were not included on the guest list.

A man approached and asked if he might join her. 'You seem to be the only person in the room, who might be enjoying yourself.'

'Hardly. The only wall flower might describe me better.'

He stood next to her. 'We can be the observers of life.'

She tilted her head. 'We observe, while they live.'

'That doesn't sound right does it? I am Adam Kashton by the way.'

'Cassie Lewis.' She held out her hand. 'Kashton...' Her eyes widened. 'Oh, you are Harvey Kashton's son. I am so sorry about your father.'

Adam nodded. 'Thank you. I can't say we were close. I never forgave him for walking out on Mum. Besides we were often at loggerheads over business decisions.' Adam grinned. 'Ha, shouldn't bore you with boring business details, I suppose.'

Cassie stared at Adam. 'I understood your father was contemplating investing in a bauxite mine.'

'That was the Premier's gambit. Dad was contemplating it, but I didn't want a bar of it. The expense would have wiped us out.' He drew in a breath. 'I really shouldn't have said anything. Pretty girl... I'm a fool.'

'Of course not. Bancroft House rules, remember.' She smiled. 'Will you excuse me for a minute. I just need to powder my nose before we go into dinner.' Cassie walked out of the anteroom. Behind her, the dinner gong sounded, and she knew the guests would be filing into the dining room. She took out her phone and rang Chris as she walked towards the main entrance.

When he answered she said, 'Something is not right... Kashton's company was in trouble, didn't have the money to buy the bauxite mine...'

There on the forecourt was the American gas guzzler. She inhaled, and the profile image in the car came back to her. 'Chris, I think the man who shot you is here. His name is Alex Sharapova. I saw him driving some huge American Ute and thought I recognised him. Then I saw lights on the coastal reserve, and I thought it might be him, but now the Ute is here, parked outside and he was in the bar... Although he seemed so nice... Gosh sorry. I'm not making sense...'

'Cassie, get out of there now! If he's there, you are not safe. I'm on my way.'

***

While dinner was underway, Susan decided to go and look for Cassie's lights on her own. Mason was busy, and she was the only person without a job. Normally, she would have had the night off. Everyone knew their roles in the evening's events. The dinner was one of many held every year at Bancroft House although the staff didn't know how important this one was to her. They just looked annoyed when she got in their way. The chef had ordered her out of his kitchen. Damn cheek.

For a while she had watched the reception on the screen in her office, but she knew the men from the government were in the manager's office watching too, and they would know she was watching. She didn't want people knowing. It felt crass.

A last glance at the guests told her the Premier was doing his job admirably. Ms Carmichael played up to him disgracefully. What would she offer? Herself or money. Susan was betting it would be her body and if that didn't work, money.

She switched off the monitor, found a coat for the evening was a little chilly, put on her walking shoes and went out into the starry night. The moon hadn't yet risen although it was light enough to see without a torch. She would just walk along the pathways to the end of the property where it gave way to coastal reserve.

When she reached the reserve boundary, she saw flashing lights off the coast. Cassie had most likely seen a boat passing. The flashing would be it bobbing up and down and she had mistaken that for car lights on the headland. Susan turned to go back to the house.

She had almost reached the hotel when the night lit up. A percussion wave knocked her onto her back. Then a whoosh of scalding air engulfed her along with a loud boom. Sounds of falling glass, and masonry, created a crackling cacophony of noise as the flames took hold.

Then she heard the screams. She scrabbled in the dirt until she managed to find her feet. Her home! Her precious home. Flames flickered above the treetops, leaping into the night as she ran towards the building, her mouth open in a silent scream.

***

Chris's phone rang. 'I'm nearly there Cassie. Where are you?'

'I'm in my car at the staff quarters, but there was an explosion. It sounded like a bomb. I'm going back. My mother...'

A fire truck pulled out of a station on the road ahead of him. Sirens sounded behind him, and he pulled over for string of ambulances and police. 'Christ, what's happened?'

'The hotel's on fire. I have to find my mother.'

The line went dead.

Twenty minutes later, as Chris approached the hotel turn off, he saw the flames. The road was choked with fleeing vehicles. He could not access the driveway for fire trucks, ambulances, and police cars.

He left the car on the side of the road and ran through the trees, cursing himself for getting Cassie involved.

The Fireys were already hosing down the flames. To one side of the forecourt people milled about. Bodies lay on the ground tended by ambulance officers. He could see some of the ASIO and AFP officers rendering assistance and controlling the zone. There was no sign of the Premier, but no doubt the AFP would have looked after him first.

Chris was more concerned with finding Sharapova and Vikki. He angled towards the edge of the property where Cassie had said she'd seen lights. A gibbous moon rose above the sea, lighting his way as he followed a path. He came across Susan Ainsworth, sitting on a garden bench, talking to herself.

She didn't recognise Chris when he approached but said, 'Oh, there you are Martin. I was looking everywhere for you. I do think we should redecorate don't you. Something in the style of that place in London we stayed at. You remember.'

'Good idea.' Chris sat down next to Susan and dialled Cassie's number. When she answered he explained where to find her mother. 'I'll just have a scout around the cliff area,' he said, 'then I'll come back to the hotel and meet you out the front. Your mother will need medical help. I think she's in shock, but otherwise she looks uninjured.'

As Chris approached the headland he saw a boat moving at speed towards the coastline. He stopped in the shadows of a tree thicket and rang another number. When the call was answered he gave the vessel's coordinates and a description.

As he hung up, he saw a man walking along the rough bush pathway. Although the night was lit only by the waning moon, he reckoned the man fitted Sharapova's description.

Chris crouched behind the tree trunk to wait, analysing the way Sharapova moved, searching for his weakness. His attention was focussed on the boat, and it didn't appear as if he had seen Chris. His left arm was held at a slight angle. Concealed weapon maybe. Most likely a shoulder strap.

As Sharapova approached, Chris rose. Sharapova reached into his jacket, but with a burst of tensile power, Chris leaped forward, shifting his weight to the ball of the front foot, and swinging his knee towards Sharapova's arm.

As Chris's shin came into contact, the man swung away, receiving a glancing blow, but it was enough to make him stagger and pull an empty hand from his jacket to maintain his balance. Chris could not allow him to reach for his gun, or it would be over.

The man was well trained. But Chris was faster, younger, and more powerful. He turned, shifted his weight, and delivered a jab to the midsection leaving Sharapova gasping for air. A low kick to Sharapova's legs caused him to stumble and Chris was behind him using a body lock, before lifting him and slamming him to the ground. He gift wrapped the man's arms around his neck, immobilising Sharapova like he was in a straitjacket of his own making.

Sharapova regained his breath. 'You attack an old man for no reason.'

The man tried to roll onto his stomach, but Chris held firm. 'You can lie still, or I can depress your carotid artery until you do.'

Sharapova lay still, confirming Chris's suspicions about his training. He knew the outcome of a depressed carotid artery.

Chris patted him down and found the pistol in a shoulder holster. Before touching it, he ripped Sharapova's folded square from its breast pocket display and used it to lift out the weapon.

'Nice. A 6P9. The smoking gun.' He stood up and pointed the pistol at Sharapova. Then he took his phone out and called Cassie. 'Can you ask a couple of those AFP blokes in the crowd to meet me on the cliffs. I have Sharapova here for them to take into custody.'

Sharapova sat up but didn't try to do more. 'What does this mean, the smoking gun.'

Chris gazed at Alex for a moment, knowing he was trying to gain information that would help him during any interrogation. He needed to know what Chris knew and would be pleasant about finding out. The man was well trained. Should he respond? What did it matter? He had enough to put the man away for murder if not espionage, and Sharapova's responses would also give Chris intelligence. 'It's just an expression.'

'I know the expression, but why do you say it?'

Chris paused for the space of a heartbeat before he said, 'In a moment the AFP will arrive to arrest you. They are law abiding citizens and will require a good enough legal reason to detain and hold you. Now, I know you set that explosive at the hotel, but you are too clever to have left any trace that it was anything other than an accident. My guess is an unfortunate gas leak. I also know you are an agent in the pay of a foreign government, a spy, but as yet I have no proof of that either, not until I bring in my CIA colleagues. However, you were carrying a concealed weapon and that is enough for the AFP to arrest you, but when I tell them that they will also find this firearm killed a man in a recent shoot out, they will be even more interested.'

Sharapova grimaced. 'Fair enough. How did you know?'

'Your pistol and a couple of moves you pulled that were reminiscent of Russian Spetsnaz systema training. I imagine you were originally trained by the old KGB, and I assume you are now working for the SVR or perhaps GRU. But you are too slow, old man.'

'Yes. This is true, I am slow. If I was younger you would not have had it so easy. But it is not what I meant. How can you say you know who I am? I have never met you before.'

'Ah, that was mostly feminine intuition. I have a very good source. And here she is now.'

Cassie ran down the pathway towards Chris, followed by two AFP officers.

Chris pulled Sharapova to his feet and handed him to the officers along with the pistol wrapped in the handkerchief. 'His weapon. You will find it killed Michael Leong.'

Before they followed the AFP back to the hotel forecourt, Chris looked out toward the sea. The boat had been stopped, and a Class 2 vessel was pulled up beside it. NSW Police Marine Area Command. Janice Burton had come up trumps. He'd have to remember to thank her.

'What is it Chris? Who or what are those boats?'

'Not sure but we will find out. I think it was Sharapova's lift out of here. Did you see where Vikki went?'

'The AFP have her in custody. They say they have enough on her, even though the whole operation was interrupted by the explosion. What happened Chris? How did they know we were after them?'

He shrugged. 'How is your mother?'

'She's in shock. They've taken her to the hospital, but she'll be okay. But I think Mason is dead. I can't find him.'

Chris placed his arm around Cassie as he saw her eyes well with tears.

'I am so sorry I put you through this.'

43. Agents and Spies

Devin sat up in his bed and stared uncomprehending at the phone in his hand. The voice was Chris's voice, but what he was saying didn't make any sense. He knew he shouldn't have started drinking whisky with Huma. She could drink any man under the table.

Next to him Tilly stirred. 'What is it darling?'

He shook his head. 'Where are you?' He spoke into the phone, asking the question not because he wanted to know but to give his brain time to catch up.

'Bancroft House, sir. I suspect Alex Sharapova's an illegal. He detonated the place. Guess he was alerted to the operation and set up a bang and blow diversion.'

'Fuck. Who?' An image arose through the fog of last night's memory. Giving in. Going to the bar. Turning back. Huma on her phone. Made a mental note to check the call's destination. 'Huma?'

'My guess sir, but I don't know how she would have known.'

Devin knew. He must have let something drop. What? Nothing came to him, but Huma never missed anything. The slightest nuance would have alerted her, but Chris didn't need to know that. Not right now. During the operation's postmortem would be time enough and would give him the space to analyse his own behaviour in the mix. At his age and with his experience Huma had still managed to bamboozle him.

'What's the damage.'

'Nine dead. Forty-three injured, eight critical.'

'The Premier.'

'Fine sir.'

'The other agents?'

'All okay. Most of the damage was contained to the kitchen and the dining room area closest to the kitchen.'

'What about Carmichael?'

'In custody with Sharapova.'

'You are talking about Alex Sharapova—Huma's father?'

'I guess so sir, although I never met her father, but the man we have has the same name.'

'Who is he working for? Blue Eagle.'

'Pretty sure it's the Russians sir. Deep cover, but we'll need to check his bona fides with our American friends. I imagine his legend must be water-tight to have lasted this long. May take a while.'

'Holy shit. I'll send some officers around to pick up Huma. You had better get back here proto, Chris. You can fill me in on the details when you arrive. In the meantime, I have some housekeeping to do.'

Devin got dressed in a hurry. He wanted to be there when the AFP arrested Huma. He kissed his sleepy wife, told her to go back to sleep then called his driver.

***

Half an hour later, he stood in Huma's living room and gazed around at the décor. There was no way she could have afforded this place on her salary alone, but then everyone knew she came from a family with money. No one had looked too closely at where the money came from, knowing Huma's stepmother's family was wealthy, and her own father had made money working for Democritus for years.

Devin was still horrified at how much he had trusted her, believed she was one of them. Never for a minute, had he thought she was anything other than what she appeared to be.

One of the AFP officers searching the apartment came out of the bedroom.

'Find anything?'

'Nothing sir.'

'Damn!' Devin turned away and raised his phone to his ear.

Chris stood next to Cassie as they inspected ground, cleared now of debris but still showing patches of charred earth. The sky over the sea looked swollen as if about to burst. To their left, the grey roof tiles of the staff quarters remained visible above the tree line. Unscathed by the fire, it would now serve as Susan and Mason's home.

Mason had been found under the rubble, barely alive. Now he needed full time care, and the low setting of the old stables turned garage, and converted into staff quarters, was the perfect place from which Susan might wheel him out into the sunshine for a turn around the garden every day.

'How's your mum doing?' Chris asked.

'Vague but okay, I think. The doctor says there is nothing wrong with her physically, but he says her mind does not want to confront the horror. A couple of the older staff members have offered to stay on to look after the grounds and take care of Mum and Mason until we decide what to do with the place.' Cassie paused before turning to face Chris. 'When are you leaving?'

A week on Monday. I head out to London for a few weeks then on to Cairo, but I'll be back, and I hope we can stay in touch.

'Can I visit?'

'I would like that.' He took her hand.

'Is it safe?'

Chris frowned. 'I am beginning to think safety is less about place and more in the company you keep.'

'You think?' She laughed. 'Can you tell me anything about what happened?'

He glanced at her. 'If anyone deserves to know it is you. What did you want to know?'

'Who is Alex Sharapova?'

'Ah. It turns out that he was once a Russian KGB officer before the fall of the Soviet Union. He absconded in early 1992.'

'But... I don't understand. Wasn't he still working for the Russians?'

'That's all I can tell you Cassie. Don't think about it or it will drive you crazy. Come I will drive you back to your apartment. Then I have to get back to Canberra.'

What Chris couldn't tell her was that that Alex Sharapova was really Aleksei Volkov, who had fled the Russian Embassy in Washington after the Soviet Union fell apart. It had taken Chris some weeks to investigate and unravel the Sharapovas' backgrounds. The information he had gleaned, along with what the ASIO officers had extracted, created an incredible legend. Alex had hidden his trail well.

Chris dropped Cassie off at her apartment, promising he would be back for the weekend before he flew out from Sydney airport. Then he headed back to Canberra. As he drove he reviewed what he had found, looking for gaps or problems. He had been through it all already at the formal Perseus Project's evaluation but since then, Chris had found out more detail.

As Soviet Russia imploded Alex had absconded from the Embassy in Washington, taking his daughter Anya Volkov born 1975, with him. Father and daughter were very close, and the mother had remained in Russia, estranged from her husband while he was at Russia's Washington Embassy. After he had fled, his wife had divorced him. She still lived in Moscow.

As a fugitive in America, Alex began leading a double life under the legend of an ex British special forces veteran, who had taken up corporate spying. At the time Russia was in internal upheaval, and no one from his side had bothered to look for him. But his corporate espionage activities drew the attention of American law enforcement.

To avoid growing FBI interest, Alex needed a new identity. He had targeted a family of refugees who had just arrived in America, befriending them until he had the information he wanted. Then it seems likely he had killed them. At any rate, they had been murdered, and according to Chris's source in the FBI, the killer or killers had never been found. Whether or not he killed them, Alex had used their identities for himself and his daughter, who became Huma Sharapova born 1980, five years after her real birthdate.

They had then moved to Texas where Alex befriended a young Australian woman undertaking a course in corporate leadership at Austin University. He set about wooing her. They married and immigrated to Australia soon afterwards. Once in Australia, Alex used his new father-in-law's connections to gain a foothold in an Australian armaments firm.

Young Anya, aka Huma, spoke several languages through having lived in so many counties as an intelligence officer/diplomat's daughter. Her father also spoke several languages and encouraged his daughters gift. So, Huma undertook study in languages at the ANU, where she excelled. It had all unravelled for Alex while Huma was at university for she had contacted her mother, still living in Moscow.

ASIO officers had interrogated Alex, and he had admitted Putin's government had finally tracked him down through Huma's contact with her mother. Russian intelligence officers from the embassy in Canberra had approached him using both carrot and stick, promising to maintain his legend with the Australians, while over-looking his desertion, in return for him working for Russia.

When Huma took a job with the Foreign Office. He began to train his daughter in spy craft using her as his asset. Her career took off after her first posting to Australia's embassy in Bulgaria where she recruited a low-level Russian diplomat as an Australian agent. In reality the man she had recruited was a double agent. Once she was well and truly compromised the double agent took over as her handler and Alex was sidelined in Australia.

She was then posted to Tehran. After that she was sent to Afghanistan. She left Afghanistan when Australia closed its embassy and had just taken up a post in London. But Anja/Huma was trapped by her father's lies.

After the Chinese found out she, or rather the refugee family whose documents her father had stolen, had Uyghurs relatives in Xinjiang they came after her. While Anya/Huma knew nothing about the relatives, much less cared about their welfare, it was too late. Her career as an Australian intelligence officer was over. Alex was brought back into service and Huma became her father's agent.

Chris surmised that when Devin was promoted, Huma saw another opportunity. She would have known the Treasurer found her irresistible, and that would have been her ticket to get back into the game. Chris was also certain she and Alex were instrumental in both Kashton and Delahanty's deaths. Alex insisted neither he nor his daughter had harmed anyone physically, although the rounds in Michael Leung's body told a different story.

Chris also reckoned Huma had recruited Roland Leung to carry out the assassinations, which would place her in the FIRB chair's position, able to recommend Blue Eagle Bank as primary investor. Blue Eagle Bank would then act as a front for the Russians through Misha Yelchin.

Alistair had blundered in with his incompetent investigation into Kashton's death, getting involved in activity beyond his capability. Now he was serving time somewhere in Silverwater Prison. Chris shed no regret for the man and his veniality.

Mèng's autopsy results had found traces of aconitine poisoning. The puzzling thing for the Perseus Project's evaluation review committee was who had killed Mèng. Roland was already dead so it couldn't have been him.

Then the AFP found an empty bottle of fùzǐ in Alex Sharapova's home. They hadn't known what it was immediately, but it had the same label as the scrap Chris had found in the pantry.

Chris could only guess that Alex was afraid of what Mèng knew and wasn't going to take any chances. Perhaps, as Roland was dead and could not carry out a Chinese contract to kill Mèng Alex took it on himself. Maybe it was fùzǐ Alex had been looking for when he ransacked the Triad offices. But all that was mere speculation. It would take time for the AFP to get it out of Alex, if they ever did at all.

Chris had also surmised that Alex had met Michael Leung through his import/export business. It seemed Alex had been shipping armaments to Africa on behalf of Misha Yelchin for some time. Janice Burton had found paperwork in Michael's possessions that seemed to support Chris's theory.

In addition, the boat that had been apprehended by the Sydney Water Police the night of the explosion and provided more intelligence. The AFP had tracked a cargo docket found on the boat to a transit dock, where containers awaited shipment onwards to Africa. The containers were filled with Russian made armaments. It was likely only one small part of a larger operation that supplied arms through East Africa to Central and perhaps onto west Africa.

Chris had been right that armaments were involved in the mix somewhere. While he hadn't ascertained for certain that it was that armaments shipment that had Walker Fitzsimmons and the CIA interested, it was likely that Fitz was following James Sinclair for that reason. He might find out more in London.

Russian, billionaires, armaments and aluminium made a lethal combination and the bauxite mine was now under intense scrutiny. Yet all of it had been a hunch rather than any specific intel, although he had been proved right, again.

He wondered what it said about him, that he was able to read the criminal mind so well. Perhaps the old saying, *there but for the grace of God go I* was apt in this wilderness of mirrors. He grinned and turned on the radio, leaned back in his seat and enjoyed the limited freedom of driving along an open road to the sounds of the White Stripes, *Seven Nation Army,* bringing back memories.

The only fly left in his celebratory beer was Huma's escape. No one knew where she was or even if she was still in the country. Poor young Anya Volkov, what a life, but with a father like Alex she had never stood a chance. Still, she was a grown woman and knew what she was doing. If she was found she would go away for a very long stretch, but first they had to find her and that seemed unlikely if she had already left the country.

She was probably in Moscow, where it would be heading into autumn now. He felt a twinge of envy. Still, he couldn't complain. The strange and unlikely Perseus Project had led to a promotion and a new posting. It had been a while since he'd last been in London or even Cairo and he was looking forward to seeing them both again.

About the Author

Gillian Long has a PhD in creative writing, and a background in publishing, psychology, politics, and executive leadership in both civil service and the not-for-profit sector. She has lived and worked in Africa, and Europe and now lives on a farm in the Australian Wet Tropics of Far North Queensland. Her previous novels, short stories, forthcoming titles, and other writing can be seen at https://gillianlong.wordpress.com

Coming in 2025...

An Uncivil War
Gillian Long

Book 2 of the Mark Anders series

An Uncivil War is a sequel to *The 9th District*, a novel about the industrial strife in the cane fields of north Queensland in the 1930s. It continues the exploration of power, money, and corruption during the 1930s lead up to the Second World War, and follows Mark Anders, now a freelance photojournalist, as he heads off to Spain to cover the Civil War. He is adamant that this time he will remain an observer and reporter leaving direct action to others. He is not there to get involved or rescue anyone, but he can't help but wonder whether Javier Cruz, his friend and fellow cane cutter, is still alive after he volunteered to join the International Brigade. Yet, despite Mark's determination to retain his neutrality, he soon finds himself immersed in dangerous subterfuge and intrigue.

The 9th District.
Gillian Long

This historical novel, the first in a series, is based on real events set in North Queensland during the great depression, when men's lives are cheap, immigrants are expendable, and a mysterious disease is sweeping through the cane fields.

Mark Anders has had enough. He challenges the powerful sugar industry, and the fight becomes brutal. But Mark's weakness is Beatrice, the daughter of his nemeses who will stop at nothing to discredit a godless Bolshevik.

Disgraced and driven from his home Mark discovers his real heart's desire. It's not his farm or the woman he loves, but does he have the courage to leave everything he built behind to bear witness to the truth?

Greenwash
Gillian Long

Dr Jack Fallon is often accused of being a loner, but that suits his role as a mining engineer, who spends most of his time in the outback. His mother disappeared under strange circumstances when he was a child, and he took solace in the riches of the earth. But its geological structures are notoriously unstable, and Jack finds himself in a race against time to expose the truth before catastrophe destroys all he holds dear, including Sophia, the woman he loves. Set in Queensland, this global conspiracy acts out through a local crime, and an environmental disaster.

Becoming Helen
Gillian Long

Magdalena von Herff barely knows what name to use before men begin to exploit her beauty, intelligence, and talents, but she soon realises that none are there to help her, except perhaps one—her enemy. *Becoming Helen* is set in Europe, Britain, and America and is a 1930s tale of deceit, disillusionment, and retribution after a British Intelligence Officer compromises a young German girl into spying on her own country, expecting her to lie, cheat and bed chosen German military targets for the Allied cause.

Dying Days
Gillian Long

Matt Reid, an ex-British Special Forces soldier, arrives in Australia in search of his biological father. He meets Alan Fletcher, a retired war correspondent, whose story about the disappearance of a Rhodesian SAS soldier in 1980, sends Matt off to Zimbabwe on a mission to find the truth. What he doesn't expect is to become a person of interest to a paranoid secret police or to uncover plots of treachery and revenge and a half century old family feud. This is a story about discovering family, falling in love and finding redemption.

The Trouble with Maggie
Gillian Long

Maggie had everything she wanted; a wonderful husband and two gorgeous kids. Her life was perfect, until the fateful moment she ignored her dead grandmother's warning, and her life changed forever. Set in rural Australia, this story is about the trials of marriage; secrets, guilt, love, and temptation, but most of all, it is a story about Maggie's journey to redemption. This is a modern tale of morality, longing, lust, and lies, filled with heroism, hedonism, hanki-panki, and hocus-pocus.

Watershed
Gillian Long

It's the end of the 2020s and Australia struggles under tyranny. The economy has collapsed as terrorism escalates. Conscript Blake Lincoln returns from an endless Middle East war, wounded and a national hero. When he meets Charlotte, all he wants is to have his old life back. Instead, he uncovers secrets that will blow the government apart. Watershed is set in Brisbane, Sydney, and Canberra, and takes in the vast wilderness of Cape York, and the raw beauty of the Kimberly region. It is a story about the insidiousness of political corruption, the dangers of social injustice, the fragility of democracy and the power of family, as one man prepares to abandon all he believes in to save the woman he loves.

www.ingramcontent.com/pod-product-compliance
Lightning Source LLC
Chambersburg PA
CBHW020946260626
47169CB00006B/1849